W9-CDZ-241

EXPL**O**RER.
ACADEMY

THE *FALCON'S FEATHER*

TRUDI TRUEIT

UNDER THE *Stars*

NATIONAL
GEOGRAPHIC

FOR JENNIE, WITH LOVE –T.T.

Copyright © 2019 National Geographic Partners, LLC
Paperback Edition Copyright © 2020 National Geographic Partners, LLC

Published by National Geographic Partners, LLC. All rights reserved. Reproduction of the whole or any part of the contents without written permission from the publisher is prohibited.

Since 1888, the National Geographic Society has funded more than 12,000 research, exploration, and preservation projects around the world. The Society receives funds from National Geographic Partners, LLC, funded in part by your purchase. A portion of the proceeds from this book supports this vital work. To learn more, visit natgeo.com/info.

NATIONAL GEOGRAPHIC and Yellow Border Design are trademarks of the National Geographic Society, used under license.

Under the Stars is a trademark of National Geographic Partners, LLC.

For more information, visit nationalgeographic.com, call 1-877-873-6846, or write to the following address:

National Geographic Partners
1145 17th Street N.W.
Washington, D.C. 20036-4688 U.S.A.

Visit us online at nationalgeographic.com/books

For librarians and teachers: ngchildrensbooks.org

More for kids from National Geographic: natgeokids.com

National Geographic Kids magazine inspires children to explore their world with fun yet educational articles on animals, science, nature, and more. Using fresh storytelling and amazing photography, *Nat Geo Kids* shows kids ages 6 to 14 the fascinating truth about the world—and why they should care. **kids.nationalgeographic.com/subscribe**

For information about special discounts for bulk purchases, please contact National Geographic Books Special Sales: specialsales@natgeo.com

For rights or permissions inquiries, please contact National Geographic Books Subsidiary Rights: bookrights@natgeo.com

Designed by Eva Absher-Schantz
Codes and puzzles developed by Dr. Gareth Moore

Paperback Edition ISBN: 978-1-4263-3817-5

Printed in China
19/PPS/1

PRAISE FOR THE EXPLORER ACADEMY SERIES

"A fun, exciting, and action-packed ride that kids will love."

—**J.J. Abrams,** award-winning film and
television creator, writer, producer, and director

"Inspires the next generation of curious kids to go out into our world and discover something unexpected."

—**James Cameron,** National Geographic
Explorer-in-Residence and acclaimed filmmaker

"...a fully packed high-tech adventure that offers both cool, educational facts about the planet and a diverse cast of fun characters."

—*Kirkus Reviews*

"Thrill-seeking readers are going to love Cruz and his friends and want to follow them on every step of their high-tech, action-packed adventure."

—**Lauren Tarshis,** author of the I Survived series

"Absolutely brilliant! Explorer Academy is a fabulous feast for mind and heart—a thrilling, inspiring journey with compelling characters, wondrous places, and the highest possible stakes. Just as there's only one planet Earth, there's only one series like this. Don't wait another instant to enjoy this phenomenal adventure!"

—**T.A. Barron,** author of the Merlin Saga

"Nonstop action and a mix of full-color photographs and drawings throughout make this appealing to aspiring explorers and reluctant readers alike, and the cliffhanger ending ensures they'll be coming back for more."

—*School Library Journal*

"Explorer Academy is sure to awaken readers' inner adventurer and curiosity about the world around them. But you don't have to take my word for it—check out Cruz, Emmett, Sailor, and Lani's adventures for yourself!"

—**LeVar Burton,** actor, director, author, and host
of the PBS children's series *Reading Rainbow*

"Sure to appeal to kids who love code cracking and mysteries with cutting-edge technology."

—*Booklist*

"I promise: Once you enter Explorer Academy, you'll never want to leave."

—**Valerie Tripp,** co-creator and author
of the American Girl series

"...the book's real strength rests in its adventure, as its heroes...tackle puzzles and simulated missions as part of the educational process. Maps, letters, and puzzles bring the exploration to life, and back matter explores the 'Truth Behind the Fiction'...This exciting series...introduces young readers to the joys of science and nature."

—*Publishers Weekly*

"Both my 8-year-old girl and 12-year-old boy LOVED this book. It's fun and adventure and mystery all rolled into one."

—**Mom blogger,** The Beckham Project

L (on port side)

THE ORION SHIP MAP

A Aquatics Room

B Faculty Offices

C Sick Bay

D Conference Room

E Classrooms

F Observation Deck

G Library

H Galley/Dining Room

I Labs

J Bridge

K Helipad

L Faculty Cabins

M Lounge

N Crew Quarters

O Explorer Cabins

P Mini CAVE

Q Atrium

R Storage/Control Room

H (on port side)

K

J

I

Q

M

N

R

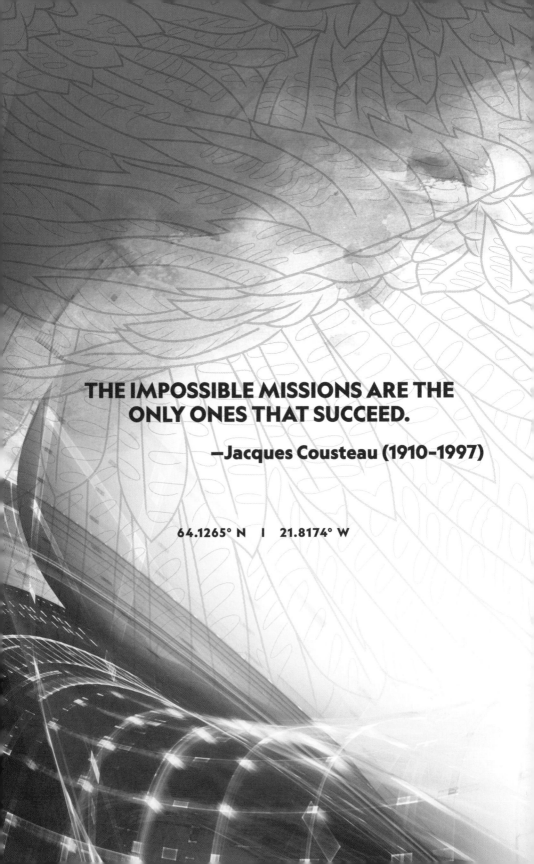

THE IMPOSSIBLE MISSIONS ARE THE ONLY ONES THAT SUCCEED.

—Jacques Cousteau (1910–1997)

64.1265° N   I   21.8174° W

NATIONAL HARBOR MARINA, MARYLAND, U.S.A.

MARYLAND

Potomac

D.C.

VIRGINIA

Potomac

Chesapeake Bay

▶**A HEAD** popped around the doorway of cabin 202, a thick hazelnut ponytail swinging from the top. "Aren't you unpacked yet?"

"Almost." Cruz gave Sailor an uncertain grin. His heart skipped as he reached for the last item in his suitcase: a ball of puffed black carbon. He hoped the treasure inside wasn't broken, but it probably was. How could it not be?

If it hadn't been damaged by Lani taking it apart, it most certainly had suffered from the overnight trip from Hawaii via mail drone. Cruz gently tapped the foam-like carbon until the seal broke, then carefully pulled the orb apart. Free of its cocoon, the palm-size silver dome looked all right. However, Cruz wouldn't know for sure until he touched it and the holo-video of his mother and him as a younger child at the beach appeared. Humming "Here Comes the Sun," he set the globe on his nightstand. He placed it between the aqua box with some of his mom's things and Mell, his honeybee drone. Cruz hesitated. Maybe now wasn't the best time to find out if the video was ruined. If it was, Lani would say it was a bad omen, a sign that his journey on *Orion* was doomed. Cruz wasn't superstitious. Still, he couldn't seem to get his finger to tap the dome.

His friend and teammate Sailor York was checking out Cruz's cabin. "You got a corner again. Sweet as! Bryndis and I are at the other end of the passage. Doesn't this place make you feel like you're seeing double?"

She had a point. Most everything in the cozy, whitewashed maple stateroom was in pairs—two twin beds, two identical navy-and-white-pinstriped comforters with shams, two maple nightstands, side-by-side dressers, a pair of navy stuffed chairs—each with a penguin pillow—and two small writing desks and chairs. Cruz loved his desk. Made of polished blue lapis granite, the deep sapphire blue stone with golden flecks and soft white splatters reminded Cruz of photographs of the Milky Way. Standing like a miniature tent on each starry desk was a note from Explorer Academy president Dr. Regina Hightower. She'd written Cruz and his roommate, Emmett Lu, nearly identical messages, wishing them an exciting, educational, and life-changing journey. However, Cruz noticed his note contained one line that Emmett's did not. Under her signature, Dr. Hightower had included her private cell phone number. *In case you need anything,* she'd scrawled beside it, then, *Please be careful.*

The school's president was one of the few people who knew about Cruz's personal mission. He was looking for a formula developed by his mother before her death. Petra Coronado had discovered a serum that had the power to regenerate human cells—a breakthrough that could have led to curing hundreds of diseases. A founding scientist with the Synthesis, the top secret scientific branch of the Society, she had hit upon the formula while working on a pain medication for Nebula Pharmaceuticals. Once Nebula learned she'd created something that went far beyond their parameters, they'd ordered her to destroy the serum and formula. As his mother had explained in her digital holo-video journal, "The last thing a pharmaceutical company making billions of dollars selling drugs wants is for humanity to never need those drugs."

Cruz's mother had been pressured into agreeing to Nebula's demands, but not before engraving the formula into black marble, splitting the stone into eight pieces, and hiding the fragments of the cipher around the world. Fearing for her life, she made a holo-journal for Cruz with clues on how to find the pieces. Soon after, she died in a mysterious lab fire that had been ruled accidental. Cruz only recently discovered his mother's death had been no accident. And worse? Nebula was to blame.

Following the first clue in her journal, Cruz had deduced the first piece of the cipher was hidden in the base of his holo-projector back home in Hawaii. His best friend, Lani Kealoha, had removed the bottom plate of the dome and, sure enough, found the stone inside.

Laser-etched with partial numbers and symbols, the black marble now hung on a lanyard around Cruz's neck. It was pie-shaped and less than an inch across at the curved edge. The segment looked like a piece to a miniature, round puzzle. With two knobs on the right side and a curved indentation on the left, it was obvious the fragment was meant to interlock with two others. Finding it had been an amazing feat, but Cruz knew he had a long way to go to complete the cipher circle. Then there was Nebula. They were still out there, still determined to make sure he didn't succeed. To help keep him safe, Dr. Hightower had increased the security on board *Orion*, and among the students, only Emmett and Sailor knew of Cruz's mission.

Sailor peered around cabin 202, dark eyes roving past the door that opened to the attached balcony, over to the closet, then, finally, to the closed bathroom door. "Is Emmett...?" She stuck out her tongue and pointed at her mouth, making what Cruz was sure was the international sign for hurling.

"Heaving chunks? Nope. So far, so good. He went up to the fourth deck to check out the science tech lab. Between you and me, I think he needs help with Lumagine."

"Still working on that mind-control fabric, huh? Hasn't he tried, like, twenty times?"

"Twenty-six, actually. That's nothing for Emmett. It took him fifty-seven attempts to invent his emoto-glasses."

"That's what my mom would call super stick-to-itiveness."

Cruz noticed how Sailor kept a hand against the wall, as if worried that any minute a giant wave would capsize the boat. "He brought a bunch of extra seasick bands. I'm sure he wouldn't mind if you wanted to borrow one—"

"I'm fine," she said, though she didn't let go of the wall.

"It takes a few days to get your sea legs," he assured her. Living in Hawaii for the past seven—almost eight—years, Cruz had spent most of his life in or on the water. He knew the swaying motion of a 364-foot ship like *Orion* could take some getting used to, but he was sure everyone on his team would adjust. They'd already had some practice back at the Academy's Computer Animated Virtual Experience simulator—the CAVE.

"Taryn says there are snacks in the galley," said Sailor. "We have a few minutes before our meeting. You want to grab something on the way?"

Cruz was a little hungry. "Sure. One sec." He snapped his suitcase shut and went to put it in the closet.

"What's this?" Sailor had picked up a postcard off Cruz's desk.

"It's from my aunt."

She frowned. "How can you tell? She didn't sign it. It says 'Begin with the birth year of Peary's first man,' and then there's a bunch of numbers."

"It's a game we play. Aunt Marisol sends me coded messages on postcards. I decode them using books, art, or music, or whatever the clues lead to."

"Sweet as! So what does it say?"

POSTCARD

Begin with the birth year of Peary's first man.

1-12-9-29-43-19-12

2-14-43-2-17-13

Cruz Coronado

Explorer Academy

Orion

"Not sure yet. You can help me decode it if you want."

She rolled her eyes. "If I knew where to begin."

Cruz crossed the room to lock the veranda door. "Rule one: Always start with the picture."

Sailor flipped the card. The photo was of a round sea creature, its mottled brown-and-white head and creamy-colored tentacles cradled in a circular shell with wavy brown and white stripes. "I know this animal," she cried. "It's a mollusk, but I can't think of the name ... Not a hermit crab ..."

"Nautilus."

She snapped her fingers. "That's it!"

Cruz grinned. "And what book or song do you know that has a naut—"

"*Twenty Thousand Leagues Under the Sea. Nautilus* is the name of Captain Nemo's submarine."

He laughed. "I told Aunt Marisol she needs to make these harder."

Cruz grabbed his tablet computer and tucked it under his arm. He nodded toward the postcard. "Bring it with."

As they left the cabin, the door locked automatically behind them. Turning right out of his stateroom, Cruz followed Sailor down the narrow passage. A tall, sturdy security guard in a black jumpsuit stood near the elevator. Her ID tag read *K. Dover.* They said hi and she said hi, but her eyes lingered a bit longer on Cruz than on Sailor. Officer Dover tipped her reddish blond head at him as if to say, *So you're the one I'm here for.* Cruz had thought having extra security on board would make him feel safer, but all it was doing so far was making him feel singled out.

Beyond the elevator, the hall opened into a sunny atrium. On the other side of the ship were the faculty staterooms. Aunt Marisol's cabin was the second door on the left side. *Not "left,"* he corrected himself, *port.* He needed to start thinking in boating terms. The bow was the front of the ship, and the stern, the back. You went fore, or forward, to the bow and aft, or backward, to the stern. If you stood facing the bow, the right side of the ship was known as starboard and the left was port. A pair of grand staircases curved up each side of the round atrium, their ornate brass rails leading to the lounge on the third deck. The open lounge had plenty of seating: plump red and blue chairs in groups of four for hanging out with friends, as well as straight-backed chairs clustered around taller tables for doing homework. A large TV screen took up the back wall. The other three walls were glass, offering a sweeping view of wherever *Orion* was going. At the moment, the ship was navigating the murky greenish blue waters of the Chesapeake Bay. Potted lemon, lime, and orange trees flanked the doors leading to the outdoor bow deck. Lush green limbs drooped under the weight of ripe fruit. Certain they were fake, Cruz reached for a lemon.

"Better not let Chef Kristos catch you or you'll be washing dishes for months."

Cruz whirled around to see a young man in a navy shirt and matching pants. "I...I...only wanted to see if they were real," he sputtered.

"Did the same thing myself when I first came on board," the man said, his Australian accent dropping the r so the last word sounded like "on bawd." "If you think this is something, have a gander at the hydroponic garden on the observation deck. Chef Kristos grows most of the veggies we eat right here on the ship."

"I know!" said Sailor. "Do you think Chef Kristos would let me help take care of the plants? I miss my garden back home."

"Can't hurt to ask." The man rubbed his chin, and the emerald green eyes of a silver chameleon on his ring winked at them. "Do I detect a bit of the Kiwi there?"

Sailor grinned. "I'm from Christchurch, New Zealand."

"Melbourne born and raised."

"Sweet as! I'm Sailor York, and this is Cruz Coronado. We're explorers."

The man ruffled his messy crop of cinnamon hair. "Tripp Scarlatos. Marine biologist, aquatics director, and *Ridley* pilot."

"The mini sub?" Cruz's ears perked up. "You drive the mini sub?"

"Yip. Best job on the boat. In fact, I'm late for a meeting with Monsieur Legrand, and he does not like to be kept waiting, though I'm sure you know that. Hooroo!"

As Sailor and Cruz passed the security station next to the purser's desk, a beefy guard with a thick dark mustache and a gold hoop earring caught Cruz's eye. The gold ID tag on his massive chest read *J. Wardicorn.* He glanced at them but did not smile or nod. Turning down the corridor that led to the galley and classrooms, Cruz could feel the guard's eyes boring into his back. More scrutiny.

Sailor was studying his postcard as they walked. "Who is Peary's first man?"

"I know that one." Cruz had just finished reading a book about explorers—a book Aunt Marisol had loaned him. Coincidence? Hardly. "It's Matthew Henson. He was the first African-American explorer to go to the Arctic. He navigated a bunch of Robert Peary's expeditions and that's where he got the nickname 'Peary's first man.'" He glanced at her. "Read the clue again."

"'Begin with the birth year of Peary's first man.'"

Okay, so you'd want to look up the year Henson was born, then go to the text of *Twenty Thousand Leagues* and search the book for the first mention of that year. Once you find it, you'd start counting the letters, according to the postcard. That's what those sets of numbers are for. See how the first number is one? The means the letter you want is going to be the first letter after 1866."

"I get it," said Sailor. "The next number is twelve, so I'd want to find the twelfth letter after 1866 and so on until I spell out a word."

"Right."

"And I bet each set of numbers is equal to one word in the message."

"Exactly."

Her face lit up. "Can I decode it?"

Cruz could tell it was a short phrase, and Aunt Marisol never put anything personal in their postcards, so he didn't see why not. "Be my guest."

They were at the galley entrance. Cruz held his gold Open Sesame wristband up to the security camera to open the door. Just inside the dining room, several baskets full of fruit, energy bars, and other snacks had been placed on a side table. Sailor grabbed an apple. Cruz chose a small bag of trail mix. They took their food and headed to the conference room down the passage. Emmett was already there. He'd saved three seats for Sailor, Cruz, and Bryndis. Letting Sailor have the first chair, Cruz slipped into the second, which also happened to be next to Dugan Marsh.

Although they had trained together back at Academy headquarters and were now on Team Cousteau together, Cruz kept his distance from Dugan. The boy from Santa Fe, who was Ali Soliman's roommate, had made it clear from the start he didn't think Cruz belonged here. Dugan often made rude comments about Cruz getting special treatment because his aunt was their anthropology professor. It wasn't true.

If anything, Aunt Marisol had made Cruz work harder to prove himself. Still, that didn't stop Dugan from needling Cruz every chance he got. It also hadn't helped that Cruz had walloped Dugan in Monsieur Legrand's Augmented Reality Challenge obstacle course—the ARC—in fitness and survival training class. Maybe being on the ship was the fresh start they needed. Cruz was certainly willing to give it a try. "How's it going, Dugan?"

"Wonderful," said Dugan with about as much enthusiasm as a sick slug.

Cruz opened his bag of trail mix and offered the bag to his teammate.

"Are we supposed to eat in here?" snapped Dugan. "Or did you get your aunt to change the rules just for you?"

Strike two. Cruz didn't need a third strike to tell him Dugan wasn't interested in a new beginning. He pivoted his chair toward friendlier territory, aka Emmett. Looking around, Cruz did not see a sign saying NO FOOD. Even so, he slid the bag into his lap and ate a little faster in case Dugan was right.

Cruz tried to ask Emmett about his progress in the tech lab; however, with his mouth full, "How'd it go at the tech lab?" came out "Half hid a goat atheck lap?"

A bewildered Emmett stared at him for a few seconds, his emoto-glasses changing from their usual solid lime green ovals to a rushing current of seafoam and sapphire. "Oh, I gotcha. Not so good. The nano-processors sync up on the computer sim runs, but in human trials, I can't get the textile to respond to cerebral cortex functional recon-structive commands—or even basic pigmentation alterations, for that matter."

"So nothing happens?"

"That's what I said."

Cruz was about to reassure Emmett that he would figure it out, when Sailor leaned behind Emmett. "Got it!" She was clutching her tablet and the postcard. "Henson was born in 1866, and fortunately,

I didn't have to read far—1866 is the third word in the book. Here you go." She handed the postcard to Cruz.

He saw she had assigned each of the numbers a letter, as he had instructed. Aunt Marisol's message read: *Welcome aboard.*

"Thanks for letting me be your cryptographer," said Sailor. "That was fun."

"Anytime."

"Good afternoon, explorers!" Taryn Secliff breezed into the room.

Taryn was their class adviser, and the "mom" of their group. She gave advice, helped solve problems, and made sure everyone was where they were supposed to be, doing what they were supposed to be doing. As Taryn passed Cruz, he saw Hubbard, her West Highland white terrier,

at her heels. The little dog was wearing a bright yellow life vest. Taryn took a seat at the head of the table. She searched their faces. "How are we all doing? Settling in? Getting your sea legs? Excited to explore the world?"

Nudging Emmett, Cruz nodded to the empty seat across from him and whispered, "Bryndis isn't here."

Bryndis Jónsdóttir, the fifth member of Team Cousteau, had come to Cruz's rescue after he had been falsely accused of cheating and expelled from the Academy. Her detective work revealed it was Renshaw McKittrick, another team member, and not Cruz, who'd hacked into their CAVE training programs and altered them. Cruz owed Bryndis a lot. Plus, he liked her a lot. Cruz was starting to think maybe she liked him a little, too.

Emmett and Cruz looked at each other. Should they say something about Bryndis?

Taryn cleared her throat to signal they were starting. "On behalf of the faculty, staff, and crew of Explorer Academy, it's my pleasure to welcome you aboard *Orion*, the flagship of the Academy's fleet. For the remainder of your time with us, this will be home. And as such, we expect you to treat it with care. Please keep your cabin and the lounge areas clean. We also expect you to follow the same rules you did back at Academy headquarters. No leaving the ship without permission or adult supervision, no visitors on board without prior approval, and all issues with roommates, teammates, faculty, homework, health, and everything else are to be brought to my attention. Most of the ship is at your disposal, so if you haven't already had a chance to take the tour and meet the crew, please do so when we finish here. Questions?" Taryn was searching their faces. "None? Moving on. Second order of business: Classes resume tomorrow two doors down in Manatee classroom at eight a.m."

There were a few groans—the biggest from Dugan.

Taryn pursed her lips. "This is not a vacation cruise. While we're at sea, you'll be expected to follow the same school schedule you did at the Academy. First period, conservation; followed by anthropology, fitness and survival training, biology, world geography, and journalism. Whenever we dock, classes will be suspended during our time in port." As they started to cheer, Taryn held up a hand. "Before you get too excited, this is because your professors and guest instructors will have missions for you to complete on shore. You'll learn more about those as we go, but don't expect a lot of free time. Questions? None? Moving on. Third item—"

Cruz couldn't take it anymore. He lifted his arm. "Taryn, Bryndis isn't here."

"That is true," she said evenly. "As I was saying, third item..."

Cruz dropped his arm. Shouldn't their adviser be more concerned that an explorer was missing? What if Bryndis had gotten lost? Or was sick? Or had fallen overboard?

Rising from her chair, Taryn moved toward a connecting door behind her. She grabbed the knob and flung the door wide open. "...your official Explorer Academy uniforms!"

Cruz's breath caught. Bryndis! The tall, fair-haired Icelander stood in the doorway, one knee bent, like a fashion model. She wore a light gray zippered jacket with a high collar. Dark gray fabric trimmed the square shoulders and cuffs. On the front of the jacket were four diagonal pockets—two on the chest and two on the hips. Pinned to the jacket above the top-right pocket was a black rectangle with the letters *EA* in gold. On the left collar was a button or pin that looked like planet Earth. Straight-legged pants matched the jacket, with light and dark shades of gray. A mock-turtleneck tee the color of moss poked out the top of the jacket. From her pinkie dangled a pair of round bronze sunglasses that looked like stacked machinery gears.

A grinning Bryndis strolled into the conference room with two women trailing behind her. The first looked a few years older than Aunt Marisol. She wore a white lab coat, a light blue button-down shirt, a black knee-length skirt, and nurse's shoes. She carried a tablet twice the size of the explorers' standard-issue computer. The other woman, about Taryn's age, shuffled in wearing shredded jeans, a faded pink tee, and red flip-flops. She'd tied a tiger-print scarf around her head and was dipping her hand into a bag of pink jelly beans.

"Explorers, please meet our tech lab chief, Dr. Fanchon Quills, and her assistant, Dr. Sidril Vanderwick," said Taryn. "They are the brains behind much of your wearable technology and are joining us to explain its main features. Fanchon?"

Cruz turned toward the lady in the lab coat, her blondish brown hair pulled back into a bun so tight it was stretching her cheeks back.

"Thank you, Taryn," said the woman with the tiger-print head scarf.

Cruz did a double take. *That* was Dr. Quills? The one who looked like a college student on her way to the beach and was eating candy?

"Please, everyone, call me Fanchon." Dr. Quills set her jelly beans on the table so she could gesture toward Bryndis. "Your Academy uniforms utilize state-of-the-art technology. The material is developed by our own Society scientists. It's designed to help keep you cool in warm climates and blocks 99.9 percent of the sun's harmful rays. It's water-repellent, bug-repellent, reptile-repellent, and antibacterial. In your lower-left pocket, you'll find a small charging port." Bryndis unzipped the pocket and brought out a tiny plug. "This converts the heat from your body to electricity to power your tablet, cell phone, or any other digital device."

"Did you see that?" Cruz pounded Emmett on the shoulder.

"I saw. I saw." Emmett's glasses were a kaleidoscope on hyperdrive.

"Notice the EA pin on the top right," continued the tech chief. "This is your communications system. Press it firmly once, then specify who you are and who you want to communicate with. You can reach a crew member, explorer, faculty member, or anyone with a similar pin within a twenty-five-mile radius of your location. The signal can be boosted, of course, if necessary. Press the EA pin twice, and it becomes a global translator, allowing you to understand and converse in more than six thousand languages. The planet Earth insignia activates your personal GPS system." Bryndis tapped the round blue-and-green pin on her left collar. In an instant, it emitted a holographic overlay of the third deck of the ship in front of her!

Cruz's bag of trail mix hit the floor.

"This will allow you to find your way around most anyplace in the world," explained Fanchon. "Your holo-map includes augmented-reality features, such as museums, historical sites, restaurants, or pretty much whatever you request. As you move, the map and elements will change, according to your position. This view is public mode. Put on your sunglasses to switch to private mode so that only you will see the display."

Bryndis placed the cog-like sunglasses on her nose, and the holographic image instantly disappeared. "I can see everything perfectly," she verified. The lenses looked cool, though Cruz wondered if Bryndis could see the real world as well as she could see the virtual one.

"I am happy to take your questions." Fanchon Quills scanned the room. The usually inquisitive explorers were speechless, including Cruz.

"Not one question?" Taryn cocked an eyebrow. "Come on. The time to ask is now, not when you're out on a mission. Speak up!"

"*Arf!*" barked Hubbard.

Everyone giggled.

"You'll find complete operating instructions for your uniform and its technology on your tablet," explained Taryn. "Please carefully review them." Her gaze settled on Cruz. "Because one day, this uniform might save your life."

Cruz understood. Only a few days ago, he had come as close to death as he'd ever been.

Malcolm Rook, Explorer Academy's librarian, had been secretly working for Nebula. Cornering Cruz and his dad in the special collections of the Academy's library with a laser, Mr. Rook planned to steal the holo-journal and kill Cruz and his father. He might have succeeded, too, had Cruz not commanded Mell to attack at the last second. The persistent stings of the faithful drone caused Rook to misfire, and the laser had only grazed Cruz's arm. He was lucky, he knew. Cruz slid the right sleeve of his tee up a few inches. The small football-shaped burn scar on his upper right arm was nearly gone.

Everyone was lining up to get their uniforms. Cruz stood, too, and waited behind Emmett. However, while his 22 classmates were bubbling with excitement, Cruz remained quiet. He was worried. Fanchon had said their uniforms were every kind of "proof" imaginable: waterproof, sunproof, bugproof, reptileproof, even germproof. But she had left one very important "proof" off that list.

Bulletproof.

ATLANTIC
OCEAN

NORTH
SEA

UNITED
KINGDOM

LONDON,
ENGLAND

IRELAND

NETH.

CELTIC
SEA

BELGIUM

FRANCE

▶ **"ANOTHER** *perfect plan failed."* The tone was cool and controlled, yet the words sent a chill down Thorne Prescott's spine. Hezekiah Brume was not a man who took disappointment well.

"Uh . . . sorry, sir," croaked Prescott, looking away from the holo-image. Not that he would have seen anything other than whatever his boss had his phone pointed toward—a vase of roses or an antique clock or, like this morning, a gold knife smoothly slicing through a fried egg.

Brume never allowed himself to be photographed. Prescott had no clue why. The owner of Nebula Pharmaceuticals was as much of a mystery to Prescott as he was to the rest of the world. Although Prescott had worked for Brume for nearly five years, he had never met him. Today was supposed to be the day he finally did. Prescott had taken the red-eye flight from Washington, D.C., to London. He had arrived at Nebula headquarters at 8 a.m., only to discover Brume was not there. Brume's executive assistant, Oona, had given him some explanation about an emergency in Beijing. And so Prescott found himself a thousand feet above the city, talking to his boss, who was five thousand miles away.

Brume's knife was tapping a gold-rimmed plate. He was waiting for an explanation. Prescott buried the heel of a snakeskin cowboy boot into the plush white carpet. "I had him cornered in the museum, but there was too much security." He put a hand to his head. The lump was nearly gone. Prescott wasn't sure who'd cracked him on the noggin when he was inches away from taking care of Cruz Coronado once and for all. He'd woken up on the floor in the basement of the museum with two guards handcuffing him and his intended target nowhere to be found. "We're back on track. He's within our grasp."

"That's what you said about Hawaii, Cobra." Brume never used his true identity, in case he was under surveillance by an enemy, and he required his field employees to do the same. Everyone had a code name. Prescott's was Cobra, for his cowboy boots. Brume's was Lion. Zebra, Wallaby, and Mongoose were on board Orion.

"Hawaii was . . . unfortunate." Prescott had to admit that trying to drown a kid who practically had fins was not his best idea. Suddenly, a strange sensation came over him. Prescott had the creepy feeling he was being watched. He let his gaze wander over the large office. Everything dripped of money, from the tornado of a crystal chandelier to the smallest gold fleur-de-lis pull to the satin drapes. Not that Prescott cared about that kind of thing. Behind the tufted, gold velvet sofa, a shellacked ebony door etched with a large N was slightly open. It probably led to the bathroom. Now, a 14-karat-gold toilet, that would be something to see!

"Perhaps Jaguar can be more helpful to us," said his boss.

"Jaguar?" Prescott did not recognize the code name.

"We have someone new, someone who can get even closer to him."

Closer? The only person who could possibly get closer to Cruz than their current crop of contacts was . . .

Prescott drew in a breath. An explorer. Brume had a spy among the explorers!

There it was again—that feeling that he was being observed. He scanned the room, his eyes moving from the desk to the bookcases to the monogrammed bathroom door. There! In the sliver of space between the two doors, he caught a shadow. And was that an eye? It was! Someone was spying on him.

"Is that all you have to report, Cobra?"

Prescott knew he could put it off no longer. "There is one other thing, sir. She . . . left something for him . . . a journal." He heard a fork hit porcelain and rushed on. "Probably filled with personal ramblings. I don't think it's anything to worry about. It could tell him nothing."

"Or it could tell him everything," growled his boss. "Get the journal. Take care of its owner. No loose ends. And do it before his thirteenth birthday, do you hear me?"

"November twenty-ninth," confirmed Prescott, though he didn't understand the significance of the deadline. What difference did it make if he finished the job on the 29th or the 30th? It must have something to do with the number 13. Brume was a superstitious man. Maybe he thought dealing with the kid after he turned 13 would bring him bad luck. With Brume, who knew?

"We have another problem." Brume was still talking. "Meerkat. I need you to handle him."

Meerkat? That was the code name for Malcolm Rook, the Academy librarian. Rook was supposed to have taken care of Cruz after Prescott had blown his chance, but he had failed, too. Following Rook's arrest, Nebula's attorneys had sprung him from jail and gotten him out of the country. Yet, now Brume wanted Meerkat out of the picture completely? Interesting.

"I understand," said Prescott, his eyes drifting to the ebony door. The eyeball was gone.

Watching his boss spread orange marmalade over a triangle of toasted multigrain bread, it dawned on Prescott that Beijing was

seven hours ahead of London. It wasn't breakfast time there. It was three o'clock in the afternoon. He was beginning to understand. Brume wasn't in China. Never had been. He might still be in London, maybe even peering at him from that bathroom 30 feet away.

"Cobra!"

"Sir?"

The toast hovered. "Hawaii and Washington, D.C. That's two strikes, you know."

Another tremor shook Prescott.

He knew.

3

CRUZ STARED at his reflection. In the lavender blue light of dawn, it seemed as if someone else was staring back. It was him, and yet it wasn't.

Standing in front of the full-length mirror attached to the inside of their closet door, his eyes slowly traveled down his angular jacket and pants, ending at a new pair of cream athletic shoes with gold stripes. He'd figured that any uniform that could become a flotation device or was packing a lightweight parachute in the back lining (or so the instructions claimed) was probably not going to be comfortable. He'd expected it to be heavy or itchy or stiff or all of those things, but it wasn't. The shirt was like skin; he barely felt it. The jacket and pants were featherlight and stretched in every direction, their linings softer than fleece. Plus, everything fit perfectly.

Cruz slipped Mell inside his lower-right jacket pocket. He stuck the honeycomb pin on his uniform next to the rectangular Explorer Academy communications pin. The tiny pin was a gift from Lani, a voice-command remote she had made for Mell. It was a going-away present. Lani hadn't wanted Cruz to go to the Academy without her, but he had gone anyway. Only the best of friends would give you such a cool gift when you were leaving her behind. That was Lani. More recently, she'd made him a protective sleeve for his mom's holo-journal. To the ordinary observer, the journal looked like a plain white piece of cardstock, but lay it flat on a surface and—watch out! First, the three-by-three-inch square emitted a security beam to scan and identify any human in its proximity. If it determined the human was not Cruz, it simply shut off. But if it *did* identify him, the page morphed into a three-dimensional orb that projected a holo-video of his mother, Petra. It was her digital journal that had sent Cruz on a global quest to find the pieces of her formula. After giving him his first clue, her holo-image had disappeared and the orb had returned to its former state—a plain, *fragile* white square of cardstock. Lani's protective sleeve was made of a super-durable material; she didn't say what it was but he couldn't bend it, so it was probably some type of carbon fiber. Picking up the journal by its edges with a towel so he wouldn't activate it, Cruz slipped it into Lani's sturdy sleeve, then tucked that into the upper-left front pocket of his jacket. He was ready for his first day of classes.

Emmett came out of the bath-room and stood next to Cruz. He looked at himself in the mirror, too. "We look fifteen," he declared.

"I do. You look fourteen, maybe," snickered Cruz, which earned him a punch in the arm.

Emmett sniffed the air. "I smell waffles."

"Before we go, we'd better…" Cruz motioned to their closet.

Along with their uniforms, the explor-ers had been issued activewear, heavy-duty backpacks,

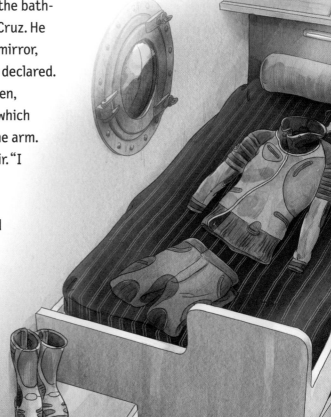

hiking boots, and deck shoes. Each also got a thick polar coat. Of all their new clothes, it was Cruz's favorite. Not only did the hooded coat keep your body temperature at a toasty 98.6 degrees in the cold weather, but it was reversible, too. One side was gray camouflage, while the other was more of a solid silvery color. The silver side might have looked a bit plain, but it had a special feature. Hit the top collar button and it glowed in the dark! Another one of Fanchon and Sidril's creations, the tech gurus had nicknamed it the hide-and-seek jacket. As Fanchon had explained, "You've got camouflage to hide and bioluminescent light to be seen!"

Not having time to organize all of their new gear, Emmett and Cruz had crammed everything into the closet they shared. It was a mess.

"We could leave it open," suggested Emmett.

"If Taryn sees it..."

"Come on." They shoved their backs against the pair of doors to get them to latch.

"Good thing they're keeping all our diving gear below." Emmett gritted his teeth.

Cruz dug in his heels. "Let's hope they don't issue us any more stuff."

"One more push and I think we've got it."

They gave it a good heave and heard both doors catch.

"We'll reorganize after dinner," huffed Cruz.

"I thought we were going to get started on the next clue to your mom's formula."

"We've got time. I told Sailor to meet us here at nine."

"Nine? That only gives us a half hour until lights-out."

"I know, but Lani's six hours behind us in Hawaii and I promised we wouldn't do any detective work without her."

In the passage, Cruz and Emmett met the same female security guard they'd seen yesterday. This time, however, Officer Dover was posted halfway between their cabin and the elevator. She was getting closer!

"Good morning," she said.

"Hi," said Cruz, scurrying past.

As they entered the atrium, Cruz was wondering if Aunt Marisol had anything to do with the guard's new position, when who should come floating down the port side of the grand staircase? Instead of her usual brightly colored clothes and high heels, Aunt Marisol was wearing a long-sleeved white dress shirt, khaki crop pants, and blue deck shoes without socks. Her long, dark chocolate brown hair was pulled back into a low ponytail.

"Awww, look at the two of you in your uniforms," she gushed, though she never took her gaze off Cruz.

Watching her eyes fill with pride, Cruz felt a warmth go through him. Emmett was grinning big-time.

Aunt Marisol bent toward him. "Cruz, can I talk to you for a minute? It's important."

"Sure. Go on ahead," Cruz instructed Emmett. "I'll catch up."

"Okay, but I can't promise there will be any waffles left when you do." Emmett took the stairs two at a time.

Hooking her arm through his elbow, Aunt Marisol led Cruz across the atrium toward the faculty passage. "I just talked to Captain Iskandar," she whispered. "He said you hadn't come by the bridge to put your … uh … valuables in the ship's safe." By "valuables" she meant his mom's journal and the first piece of the cipher. "Did you forget?" she pressed.

"No."

"Do you want me to take care of it for you?"

"No. I've … uh … decided I'm not going to put them in the safe after all."

She stopped. "Why not?"

"I thought I'd … keep them with me."

"*With you?* Are you kidding?" When he shook his head, she hissed, "Cruz, that's a bad idea."

"You don't think I can handle it?"

"It's not that," she said, but her flashing eyes made it clear it was that. "A million things could happen to them in your possession. What if you lose them?"

"I won't."

"What if someone steals them?"

"They won't."

"What if you fall into a stream or forget them in your pocket when you send your pants to the laundry or leave your jacket on shore—"

"*I won't!*"

"Cruz!"

"A million things could happen if I *don't* have them with me." He matched her fire with his own. "What if I need to check a clue in the journal? Or find the next piece of the formula? In her journal, Mom told me to show her each piece so she could confirm it was genuine. Only then can I unlock the next clue. That means I'll have to come all the way back to the ship and get the captain to open the safe for me. I *have* to have it with me. Besides," he rushed on as Aunt Marisol opened her mouth to argue, "how do we know the safe is really, you know, *safe*? Do you know the combination?"

"Well, no, but I'm sure Captain Iskandar would never—"

"I thought Mr. Rook would never, either. Look how that turned out."

Her gaze dropped to his arm. "I know you want to protect your mom's work, but you can't do it alone. There are people here who want to help. You need to trust them."

"I trust *you*." He stood taller. "And Emmett and Sailor. Nobody else."

"So that's it, then? Your mind is made up? You won't consider using the ship's safe."

"I'll...consider it," he lied. Cruz didn't want to seem inflexible. And he didn't want her to be mad at him.

"Maybe you should talk to your dad about it? See what he thinks?"

"Okay." Another lie. Cruz didn't know why he said it, except second lies are always easier than first ones.

"Go get something to eat." She spun him toward the stairs. "I'll see you in class."

He spun back. "Aunt Marisol?"

"What?"

He gave her the softest, widest doe eyes he had. "I love you."

"I love you, too, Cruz Sebastian Coronado, but all the sweet words in the world won't help you if you lose—"

"I *won't*."

Cruz may have lied when he said he'd consider placing the journal and cipher in the ship's safe, but he had told the truth about why he wanted to keep the items close to him. It was important to be able to access them at a moment's notice. Yet there was more to it than that. He didn't know how to explain it. His aunt would probably think it was silly, but Cruz needed the stone. When he sat quietly in the bubbled observation deck watching the sun slip from the horizon, he needed to slide his thumb across the engraved equations. When he hiked up a mountain trail through a thicket of snow-flocked trees, he needed to feel the rhythm of it bumping against him like a second heart. And as Cruz uncovered the other pieces, he knew he would need them, too. Every. Single. One. They were his only—his last—connection to his mother. Once he'd found all the fragments and the formula was complete, he knew what was likely to happen. His mother's prerecorded digital journal would instruct him to turn them over to the Society and his mission would end. There would be nothing to keep them together. He would continue on and his mom would evaporate from his life forever. Was it so wrong to want to hold on to her for as long as possible?

"Cruz?" Zane Patrick was looking at him oddly.

Cruz glanced around. He was at the end of the passage on the third deck. He'd gone past the galley, the conference room, the faculty offices, and the classrooms, with no recollection of doing so.

"You okay?" asked his friend.

Cruz's hand flew to his chest. The stone was there. Safe and sound. "Uh . . . yeah. I'm good."

DR. BRENT GABRIEL welcomed Cruz to Manatee classroom with a wide grin. "I'm sure glad to see you."

"Thanks."

"I'd like to apologize... about everything that happened." The conservation professor lowered his voice. "When I heard the CAVE training software had been compromised and the hack had been traced back to your tablet, I... I didn't want to believe it. But it seemed so cut-and-dried. I am truly sorry. I should have pressed for a more thorough review."

"It's okay." Cruz was trying to put it all behind him.

"And then to have to endure that whole ordeal with Rook..."

To protect Cruz, Dr. Hightower had not revealed to anyone the full truth behind Malcolm Rook's attack on Cruz and his father. Instead, she'd told the students and staff of the Academy that the librarian's actions had been caused by stress and that he was now receiving counseling.

"Well, after that nightmare, no one would have blamed you if you'd wanted to get as far away from the Academy as possible," finished Dr. Gabriel. He was buffing the back of his bald head with his fist the way he always did when something bothered him.

"Not a chance," replied Cruz.

"That's the spirit." Professor Gabriel backed away. "Oh, and don't forget to see me after class for your makeup work."

"M-makeup work?"

"You missed three assignments and a test on global water issues."

"But I was unfairly expelled. And injured, too!"

"Which is why I'm giving you an extra week to do the work."

"But—"

"You need to know the material. I have complete faith that you'll rise to the challenge."

That wasn't fair. How was Cruz supposed to argue with praise?

Unfortunately, his other teachers also expected him to do the work he'd missed. Even Aunt Marisol had him reading 50 pages in preparation for a quiz tomorrow on basic archaeological terms. *Tomorrow!* Cruz wanted to run up to Dugan and say, "See? I am not getting any special treatment!" But of course he didn't. By the time their journalism professor, Dr. Kira Benedict, dismissed the last class of the day, Cruz felt like he'd been hit by a homework avalanche. He was buried up to his neck in reading, projects, essays, assignments, and test prep.

On their way out of Manatee classroom, Cruz turned to Emmett. "Do you mind waiting to reorganize our closet? I thought I'd go to the library and try to catch up on all the work I missed last week."

"No problem. I've got plenty to keep me busy with Lumagine."

Orion's library was on the fifth and top deck of the ship, between the bridge and the observation deck. It wasn't as grand as the library back at Academy headquarters. No towering rotunda painted like the night sky, life-size bronze statues of famous explorers, or acres of shelves. Yet the two-story mahogany-paneled room with a curved staircase was elegant in its own way. The bookcases were built into the walls. Each case was lit from within and had a set of double glass accordion doors—to keep the books in place when the seas got a bit rough, Cruz figured. Along the starboard wall, bronze fan-shaped sconces and plump navy chairs invited readers to settle in next to the windows. Navy drapes had been swept aside by gold tassels to let in the afternoon light.

As Cruz tried to decide where to sit, a woman poked her head around a mahogany pole. A wave of black hair swung over her shoulder. Coral lips slid upward. "Hi, Cruz." Her blood-red cat-eye glasses sat slightly tilted on a freckled nose.

"Hi, Dr. Holland," he said shyly. Back at the Academy, Dr. Holland had been the assistant librarian. She had worked alongside Mr. Rook. However, she did not know the truth about him. Cruz hoped Dr. Holland didn't hold it against him that her friend and colleague was no longer working at the Academy.

"First time using the ship's library?" asked Dr. Holland.

Cruz nodded. He'd peeked in on the tour, but that was it.

"We have more than a thousand titles on board to check out, as well as digital access to pretty much any book in print. You're welcome to use one of our e-readers or have the book uploaded to your tablet. We also have full Wi-Fi, document-size printers, and tabletop computers to view maps. In other words"—her smiling green eyes glanced up—"you have the world at your fingertips."

Cruz followed her gaze. A giant glass map covered the entire oval ceiling! Lit from a skylight above, the planet's continents, islands, and oceans glowed. The sea currents looked as if they were really in motion! Tipping his head all the way back, Cruz did a slow circle.

"I'll let you settle in," said the librarian.

Cruz chose a chair by the window and spent the next several hours trying to focus on homework and not stare up at the cool backlit ceiling map. He was almost done with Aunt Marisol's reading assignment on absolute and relative archaeological dating methods, when his nose began to twitch. Cheese. He smelled warm cheese. His stomach gurgled in confirmation. Emmett was in the doorway, holding a grilled cheese

sandwich. His roommate held up the plate, indicating it was meant for Cruz. The clock on Cruz's tablet read 20 minutes to seven. The galley closed at 6:30. He had worked right through dinner! Quickly packing up, Cruz made a beeline for the sandwich and the friend who was kind enough to bring it.

Cruz reached for the brown triangle. "I'm starving."

"I figured. I got to the galley just in time. I've got another surprise."

The first thought that popped into Cruz's mind was chocolate cake, but Emmett's other hand was empty. Shoot!

"It's back in our room." Pink dots were rapidly chasing turquoise streaks in Emmett's circular frames. If Emmett was this excited, maybe it was better than cake!

They headed down three decks to their passage on the atrium level. Cruz was already into the second half of his sandwich when they passed Officer Dover in the hall. Emmett held his OS band up to the security camera in front of cabin 202. The lock unlatched, and the door swung open. Cruz froze mid-bite.

It looked as if a hurricane had struck their room!

SEEING their cabin turned upside down was not the surprise Cruz had expected. And by the look on Emmett's face, it wasn't the one he'd planned. Every drawer had been ripped from its dresser, desk, or nightstand, its contents dumped on the floor. Shirts, jackets, pants, jeans, socks, and shoes were strewn everywhere. The beds had been stripped, chairs overturned. Like the first snow of winter, a thin layer of white covered everything. It took Cruz a moment to identify the coating. Carefully navigating the mess, he found what was left of his pillow between one of the stuffed chair cushions and the wall. The violent slash marks that shredded his pillowcase sent a shudder through him.

"So much for reorganizing the closet," said Emmett flatly. Apparently, that had been his surprise. His roommate looked at him through frames that were churning storm clouds. "Nebula?"

"I guess Mr. Rook told them about Mom's journal and the cipher."

Emmett gasped. "You didn't...?"

One hand went to his chest, the other to his pocket. Just to be sure. "I've got them. But I did leave..." Cruz's gaze swung to his nightstand. It was gone! He dived into the tangle of sheets at the foot of his bed. "Oh no! *No!*"

"What's wrong?" cried Emmett

"My holo-video," he called from inside his comforter.

"The one that had the first piece of the cipher hidden inside?"

"Yes, Lani sent it, along with the cipher. I put it on my nightstand when I unpacked yesterday. They must have thought it was the journal. I should never have left it out!"

"Maybe it just got knocked off." Cruz could hear Emmett rummaging through stuff. "It's silver, right?"

"Yes, with a round top and a flat bottom." Cruz fought his way out of the sheet. He peered under the bed. Frantic, he checked behind the nightstand, which was bolted to the floor. Nothing. Out of breath, Cruz started pawing through a pile of clothes. It had to be here. It just had to. He'd never forgive himself if he lost it. Neither would Aunt Marisol.

"Got it!" Emmett's arm rose from beneath a mound of clothes, the dome in his palm.

Cruz rushed to scoop the holo-projector from Emmett. "Thank you, thank you!" He gently placed the dome on his starry-night granite desk. Cruz was glad it hadn't been stolen, but he knew he wasn't out of the woods. Could the video have survived Lani's surgery, a cross-country mail-drone flight, *and* an intruder's attack? It hardly seemed possible.

Emmett was beside him. Cruz reached out. Reluctantly. He wanted to know, yet he didn't. He felt cool metal under his fingertips. Cruz waited. For a moment—a very long moment—time stopped. Nothing happened. His head fell. It *was* broken.

"There!" cried Emmett.

Cruz saw a flutter, and his mother's face appeared. The image flickered for a few seconds before stabilizing. Cruz watched the scene at the beach he'd viewed a thousand times unfold before him: his toddler-age self digging his own island in the sand, then calling for his mother to rescue him, which she happily did. Only when the video finished and went to black did Cruz let himself exhale. It hadn't been damaged. Everything was all right.

"Nice memory," Emmett said softly.

Overcome with joy and relief, Cruz could only nod.

One crisis over, they turned their attention to the next.

"It had to be somebody from maintenance or housekeeping, don't you think?" Emmett stepped through the wreckage. "Someone who wouldn't raise suspicions from security."

"Or even someone *on* the security team."

"We can't trust anyone."

"That's what I told Aunt Marisol."

"You did? When?"

"When she said I should put the journal and cipher in the ship's safe. I told her I could look after them myself, but now"—he reached for his overturned desk chair—"I'm not so sure."

"I could check the security logs and footage from the passage," said Emmett. "Although I have a feeling that whoever did this knew how to cover their tracks."

"Agreed." Cruz saw a split in one of the legs of his chair that hadn't been there before, and the realization hit. This was more than someone looking for something—the intruder could have done that without them ever knowing he or she had been in the room. No. This was a message from Nebula. And the message was: *We can get to you anytime we want.*

Emmett gently took the chair from Cruz's hands. "Let's put the room back together before somebody sees."

Fortunately, Cruz's other keepsakes from his mother weren't damaged. Someone had opened the aqua box and flung its contents on the floor; however, everything was next to his bed: a jewelry box key, an Aztec crown charm, a photo of Cruz with the code scribbled on the back, a pair of washers (one ridged and one smooth), a pad of cat-shaped sticky notes, a box of bandages, pens and pencils, and even a bag of almonds. Nothing was opened, damaged, or missing. Cruz carefully put all the items back in the box and replaced the top. He started to put it back on his nightstand but instead slid it under his bed.

At a quarter to nine, there was a knock at the door.

Emmett's head popped up from the side of his bed. He'd been tucking in his comforter. "Too early for Sailor."

Cruz hung up his hide-and-seek jacket on a hook inside the closet door, then surveyed the room. Not bad. No one would have ever guessed that an hour ago cabin 202 was in total shambles. He went to answer the door.

"The vac!" hissed Emmett a second before Cruz would have tripped over it.

Cruz dived for Aunt Marisol's handheld mini vacuum. With a silent prayer of thanks that she'd insisted he bring it, Cruz tossed the appliance to Emmett, who pitched it into the closet.

Another knock. "Hey! You guys there?" It *was* Sailor. Cruz opened up, and she flew past. "We're in a time crunch, so let's get cracking."

"We have to wait for Lani," said Cruz firmly. He stifled a yawn, which probably caused Emmett to yawn, which then triggered a full yawn from Cruz. Yawns really were contagious!

Sailor glanced from one roommate to the other. "You two look knackered."

"If 'knackered' means 'tired,' you nailed it." Emmett flopped onto one of the overstuffed chairs. He put his feet up on the little round table, tipped his head back, and closed his eyes.

"Maybe I should let you guys go to sleep. We can do this another time."

"No!" burst Cruz. He wasn't about to postpone something this important. He lightly smacked Emmett's foot to get him to open his eyes. "We've been cleaning, that's all."

"And cleaning and cleaning ..." groaned Emmett, his eyes still shut.

She made a face. "We've only been on the ship two days. How dirty could your room have gotten?"

"Somebody ... broke in," confessed Cruz.

"Nebula," added Emmett. "They trashed the place."

Sailor's head swiveled. "Did they get the—"

"The journal and cipher are safe," said Cruz.

"Nothing's safe." Emmett opened his eyes, sat up straight, and planted both feet on the floor. "We should know that by now. And I should have done it first thing yesterday."

Cruz turned his desk chair around so he could join them. "Done what?"

"Set up some security in here."

"You mean, like a camera?" asked Sailor. "You could use Mell."

"That's a start, but I was thinking bigger, you know, motion detectors, thermal sensors, infrared beams—the works." Emmett's glasses had morphed into bright turquoise teardrops.

If Emmett could secure their cabin, then it meant Cruz could keep the journal and cipher close *and* safe. It was worth a try. "Okay," said Cruz. "Do whatever you have to do."

At 9 p.m. on the dot, Cruz's tablet chimed. Lani appeared. He turned the screen so everyone could say hello to her.

"You cut your hair," squealed Sailor.

Lani shook her angled, chin-length bob. "Do you like it?"

"Love it!"

Cruz pretended to look confused. "What's with the white skunk stripe?"

Tucking the lock of silvery white hair at her temple behind one ear, she lifted her chin. "The color is called Moondust. It'll wash out. Now, the tattoo I got is another story—"

"*What?*" He spun the tablet.

Her lips turned up at the corners. She was kidding. He should have known better. Lani wasn't about to let him get away with that skunk remark. He knew only one way to top her! Cruz slipped his mother's paper journal out of Lani's protective sleeve and placed it on his desk. Seconds later, the page emitted its orange beam. Cruz stayed still while the ray scanned him. Once it had identified him, the journal began its origami-like transformation from rectangular pancake to pointed orb. This being

41

Lani's first time witnessing the transformation, Cruz kept his eyes on her eyebrows as they inched upward and her mouth formed a perfect O. Once the conversion was complete, one of the orb points projected an opaque image of Cruz's mother. Only then did he shift his gaze away from Lani. "Hi, Mom," Cruz said to the blond woman hovering before them.

"Hi, Cruzer."

"Mom, can you repeat the clue to the second piece of the cipher?"

"Travel north to the land of skrei and heather, Odin and Thor. Seek the smallest speck, for it nurtures Earth's greatest hope." The outline of what looked to be a jagged arrowhead appeared next to her. "If you run into trouble, go to Freyja Skloke. Good luck, son!" Pixel by pixel, her image dissolved. Then the orb began deconstructing itself, returning to its flattened rectangle within seconds.

"Whoa!" said Lani. "Impressive."

"Odin and Thor are Norse gods, so she must mean a Nordic country, but that's as far as I got," Cruz said to his friends. "I need to know which country she meant so I can tell Captain Iskandar where to sail Orion. Do we go to Sweden, Denmark, Norway, Finland, or Iceland?"

"Don't forget Greenland," clipped Emmett.

"Or the Faroe Islands," added Sailor.

"There's also the Åland Islands, in the Baltic." Emmett had pulled up a map of the North Atlantic on his tablet.

Glancing over his roommate's shoulder, Cruz rubbed his chin. "That's quite a list."

"Maybe we can rule some out," said Sailor. "Is Greenland truly Nordic? I know it was settled by Erik the Red, but geographically, it's considered part of North America."

"It's Nordic," replied Emmett. "It's a self-governing country under the authority of Denmark. Its major languages are Danish and Greenlandic. Its currency is the Danish krone."

"Okay, okay," Sailor surrendered. "It's Nordic, but it's also eighty percent ice."

Emmett frowned. "What does that have to do with anything?"

"Do you really think Cruz's mother would hide a chunk of the cipher in Greenland?"

"Why not? She's got to make it tough to find."

"But it's his *mom*."

"So?"

"Your mother never wants you to do anything *too* dangerous."

"I don't think she had much choice," sighed Emmett. "This *is* Nebula we're talking about."

"Still..." Sailor raised her hand. "I vote we rule out Greenland."

"And I vote we don't." Emmett shot her a glare. "Cruz?"

Two heads looked to him to cast the deciding vote. Cruz didn't know what to say.

"Skrei!" It was Lani.

Cruz had almost forgotten she was here. He glanced at his tablet. "Huh?"

"Sorry it took me so long. The spelling threw off my search. It's pronounced 'skray,' but spelled *s-k-r-e-i*. It's a type of codfish caught between January and April as it migrates from the Barents Sea to its traditional spawning grounds along the *Norwegian* coast."

A three-way cry went up from cabin 202. "Norway!"

"Let's keep going," said Cruz, his pulse picking up speed. "So we're supposed to go to Norway to seek the smallest speck that nurtures Earth's greatest hope. The smallest speck. What is a speck? It's a crumb...a dot...a grain of sand or dirt—"

"Dirt." Sailor snapped her fingers. "As in, archaeology. The jagged arrowhead-looking thing in the clue could be a Viking artifact."

"It could have been something important to their culture," continued Lani, "like a tool or a piece of technology that advanced their civilization."

"Locate it and we'll find the next piece of the cipher," concluded Emmett.

Everyone cheered, except Cruz. He was already a step ahead of them. The first time he'd seen the squiggled outline in his mother's journal, he'd suspected the shape might be an artifact. He'd shown his drawing to Aunt Marisol before they sailed. After all, she was one of the top archaeologists in the world. If *she* couldn't identify it . . .

Hunching over his tablet, his aunt had carefully studied every detail with her loop. "Do you know what it's made of?"

"No."

She'd moved the magnifying glass. "By the rough edges and the deep cuts, I'd say it's wood. See, it has some serious deterioration here that you're not likely to see on metals. Do you know the time period? Nordic Stone Age? Viking Age?"

"No. Sorry. It is an arrowhead, isn't it?"

"Could be. It could also be an ax head, a cooking utensil, a piece of jewelry, a hair comb—"

Cruz had stopped her with a groan. "So it could be anything."

"Afraid so." She'd bent over the drawing again, her dark hair blanketing his tablet. "Shape alone doesn't give us much to go on. Only the Archive has the technology to make a match, and even then, it'd be a long shot . . ."

"Archive? You mean, the database at the Society's headquarters?"

Her head had shot up. "Did I say Archive? No, I didn't."

"Yes, you did." He'd chuckled. "I heard you."

"You have to forget that I said it and you heard it."

"Why?"

She'd winced and said weakly, "Because I said so?"

"Aunt Marisol!"

"Someday I'll explain it to you. For now, you have to trust me. Don't write it. Don't say it. Don't even think it. Do you understand?" He had been able to tell by her glare that she was deadly serious.

"I do," he'd said, but of course he didn't. How could he? His brain wasn't one of those old-fashioned whiteboards. He couldn't simply erase it at will. The Archive. Could it be some kind of secret library?

Sailor, Emmett, and Lani had finished celebrating and were staring at him.

Cruz swallowed hard. "Uh ... sorry ... where were we?"

"Trying to figure out where the artifact is," said Emmett. "And what it is."

"Right. Aunt Marisol is checking into it, but she says it's going to be tough to ID by shape alone. I'll email you all my drawings, and we can start researching." He clicked on a folder in his tablet marked *Hawaii Photos*. It held photos of his dad, their surf shop, and their hikes and adventures. Scrolling down, he found the file marked *Surfing* and opened it—a good hiding place, he thought, for a secret drawing. "Emmett, how about if you search the Society's museum database? Sailor, you connect with the Academy's main library. And, Lani, you search Viking museums in Scandinavia. I'll check *Orion*'s library. If anybody finds anything, get in touch, okay?"

"Sounds good," said Lani.

Sailor and Emmett were nodding, too.

Suddenly, Sailor popped out of her chair. "Oh, gosh, I gotta scram. It's nine twenty-six. Four minutes to lights-out." She bolted for the door. "Good night, C and E. Good afternoon, L."

"Bye!" called Lani.

Emmett was already heading into the bathroom to brush his teeth. The cabin lights flickered twice—Taryn's signal that they had a few minutes to get in bed before the lights went out for the night. Cruz picked up his tablet. "Lani? You still there?"

"Uh-huh."

"Sorry I teased you about your hair. It really does look nice. Even the Moonrocks color."

She giggled. "Moon*dust*. And thanks, 'cause I lied. It won't wash out."

Cruz glanced at his headboard, where his pillow should have been. What remained of it was now wrapped in a sheet under his bed, waiting to be thrown out. He wondered if he should tell Lani about the break-in. No. It would only scare her.

"Oh, I almost forgot," said Lani. "I'm sending you a care package. Grandma made your favorite."

"Liliko'i jelly?"

"Yep."

Closing his eyes, Cruz sighed. He loved passion fruit. It had been a long time since he'd sliced open one of the yellow melons and scooped out its sweet, tangy pulp. He missed the taste. He missed everything about home—the trade winds feathering the palm trees, the citrusy fragrance of white ginger growing wild along the road, the warm grains of white sand sifting through his toes. And the surf. Cruz could almost hear it lapping against the shore, its rhythm easy and soothing. The sound could calm him like nothing else could. The waves against the ship at night were nice, but they weren't the same as home. Nothing was.

"*Aloha po, hoaaloha.*" Lani was saying "good night, my friend" in Hawaiian.

"*Aloha po, hoaaloha,*" he returned.

It felt good to hear the words. And to say them. Like a favorite old song you come back to again and again. Cruz held on to the image of Hanalei for as long as he could.

When at last he opened his eyes, the cabin was dark.

5

FLINGING open the door to his aunt's office on the third deck, Cruz cried, "Norway!"

Aunt Marisol, who was bending over a box, jumped. She smacked her elbow on her desk. "Ow!"

"Sorry, sorry." He flew to rub her arm, as if his touch could magically heal the injury.

"What about Norway?" she asked, wincing.

"That's where we have to go. We figured out the first part of Mom's clue."

"Careful! Dugan just left."

"Hold on." Tapping the honeycomb pin on his lapel, Cruz said, "Mell, on." He opened the lower-right pocket of his uniform to see the drone's golden eyes blinking at him. "Mell, security mode. Remain near the ceiling in this outer passage and record all activity, then alert me if anyone stops near this door." The MAV flew out of his pocket and zipped up to the top of the jamb. She helicoptered there for a moment before landing on the thin horizontal wood frame. He shut the door. "All secure."

His aunt nodded her approval. "So, Norway, huh?"

"It's the land of skrei and heather, Odin and Thor." He grinned.

"So it is." She tapped a glittery white nail against her chin. "So it is." He could tell she was thinking of how to incorporate this new destination into their curriculum. "And just where in Norway are we headed?"

"Uh … that's the part we haven't figured out yet. We still don't know what the artifact is or where it came from." Feeling the slight vibration of the engine under him, Cruz blew out a big breath of air. "I know, I know, we have to hurry so we can tell Captain Iskandar."

She tipped her head toward the porthole. "That's the Jersey coast off the port bow. You have time."

Maybe, but the sooner he figured out their destination, the better. Cruz felt restless, and not in a good way—not like when you can't sit still because you're waiting for something exciting to happen. He couldn't shake the feeling that instead of a new beginning, something was ending. Not that he had any idea what *it* was. The whole thing was unsettling. Someone breaking into your room will do that to you, he supposed. That, and not enough sleep. He had tossed and turned through his first two nights on *Orion*.

Aunt Marisol was studying him. "Something else on your mind?"

There was, but...

She crossed the cramped office in two steps. Taking him by the shoulders, she turned him toward the only place to sit in the small office besides her desk chair: a bright red love seat. She plunked him down against a white pillow with a cross-stitched gold crown, then took the place beside him. "Don't think I don't know what's going on in that head of yours. Your curiosity is one of the things I love about you— probably because it reminds me so much of your mom—but you have to listen to me." She waited until he'd lifted his eyes to meet hers. "I can't give you any more information about the department that I never mentioned and you never heard me mention. I wish I could, but I can't. Not yet."

"I know." Cruz could accept that she couldn't tell him more about the Archive for the time being. Besides, that wasn't what he'd been planning to talk to her about anyway. Cruz had something else on his mind. "I was wondering...are you...allowed to...I mean, can you tell me about the Synthesis?"

"The Synthesis?" she asked. "I can tell you what I know, which is

basically what you know, since your mom was one of its founders. The Synthesis is a top secret scientific branch of the Society. It's focused on researching the potential of the human mind and body. I'm not in the inner circle, but I know they've made progress in the areas of artificial intelligence and human strength and endurance—"

"What would they want with me?"

Her eyebrows shot up. "You?"

Cruz let out a cleansing sigh. It felt good to say it to someone. Finally.

She tipped her head. "Cruz, has something happened? Has someone from the Synthesis contacted you?"

"I wasn't sure if I should tell you—"

"You weren't sure if you should tell me?" Her lips became a thin, red line. "We can't have secrets between us, Cruz. If you're going to be anything less than candid with me, then this...this finding the cipher to your mother's formula isn't going to work."

He wrung his hands. "I should have said something before now. It's just that with being expelled and getting attacked by Mr. Rook and coming on board the ship—"

"All right." Her expression softened. "I didn't mean to jump on you. Go on. Tell me how the Synthesis got in touch with you."

"It happened after I was expelled...on the day I went to the museum to hang out and wait while you were investigating the CAVE hacking. I was in the museum, when the guy from Nebula, the one in the cowboy boots, grabbed me."

"You told me you got away from him."

"I did, but I didn't stomp on his foot and run, like I told you. The truth is, I had...well, I had some help. See, the guy had me cornered in the basement and I thought I was a goner. Out of the blue, Jericho showed up and whacked him on the head with a dinosaur bone." Cruz snickered. "It knocked him out cold. You should have seen it, Aunt Marisol. Jericho got there in the nick of time—"

"Jericho?"

"Jericho Miles. He's a tech with the Synthesis. At least, I think he is. He's pretty secretive about what he does. Emmett, Sailor, and I met him when we stumbled into the Synthesis lab ... That's why we were late for our first CAVE mission." Her forehead was starting to get pruny, so he figured he'd keep talking. "Anyway, the reason Jericho was in the right place at the right time was because he was looking for me, too—not to kill me but to get a sample of my blood."

"What?"

"Jericho said his boss had sent him, but he didn't know why. I think he was telling the truth, because he ... he changed his mind. About getting my blood, I mean. He let me go without getting the sample. Jericho took it from his own arm instead and told me to get out of there, which I did. Still, ever since it happened I've been wondering—"

"What does the Synthesis want with your blood?" Aunt Marisol was tapping her chin again. "I've never heard of this Jericho Miles, but I'll certainly look into it ..."

Cruz was suddenly flooded with fear. What had he been thinking? He'd made a mistake—a huge mistake—telling her. Hadn't his mother said in her journal she didn't know if the Society was friend or foe? Maybe someone in the Synthesis was working for Nebula, maybe even the entire lab! Now Aunt Marisol was going to start asking questions—questions Cruz was pretty certain nobody there wanted to answer.

"... one way or another," she was saying, "we'll get to the bottom of this—"

"No!" he cried. "Don't, Aunt Marisol. Don't ask anybody about anything."

"But I thought you wanted to know why—"

"No, I ..." His voice broke, tears springing to his eyes. A lump rose in his throat. His heart yelled out what he could not: *I don't want to lose you. I couldn't handle that. Not after Mom. Not both of you.*

Her arm went around him. "It's all right, Cruz. Nothing will happen to you."

"It's not me ... I'm worried about. Promise me you won't do it, you won't look into it." He fought back tears. "You have to promise."

He saw the terror on his face reflected in her eyes. "Okay," she soothed. "We'll leave it be for now. I'm glad you told me what happened."

He laid his head against her shoulder. They stayed that way for a while, listening to the sounds of the ship—the steady hum of the engine, the clatter of dishes from the galley next door. *Orion* gently rocked the little red sofa and its two occupants, adding to the marine lullaby. Up and down. Up and down. Cruz never planned on falling asleep on his aunt's shoulder.

But he did.

IT WAS SUNDAY MORNING and Cruz was lying on his side on top of his comforter, his elbow forming a triangle between the mattress and his head. He was reading an article Dr. Ishikawa had assigned in biology class about nucleic acids, the building blocks of all living organisms. The article explained how deoxyribonucleic acid holds the genetic code for every single cell in the body, carrying that information from one generation to the next. Cruz ran his finger over the illustration of a DNA molecule. He sat up and turned his arm over, his gaze slowly moving from the rosy, twisted-ladder birthmark on the inside of his wrist to the spiraling rungs of DNA in the drawing.

Cruz had known for some time that his strange birthmark resembled a strand of DNA. It was his dad who'd first made the comparison when Cruz was much younger. "It means you're unique," explained his father, except Cruz didn't feel unique. All he felt was weird. At school, kids teased him about the strange reddish pink blemish, so Cruz had become an expert at hiding it. He'd stuff his hands in his pockets or cover it with long sleeves, bracelets, watches—even duct tape. Since Cruz had come to the Academy more than a month ago, not a single person had mentioned it, except Taryn when she'd fitted him for his

Open Sesame band. Instead of kidding him about it, she'd said it was cool. The band only hid a little bit of his birthmark. Cruz wondered, had he become so good at hiding it that no one else at the Academy had noticed? Possibly. Emmett, being his roommate, *must* have seen it. If so, he hadn't said a peep.

Said roommate was now crouched next to Cruz's dresser. His neck bent, Emmett had one eye closed as he lined up one white cube with an identical one he'd placed on Cruz's nightstand. Squinting, Emmett slid the giant white ice-cube-size sensor an inch to the right.

"How's the security system coming along?" asked Cruz.

"Almost done with the infrared beams." Emmett tapped the cube a hair more to the right. "Let's fire it up. Go outside. I'll give you the signal to come in."

Cruz obeyed. Once in the passage, he waited for Emmett to shout "Okay!" then opened the door. Nothing happened. "Uh-oh. Is it broken?"

Emmett squished up his lips. "You have to cross one of the beams."

"Oops." Cruz took a step in.

Wee-ooo-wee-ooo-wee-ooo!

Slapping his hands to his ears, Cruz felt a twitch at his hip. Suddenly, Mell flew out of his pocket. Hovering at eye level, she flashed her golden eyes at him: three short bursts, three longer ones, then three short ones again. She circled him, then repeated the pattern.

"Morse code," yelled Emmett, shutting off the siren. "Mell is blinking the international distress signal to let you know we've had a security breach."

"How in the world did you—"

"I also rigged it so when a sensor is tripped it sends out a high-frequency sound wave. It's pitched at eighty kilohertz, so pretty much only bats and Mell can hear it."

Did he say bats? Cruz's ears were still ringing.

Emmett's glasses had turned to round orbs of sunshine. "We've got eight sensors and four beams. One inside the door, another one a few feet beyond that in case our intruder gets past the first one, one from your dresser to your nightstand, and one to cover the veranda door to keep anyone from slipping in from the balcony."

"Brilliant," said Cruz, his hearing almost back to normal.

"I'm not done. That's Phase One. We can only use them at night, when we're the only ones here. See? That's why I left us a clear path to the bathroom. Phase Two is cameras. Fanchon loaned me some that she designed herself. Check these out." Emmett took a small rectangular box from his pocket, lifted the lid, and held it out to Cruz.

He peered in. "These are cameras? They look like seashells."

"Wicked, huh?" Emmett gave him a proud grin as he reached in for what appeared to be a polished white conch shell. "And we can rig them up to our communicators so when *anyone* enters, we'll get a voice alert; then we can switch over to our tablets to see who it is in real time. As soon as I place these, I'm going up to the tech lab so Fanchon can help me connect every-thing. Want to come?"

"I'll leave it to you. You're the experts. Besides, I want to go see the submarine." Cruz left Emmett to place the camera shells and headed down two decks to B deck. He went past the cargo hold and through a door marked AQUATICS. Cruz followed the arrow below the words SUB DOCK and took a sharp left, then a right. A few steps inside a large room, Cruz stopped short. His eyes slowly traveled up what looked like a giant olive green egg. *Ridley!*

Cruz rested a hand on the metal exterior of the submarine. He'd read everything about it he could possibly get his hands on. Named after one of the most endangered turtles on Earth, the Kemp's ridley, the Neptune II–class deep submergence vehicle, or DSV, was 15.8 feet high and 40.2 feet long. *Ridley* had a reinforced hull that was almost impenetrable, four robotic arms, and six high-definition cameras. Inside, there was room for a pilot,

copilot, and about eight passengers. The vehicle could travel up to 25 miles at eight knots and dive to the seafloor at the deepest part of the ocean—almost seven miles down!

The top hatch was opening. Embarrassed, Cruz jumped back.

Tripp Scarlatos's ruffled head appeared. "She's a beaut, ain't she?"

"She sure is! Am I bothering you? You said I could come by—"

"No worries, mate. Just running diagnostics. Come on down and have a look around."

Cruz pointed to his chest. "You mean . . . me . . . in there?"

Tripp's head slipped below. Only his hand remained, motioning for Cruz to follow. Cruz climbed the ladder on the side of the sub and carefully lowered himself into the pod. It was tight inside but not claustrophobic. The curved walls were covered in panels all filled with levers, switches, buttons, and dials.

"Give her a try." Tripp gestured for Cruz to sit in the pilot's seat.

Cruz eased himself into the leather chair behind the U-shaped steering column.

"There's your forward thruster and reverse." Tripp tapped a lever to Cruz's right. "On your right is your main control panel—forward, reverse, dive. To the left are your robotics. You can also wall off the back section to create an airtight seal so you can send out your dive team."

"What's this little yellow button for?" Cruz reached out.

"Don't touch that!"

Cruz quickly drew back. "Sorry."

"Just kiddin', mate." Tripp pressed his thumb into the yellow button, and the wall in front of them glowed. "Headlights."

Cruz laughed. "How many dives have you done in *Ridley*?"

"Gosh, I dunno, hundreds. It's been a few years since I've had my lemonade bath."

"Your what?"

"New pilots always get doused with a bucket of lemonade after their first dive. Rite of passage. Rather a sticky rite, if you ask me."

"It'd be worth it to be able to drive *Ridley*. I'd give anything to learn."

Tripp spun his chameleon ring around his finger. "I could teach you. If you wanted."

If *he* wanted? To drive *Ridley*? Was Tripp kidding? Of course he wanted!

"That would be gramazing." Cruz let out a snort. "Gramazing! I couldn't make up my mind whether to say 'great' or 'amazing,' so I said both!"

"Crackin' term. Say, I've got a bit of time now. Want your first lesson in DSV operation?"

Cruz did not need to be asked twice. Lani was never going to believe this. He could hardly believe it himself!

Tripp slid into the copilot's seat. "Let's start with propulsion basics..."

OFF THE COAST OF MASSACHUSETTS, U.S.A.

N.H.

ATLANTIC OCEAN

MASSACHUSETTS

CONN. RHODE ISLAND

"SERIOUSLY?" Lani slapped a hand to her cheek. "You got to drive the sub?"

"Not yet, but Tripp says after a few lessons I'll be ready to be his copilot on a real dive."

"Ah, maaaan!" Emmett's glasses were a carousel of oranges, yellows, and greens. "I should have gone with you."

"I have another lesson next Sunday!" exclaimed Cruz. "I'll ask if you can come along."

Lani sighed. "I wish I could come, too."

She looked so disappointed; Cruz felt terrible. He didn't know what to say. Maybe he shouldn't tell her *every* incredible thing that happened to him. It would only make them both feel bad—Lani because she wasn't here and Cruz because he was. But Lani was his closest friend in the world. How do you keep the best stuff from your best friend?

"Taryn to explorers!" Cruz was startled by the voice coming through the EA pin on his lapel. He was still getting used to the thing. "All explorers, please report to the third-deck conference room in ten minutes. Repeat. Third-deck conference room in ten minutes."

"I thought Sundays were our free day," groaned Emmett.

Cruz shrugged. He'd thought so, too.

"You'd better go." Lani's voice dripped with longing.

"Bye, Lani. I'll call you later." Cruz waved to her, before tucking his tablet under his arm.

In the passageway, Cruz and Emmett joined the explorers streaming toward the atrium. Cruz caught up to Zane, who was at the front of the group. "Do you know what's going on?"

"Not a clue."

"Maybe it's a muster drill," said Ali. "You know, so we can practice going to our lifeboat stations and evacuating the ship."

"We'd have heard an alarm for that," interjected Emmett.

When they filed into the conference room, Taryn was already there. She stood at the head of the table. Instead of her usual warm greeting, she said, rather crisply, "Please divide into your teams and have a seat. Team Magellan, take the back right; Team Cousteau to the back left; Team Earhart, sit to my right; and, Team Galileo, you will be here on my left."

Cruz took a seat between Emmett and Bryndis. Dugan sat next to Bryndis, and Sailor slipped into the chair beside him. All the teams but theirs were comprised of six explorers. Renshaw McKittrick had been their sixth member, until he'd been expelled. Cruz wondered how things would work now that Team Cousteau was down a member.

"It's been brought to my attention that we have a serious problem on board *Orion*." Taryn placed both hands on the table. "It must be dealt with as soon as possible."

Cruz shifted. What could they have done? Taryn rarely got this stern with them. Bryndis's face, already naturally pale, had gone chalk white. Emmett's emoto-glasses were turning a filmy gray. He was scared.

"I did not think something like this would happen so soon." Taryn's jaw was tight. "I mean, you've been on the ship for less than a week and yet"—her eyes narrowed and roamed the room—"everyone is looking *so* stressed out!"

It took a few seconds for her words to sink in. Wait a minute … was she saying …?

As a slow smirk began to replace Taryn's grim expression, all the explorers, including Cruz, began to breathe normally again. No one was in trouble! Cruz noticed the pink was coming back into Bryndis's cheeks and the green returning to Emmett's glasses.

"From now on," said their adviser, her calm tone back, "Sunday is officially *Fun*day."

Bryndis bent toward Cruz. "What's a fundy?"

"*Fun day*," enunciated Cruz. "It's a made-up word."

"*Já!* Learning scientific terms in English is hard enough—now I have to worry about made-up words, too?"

Cruz realized their studies must be more than a little challenging for those explorers whose first language wasn't English. He smiled at her. "You're doing fine."

Bryndis shyly returned the grin, a dimple appearing on each cheek.

"Every Sunday afternoon, we're going to meet here to do an activity together," Taryn was explaining. "We may build a miniature robot or a gingerbread Taj Mahal. We may tie-dye socks or learn to tie sailing knots. We're going to do all kinds of things. Some you may love and some may not be your cup of tea. That's okay. But you are explorers after all, and that means discovering what lies within as well as beyond."

Dugan's hand shot up. "Do we have to—"

"Yes." She cut him off kindly, but quickly.

"Mandatory merriment," Emmett joked to Cruz.

"Our first Funday event is a scavenger hunt," said Taryn. "Sort of. You'll see what I mean soon enough."

"We've got this," Cruz muttered to Emmett.

"I almost forgot," said their adviser. "Each member of the winning team will get a prize."

"What kind of prize?" asked Tao Sun.

"You'll have to win to find out." Taryn took some envelopes from her tote bag. Circling the room, she gave one to a member of each team. She handed Team Cousteau's to Cruz. "Here are your instructions. Do not open them until I give the signal." Her eyes gleamed. "Remember, the whole point is to have *fun*."

Cruz put his finger under the flap. The room went deadly still.

"Ready?" Returning to her spot, Taryn held her hand up like she was going to start a marathon. "Set? Go!"

Cruz ripped open the envelope. He pulled out two pieces of paper and gave one to Sailor. Unfolding hers, Sailor read it aloud:

Welcome to
Taryn's Traveling Teasers:
A SCAVENGER HUNT WITH A TWIST!

Your mission: Solve a series of puzzles and collect several objects on your way to your final destination somewhere on *Orion*!

Step 1: Solve a puzzle, then proceed to the destination indicated in the solution.

Step 2: Once you arrive, look for a person wearing a red carnation. He/she will give you an **object** and a **new puzzle** to solve. Take your object with you.

Repeat Steps 1 and 2 until you have **three** objects. These objects and your last puzzle will guide you to your final destination. The first team to arrive at the final stop with all the correct objects WINS! Your first puzzle is enclosed in this envelope.

Good luck!

"I've got the puzzle," said Cruz, holding up his paper. "Let's solve it somewhere else." Hurrying from the conference room, they headed to a corner of the lounge. Cruz smoothed the page out on a table, and the rest of the team clustered around.

"It's a rebus," announced Emmett. "We have to figure out the word each picture symbolizes, then put all the words together to form a phrase."

Bryndis tipped her head. "Is that first picture dirt or sand?"

"I'd say sand," answered Cruz. "It looks like the beach."

"Sand twins beat," cried Dugan. He clapped. "I got the top line. Sandwich meat!"

Emmett frowned. "I don't think they're twins, Dugan. Their hair is different. They look like sisters to me."

"I think it's whisk, not beat," said Sailor. "The whisk isn't in motion."

Dugan yawned. "Whatever."

"The fourth one is a bunch of clothes," said Bryndis.

"The pile of coins must be treasure," offered Sailor.

Bryndis squinted. "Is that a bear den?"

"The last one looks like a gate." Cruz tipped his head. "Or a fence."

"No, wait—gold," muttered Sailor. "Yeah, gold makes more sense."

"None of it makes sense, if you ask me," Dugan grunted. "Who cares what it is? We're not even getting graded on this. I heard Chef Kristos is making homemade chocolate ice cream. I say we bag this lame game and go see if he's done—"

"Probably just a den," said Bryndis.

"Most likely friends," mumbled Emmett.

"Definitely a gate," declared Cruz.

"This is dumb." Dugan flopped into a chair. "We're never gonna get it."

"I got it!" called Cruz. "Everyone, when I point to you, say the word you think best fits your picture. I'll start. Sand." He pointed to Emmett, who said "friends"; then to Sailor, who said "whisk"; Bryndis, who replied "clothes"; back to Sailor for "gold"; Bryndis for "den"; and Cruz finished off with "gate." Cruz looked at Bryndis. "Now say the whole thing through."

"Sand, friends, whisk, clothes, gold, den, gate." She giggled.

"Say it again. Faster."

"Sandfriends, whiskclothes, golden gate." She gasped. "San Francisco's Golden Gate!"

"It's the bridge," cried Sailor. "We did it. We solved it. Sweet as!"

"Let's go!" Emmett sprang up.

Dugan blew a raspberry. "How are we gonna get to the Golden Gate Bridge from here?"

Sailor slapped a palm to her forehead.

"Not that bridge, Dugan." Cruz pointed up. "*That* one."

"Oh."

Captain Iskandar met them at the entrance to the bridge, a red carnation tucked into his name tag. As usual, the gold buttons of his pressed white uniform were stretched to capacity over his round stomach. Deep-set eyes crinkled in the shade of a bushy unibrow. "Well done, Team Cousteau!"

"Are we the first group to show up?" prodded Emmett.

"Can't say. Sworn to secrecy. Your object." He handed Emmett a yellow rubber ball. "And your next clue." He placed a small cardboard box in Sailor's hands.

"Thanks, Captain Iskandar!"

Sailor was already peering into the box. "It's a jigsaw puzzle."

Racing back to the lounge, they dumped out the pieces on a table and began putting them together. The puzzle had about 50 pieces; most were green and none had corners! With the five of them clustered around, Cruz figured it took twice as long to put the round puzzle together as it would have if only one person had done it. As they clicked the pieces in place, one after the other, Cruz recognized the photo. "It's *Ridley!*"

They took off for the aquatics room. As they scrambled down the starboard side of the grand staircase, Team Earhart was running up the port side.

"I hope they're not ahead of us," said Emmett.

Halfway down, Cruz stopped. "Where's Dugan?"

"He was behind me," called Bryndis. "But he was still griping about ice cream."

"Oh, crikey," gasped Sailor. "That boy!"

"Chillax, I'm here." Dugan was at the top of the stairs. He oozed his way down to them.

Cruz was starting to get annoyed at Dugan's half-hearted effort, and he could see he wasn't the only one. He started to say something but stopped himself. Taryn had said this was supposed to be a fun activity, and besides, it wouldn't do any good to start arguing. Cruz led the team down to B deck, past the control room and cargo hold, into aquatics.

Tripp Scarlatos was waiting next to the DSV, a red carnation tucked behind his ear. He batted his eyelashes like he was in a beauty pageant. "Here ya go, mate." Tripp handed Emmett a red-and-gray-plaid scarf. "And your clue is coming right up."

Tripp turned out the lights, then flipped a switch on his computer, and a holographic message appeared before them. It was just one sentence, the glowing words floating above Cruz's shoulder: *Which building on Earth has the most stories?*

Sailor was the first to speak. "I bet it's One World Trade Center. It has more than a hundred stories."

"The Shanghai Tower is taller," countered Emmett.

"Is not."

"Is too."

"Do you always have to contradict everything I say?"

"I only contradict you when you're wrong. Can I help it if you're wrong a lot?"

Sailor let out a shriek.

"One World Trade Center has a hundred and four stories," cut in Cruz. While the two of them had been bickering, he'd flipped open his tablet to do an online search. "Let's see ... The Shanghai Tower has a hundred and twenty-eight stories."

"Told ya," snapped Emmett.

"However, the tallest building in the world is"—Cruz gulped hard—"Nebula Tower in London."

"So we're *both* wrong," declared Sailor happily. The information sinking in, she put a hand to her mouth.

"London?" A vertical crease formed between Bryndis's eyebrows. "There's no London room on the ship, is there?"

"No," shot Emmett. "Cruz, are you sure there's no other building that's taller?"

Cruz was typing as fast as he could. "Checking."

"You're wasting your time," drawled Dugan. He was leaning against a post behind them.

"Yeah?" Sailor folded her arms across her. "If you're so smart, then what's the answer?"

"Ignore him, Sailor." Emmett's frames morphed into a pair of squares the color of a campfire. "He's only trying to get under our skin."

Dugan whistled. "Okay, if you don't want to know ..."

"We're supposed to be a team," reminded Cruz. "Dugan, if you have something to say that can help solve the puzzle then say it."

Straightening, Dugan sauntered toward them. "The building on Earth with the most stories is ... drumroll, please ... *a library.*"

Cruz could have kicked himself! Dugan was right. This was a *puzzle*, not a quiz in geography class! A proud Dugan trotted out of the room. The rest of Team Cousteau exchanged shocked expressions. Had their laziest member actually solved a riddle?

Dugan popped his head back in. "You guys coming or not? This is a race, you know."

Hurrying down the passage of B deck, Cruz slapped Dugan on the back. "Nice work."

He got a contorted smirk in return, which, coming from Dugan, was progress.

The library was five decks up, behind the bridge. By the time the explorers stumbled through the door, they were out of breath. Cruz saw none of the other teams, so they were either doing extremely well or extremely poorly. Dr. Holland waved them over to the checkout desk. A red carnation was attached to the front of her black sweater. The librarian handed Cruz a piece of paper. "This is your last puzzle." Glancing at the page, he showed it to his teammates.

Sailor groaned. "An unmarked map?"

"All I can tell you is that it's a country in the Northern Hemisphere." The librarian held out a basket to Dugan. "Now, for your last object. Pick one, please, then retrieve the item it leads you to. You may take it from the library, but please return it when you're done with the game."

Dugan reached in and pulled out a strip. "It says 823.819 Doyle."

"Card catalog system," Cruz and Emmett said in unison. They'd been down this road before.

"Bryndis, Sailor, and I will find the book," directed Dugan. "You guys find the country."

Emmett and Cruz raced to one of the two map tables at the back of the library. The table was actually a gigantic computer built into a desk frame, so the horizontal screen faced the ceiling. The touch screen allowed you to easily and quickly scroll to any location on Earth. Cruz placed the unmarked puzzle map over the screen, while Emmett started scrolling. They began scanning the world's oceans and continents, searching for a match.

"It's surrounded by the sea on three sides," said Cruz.

"It's got a lot of islands around it, too," added Emmett. "It's a big world. This could take us forever."

"Let's hope the book the guys are looking for will help us." His eyes darting from the map to the computer, then back to the map again, Cruz got a strange feeling. It felt like he'd seen this map, or one like it, before. But where? He caught something out of the corner of his eye. "Emmett, stop!" As Emmett drew his hand back, Cruz scrolled back from Eastern Europe to the North Atlantic. He slid the puzzle map over the United Kingdom, adjusting the zoom to line up the borders. "Bingo!"

It was a match. Their map was Scotland. Cruz and Emmett bumped fists!

"We got it!" Emmett shouted up to their teammates, who were running around the perimeter of the balcony.

"Same here," yelled Sailor over the rail. "We're coming down."

Cruz stared at the puzzle map, the light from the computer screen illuminating the craggy border. There was something so familiar about it...

Cruz let out a moan. How could he have been so blind?

Emmett heard his revelation. "What's the matter?"

"The artifact. I just realized—"

"You're thinking about that *now*?"

"Emmett, what if it's not what we thought? What if it's not a Viking relic?"

"Then what—"

Cruz held up the puzzle map.

Emmett's jaw, tinged blue from the glow of the Atlantic Ocean, slowly fell. "If that's true, then all this time, you've ... I've ... we've..."

Cruz swallowed hard. "Been looking for the wrong thing."

7

WITH DUGAN, Sailor, and Bryndis
barreling toward them, Cruz and Emmett knew any further discussion
about the cipher clue would have to wait. Braking, Dugan thrust out an
arm to show Cruz and Emmett the cover of the book. It was *The Hound
of the Baskervilles* by Arthur Conan Doyle. "What did … you guys …
find?" huffed Dugan.

"Scotland," said Cruz. "The puzzle map is Scotland."

"We're supposed to put these clues together with the objects we've
collected to reveal our final destination," huffed Sailor.

At that moment, Team Magellan stormed into the library. Zane, Yulia
Navarro, Ekaterina Pajarin, Tao, Ali, and Matteo Montefiore hurried to
Dr. Holland.

"Let's get out of sight," ordered Emmett. "Behind that post…"

"*Flýttu þér!*" hissed Bryndis. "Hurry!"

Before taking refuge with the rest of his team, Cruz scrolled the
computer map to Antarctica. In their huddle, Emmett dug into his
pockets, bringing out the yellow ball and plaid scarf. Cruz waved his
map of Scotland. Dugan held up *The Hound of the Baskervilles*. It took
Cruz only a few seconds to it figure out. A ball, a tartan scarf, Scotland,
and a book with a dog in the title could only lead to one conclusion:
Hubbard, Taryn's West Highland white terrier.

"Sweet as!" cried Sailor. "It's—"

Emmett slapped a hand over her mouth. "Don't say it."

"Let's haul!" cried Dugan, and they charged for the door. Dashing down the passage, they met Team Galileo coming from the other way. That left only one team unaccounted for. Where could Team Earhart be?

"I bet they're ahead of us." Dugan led the pack. "Pick up the pace, people." They zipped down three flights of stairs and took a sharp left into the explorers' wing. Dugan was going so fast he would have skidded into the wall if Cruz hadn't grabbed his shirt. Taryn's room was the first one on the port side. Her door was open! Inside, they found Taryn sitting in a light blue chair, calmly knitting. At her feet, Hubbard was sleeping in his red-and-gray-tartan doggy bed, which matched the scarf Emmett had wrapped around his own neck.

Pink knitting needles paused. "Do you have some items for me?"

Emmett unwrapped the scarf and gave it to her, along with the ball. Dugan handed over the book.

"It's Hubbard . . . the answer to all the clues is Hubbard." Bryndis gasped.

Taryn took their items and placed them in an empty tub beside her. "Your answer is correct, and you have all of your objects. Excellent work. However"—she gave them a pained look—"unfortunately, I must tell you the game is over . . ."

Dang! Team Earhart had gotten there first.

". . . because YOU WON!"

Cruz was instantly locked in a group hug, bouncing in a victory dance that lasted until Team Magellan showed up a few minutes later. They had done it. At last! After three CAVE training sessions back at the Academy and one game on *Orion,* Team Cousteau had finally come in first! And with only five members, too. Maybe being at a disadvantage, or believing you are, isn't such a bad thing, thought Cruz. It certainly had motivated *him* to work harder.

Once all the teams arrived and they couldn't possibly jam one more person into Taryn's room, their dorm adviser quieted the group. "Terrific job! You were much faster than I expected, too, but then, I should have known. You *are* the best and the brightest. Did everyone have fun?"

"Yes," Cruz eagerly chimed in with everyone else. Even Team Earhart, who'd gotten off track and somehow ended up in sick bay, was nodding and grinning.

"Now for your reward." Taryn reached for her yarn basket. "Team Cousteau, please step forward and hold out your hands."

Standing between Emmett and Bryndis, Cruz cupped one hand in the other. His imagination was already considering the prize possibilities. Maybe they'd get bones from a newly discovered dinosaur or a talking plant from the Amazon rain forest or rocks from Mars! As Taryn came down the row, his heart began to thump faster.

"What is it? What did you get?" the explorers behind them kept asking.

Cruz felt something fall into his palm. As Taryn stepped away, he glanced down. He was holding a purple capsule, like the oblong gel caps that contain cold medicine. This pill was twice as big as a normal capsule. Cruz hoped he wasn't supposed to swallow it. He'd never get this down his throat!

"Well?" pressed Ali from behind them.

"It's a spherocylinder," announced Emmett.

"Huh?"

"A capsule." Emmett held it up between his thumb and index finger.

Ali's smile faded. He wasn't the only one. Cruz rolled the sphere around his palm with a fingertip. Of all of the incredible things he'd pictured they might get, this was not among, oh, the top million.

"It looks like my allergy medicine." Dugan was poking at his.

"Don't eat it," warned Taryn. "That's not what it's for. Each of you holds a time capsule, a computerized device that can hold a memory—literally. It's easy to use. Place it in your palm and make a tight fist. When you feel the capsule shake, think of something, someone, or someplace you want to remember. The capsule captures the recollection so that you, or anyone you choose to give it to, can relive your moment in time."

Twenty-three explorers stared at her in awe. Cruz glanced at his capsule. Taryn had to be joking. It hardly seemed possible that something so ordinary could do something so extraordinary. Cruz could tell Emmett was skeptical, too. He'd raised his arm so his nose was up against his wrist and was studying the oblong device from every angle.

Taryn smiled. "Not a bad prize, huh?"

Once they realized she wasn't kidding, an excited buzz swept through the cabin.

"Right now, as you hold it, the capsule is syncing up with your own personal bioelectromagnetic signatures," explained Taryn. "Let me show you how it works." Picking up a capsule, she closed her hand around it. Taryn shut her eyes. Thirty seconds later, she opened her eyes and her palm. The purple spherocylinder was glowing!

Everyone gasped.

Taryn took Cruz's right hand, put the capsule in it, and wrapped his fingers around it. "Close your eyes."

Cruz did as she instructed. In his mind, he saw a flash of white, like one of those starburst firecrackers that explodes on the Fourth of July. As the flare vanished, he saw himself coming through the front door of the Academy. He was with Aunt Marisol and Sailor. He had his suitcase. So did Sailor. It was his first day! The scene was familiar yet also different. He was watching everything from a distance. Cruz saw himself roll his suitcase through the lobby and get in line to check in. It was strange, not to mention a bit creepy, until Cruz remembered, this was Taryn's memory, not his. It was how *she* saw *him* from behind the front desk on that day back in September.

"Where are you?" Taryn whispered into his ear.

"Back at school in D.C." Everything unfolded as he remembered it, though from a new perspective. "It's my first day. I'm waiting in line to check in ... Oh, there's Dugan ... Oh, yeah, he's bragging about winning the North Star award ... Now it's my turn to check in. I'm petting Hubbard, and now I'm talking to you. I look scared!"

He heard laughter.

"Open your eyes."

Cruz's eyelids fluttered. The other explorers were looking at him, transfixed. They were waiting for him to say something. "It wasn't like a dream," he struggled to try to explain the experience. "It felt real, like I was living it all over again."

"That's the idea," said Taryn. She turned to the rest of Team Cousteau. "Questions?"

"Can we only use them once?" asked Bryndis.

"You may use your time capsule as often as you like, but it will only hold one memory at a time. Also, other people can view it, but only you can change it. It should last ... well, as long as you do."

"Thanks, Taryn." Cruz held his fist against his heart. "This is the best prize I've ever won."

The rest of the team agreed.

"You're most welcome." Clasping her hands in front of her, Taryn bowed. "And now I pronounce Funday officially complete. If you'll all scoot, I'd like to finish my knitting in peace. Besides, I'm sure you have homework."

While he waited for the cabin to clear, Cruz knelt to pet Hubbard. He couldn't wait to call Lani and show her his time capsule. Like Emmett, she was always tinkering with technology. She would love this! On second thought, maybe he shouldn't. After her reaction to his news about learning to pilot *Ridley,* it would be one more thing he got that she didn't. Still, if he didn't tell her, she'd be upset when she found out, and he couldn't keep something like this a secret. Could he?

Things with his best friend were getting ... challenging. Next to his dad and Aunt Marisol, Lani was the most important person in his life, but she was there, in Hawaii, and he was here, on *Orion*. The distance between them was growing, and it involved more than miles. When Cruz had left for the Academy, he'd known his life was going to change, but he'd had no idea how much. Or how fast. Cruz didn't want to lose Lani, but he also didn't want to hurt her. There had to be a way to include his best friend without making her feel like she was missing out. He just had no clue how.

Emmett was bumping his fist lightly against Cruz's shoulder. "Library?"

"Uh-huh."

They needed to see if they could determine if the image from his mom's journal was, in fact, a place. Cruz gave Hubbard one last scratch before leaving Taryn's cabin. Now, with nothing at stake, the pair could take their time going up three decks. Fortunately, when they walked into the ship's library, the place was practically deserted. There was only one other person there besides Dr. Holland: Chef Kristos, reading in the corner. Upon second glance, Cruz realized that, behind his book, Chef's eyes were closed.

As they headed to the same map table they'd used during Taryn's scavenger hunt, Cruz whispered to Emmett, "Shouldn't he be fixing dinner?"

"Must be his day off. If it isn't, it looks like we'll be making our own PB and Js."

At the map table, Cruz tapped his tablet screen to bring up the file of his drawing. Emmett scrolled the map to the southernmost point of Norway.

"I'll take the east side of the country. You take the west. We'll work our way north." Cruz placed his tablet between them, and the pair began their search.

An hour later, they were still looking.

"Norway must have a million islands." Cruz rubbed his screen-weary eyes.

Emmett took off his glasses to do the same. "And an endless coastline."

"Second longest in the world," added a new voice.

Cruz jumped. "Uh ... hi, Bryndis."

"Only Canada has more kilometers of coast than Norway," explained Bryndis. "What are you guys doing? Did I miss a geography assignment?"

"Nope." Cruz began walking his fingers across the map toward his tablet. The drawing was in plain sight. All Bryndis had to do was lean over a bit and look down. "Um ... we heard a rumor that we might be sailing to Norway, so we thought we'd take a look first ..."

She sighed. "Norway's beautiful. Oslo has a great Viking ship museum."

Cruz casually rested his hand on his tablet screen. "Can't say for sure."

"I suppose we'll find out soon enough. *Bless.*" She turned away.

Bless was Icelandic for "goodbye."

Whew! That was close. Cruz drew the back of his hand across his forehead to signal as much to Emmett. His roommate's eyebrows bounced a few times behind dark purple, oval frames.

"I don't mean to intrude, but"—Bryndis twirled back—"if you're looking for Spitsbergen, you're not going to find it there."

Cruz slapped his palm back onto his tablet. "Huh?"

"Spitsbergen." Her lips slid up one cheek. "That is what you're hiding, isn't it?"

"Hide? Us?" Emmett tried to toss off a light laugh. It didn't work.

Caught, Cruz took his hand away. He was trying to figure out a way to tell her without *telling* her, when she said, "Ohhh, I get it."

"You do?"

"It's another puzzle map, right?"

"Uh ... yeah," sputtered Cruz. "Taryn gave it to us. What did you say it was?"

"Spitsbergen." She hurried around the table. Emmett scooted closer to Cruz to give her room. Bryndis scrolled the map well north of

Norway to a group of islands in the Arctic Ocean. She zoomed in. "It's the largest island in the Svalbard archipelago. See?"

The moment Bryndis straightened, Cruz's heart nearly stopped. By now, he knew every corner, curve, and cranny of the image from his mom's journal. There was no doubt in his mind that this island was what they had been looking for!

Bryndis bent over Cruz's tablet. "It was these two inlets, Van Mijenfjorden and Van Keulenfjorden, that helped me identify it. When I see them together, they always remind me of an alligator's open jaws."

"So you've been there?" wondered Cruz.

"*Já.* A couple of years ago, I went with my family during the summer. We flew to Longyearbyen." She pointed to the map. "We took a boat tour around the island and saw a pod of orcas. It was pretty great. My brother wanted to take a tour of the seed vault, but they won't let you go inside unless you have a deposit. It's like a real bank ... Well, I guess it is a real bank, except instead of being full of money it's full of seeds."

"That's right." Emmett's eyes widened. "The Svalbard Global Seed Vault."

"It's nicknamed the Doomsday Vault," said Bryndis. "Norway built it so we'd have a backup supply of seeds in case a disaster ever wipes out our food supply. Countries from all over the world send samples of their seeds there for safekeeping. Of course, it's not the only seed vault in the world. There are many others, but I think this one is pretty cool."

"Seeds." Emmett gulped. "Did you hear that, Cruz?"

"I think I remember seeing something about it on the news," said Cruz. "Didn't some countries in the Middle East make withdrawals?"

Bryndis nodded. "That's right. Syria was the first, I think. A research center stored grain seeds there during their drought and civil war."

"Seeds, Cruz, *seeds,*" hissed Emmett.

Cruz gave his friend a puzzled look. Why did Emmett keep saying that?

"The vault is built into the side of a mountain, at the site of an old coal mine," said Bryndis. "A Norwegian artist created artwork for the entrance with reflective triangles and lights. At night, the vault glows. To me, it looks like they captured a thousand stars and put them in a box made of turquoise glass. You can see it for kilometers..."

Emmett was poking Cruz in the side. "Seeds."

"I *know*!" He was starting to get annoyed.

"Don't you get it?"

"What?"

"Seeds are the smallest specks."

Cruz snapped his head around so fast his neck popped. It was the clue from his mother's journal: "Seek the smallest speck, for it nurtures Earth's greatest hope." Seeds! That was the answer. She was telling him to go to the Svalbard Global Seed Vault. That's where she'd hidden the second piece of the cipher!

"...but if Taryn gave you that map, it has to be true," Bryndis was saying. "We must be going to Svalbard."

With a knowing glance to Emmett, Cruz gave her a nod. His heart was racing. "Must be."

"Some people say it's too cold and rugged, you know, too wild, but that's why I like it," said Bryndis. "The mountains and glaciers and tundra—and all the animals: the orcas, arctic foxes, and polar bears. It's nature, pure and beautiful." She smiled, her palest of pale blue eyes meeting Cruz's. "I think you'd like it, too."

He already did.

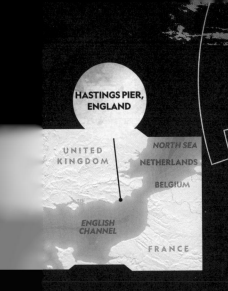

HASTINGS PIER, ENGLAND

UNITED KINGDOM

NORTH SEA

NETHERLANDS

BELGIUM

ENGLISH CHANNEL

FRANCE

8

THE GLARE of the early morning sun off the water was giving Thorne Prescott a headache. He was alone on Hastings Pier but for a few noisy seagulls circling. Walking across the planks of the football-field-size boardwalk, he readjusted his phone's earpiece. "Zebra, what do you mean there's no journal?"

"We've searched everywhere. It's not here."

Prescott turned from the lapis blue waters of the English Channel. "What about Jaguar?"

He had a feeling they would get their most reliable intel from their youngest spy.

"Working on it, but nothing so far."

Prescott raked a hand through his hair. The journal wasn't at the aunt's house or the Academy. Nebula's spies had searched the school.

"It is possible there never was any journal," said Zebra.

Prescott was starting to wonder the same thing.

"Meerkat lied to us," added Zebra. "Or stole it himself."

Prescott glanced up at the stark white hotel at the head of the pier, its blue-and-white-striped awnings billowing in the sea breeze. "There's only one way to know for sure."

"I could have Mongoose take care of the kid. If he's hidden the journal, it'll stay hidden."

"No!" Hezekiah Brume had said no loose ends, and right now there were far too many of them. A young couple was coming toward him. Moving to the rail, Prescott held up his cell phone and pretended to be a tourist. He took photos until they were out of earshot. "Zebra, confirm, once and for all, if the journal exists," he growled into the phone, his temper starting to simmer. "If it does, destroy it. Once that's taken care of, then you can finish the job." Prescott hung up, his head pounding. It should not be this difficult to outwit a 12-year-old. He walked briskly back toward the shore, tapping his screen.

"Hello, Cobra." A husky female voice, polished with an English accent, tickled his ear.

"Swan, I need access to room five-two-seven of the Conqueror Lodge in two minutes."

"Certainly," said the woman, who sounded an awful lot like Oona, Brume's assistant.

Carefully slipping his phone into his coat pocket, Prescott crossed right in front of the hotel. He trotted up the steps, scuffing his unspoiled cowboy boots on the mat. To avoid camera surveillance, he zigzagged through the hallways of the seaside resort. Taking the stairs up to the fifth floor, he pressed his thumb on the pad that read "five-two-seven" and waited for the green light. Easing the door ajar, he put one hand on the weapon in his chest pocket. Prescott moved slowly at first, his eye behind the gun barrel, then charged into the room. "Freeze, Rook!" You've got five seconds to—"

Luckily, the made bed was empty. The white comforter was yanked taut under four plump pillows. A tray of mints lie on top, indicating no one had slept there last night. Prescott tip-toed silently over to the bathroom and kicked open the door. Also empty. If Rook had been there at all, he left hours ago. Prescott sat on the narrow edge of the bed. Dropping his head, he slid his index finger down the ridge of his forehead, trying to push away the permanent ache. He could always take care of Rook later. After all, Prescott was never truly convinced the librarian had the journal anyway. He gripped the end of his pistol and tucked it safely in his pocket. With everything he knew about Cruz, there was only one other place he really could think to look. Prescott reached for his phone.

"Hello, Cobra."

"Swan, I need a plane ticket to Kauai."

"A first-class ticket from London to Kauai will be waiting for you at Gatwick Airport. Departure is at two thirty p.m. today." Funny. It was almost as if she had known what he was going to request. "Have a good flight." Swan hung up.

Before leaving room 527 of the Conqueror Lodge, Prescott made one last call.

"What now?" hissed the voice on the other end. Prescott heard a series of beeps in the background, as if someone was backing up a forklift. "I can't talk."

"Everything I said earlier about the journal? Forget it."

"You mean . . . ?"

"Get rid of the kid."

9

▶ **"YOU DID IT!"** cried Lani. "You solved the mystery!"

"*We* solved the mystery," corrected Cruz, holding up his tablet so its built-in camera could include his roommate in the shot. "I may have zeroed in on the map, but Bryndis clued us in about Svalbard, and then Emmett made the link between Mom's clue and the seed vault."

Emmett looked up from the Lumagine calculations on his desktop computer and waved. "Team Cousteau rules!"

"Wait!" Lani frowned. "You mean, Bryndis knows...?"

"Not about the cipher," Cruz assured her. "She helped us find the island, that's all. She has no idea why we need to go there. I can't talk long, but I had to tell you."

"I'm glad you did. What's up? Are you going on an expedition?"

"I wish. I have a boatload of homework."

"Ha! I got that. *Orion*? Boatload?"

Cruz laughed. He hadn't intended the pun. He was being honest. It was Sunday night, and he had a ton to do for school: an assignment on alternative energies for conservation class (due Wednesday), a profile of a modern-day explorer for journalism (due Tuesday), and a quiz on the history of archaeological dating methods in Aunt Marisol's class (tomorrow!).

"Did you tell your dad?" Lani was asking.

"Called him just before I called you."

"I'm sorry I wasn't more help," said Lani. "I should have—"

"Are you kidding? You were a huge help! If you hadn't figured out what in the world skrei was, Sailor and Emmett would *still* be debating about Greenland."

The corners of her mouth turned up. "Yeah. Maybe. I'll do better next time. If there is one."

"What do you mean *if*? I still have six more pieces to find after this one. Of course there will be a next time." He studied her. "Unless..."

"Unless what?"

"You're trying to say you don't *want* to help me search for the rest of the cipher."

"Why would I say that?"

"I don't know. You're the one that said *if*—"

She groaned. "I meant because you don't *need* me. You've got your aunt and Emmett and your teammates—"

"They're great, everyone's great, but they're not *you*." Cruz's voice cracked. "I never said I didn't need you, Lani."

"I never said I didn't want to help."

"Okay."

"Okay."

Had they just had an argument? And if so, had he won or lost?

Lani was looking down, her eyes hidden by her curtain of hair. "So... uh... now you're heading to Svalbard?" Her tone was soft. Apologetic.

"Yeah, but first Aunt Marisol is taking us on an archaeological mission at a Viking settlement in Newfoundland." Cruz glanced at the clock. He had to hang up soon, and he didn't want to spend the whole call talking about himself. "How was your weekend?"

"Same old, same old. Bused tables most of yesterday." Lani's family owned the Purple Orchid, the fanciest restaurant on Kauai. Lani bounced on her bed. "But this afternoon I'm going horseback riding." She loved horses. Her uncle owned a small ranch at the south end of the island, where he gave riding lessons and took tourists on the local trails. Lani went there whenever she could, usually with her brother Tiko.

"At your uncle's in Koloa? With Tiko?"

"No…um…at Kilauea Point…with a friend. Remember last year when we worked on that habitat restoration project on Mauna Kea and planted, like, a hundred silverswords? I met him then."

"Him?" He couldn't resist teasing her.

She rolled her eyes. "Haych is just a friend. Don't worry. You're still my best friend."

Cruz wasn't worried. Over the course of their friendship, they'd each had their share of crushes here and there, but no one had ever come between them. He felt sure this time would be no different. Cruz smiled. "Back at ya, *hoaaloha.*"

"She's your best friend? That hurts me to the core," cried Emmett, dramatically flinging a fist to his chest and lurching forward as if Cruz had plunged a dagger into his heart.

"Poor, friendless Emmett." Lani laughed.

There was a muffled noise coming from his computer.

Lani's mom was calling her.

"Coming!" she yelled over one shoulder, then to Cruz, "Gotta go." She jumped up, knocking her laptop over on her bed. Her room tipped sideways. A second later, her faced appeared, also sideways. "Aloha, Ems and Cruz."

"Have fun." Cruz waved. He was glad to end the call on a happy note. Cruz scooted back against his headboard. He plumped up his pillow to settle in for an evening of studying. His first task was to read a chapter for Aunt Marisol's quiz.

In archaeology, stratigraphy is the study of layers of rock, soil, decomposing plants and animals, and other matter at a given site. These layers, or strata, are laid down over time. The bottom strata contains the oldest artifacts, while the youngest artifacts can be found in the top layers. Cut in a cross section, strata resemble the layers of a cake. Stratigraphy may provide archaeologists with valuable clues to the relative age of an artifact or site . . .

Cruz tipped his head back. He let a stream of air sputter through his lips. What kind of a name was Haych anyway?

AUNT MARISOL was four minutes late to class. She was never late.

Seated in his usual spot (second row, last chair) next to Emmett in Manatee classroom, Cruz pushed his arms up and arched his back for a good stretch. It was Monday morning, and he'd nearly fallen asleep in conservation class first period. Professor Gabriel had not been pleased to find Cruz nodding off during his lecture on geothermal energy. Cruz was sorry, but he couldn't help it. He'd stayed up late studying. And then he'd just stayed up. It was Lani's fault. Staring at the clock at half past midnight, he'd wondered if she was back from horseback riding. He'd almost called her. It was only 6:30 back in Hanalei. She would be having dinner, so it wouldn't have been a big deal. He didn't call her. She would have seen right through him and known he was checking in on her. Checking *up* on her, was more like it. Cruz knew Lani didn't mean to replace him with a new best friend any more than he'd meant to leave her behind when he'd come to the Academy. But sometimes things happen, whether you intend for them to or not. What if Lani had a crush on this Haych? Or worse, more than a crush?

Emmett was tapping his arm. "The ship has picked up speed."

Cruz glanced out the window. They *did* seem to be moving faster.

"Good morning, explorers!" Aunt Marisol swept into the room.

She wasn't alone. Trailing her were Professor Gabriel, their conservation teacher; Professor Ishikawa, who taught biology; and Monsieur Legrand, their fitness and survival instructor. What was going on? Were they going to teach together?

The class quickly settled.

"Sorry I'm—we're—late," said Aunt Marisol. "I know I promised we'd be going ashore in Newfoundland to help map a Viking settlement site. Unfortunately, we're not going to be able to do that."

Everyone moaned. So much for their first big adventure.

Aunt Marisol lifted a hand. "I can understand your disappointment, but we'll have plenty of opportunities to participate in archaeological expeditions on our travels. I promise. Right now, the Society needs our help."

Their help? Cruz sat forward, now very much awake.

Professor Ishikawa cleared his throat. "This morning, I received a distress call from a friend of mine, a Canadian conservation biologist. While doing research in southern Nova Scotia, he discovered that some North Atlantic right whales that they've been tracking have become entangled in fishing gear."

Everyone gasped.

"My friend sent me a brief clip of drone footage." Their instructor plugged his phone into the computer connected to the projector. "One moment, please."

"It's not uncommon for larger marine animals to get snagged in lines and nets," explained Dr. Gabriel while they waited. "Unfortunately, bycatch is a serious global threat. More than three hundred thousand whales, dolphins, and porpoises die this way every year—that's one death every two minutes."

"This clip is from the Bay of Fundy," said Dr. Ishikawa. "The bay is a major feeding ground and nursery for a number of whale species, including the North Atlantic right whale—the most endangered whale on the planet. We estimate their global population at less than three hundred and fifty."

Ali put his hand up. "Why are they called right whales?"

"Back in the heyday of the whaling industry, between the thirteenth and seventeenth centuries, they were considered the *right* kind of whales to hunt," explained Dr. Gabriel. "They are baleen whales, so they feed by swimming through plankton with their mouths open and their heads just above the surface. They swim slowly and close to the shore, which made them an easy target for whalers. Plus, they had a high blubber content. Their fat was valued for lamp oil. The blubber kept the whales afloat after they'd been killed so they could be towed to shore."

"Although whaling is now against the law in the U.S. and Canada, these days right whales are at risk for being hit by ships and getting snared in fishing lines," said Dr. Ishikawa. "Okay, I think it's uploaded."

Aunt Marisol lowered the lights. On the large view screen, they saw an aerial shot of the bay. Soaring about 30 feet above the water, the drone zeroed in on a pod of black whales gliding through the choppy, white-tipped waves. There must have been a dozen right whales— maybe more—of different sizes, yet the mammoth creatures moved easily and gracefully together with barely a few feet between them.

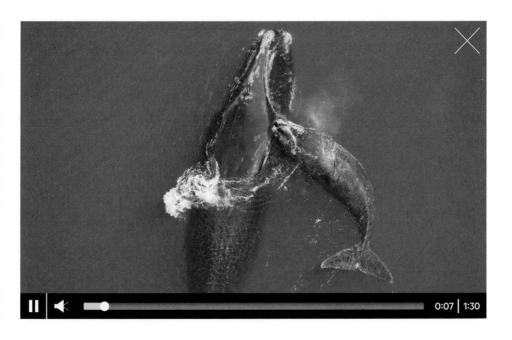

Every now and then, one would surface, sending up a large, V-shaped cloud of spray. As they breached, the sun glistened off their shiny slate-colored backs. Cruz noticed the whales had bumps on their heads and no dorsal fins.

"A calf!" cried Sailor.

As the baby flicked its tail and happily bumped what was most likely its mom, everyone sighed. The drone banked left and the explorers' "awws" turned to horrified "oohs." A wide, dark green fishing net was wrapped around the left side of the mother whale's body, strapping her fin to her side. Another whale came into frame with netting wrapped around its tail. A red buoy was attached to the net and was being dragged behind the creature. The video abruptly ended. "That's all he was able to send," said Dr. Ishikawa. "But it's enough to tell us we have a pod in trouble."

Zane raised his hand. "The ones caught in the nets looked like they were keeping up with the others all right. Maybe they aren't hurt too badly."

"We hope not," sighed Dr. Ishikawa, "but don't be fooled. Whales are large, powerful animals. They may continue swimming after they've been snarled; however, if they're unable to break free in time, it can lead to serious injury or even death. The ropes can slice through their skin and cause infection. They can deform bones, cut off part of a tail, and restrict breathing, swimming, and eating."

"Plus, nets are often attached to other gear—traps, hooks, anchors, and buoys, like the one you saw in the video," added Aunt Marisol. She flipped on the lights.

"A snagged whale may be able to survive for a while," said Professor Gabriel, "but it is a long and painful way to die."

Cruz couldn't stand it anymore. "We are going to help them, aren't we?"

"We are." Dr. Ishikawa clasped his hands. "*Orion* is at this moment headed to the specified coordinates as quickly as Captain Iskandar can get us there."

Cruz and Emmett exchanged looks. Emmett had been right. The ship *was* moving faster.

"We should reach the bay in forty-eight hours," said Dr. Ishikawa. "Time is of the essence. The whales will be starting their fall migration soon. Monsieur Legrand?"

Stepping forward, the rugged French survival instructor placed his hands on his hips. "I will be leading the rescue effort. I will need several explorers who are willing to dive with me to remove the fishing gear. I must tell you this will not be an easy mission..."

Cruz held out his left fist. Emmett bumped it with his own. They were in.

"Any time you are dealing with a wild animal, especially one that weighs seventy tons or more and may be injured, it is dangerous work..." continued Monsieur Legrand.

Bryndis and Dugan had spun in their chairs. Sailor, on the other side of Emmett, was leaning forward. The three of them were eagerly nodding at Cruz. That's all the encouragement he needed. He threw his arm up. "Team Cousteau would like to volunteer. We'll dive with you, Monsieur Legrand."

"*Très bon!* Courage. That is what I like to see."

Professor Ishikawa turned to the rest of the class. "We have jobs for the rest of you, too."

"Just tell us what to do," said Zane.

In a few minutes, it was settled. Team Magellan would handle dive support. Under the guidance of aquatics director Tripp Scarlatos, they would help the rescue divers safely launch from *Orion* and monitor their progress. Team Galileo would be spotters, using high-powered computerized binoculars, drones, and radio tracking to help locate whales. Professor Gabriel would be in charge of them. Finally, Professor Ishikawa and Team Earhart would be standing by in a smaller boat with a veterinarian to render aid to any injured whales, and to help Team Cousteau remove and recover the fishing gear.

"Each team, please report to your adult leader's office at four p.m.," instructed Aunt Marisol. "You'll get further details and instructions for your part of the mission."

Cruz was so pumped for Team Cousteau's meeting with Monsieur Legrand, he could barely concentrate on his classes. However, he did manage to get an almost perfect score on Aunt Marisol's archaeology quiz, missing only one question about stratigraphy.

That afternoon, Dugan, Bryndis, Sailor, Emmett, and Cruz met in Monsieur Legrand's office down the passage from Manatee classroom. As their fitness instructor explained more about the creatures they would be dealing with, he played Dr. Ishikawa's short video for them again.

"Right whales are slow swimmers and shallow divers," Monsieur Legrand informed them. "However, as you can see, they are large animals, up to fifty feet long. Also, they tend to swim in tight groups of six to fifteen, which could make things challenging as we try to move into position. They are social animals, but it is important we take our time so we don't scare them. We must remain patient and earn their trust, or they will not allow us to help." Seeing the explorers nod, Monsieur Legrand continued. "I'm going to assign each of you a dive position. You'll take this spot for each assessment. Once we approach a whale, you will carefully move to your place, inspect the animal for snared lines, injuries, or other issues, and report it to me via the video and voice communications system in your helmet. Bryndis, I want you to position yourself on the upper-right side of the whale, above the fin. Sailor, swim to the opposite side near the left fin. Emmett, you will take the back right, and Dugan the back left. Once you have all checked in to report what you see and I have a clear picture of the problem, I will lead you in removing the fishing gear. You must listen carefully and obey my instructions to the letter. No one does anything without my permission, *comprenez-vous?*"

Yes, they understood.

"Now, in order for us to be successful, there is one more thing—"

"Scarlatos to Monsieur Legrand." Tripp Scarlatos's Australian accent crackled through their instructor's communications pin.

"Legrand here."

"I'm ready when you are, mate. Bring 'em down anytime."

"We're on our way. Legrand out." The instructor stopped the video. "Tripp is waiting for us in aquatics. We're going to check our dive equipment. Also, I want you to go inside *Ridley* so you'll be familiar with how we will exit and return from the dive."

Biting his lip, Cruz looked out the porthole. Monsieur Legrand had forgotten to give him a job. Or maybe he hadn't forgotten. Maybe there wasn't anything for him to do.

"Wait!" called Sailor as they started to get up. "Monsieur Legrand, what about Cruz?"

"Yeah," said Emmett. "You forgot Cruz."

Their instructor let out a chuckle. "Hardly."

Cruz let out a breath. So Monsieur Legrand *did* have something for him to do. He didn't care how insignificant it was. He just wanted to help any way he could.

"As I was about to say before Tripp checked in, the key to a successful rescue mission lies in having a good cetacean ambassador," said Monsieur Legrand. "That will be your task, Cruz."

Cruz was confused. "I'll do what?"

"You'll be our cetacean ambassador."

That's what he thought he'd said. What in the world was a—

"In other words"—Monsieur Legrand clamped a firm hand on Cruz's shoulder—"you're going to talk to the whales."

10

THE LIGHTS were low, the blinds pulled over
the portholes, as Cruz and Emmett stepped through the door labeled
TECHNOLOGY LAB. It was torture for Cruz, waiting for his eyes to adjust. He
couldn't wait to look around the place Emmett had not stopped raving
about since they'd left port a week ago.

"Hello?" called Emmett. "Fanchon? Sidril?"

As Cruz became accustomed to the dimness, a sea of cubicles
appeared. The lab was the size of two classrooms, the dividers stretching across the entire compartment. Directly ahead, in the first cubicle,
a giant glass globe stood on a pedestal. Dozens of curling tubes fanned
out from the center of the clear orb. It reminded Cruz of a giant Pacific
octopus. A burgundy fluid bubbled inside the octopus's stomach, the
twisty tentacles bringing in and taking away the blood-colored liquid
to places unknown. In the cubicle next to it, Cruz saw a robotic forearm
on the table, palm up, its fingers moving to tap the thumb in slow suc-
cession: index finger, middle finger, ring finger, pinkie. Repeat. Wires ran
from a plain black box to the circuitry of the arm.

"She must be in her office." Emmett motioned for Cruz to follow
him.

Navigating the maze of cubicles, they passed gurgling beakers,
spinning test tubes, rotating platforms, and more than a few baffling
objects, like a half-accordion, half-pasta-strainer contraption that was

expanding and contracting while filtering something that looked like beef stew. Cruz dared to pause at the only station that looked some-what normal. Beside a microscope sat a tray of a dozen or so petri dishes. Each of the shallow dishes held a cross section of a grapefruit inside a peach-colored gel.

"Weird," whispered Cruz, leaning over the tray.

"I bet you're not dessert." As he watched, the gel began to turn a deeper shade of orange until it resembled the coils of a hot stove. The gels in the other dishes started changing color, too. Soon, the whole tray began to vibrate. "This can't be good," muttered Cruz a second before the first sample exploded in his face.

"Whoa, whoa, whoa!" Fanchon was rushing toward them, a cheetah-print scarf in her hair and long metal cylinders swinging from her ears like wind chimes in a storm. Over a pair of jeans and a candy-cane-striped long-sleeved tee, the young scientist wore a black apron with a white outline of a grinning cat. "What are you doing?"

"I'm s-sorry," sputtered Cruz. "I didn't mean to—"

She put a hand to her bandanna. "Did you talk to it?"

Cruz was trying to get slime out of his nose. "Uh ... no ... I don't think so."

"You must have said *something*."

"Well, I might have ..."

"Stay here." She grabbed the tray and raced back into the labyrinth of cubicles, worn-out sneakers smacking the tile floor.

Cruz gave Emmett a horrified look. "I didn't know it would do that."

"How could you?" Emmett was reaching around one of the dividers.

"Be careful." Cruz wiped his mouth on his sleeve. "Who knows what's lurking—"

"Argggh!" shrieked Emmett, beginning to shake violently.

"Argggh!" echoed Cruz, horrified at seeing his friend's eyes roll back. Cruz latched on to Emmett's waist to drag him from the clutches of whatever freakish lab experiment had him in a death grip. "I've got you," cried Cruz. "I won't let go!"

"Good, because…" Emmett suddenly stopped thrashing. He whipped his arm back to reveal what was attached to it: a roll of paper towels. "I gotcha, too."

"Not one bit funny," scolded Cruz, though he had to admit it was a *tiny* bit funny. He ripped off a couple of sheets from the roll to clean his face. "What kind of place is this anyway?"

"I'm so glad you asked!" called Fanchon, her strong voice arriving a few seconds ahead of her. "This is a place of innovation. Of determination. Of transformation. Of anticipation. This is a place for those who dare to dream new dreams." She patted Emmett's back. "Like this bright explorer here."

Cruz vigorously nodded. He admired Emmett, not only for his intelligence but for his ability to see the potential in even the simplest things, things most people took for granted, like a pair of glasses or a piece of fabric.

Fanchon undid the knot of her cheetah head scarf and a wave of wild, dark caramel-colored curls sprung from the fabric. The tips looked as if they had been dipped in pink lemonade. "Cruz, it looks like I'm the one that owes you an apology."

"Sorry?"

"Your … interaction … confirmed my suspicion that my sensotivia extract was, perhaps, a little *too* sensitive."

"So, I didn't ruin—"

"The samples are fine." She retied her scarf. "I talked to them and they calmed right down."

Cruz was dying to ask what exactly you say to soothe a tray of angry orange slime, but thought better of it.

"I've been meaning to tell you"—Fanchon leaned in, as if to tell him a secret, though the trio seemed to be alone—"I am a great admirer of your mother."

"My … mom?" Cruz was taken aback.

"I mean, I didn't know her, but I've read all of her papers. She was an incredible role model for girls like me who love science. In fact, it was her work that inspired something I'm developing right now..." She gave an awkward smile. "But enough about me. I know why you're here. Hold on. It's ready." Sliding by Emmett, she went around a corner.

Cruz wasn't sure what to expect. All their survival instructor had told him was that the tech lab chief had designed a device that could convert human language to cetacean-speak and vice versa. Cruz hoped it wasn't anything that required him to mimic the animals. The only foreign language Cruz knew was Spanish, and he doubted that had much in common with the squeaks, squeals, and groans the large marine mammals used to communicate.

Fanchon was back, holding a shiny black dive helmet and a matching candy-bar-size controller. "I present to you the Uck."

Cruz twisted his mouth. "The yuck?"

"*U-C-C*. It stands for Universal Cetacean Communicator. It works like my standard rebreathing dive helmet; however, when you come within twenty feet or so of a cetacean, the onboard computer kicks in. It identifies the species and selects the corresponding vocabulary program. Once it has, you'll see a green light flash above your left eye. That's the signal that the translator is ready and you may proceed."

"Then I just talk inside the helmet?"

"Yes. Speak in your normal voice, but use simple words and short phrases, if you can. It'll help the translator work faster

94

and more efficiently. It takes about ten seconds for the computer to record your phrase, translate it, and broadcast it to the animal. Since most cetaceans have excellent hearing, the noise it produces will be low and won't interfere with your normal hearing. Likewise, when the whale sings, the UCC will record it and translate what it can for you. While that's happening, you'll see a blue light. For the translation, it's my voice you'll hear in your helmet."

Maybe talking to the whales wasn't going to be as difficult or complicated as he'd thought.

"One other thing," added Fanchon. "Don't expect it to say, 'Hi, Cruz, how are you?' That's not how it works. You'll likely get a set of descriptive words to convey what the animal is feeling or thinking. You may have to do a little guesswork to figure it out. The best advice I can give you is to go with your gut."

"Okay." So much for easy and uncomplicated.

"What's the controller for?" asked Emmett.

"It allows you to switch between human and cetacean communication. It clips on your diver's belt. You'll always be able to hear your team, Cruz, but in UCC mode, you won't be able to speak to them, I'm afraid. I'm still working on that feature. Flip the toggle to the left to activate the UCC, then move it to the right to talk to your team." Fanchon handed the helmet and control to him. "I think that's everything. I just completed the final upload so you'll be able to interact with more than eighty types of cetaceans, from the blue whale to the narwhal." She bit her lip. "At least, I hope so. After all, it *is* a prototype."

Cruz furrowed his brow. "You have tried it out, though, right?"

"Yes ... and no. I did have some interesting conversations with the bottlenose dolphins at the National Aquarium, in Baltimore. However, you'll be the first human to use it in the wild. And with a whale. I'd planned to do more testing before deployment, but this is an emergency—"

They heard a series of short beeps. They were coming from the far end of the lab.

"I'd better go ... uh ... take care of that," sputtered Fanchon. "You'll do fine, Cruz. Right whales are friendly, or so I've been told by some dolphins I know." She grinned.

He did his best to return the smile.

Beep. Beep. Beep. They were coming faster.

"Fanchon!"

"Be right there, Sidril." Backing away, the tech chief nodded to Emmett. "By the way, I took a look at your latest Lumagine equations. I've got a few ideas, if you want to kick it around a little."

"You bet!"

"I've got time tomorrow night." She disappeared around a corner. "How about seven?"

"Thanks, Fanchon." Emmett grinned. "I'll be here."

Bright red fingernails appeared above a partition. "Oh, and, Cruz, if you experience any unusual symptoms in the next few days, you know, from the sensotivia gel, come on back. I've got a cream that'll fix you right up."

Cruz put a hand to his chin. It was sticky. "Cream for *what*?" he called, but Fanchon Quills had already vanished into the jungle of cubicles.

CRUZ WAS ALONE at the rail on the third deck, watching the ship's bow slice through the glassy sapphire waters of the Atlantic. To his left was the craggy coast of Maine, its line of evergreen trees broken up now and again by long stretches of white sand. Occasionally, the ship would pass a small island, and Cruz would scan for the white column of a lighthouse rising from its rocky shore. The mid-morning October sun and brisk, salty wind felt good on his face. At breakfast, Captain Iskandar had made an all-ship announcement that they should arrive in the Bay of Fundy around noon. Classes had been canceled for the day. Taryn had instructed the explorers to eat lunch early and rest in their cabins, but Cruz could do neither. He was too nervous. He had come to the outdoor deck to practice what he'd say to the whales. Short and simple, that's what Fanchon had said.

Hello. My name is Cruz. Did whales have names?

Hello. We have come to help. That sounded better.

It was the listening part that worried him. What if he didn't understand the whales? What if he misinterpreted a message? What if the translator malfunctioned? The what-ifs had woken him up at 2 a.m., ping-ponging around his brain, and hadn't stopped since. What if he said the wrong thing? What if he frightened the whales and they swam away before his team could remove the fishing gear? What if he frightened them so much they never trusted humans again?

His mind reeling, Cruz curled his cold fingers around the rail. This was wrong. This was all wrong. Being a cetacean ambassador was too big of a responsibility. Fanchon should be the one to do it, or Tripp, or, better yet, Monsieur Legrand. Yes, yes, he was the survivalist. Their instructor had done everything from paragliding over the Alps to diving to the ocean floor in the Mariana Trench. Cruz had been nowhere. Done nothing. He wasn't ready! From the rolling bow of *Orion*, Cruz tilted his head back, looked up at the swooshes of wispy clouds, and yelled into the wind: "I CAN'T DO IT!" He half expected someone to shout something back. No one did.

Closing his eyes, Cruz slid his hand inside the lapel of his jacket. Through his shirt, his fingers found the stone cipher. He could feel his heart slamming against it. Sometimes he felt so unsure of himself. Cruz wanted so much to fulfill his mother's wish and find all the pieces of the cipher, but what if he couldn't? What if he wasn't as brave as his mother? What if—

"Cruz?"

He turned, the wind whipping his hair into his eyes. He had to brush it away first before he could see Emmett.

"It's freezing out here." Emmett hugged himself. "Come inside. We got our first mail delivery. Your care package from Lani came."

Taryn had mentioned that snail mail would be flown in from the Academy once a week. Had it been a week already?

Prying his hands from the rail, Cruz followed Emmett into the lounge. Along with Lani's box, there were two envelopes on a table. One envelope was from his dad. The other had his name and address printed by computer on the front and no return address. Sitting down, he reached for Lani's box first. The moment he slid it close, Cruz had an overwhelming sensation of familiarity, as if he'd been somehow, magically, transported back to Kauai. Once he split open the top seam of the box, Cruz understood why. Lani had sprinkled the shredded recyclable packing paper with pink plumeria petals. Cruz inhaled. It smelled like fresh apricots and roses. And home. Sweeping aside the blossoms, he picked up her note.

> Hi, Cruz,
> Here are a few reminders of the Garden Isle.
> These will have to do. I couldn't fit a pepperoni and
> sausage pizza in the box. Don't forget
> me while you're out there on the
> big blue ocean.
> Love, Lani

As if he could forget her.

Beneath the note was a small clear jar with a gold lid. Lifting it, Cruz snickered. Grandma Kealoha's orange liliko'i jelly bore a striking resemblance to Fanchon Quills's sensotivia gel (pre anger mode). Next was a small loaf of bread wrapped in cellophane. He put it to his nose. Banana bread! Beside the bread was a key chain with a miniature blue surfboard attached. When you pressed the side of the board, a light came on. Cool! The last item was a bag filled with macadamia cookies—his favorite—tied with a white-and-lavender ribbon. Cruz knew Lani had made these herself because the edges were on the crispy side. Lani was a top-notch scientist, inventor, pianist, and surfer. She was, however, a less-than-top-notch baker. Cruz put everything back in the box. He'd have to be sure to call Lani soon and thank her for the goodies.

His dad's letter contained the usual news from home: The weather was on the rainy side, Cousin Santino's wedding was beautiful (if rainy), the new line of round beach towels was selling like mad at the Goofy Foot. *Business is going well,* wrote his dad. *I've got several students signed up for my surfing class, too. It will be fun to teach again. Looking forward to hearing how your travels are going (that means call me soon!). Miss you. Love, Dad.* Cruz folded up his dad's letter and reached for the mystery envelope. Turning it over, he slid his finger through the top fold. He took out the light blue page inside.

> *Dear Cruz,*
> *I hope I am not too late, but this was the only way*
> *I could be certain my message would reach you with-*
> *out being intercepted. Even now, I am not sure it will.*
> *Someone on board* Orion *is going to try to kill you. I*
> *don't know who. I don't know when. I only know the*
> *plan is to steal your mom's journal, then get rid of you*
> *before you turn 13. Do not take any unnecessary risks.*
> *I hope to one day meet you, if I live that long . . . and*
> *you do, too.*
> *—A friend*

"What's wrong?" asked Emmett.

Stunned, Cruz handed the letter to him. As his roommate read it, his glasses turned from robin's egg blue triangles to deep purple half-moons. "Where did this come from?"

Cruz flipped the envelope. "The postmark is from London, England."

"Do you know anyone from there?"

"Nobody, except Weatherly, but she couldn't have sent it." Weatherly Bright, an explorer on Team Galileo, came from London. However, she had been enrolled at the Academy since September along with Cruz and everyone else, so she could hardly have mailed him a letter from England a few days ago.

Emmett read the letter again. "I get why they might want the journal, but what does your birthday have to do with it?"

"I don't know. Maybe he means by doing away with me they also get rid of the last trace of my mom. I know one thing for sure. I don't scare as easily as I used to."

"You'd better tell your aunt—"

"No." Cruz snatched the page from his roommate. "I'm not telling anybody about this and neither are you." He had come to Explorer Academy to experience the remarkable, to find his passion, and to push himself to discover all he was capable of achieving, but he couldn't do any of those things if he let fear rule his every move. "Besides, we don't know who sent it. It's probably not even true."

"I know what you're up to." Emmett raised an eyebrow. "You just don't want anything messing up your chance to talk to the whales."

Lifting a shoulder, Cruz grinned. Now that *was* the truth.

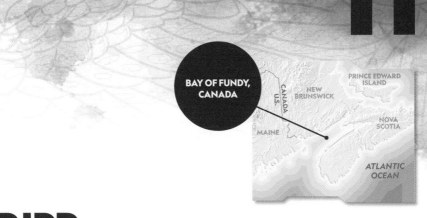

BAY OF FUNDY, CANADA

PRINCE EDWARD ISLAND
NEW BRUNSWICK
CANADA
U.S.
MAINE
NOVA SCOTIA
ATLANTIC OCEAN

TRIPP

Scarlatos adjusted his headset and turned in his pilot's seat. "Everybody ready? Too bad if you aren't, mates, 'cause here we go!"

Seated in the back section of *Ridley*, Cruz stretched his neck to peer through the front oval porthole. The massive steel door on *Orion*'s hull was sliding slowly open. Seawater was pouring into the bay. They were about to launch!

Next to Tripp in the copilot's seat, Monsieur Legrand puffed up. "My team is more than ready." Their instructor glanced back to survey Cruz and his teammates, packed hip to hip on the curved bench in the dive section of the sub. Monsieur Legrand gave them a thumbs-up.

In their lightweight wet suits, Team Cousteau returned the signal, though it was obvious no one was as confident as their leader. Sailor was chomping the life out of at least four pieces of gum, Dugan's heels were fidgeting faster than a hummingbird's wings, and the red and black streaks pulsing through Emmett's trapezoidal-shaped glasses were moving faster than a race car. Seated between Dugan and Bryndis, Cruz was clutching his UCC dive helmet to his chest so tightly he was sure it was going to burst into a million pieces. Everyone knew what was at stake. This wasn't a CAVE simulation. They wouldn't get a second chance. If they didn't focus, if they didn't cooperate, oh man, if they made even a single mistake...

Cruz took a ragged breath and tried not to think about it.

With *Ridley* now fully submerged, Tripp released the holding clamps. They were moving! The pilot delicately maneuvered the sub through the hull opening. Peering out the starboard porthole next to him, Cruz saw a murky blue horizon.

"*Ridley* to *Orion*," said Tripp. "We have cleared the ship. Operation Cetacean Extrication is under way."

Sailor started clapping. Cruz joined in. Sitting behind Tripp, the three members on board from Team Magellan—Ekaterina, Tao, and Zane—were applauding, too.

Bryndis was nudging him. "Now *this* is a fundy."

"What?"

"Remember when we played Taryn's game and I asked you what a fundy was?"

"That's right." He snickered. "Here's hoping we have a fun day in Fundy."

"We will." She patted his shoulder. "It's *örlög*."

"What?"

"Örlög. It means 'destiny'—you know, doing what you were meant to do. It's from Norse mythology."

Cruz liked the sound of that. He leaned back so he could get a better look through the porthole. Above them, the afternoon sun painted the rippling waters near the surface a light aqua. As his eyes moved downward, the water changed color. It went from aqua to turquoise, then cobalt.

"You know there are sharks in these waters." Dugan's head was inches from Cruz's. "A great white can rip your leg clean off."

"It can," agreed Cruz matter-of-factly, "but only because it mistakes you for food. Good thing I'm from Hawaii and not from, say, New Mexico, or I might not know what to do if I ever came nose-to-nose with a shark." Cruz couldn't resist ribbing Dugan, whom he knew was from Santa Fe.

"I know what to do," shot Dugan.

"Sure you do." Cruz pointed to the gold chain hanging over the neck of Dugan's wet suit. "That's why you won't forget to tuck that in before we get out there, because you know sharks can mistake jewelry for fish scales, especially on a sunny day."

"They can?" Was that a tiny crack in Dugan's tough outer shell?

"Uh-huh. Sharks find their prey mainly by smell. They see well in low contrast but have a harder time with high-contrast objects," explained Cruz. "They can be attracted to jewelry, bright swimsuits, or surfboards with contrasting colors, thinking they're fish."

Dugan eyed him suspiciously. "You're teasing."

"I'm not. Honest."

"You think you're so smart because Monsieur Legrand picked you instead of me to be the crustacean ambassador, but you're not."

It was on the tip of Cruz's tongue to correct him, but he didn't.

Bryndis did. "It's cetacean, Dugan, not crustacean. Crustaceans are crabs and—"

"I know what they are," bit Dugan, turning away.

"We've locked on to the pod." Monsieur Legrand was coming toward them with Ekaterina, Zane, and Tao close behind. "Get into your gear, team."

Cruz reached for his buoyancy vest. He slipped the outer strap over his oxygen tank. Zane was there to give him a hand, lifting the tank so Cruz could slip his arms into the vest. Cruz picked up his helmet and turned the dial above the left ear clockwise to switch on the helmet's computer system. They were using Fanchon Quills's watertight rebreathing helmets. When a diver exhaled, the helmet filtered out the carbon dioxide, recycled the oxygen and nitrogen, then added fresh air from the tank before cycling it all back into the helmet to be inhaled. Cruz clicked the dial over the right ear clockwise to turn on his microphone. While Zane connected the hoses from his tank to his helmet and the emergency regulator attached to his weight belt, Cruz checked to make sure the UCC controller was securely clipped to the belt. He set the toggle to human communication, as Fanchon had instructed. Zane slid the helmet over Cruz's head. Cruz could hear him flipping latches, attaching the helmet to his wet suit to create a water-tight seal.

"You're set," called Zane, tapping his back. "Check your level and test, please."

On the bottom of his view screen, Cruz spotted the air tank gauge. It read 100 PERCENT. Cruz took a few deep breaths to make sure the unit was functioning, before giving Zane a thumbs up. All that was left was to put on his fins and gloves. As he did, he saw Dugan unzip the top of his wet suit and slip his gold chain inside.

Once everyone from Team Cousteau was suited up, Team Magellan backed away and took their seats in the front section of the sub. With a final thumbs-up to the dive team, Tripp hit a switch on his console. The watertight wall began moving, separating the dive section from the front of the sub. A few moments after the wall locked into place, water began coming in through vents at their feet. Cruz's pulse quick-ened as the water rose to his ankles, his shins, his knees ...

"Team Cousteau, check in." Monsieur Legrand's voice was in Cruz's helmet.

"Cousteau One here," responded Cruz.

"Cousteau Two," echoed Sailor.

"Cousteau Three," called Bryndis.

"Cousteau Four," said Emmett.

Silence.

All heads turned to Dugan. He put his hands out, palms up, as if to say, *What?*

Cruz reached for the dial on Dugan's helmet and turned it clockwise.

"I said, *I'm here!*" Dugan's voice pierced their eardrums.

Monsieur Legrand sighed in that way teachers do when they wish class was over already. The dive section now completely flooded, Monsieur Legrand swam to the upper hatch and spun it. He pushed the door upward and kicked through the circular opening. As the webbed tips of his fins disappeared, Team Cousteau followed. Cruz went up after Bryndis. The moment he was in open water, he felt himself relax. He hadn't been diving since last summer. It felt good to be in the sea again—featherlight and free. He loved the buoyancy of water. Maybe Bryndis was right. Maybe this was his örlög. Cruz did a few somersaults for fun.

Monsieur Legrand closed the hatch behind them. "*Ridley,* we're clear."

"Roger that," confirmed Tripp. "The electromagnetic shark deterrent is on, so you should be protected. We'll be here in case you need anything. Team Earhart is on the surface and is tracking you. *Ridley* out."

Monsieur Legrand glanced up from his sonar receiver. "Looks like the whales have turned and are heading closer to shore. Follow me. Visibility isn't great today, so remember your scuba training and stay with your buddy." He motioned for Dugan, who was his partner, to join him. They took the lead. Sailor and Emmett fell in behind them. Cruz swam to Bryndis. Shoulder to shoulder, they brought up the rear.

The pair kicked in an easy, steady rhythm, their heads slowly turning as they scanned the seascape. Monsieur Legrand was right; visibility *was* low. For a while, the only thing Cruz saw was Sailor's and Emmett's fins stirring up a silty blue fog ahead of him. Suddenly, to his right, a silver blur. Cruz pulled up. A giant group of small, shimmery gray fish made an abrupt yet smooth turn to avoid him. There must have been thousands of fish in the school, maybe *tens* of thousands, but they seemed to move as one.

"Herring," identified Bryndis. "I read that they can communicate by farting."

Cruz tried to keep from giggling. That *had* to be an Icelandic word that meant something very different from what it meant in English.

"When they break wind, it makes a high-pitched buzzing sound that humans and other fish can't hear," she said. "Although it's possible whales and dolphins *can* hear it, in which case the gassy herring are advertising themselves as dinner. Weird, huh?"

"Tooting fish," laughed Cruz. "Who knew?"

"You *do* know we can hear you guys," Emmett said drily.

"Farts and all," added Dugan.

Cruz and Bryndis exchanged sheepish grins.

"Up ahead!" It was Monsieur Legrand. "We've found our pod, explorers!"

Cruz and Bryndis swam faster to catch up with the others. Reaching Monsieur Legrand, Cruz spotted about seven or eight dark masses perpendicular to their position. They were drifting near the surface. Suddenly, a diagram of a North Atlantic right whale popped up in the corner of Cruz's viewer. The light next to it turned green. The UCC was ready!

"Cruz, you're up," said his instructor.

This was it!

"I'm switching over to UCC communication only now." Cruz tried to sound composed, but it was hard to keep his voice steady with his heart booming against his rib cage.

"Copy that," said Monsieur Legrand. "We'll let you know if we need to speak again."

Cruz flipped the toggle. He began swimming toward the group, kicking gently and keeping his arms close to his body so he didn't spook them. He chose a whale on the outside of the group and glided toward its head. He wanted the animal to be able to clearly see him with the eye on that side. The black whale was enormous—bigger than a school bus! Its long, smooth body sloped to a massive, notched tail that was lazily fanning the water. Several white patches were splattered across its belly. The whale's mouth scooped down below a large black eye, then up toward the nose to form a giant upside-down U. Sandy white bumps dotted the head and swooshed over each eye, like a thick eyebrow. Yesterday in class, Dr. Ishikawa had explained the bumps were hardened patches of skin called callosities. These rough patches of calcified skin were a distinguishing feature of right whales. No two whales had the same pattern.

For a moment, Cruz could only stare at the 70-ton animal. Mesmerized by its size and beauty, he felt so tiny. So ordinary.

Cruz should probably say something, shouldn't he? As he started to speak, he heard a noise that sounded like a baby elephant trumpeting. Had that come from the whale? The blue light in his helmet went on. It had! Cruz held his breath, eagerly waiting for the translation.

"Human." It was Fanchon's voice in his ear. It was comforting to hear her.

Cruz heard another lonely wail, this one longer and from farther away.

"Caution," came the translation.

A dark eye was moving, studying him. Cruz's mind suddenly went blank. It took him a few seconds to remember what he had practiced. "We've … uh … we have come to help," Cruz said too loudly. "To take off the nets."

As the UCC broadcast his message, Cruz heard a long *whooooooooom*, like a lone trombone, sliding from one low note up to the one above. The noise was not loud; however, Cruz felt like his head was stuck inside a stereo speaker.

The message came back: "Help."

The whale turned its head toward Cruz, seeming to acknowledge him, before slipping lower in the water. Out of the corner of his eye, Cruz saw a flash of red. Was that a buoy? Could this be the snarled whale from Dr. Ishikawa's video? The pod parted, allowing Cruz to move between them. He kept his arms in, fluttering his fins slowly and steadily through the cloudy blue-green water. Surrounded by creatures that were 10 times his body length, Cruz didn't feel crowded or jostled or even scared.

There! A red buoy was trailing a whale. It was attached to a clump of twisted fishing net wound several times around the whale's lower belly and tail. The net was so tightly wrapped, it was bending one of the tail flukes. The sight of it made Cruz wince.

Cruz heard a soft, mournful wail. It seemed to go on forever.

As the whale's tail sank, the translator spoke: "Struggle. Tired. Pain."

"I understand!" cried Cruz. "Yes! Hold on. Do not give up!" Cruz got so excited he nearly forgot to switch his controller. "Monsieur Legrand, I'm pretty sure I've found the whale from the video, the one with the buoy. Swim through the space that I took and you'll see us. Hurry, hurry, hurry!"

"Easy there, Cruz," answered his instructor. "Tell him to stay still. We're coming."

Cruz flipped the toggle on his UCC to relay the message, then moved in a bit closer. He put a hand on the whale's body, next to a long, wide pectoral fin. "You will be all right. My friends will help. I am right here. Stay still, if you can." He was probably talking too fast and saying too much. *Slow down,* he told himself. *If you're calm, it'll be calm.* But he was touching a whale! How do you not freak out about that?

Through the haze, Cruz saw one helmet, then another, appear. "Here they come!"

The team members took their positions on each side of the whale. Sailor drifted into place next to Cruz. As their eyes met, hers widened as if to say, *Can you believe where we are?*

"Cousteau Two, report," commanded Monsieur Legrand.

"No netting up here near the left fin," replied Sailor, moving along the whale's body. "I see no injuries."

"Cousteau Three?"

"Same report from the right side," explained Bryndis.

"Cousteau Four?"

"Netting is wrapped around the lower body," said Emmett. "There is a small cut here on the belly, but it doesn't look deep."

"Cousteau Five?"

"Netting here, too, but no injuries," reported Dugan.

"The tail is bent, but I see no wounds," reported Monsieur Legrand. "Team members two through five, please slowly swim back to the tail to assist me. Cruz, please continue to keep our patient calm."

Cruz stroked the animal. Its skin felt rubbery smooth over a firm, muscular body. "You are doing well," he said into his translator. "We are going to take off the net now."

I wonder what you're thinking, Cruz thought as the dark eye roved over Sailor, then him.

The whale's tail and fins had stopped moving. It was floating. Waiting. Maybe even trusting?

Their instructor ran his hand across the net. He looked to be probing for a loose section. "We'll start here," said Monsieur Legrand, taking a knife from his belt. "Dugan, hold this piece up while I cut it. Good. Now, Emmett, gently unravel that side. Sailor and Bryndis, can you gather up what we cut away?" Little by little, piece by piece, they peeled away the netting. The whale did not flinch, even when the tips of Emmett's flipper slid along its belly. Everyone moved cautiously and carefully, and for Cruz, it was like watching a dance in slow motion— an amazing dance in a dreamy blue-and-black world. In less than 10 minutes, the explorers had removed every last bit of knotted rope. Monsieur Legrand contacted Dr. Ishikawa and Team Earhart to tell them they were bringing the debris to the surface.

Cruz looked directly into the whale's eye. "We are done. You are free."

He heard a ghostly moan, then saw an easy flick from a tail that was no longer bent. It was as if the mammal was testing to see if it was true.

A fin seemed to reach out to Cruz. It trailed along his chest. "Gratitude," said his translator.

Cruz could hardly contain himself! It was all he could do to keep from doing a somersault in the bubbles. They had done it. They had actually rescued a whale! Cruz snapped to attention when he saw the blue light. His UCC was translating again: "More."

More what? More netting? Cruz's eyes darted to inspect the whale. "It is all right," he confirmed. "We have taken off all the nets."

Cruz heard it again: "More."

He was confused. He didn't know what to think. Or say. Had they missed something? Could there be a hook in its mouth or some other injury they had missed? Maybe the whale had been snarled in the gear so long, it felt like it was still attached to it. Should Cruz say something to Monsieur Legrand? He reached for the toggle switch on his belt.

"Cruz!" Emmett was pointing over Cruz's shoulder.

Turning, he saw three whales gliding toward them. They must have splintered off from the main group and circled back while Team Cousteau was busy. The whale on the end had a long rope wrapped several times around its nose! Cruz remembered how Professor Ishikawa had told them right whales feed on zooplankton and krill by skimming the surface, opening their mouths to take in water, and filtering their prey with baleen plates. Sailor read his mind. "How can he possibly eat like that?" she said.

"It isn't easy," said Monsieur Legrand.

"It's a good thing we got here when we did," added Emmett.

Next to him, Cruz was certain, were the two other whales they'd seen in Dr. Ishikawa's video: the mother whale, a tangle of netting lashing a fin to her side, and her calf.

Cruz's translator spoke for them all: "Help."

Cruz smoothly pushed his arms through the teal waters to reach them. "We are here to help," he said. "Do not worry."

This time, instead of cutting the nets himself, Monsieur Legrand handed his knife to the explorers. He guided Bryndis and Dugan on how to snip away the ropes from the first whale; then it was Emmett and Sailor's turn to release the mother whale. Cruz held his breath as he watched them work. They had to be so, so precise.

Cruz felt a bump on his hip. It was the calf. The young whale was less than half the size of his mom and not quite as dark, but with similar callosities on his head, above the eye, and on the tip of his nose.

Cruz grinned. "Hello."

He heard several short clicks, which were soon translated: "Worried. Mother."

Cruz wondered how long his mother had been tangled in the fishing gear. The calf rolled, revealing his belly patches, and tapped his mother's side with his nose. Cruz heard a long warble. It reminded him of the way a singer holds out the last note of a sad song. The note faded away into an eerie silence.

"Love," said his translator.

Cruz swallowed past the lump in his throat.

"Gently, gently, almost there," coached Monsieur Legrand softly as Emmett cut away the last of the rope.

Cruz watched the mother whale's fin spring from its tether and felt his own heart leap with joy. His team let out a collective "Whoop!"

"That should do it," announced Monsieur Legrand. Emmett and Sailor swam backward with the net in tow. "Everyone in this group is clear with no discernible injuries. I'd say Operation Cetacean Extrication was a success. Team, let's get all this junk up to the boat."

Cruz saw that Bryndis was wrestling with a clump of netting. He grabbed one side of it, and they swam up together. As the five explorers and their instructor surfaced, the pod breached, too.

Several of the whales curled forward, diving and surfacing and diving again as if on a roller coaster. Others spun sideways, their flapping fins making it seem like they were waving. Maybe they were! As they frolicked, the whales took turns blowing huge bursts of air and water into the sky. Treading water, Cruz watched the calf and his mother break through the deep blue waves. Cresting together above the whitecaps, they pitched forward and dived, slapping their tails in unison. It was an incredible sight to see such powerful yet graceful beings swimming strong and free. What was the word Bryndis had used? Örlög. It may have been an ancient idea, but it fit. This was nature's destiny.

Now on the surface, Cruz could no longer hear the whales' song, but his translator could, and it kept repeating one word: "Joy."

Joy.

Joy.

Tears clouded Cruz's vision. He was breathless. And speechless.

Team Earhart, coming around the back side of the pod in a small powerboat, got soaked from all the thrashing and spraying, but didn't seem to mind. They cut their engine so they wouldn't scare the whales. Explorers Kwento Osasona, Femi Touitou, and Kendall Pierson were all smiles when they leaned over the port side to haul up the net from Cruz and Bryndis.

"Well done, Team Cousteau," said Monsieur Legrand once they'd heaved the last of the fishing gear into the boat. "Let's go back down to the seafloor for one last check. We don't want to leave any debris behind."

As they dived, Cruz and Emmett bumped fists. The mission couldn't have gone any better. Pairing up with their partners once again, Team Cousteau swept the seafloor. They scanned for any fishing gear that may have floated away while they were cutting the whales free. Cruz and Bryndis didn't spot anything. Neither did anyone else.

"Looks good." Cruz heard Monsieur Legrand's voice in his helmet. "Time to head back to *Ridley*."

Swimming beside Bryndis, Cruz couldn't wait to get back to the ship. His adrenaline was pumping. He was excited to tell Aunt Marisol, Lani, and his dad everything that had happened. He'd *talked to whales*!

Plus, Fanchon would want to know how the UCC had done. Cruz couldn't wait to tell her how well it had performed—

Cruz's viewer was blinking. He slowed his kicks so he could read the words that had appeared beneath the right light: AIR PURIFICATION MALFUNCTION.

"Bryndis, I may have a problem," said Cruz, deliberately keeping his voice steady.

In seconds, she was at his right shoulder. "What's up?"

"I'm getting a warning light on my rebreathing system."

"You're breaking up ... say again?"

More words were flashing on his viewer: WATER SEAL BREACH. His visor was beginning to steam up. Hearing only static, Cruz put a hand out for Bryndis. She wasn't there. His neck felt wet. He dropped his eyes. His helmet was filling with water! Cruz told himself not to panic. His training kicking in, Cruz went through the checklist of everything he needed to do: remove his helmet, grab the emergency regulator on his belt, put it to his mouth, and turn the valve. That would give him enough air to make it to the surface.

Cruz reached for the first of four latches that attached his helmet to his wet suit. He easily unsnapped three of the clamps, but the last one wouldn't pop. He tasted cool salt water. Lifting his chin, Cruz used both hands to try to pry up the latch. It refused to budge. Cruz felt light-headed. Inside the helmet, it was like a greenhouse in summer. He could no longer see anything. Everything was happening so quickly. He could feel his energy draining. Cruz drew one last, deep breath into his lungs. The flashing lights and warnings stopped. Everything went black. His helmet was dead.

Cruz knew that in a matter of seconds, he would be, too.

12

CRUZ TIPPED his neck back to keep his head above the water rising inside his helmet. Had something grabbed his arm? He couldn't be sure. His limbs were going numb. His brain, too. Like the mixed-up pieces of a jigsaw puzzle, thoughts cluttered his brain. He couldn't pick one out. Random sensations ping-ponged around his head. The minty scent of Dad's aftershave. Being squished in one of Aunt Marisol's hugs. Emmett's glasses. Lani's smile.

He started to choke. Water had gone up his nose. Cruz knew he couldn't hold on much longer. His brain slowed. His arms and legs were lead. His chin dipped below the water line. Cruz exhaled the last bit of air left in his lungs, listening to his breath become bubbles.

Bubbles. Funny. He never expected that to be the last sound he ever heard.

Cruz's head was lighter suddenly. His hair felt strange, as if it was floating away from his skull. Something was being shoved into his mouth. He tasted rubber, felt a breeze go across his tongue. Breeze? Air. *Air.*

A voice within him cried, *BREATHE!*

And he did. Cruz felt his shriveled lungs expand. He exhaled, then inhaled. Was this real? He wasn't sure. He just kept breathing. Feeling the fog in his head begin to thin, Cruz opened his eyes. The salt water stung, forcing him to partially close them again, but he was able to make out the blurry shapes of Monsieur Legrand and Bryndis. His instructor was pointing up. Cruz realized he was moving upward—

no, being moved upward. Cruz turned his head slightly and saw that Emmett had a hold of his left arm. Dugan was on his right. Bryndis was directly in front, one hand holding the regulator now in his mouth. Cruz could feel a firm grip on his waist. Sailor. With each breath, he gained energy. As the feeling returned to his legs, Cruz began to kick.

By the time they reached the surface, Cruz's mind and body were starting to work in tandem. Several minutes later, he made the okay sign to let Dugan, Emmett, and Sailor know they could release him. The trio did, however, they stayed close. He knew they were watching to make sure he was able to tread water on his own. Cruz kept the regulator in his mouth so he didn't accidentally swallow water. The team kept their dive helmets on, most likely an order from Monsieur

Legrand to keep them from gulping water and to ensure they stayed in touch. It was weird, though. He was with his team yet separated from them. Cruz could only communicate using hand signals. The bay was quiet, the only sound waves sloshing against wet suits.

Bryndis was fiddling with something on her dive belt. Cruz felt a jerk on his waist and realized he was tethered to her! Running his hand down the hose connected to his mouthpiece, Cruz discovered he was also using her emergency regulator. Bryndis probably didn't want to gamble with his air supply, so she had reached for her own instead. The team's quick thinking had most certainly saved his life. That, and unfastening that fourth, stubborn latch on his helmet.

His helmet! Cruz's eyes darted from Monsieur Legrand to Bryndis to Emmett to Dugan, trying to see if anyone bobbing in the water was holding his headgear, though he knew it was pointless. To ensure his safety, they would have let the helmet go. It was no doubt now resting at the bottom of the Bay of Fundy. Cruz let his head tip back until he felt water in his ears. Fanchon's prototype UCC—gone!

And yet...

He *was* here. He was alive. Cruz looked up at the lacy cirrus clouds whitewashing the sky a pale blue. He remembered how, at Academy orientation, Dr. Hightower had told the explorers not to take their CAVE training lightly, that the skills they learned in the simulator would prepare them for the dangers that awaited in the real world. Not until this moment had Cruz truly considered what that meant. Staring up, his tired body rising and falling in the choppy surf, he had more than enough time to think about it. Cruz understood now that every member of Team Cousteau held every other member's life in his or her hands. From now on, *this* is how it would be. It was a huge responsibility—and one that he would never again take for granted.

Bryndis was tapping his shoulder. She pointed at him, then made the okay sign.

Yes, he was all right. More than all right. Cruz was thankful. For his team. For his family. For everything. Of course, he couldn't say that. Or anything, thanks to the regulator in his mouth. Attached to a girl he liked more than he was willing to admit, Cruz was relieved that all he had to do was nod.

"DEEP BREATH. SLOW EXHALE."

Cruz obeyed.

"Once more, please."

Cruz felt the chill of the stethoscope move from the right side of his back to his left. "Dr. Eikenboom, there's nothing wrong with—"

"Quiet, please."

Cruz let out a long, frustrated sigh, which also fulfilled the doctor's request. He felt perfectly fine. Okay, maybe not *perfectly* fine. A little food and a long nap was all he needed.

"Your lungs are clear," said the ship's doctor.

Cruz started to slide off the elevated bed.

Dr. Eikenboom reached for his elbow. "Not so fast."

"But you just said my blood pressure was normal, my heart sounded good, and my lungs were clear."

A pair of white eyebrows knitted into one. "I'd like to keep you under observation for the rest of the day."

"Observation? You mean like a bug under a magnifier?"

Wrapping his stethoscope around his neck, the doctor chuckled. "Something like that."

"But I don't see why—"

"Cruz." Sitting opposite him, a scowling Aunt Marisol folded her arms.

He didn't need a translator for that. Cruz flopped back against the pillow. He wasn't really mad at her. How could he be?

When his team had returned with Team Earhart in the rescue boat, his aunt was waiting at the port rail of *Orion*. One by one, the explorers and their instructors had gone up the ladder. As each member of Team Cousteau climbed aboard, Aunt Marisol draped a towel over his or her shoulders and said, "Great job, explorer. So proud." When Cruz's bare feet hit the deck, she was there for him, too. Looking into frightened brown eyes, Cruz could tell she wanted to throw her arms around him. But she didn't. Instead, she gently placed a towel around his shoulders. "Great job, explorer. So proud," she said, the break in her voice the only evidence of her feelings.

Uh-oh. Aunt Marisol was on her feet and unfolding a blanket. If Cruz didn't act fast, she was going to have him tucked in before he could say the explorers' motto: *With all, cooperation. For all, respect. Above all, honor.*

"Dr. Eikenboom?" gulped Cruz, sitting up. "If I promise to take it easy and come back if I don't feel well, would you let me go then?"

Glancing up from his tablet, the ship's doctor twirled one end of a thick white mustache. "Tell you what. Let me go check the results of your body scan. If everything looks good, I'll consider releasing you. For now, you can go and get into dry clothes."

Aunt Marisol and Dr. Eikenboom stepped out of the exam room to let him change. Cruz peeled off his wet suit and put on the sweatpants and sweatshirt his aunt had brought for him. When he heard a knock at the door, Cruz flung the privacy curtain aside.

"How's our whale whisperer doing?" Tripp Scarlatos was leaning against the doorframe.

"Hey, Tripp. I'm fine. I keep telling everyone that."

"That's good, 'cause I'd hate to lose my best copilot. I'd have been by sooner to check on you, but I had an errand to run." He brought up his arm that had been behind the wall. "Forget something?"

"My helmet!" cried Cruz. "I can't believe you got it."

"Piece of cake. *Ridley*'s robotics can pick up almost anything."

"Thank goodness. I was dreading having to tell Fanchon I lost her prototype UCC. Do you think it still works?"

"Can't say, mate, but if anyone can fix it, it'd be Fanchon. I was on my way to the lab to take it to her and thought I'd pop in here to give ya the good news."

"Thanks!"

"Anytime. Get some rest. I'll see you later. Hooroo!" With a wave, the sub pilot was gone.

Cruz was putting on his socks when his aunt and the doctor returned. "Well?" he asked.

"Everything seems to check out okay," said Dr. Eikenboom. "I'll go ahead and release you, but I want you to take it easy. No running around the ship or doing any stunts like paragliding in the CAVE. And I want to see you back here if you start coughing or wheezing, have trouble thinking, or feel sick to your stomach."

"I promise." His stomach gurgled, as if to agree. Cruz clutched his belly. "That wasn't sickness, honest."

"When was the last time you ate?"

Cruz twisted his lips.

"I'll have Chef send down some chicken soup," interjected Aunt Marisol.

Cruz hurried out of sick bay before either of them could change their mind.

"I'll check in on you later," said Aunt Marisol, squeezing his arm as they parted at the base of the grand staircase. "Go back to your cabin and get some sleep."

"Okay." But that was easier said than done. The moment Cruz entered the explorers' passage, the news spread like a wildfire on a windy August day. His classmates began pouring out of their cabins. Cruz assured everyone, including Officer Wardicorn, who insisted on escorting him down the hall, that he was all right.

"What was it like to talk to the whales?" asked Zane.

"Incredible," answered Cruz, squeezing between Seth Moller and Kwento.

"What was it like to almost die?" called Ali.

"Scary."

"We're all glad you're okay," said Matteo, slapping Cruz on the back.

"Just what happened down there anyway?" That was Dugan.

"It was an accident," said Cruz, tensing up.

"You must have done *something*. Did you check your gear?"

His mind spun. Maybe he had missed something. "I . . . think so."

"You *think* so." Dugan snorted. "Don't you know?"

Taryn, who had stepped into the passage, was clapping. "Dr. Ishikawa just called down and said your team mission reports on Operation Cetacean Extrication are due tomorrow morning at the *beginning* of class."

There was a chorus of groans. With a wink to Cruz, Taryn began shooing everybody back into their rooms. Officer Wardicorn ushered Cruz to his cabin. "Sounds like I need to take scuba lessons," he teased, tugging on the gold hoop in his ear. "Seriously, though, I'm glad the team is all right."

"Thanks."

Emmett was waiting in the doorway. He shut the door behind Cruz.

"Home at last." Cruz collapsed onto his bed.

Emmett sat down across from him on his own bed. "So?"

"As Sailor would say, I'm sweet as!"

"What about your aunt? What did she say?"

"She freaked out a little when I told her my helmet went dead—"

"I meant about the note."

"Note? Oh, you mean the one from London?"

"Of course, the one from London." Emmett's glasses went from lavender circles to a pair of deep orange squares with flashing red sparks. "What other one would I mean?"

"I told you I wasn't going to tell *anyone*."

"Yeah, but I figured after what happened today . . . Oh, forget it."

Cruz turned, raising himself to one elbow. "Emmett, are you mad at me?" He wasn't sure why he asked a question he already knew the answer to.

"You could have died today," spit his friend. "And you know as well as I do that what happened out there was no accident. We *triple*-checked our gear."

"Maybe, but remember what Monsieur Legrand says: No matter how well you plan, you should always plan for something to go wrong. It could have happened to any of us."

"But it didn't. It happened to you. Just like the letter said." A little vein in Emmett's jaw started to throb. "I don't like this, Cruz."

Truth was, Cruz didn't like it, either. He hadn't let himself think about the possibility that someone might have tampered with his dive gear. He sat up. "I don't know if it was an accident or not, Emmett. The only thing I know for sure is that I'm here, thanks to you and Team Cousteau, and we're headed to Svalbard. By this time next week, I'll have the second cipher from the seed vault and we'll be on our way to wherever the third clue in Mom's journal leads. Let's just focus on that, okay?"

Emmett raised an eyebrow. "I still think—"

"By the way, your right sleeve is red."

"Huh?" Emmett glanced down. "Oh my gosh! It is! It *is* red! I was thinking how I was so angry with you I could see red . . . and I must have triggered the Lumagine . . . Do you know what this means?"

"You're going to have to buy a new uniform?"

"The iridocytes work!" cried Emmett. "Fanchon was right. She said I should try a different approach; instead of developing a transitional fabric, why not try camouflaging the material, you know, the way squids use reflective chromatophores to change colors?"

"Squids?"

Rushing to his desk, Emmett began mumbling to himself. "Okay, so now I know the platelets work, I've got to figure out the precise coating thickness ... This is going to be tricky. Too little and nothing will happen. Too much and your clothes will explode ..."

"Night, Emmett," whispered Cruz with a chuckle.

Cruz thought about calling his dad, but he *was* tired. Besides, it was mid-morning in Kauai and his father would be busy at the Goofy Foot. He figured he'd call early tomorrow, before classes started, when it would be late at night back home.

Cruz stretched to grab the navy knitted throw neatly folded across the foot of his bed. He pulled the blanket up to his shoulders and turned onto his side. Letting his head sink into the pillow, he curled his hand around the single chunk of stone that fell from his neck. Cruz looked out the porthole beside his bed. The milky blue sky was gone. Dark clouds were gathering above the ship.

A storm was coming.

HANALEI BAY, KAUAI, HAWAII, U.S.A.

PACIFIC OCEAN

Kaua'i

HAWAI'I

O'ahu

Maui

PACIFIC OCEAN

Hawai'i

13

►THORNE

Prescott had just bitten into his ginger chicken sandwich when he felt the vibration. Sliding his phone out of his back pocket, he placed it on the table. Prescott's eyes quickly surveyed the outdoor café. It was lunchtime. The place was packed. He scooted the phone closer to his plate and saw he had a text from Zebra. Finally!

Prescott had been in Hanalei for four days. Two days ago, he'd slipped into the Coronados' home above the Goofy Foot to search for Petra's journal while Marco was in the shop. He had not found it nor anything to indicate Marco Coronado was in possession of it: no safe, no fire security box, not even the key to a bank vault. The place was clean. Prescott's finger hovered above the screen. This was the text he had been waiting for, the one that would confirm Cruz Coronado was out of the picture. At last, he could put this whole ugly mess behind him—well, after he got rid of the kid's father . . .

Taking a swig of his iced tea, Prescott opened Zebra's message: Mission failed. Call me.

Prescott nearly spit out his tea. He shoved his wicker chair away from the table. It made an angry squeal. Pulling out his wallet, he tossed a 20-dollar bill on the pink hibiscus tablecloth and made a beeline for his hotel next door. Inside his room, Prescott made the call. "What the devil happened?"

"I don't know. We rigged his helmet and emergency regulator to fail."

Prescott rubbed the spot on the back of his head where he'd been clubbed back at the Academy. "That kid sure gets lucky a lot."

"We've got another problem."

"Besides the fact that he's still alive?"

"Jaguar says the boy has access to the journal—"

"What? I thought you said you'd searched the ship."

"We did. I don't know how he's doing it—"

"Just finish the job," barked Prescott.

"I'll need a little more time to sort it out."

"A little is all you've got."

"I'm taking a big risk here."

"Aren't we all?"

"I mean, I'm jeopardizing everything I've worked for."

Prescott stiffened as the realization set in. "You want more money."

Zebra didn't confirm it. Or deny it.

"How much?" clipped Prescott.

"Twenty percent. Lion can handle that."

"You're playing with fire, Zebra."

"Aren't we all?"

Prescott ended the call. This was all he needed. Not only had their plans unraveled, but now Zebra was getting greedy. Brume was going to be furious. Prescott knew he should probably get back to Washington, D.C. However, before he left Hawaii, he had one last place to search for the journal. Prescott headed downstairs and through the lobby, turning left out of the hotel. Breaking into a business at night was tricky. The Goofy Foot was on the first floor. If he could have a look around now, see what kind of alarm system he was dealing with, it could be done.

A few blocks down, he spotted the purple sign on the other side of the street. In the front windows, tanned mannequins in sunglasses modeled wet suits, shorts, and tees, while coolly leaning against their surfboards. He stepped inside the corner shop, a tiny bell on the door announcing him.

"Good afternoon," said a muscular, dark-haired man behind the counter. He wore a lime-and-yellow Hawaiian shirt that was so bright it stung Prescott's eyes. "What can I do for you?"

"Do you rent surf equipment?"

"We do, when surfing conditions are safe, as they are today. What are you in the market for? Shortboard? Longboard? Hybrid? Foil board?"

"Um . . . I have to confess, I'm sort of new at this."

"I figured," he chuckled. "We don't get cowboy boots in here too often."

"You must have heard my story a million times: High-powered business executive trades in the pressure-packed corporate world for the simple life in paradise."

"Know it?" He threw out his arms. "I'm living it."

Prescott gave an easy grin. "I hope to do the same."

"Anything's possible, if you're willing to work for it. That's what I always tell my son."

"You have a son? Me too. He's twelve."

"No kidding? Mine is twelve, too, though he'll be thirteen soon." He made a terrified face. "Teenagers!"

Laughing, Prescott held out his hand. "Tom London."

The man took it. "Marco Coronado. By the way, I give surfing lessons, if you're interested."

"I am," said Prescott. "I definitely am."

14

LONGYEARBYEN, SVALBARD, NORWAY

ARCTIC OCEAN

Nordaustlandet

Spitsbergen

Barentsøya

Edgeøya

GREENLAND SEA

SVALBARD (NORWAY)

BARENTS SEA

▶**STANDING** at the top of the gangway, Cruz gazed out at the fishing village of Longyearbyen, Svalbard. *Orion* had reached the northernmost point of human civilization! Being only about 650 miles from the North Pole, Cruz had expected Longyearbyen to be a lonely place: cold and icy and barren. It wasn't. It was beautiful, just as Bryndis had said. And colorful, too.

His eyes swept from the dark teal waters of the harbor to the cocoa-colored tidal flats to the steep, snow-covered hills that surrounded the port town. And everywhere, the color red—red roofs, red homes, red buildings. Cruz wondered if the bright red was meant to help the villagers brave the dark winters. It was not yet 3:30 in the afternoon, but the setting sun was already painting the flat-topped mountains a rosy pink. They'd only had daylight for about six hours today. In geography class, Dr. Modi had explained that in another two weeks, there would be no sunrise at all in the Arctic. During the polar night, the sun would remain below the horizon until mid-February. It was a stark contrast to the polar day of the spring and summer months, when the sun never set here. How weird it must be, Cruz thought, to live in a place with no sunlight in the winter and no darkness in the summer. Weird, but fun. No one to tell you when to go to bed or when to wake up! A gust of Arctic wind sliced through him, and Cruz zipped up his hide-and-seek jacket. He was wearing it camouflage side out, as were the rest of the explorers. The temperature, which had barely gotten out of the teens during the day, was quickly plummeting. Cruz heard a muffled voice. Next to him, Emmett was bundled up in his jacket, too. He also wore a thick butter yellow knit cap with a mouth covering, a matching bulky scarf, and a pair of gloves that could have doubled as catcher's mitts. The only thing visible was his glasses: two fogged-over powder blue trapezoids.

"Did you say something?" laughed Cruz.

His friend pulled down his mouth mitten. "I said what are you waiting for—sunrise? I'm freezing back here!"

"Sorry!" Cruz hurried down the gangway to the line of four small, self-driving electric SUVs parked next to the dock. His team had been assigned the first one. When he opened the door, Sailor and Dugan were already seated in the rear section. Bryndis was at the other end of the middle seat. Cruz scooted in next to her, and Emmett slid in beside him. They clicked on their seat belts. A few minutes later, Dr. Ishikawa got in the front passenger seat. Cruz watched his aunt get into the SUV behind his. Once the cars were full, the automated vehicles set off through Longyearbyen.

Bryndis had been correct when she'd said the seed vault wasn't typically open to the public. However, Dr. Ishikawa knew an oceanographer who knew a zoologist who knew an archaeologist who had worked on the team that had designed the vault. As luck would have it, that scientist was in town that very week and had volunteered to give the explorers a private tour.

Bryndis was staring out the window. She'd taken off her black gloves. Her right hand rested on her knee, her index finger tapping out her own beat.

Cruz leaned over to whisper to her, "I've been meaning to thank you, dive buddy."

Turning from the glass, she brushed a strand of white blond hair from her face. "I'm just glad we weren't on our own down there. I had trouble getting your helmet off. One of the latches was stuck. Sailor got to us first and helped me get it undone."

"Good thing your roommate can swim faster than mine," joked Cruz. He nodded to Emmett, wrapped up like a caterpillar in his chrysalis of clothing. Emmett was a great guy and all, but he was no superhero.

Bryndis wasn't laughing. In fact, her pale blue eyes were glazing over. She was on the verge of crying.

"It's okay," he quickly tried to reassure her. "I'm all right, see?"

"I was so afraid, Cruz. I've never been so scared in my life. I thought we were too late. I thought you were going to...to..."

Cruz didn't plan on doing what he did next. It just sort of...happened. His hand, resting on the outside of his leg, slid to touch hers. Bryndis curled her pinkie around his. Cruz could hear his heart thumping. Could she hear it, too?

"There!" called Dr. Ishikawa. "See the lights? That's the vault."

On the hill a few hundred feet above them, a square of bright turquoise and white lights glittered in the twilight.

"The art piece is titled 'Perpetual Repercussion,'" explained their professor. "A Norwegian artist created it with steel, glass, and mirrored triangles, along with hundreds of LED lights to make it glow at night."

"You're right." Cruz leaned toward Bryndis. "It *does* look like they captured a thousand stars and put them in a glass box."

That got her dimples to appear. She wiped her eyes.

The car turned left off the main road at a simple white sign that read GLOBAL SEED VAULT, and came to a stop in a parking lot barely big enough for a dozen cars. Everyone piled out of their SUVs and tramped through the snowy lot toward the tall, thin steel rectangle sticking out of the side of the mountain. The vault reminded Cruz of the back end of a semitruck, if a truck were 20 feet tall. The square of twinkling triangles took up the top third of the back of the truck-like entrance. The aqua and white lights illuminated a pair of locked doors below, along with the short steel bridge leading to them.

A snowmobile was cutting through the parking lot. The driver expertly swung into a small space next to the group of explorers, sending up a fan-tail of snow, then cut the engine. Throwing back the fuzzy hood of a black jacket, a man ran a tan hand through a head of thick wheat blond hair. "Welcome, Explorer Academy!" His booming voice could have set off an avalanche. "I'm Archer Luben, tour guide to the seeds."

Everyone laughed.

Dr. Luben got off his snowmobile. Dr. Ishikawa introduced himself and Aunt Marisol. They shook hands. "Thank you for showing us around inside the seed bank," said Dr. Ishikawa. "It's an amazing experience for our explorers."

"Happy to do it." The archaeologist grinned broadly, revealing a set of teeth as white as the snow at their feet. Dr. Luben had vivid green eyes with deep creases at the corners, a stubbled square jaw, and a slightly bent nose. He struck Cruz as a guy who'd be into outdoor sports with more than your usual amount of danger, like cave diving or BASE jumping.

Dr. Luben led the way up the short ramp and brought out a key to unlock the door. "You know, I was once a student at the Academy myself. If it weren't for many an intrepid explorer taking time out for me, I wouldn't be where I am today."

"Freezing your butt off in the Arctic?" muttered Dugan.

Sailor smacked him.

Cruz sucked in his lips to keep from grinning.

The explorers followed Dr. Luben inside the vault and huddled inside the entry to the tunnel. Cruz craned his neck to see around his class-mates. He spied a couple of benches, a rack of hard hats, and a trolley cart. Straight ahead, a long hallway sloped gently downward. Every 10 feet or so, a grid of white lights dangled from the ceiling to light the way.

"A bit of history for you as we go," said their guide, walking backward down the narrow corridor. "Svalbard was chosen for this Doomsday Vault because the temperatures and permafrost here in the Arctic make it a prime location for cold storage. The vault rooms are located almost four hundred feet into the mountain, so even if the cooling system fails or we see dramatic climate change outside, the vault rooms will remain naturally frozen. Most of the seeds stored here should be viable for many centuries…"

Cruz felt a hand on his right shoulder. Aunt Marisol had her other hand on Emmett's shoulder. She was signaling them to slow down, to let the others go by. They did. Sailor hung back, too.

"Once we get into the vault room, look for the U.S. bins," Aunt Marisol whispered to the three of them. "It's not a big place but it's extremely cold, so we won't be able to stay long. Inside the bins, the seed samples are stored in foil pouches. The cipher could be anywhere, tucked in a corner or even inside a seed packet. Sailor, I think you and I ought to run interference and do our best to keep people out of the area while Emmett and Cruz conduct their search."

"All right," said Sailor.

Aunt Marisol looked from Emmett to Cruz. "Remember, you won't have much time—ten minutes, tops."

They nodded.

The explorers had reached a security checkpoint. Dr. Luben slid a card through a black box that resembled a credit card terminal. He punched a code into the keypad.

"Looks like a graphene door," Emmett hissed to Cruz. "Virtually impenetrable." In other words, there would have been no way the two of them could have gotten inside on their own.

The door led into a large, round corrugated-steel tunnel. They continued farther into the mountain, their path lit by eerie blue lights. A couple hundred feet later, the tunnel opened to a sandstone chamber. The ruddy walls sparkled with ice. Cruz shivered. It was getting colder.

"Almost every country in the world stores seeds here," explained Dr. Luben. "There are three vault rooms, which can hold a total of more than two and a quarter billion seeds."

Cruz whistled quietly. That was a lot of seeds!

"Only the middle room is stocked so far." The archaeologist held up a hand. "Ready to go in?"

"Yes!" cried the explorers.

"Thank goodness we have our jackets to keep us warm," Emmett said to Cruz.

"I wonder what their maximum cold temperature is," answered Cruz.

"I think we're about to find out."

"The optimum temperature for seed storage is minus eighteen degrees Celsius, or zero degrees Fahrenheit," said Dr. Luben, his gloved hand opening a gray door frosted with ice.

Cruz felt his pulse quicken. He put his hand to the hunk of rock hanging around his neck. In a few minutes, they would be inside the vault room, and a few more minutes after that, he would have the second piece of his mother's cipher. The suspense was killing him!

They went through one more door and a locked gate before they finally got their first peek at the storage room. Aunt Marisol was right. It wasn't big—maybe 30 feet wide by 80 feet long—with five rows of metal shelving that reached almost to the top of the 20-foot domed ceiling. From what Cruz could see, almost all the shelves were filled with boxes and bins.

"These containers may look ordinary enough, but their contents are as valuable as gold—maybe more." Dr. Luben's voice echoed through the icy stone cavern. He stepped into the middle aisle. "You are standing among the most diverse collection of food crop seeds in the world. Next to me is a box of maize from Africa, and over here, eggplant from South America, and there, rice from Asia. Did you know that biodiversity in crops has decreased to the point that only about thirty crops provide ninety-five percent of the world's food supply? The U.S., for example, has lost over ninety percent of its varieties of fruits and vegetables in just a little over a century. This lack of biodiversity makes crops more susceptible to threats such as drought, frost, and disease. It's one of the many reasons why this seed bank is so crucial. Feel free to walk the aisles yourself and read the containers, or you can come with me and I'll show you some of my favorite samples. It's quite cold in here and you'll start to feel it pretty soon, if you haven't already, so we won't be staying long ..."

Cruz and Emmett sped for the first row. Cruz went down the right side, and Emmett the left. They moved as quickly as their eyes could scan the labels on the containers. Cruz saw bins marked SOUTH KOREA, COLOMBIA, IRELAND, SWITZERLAND, and PERU but no UNITED STATES. Aunt Marisol was keeping an eye on them from the opposite end of the row. When Emmett and Cruz headed to the second row, his aunt and Sailor did the same. Femi started to come their way, but Sailor said something to her and Femi turned back. *Whew!* That was close. Cruz and Emmett kept searching. CANADA, KENYA, ISRAEL, AUSTRALIA—there! The American flag! About a dozen white bins and one black one on the bottom shelf were marked UNITED STATES, each stamped with a sticker of the Stars and Stripes.

"Psssst!" Cruz alerted Emmett, who was still a good 20 feet back, to join him. Kneeling, Cruz reached for one of the white bins.

In seconds, his friend had closed the distance between them. "No, not that one! The black one with the yellow top from the Archive."

Cruz's head shot up. "What did you say?"

"I said ... uh .. pick the black one."

"From *the Archive*. How do you know about the Archive?"

Emmett cocked an eyebrow. "How do *you*?"

"My aunt let it slip ... Hey, I asked you first."

"I just know, okay?"

Cruz scowled. Emmett had said the same thing when they had stumbled into the Synthesis lab back at the Academy. His friend sure seemed to have a lot of secrets, not to mention being pretty secretive about how he'd come to have such secrets. Cruz was getting tired of all the games. They were supposed to be friends.

"So what is it?" pressed Cruz.

"Explorers!" called Professor Ishikawa. "Gather back up here, please."

"No!" yelped Cruz. Yanking out the black bin, he flung open its hinged top. The container was full of foil seed packets. They were organized into several rows.

"You start on that side; I'll take this one," said Cruz, peeling off his gloves.

Emmett did the same. "What am I looking for?"

"I don't know. Her name or maybe mine or my dad's?"

"Cruz, there's not enough time. There's got to be a hundred packets here—"

"Just go!"

They began flipping through envelopes.

"Nope," said Emmett with every flick. "Nope, nope, nope ... I can't feel my fingers anymore."

Cruz's hands were going numb, too.

Sailor was rushing toward them. "You guys, come on!" she hissed.

"We're not going to find it, Cruz," said Emmett. "There are too many."

Cruz froze when he saw the words on the top of a package: HERE COMES THE SUN.

"Cruz, did you hear me? We have to get out of—"

"Got it!" Cruz plucked out the pouch.

"No way. You couldn't possibly have—"

Cruz swung the label toward Emmett.

He frowned. "I don't get it."

"Mom's favorite song."

"Good thing *you* got that row. I would have gone right past it."

"My lucky day," said Cruz. Ripping off the pull seal, he opened the zip-top closure with his thumbs. Cruz turned the packet upside down and waited for the little black stone to drop into his palm. It didn't.

"Come on, explorers!" Dr. Ishikawa was clapping his hands. "Time to go!"

"No. *No!* It *has* to be here!" Cruz lifted his arm to peer up into the silver sleeve. He shook it, and this time, something *did* fall out: a black-and-white feather. Catching a wisp of a breeze, the striped feather hovered between Emmett and Cruz for a moment before drifting down, down, down to land on the cold, hard floor.

15

"A FEATHER?" Lani scrunched up her
nose. "That's it?"

"This is it." Cruz held the feather close to the camera so she could
get a good look. "Professor Ishikawa thinks it came from a gyrfalcon."

"A jer-what?"

"Gyrfalcon," said Emmett.

Cruz shook his head. "I'd never heard of it, either."

"It's an arctic bird—the largest falcon on Earth," explained Sailor.

"Cool," said Lani. "So what does the gyrfalcon feather mean?"

Ever since leaving the seed vault two days ago, Cruz had been rack-
ing his brain over that very question. *Everything* had pointed to the
cipher being inside the seed packet, and when it hadn't been, it was a
crushing disappointment. "No clue," he answered.

"It has to be a symbol for something," she insisted. "Let's see...
feathers float... feathers get ruffled. I'm sure we can figure it out if we
think it through."

Cruz groaned. That's all he'd been doing since Thursday. He had no
think left in him.

"Birds of a feather... light as a feather... feathers are quills..."
Lani was still brainstorming. "Hey, what about that Freyja person your
mom mentioned? Remember, she said—"

"If you run into trouble, go to Freyja Skloke." Cruz knew it by heart.

"Well, if this isn't trouble, I don't know what is." Lani was twisting a lock of hair. "All you have to do is—"

"Do an internet search," finished Sailor. "And when that turns up nothing, you search the population databases for Greenland, Iceland, Norway, Sweden, Denmark, Finland, and the Faroe and Åland Islands."

Cruz sighed. "Guess what we've been doing for the past forty-eight hours?"

"We found a Freyja Skyberg and a Freyja Sklar," said Emmett. "And what was the one from Stockholm?"

"Frieda Skall," said Sailor.

Lani scowled. "You mean ...?"

"There is no Freyja Skloke," bit Cruz. It came out harsher than he'd intended, but he was frustrated. "Maybe there once was, seven years ago, but not anymore. Either she isn't from this part of the world or she moved or—"

"She carked it." Sailor again.

"Died?" Lani dropped her hand and her twist of hair quickly unwound. "Nebula?"

"Probably," said Emmett.

"Maybe," corrected Cruz.

"You really *are* stuck," said Lani.

Cruz spun the feather between his thumb and index finger until the black-and-white vane became a gray blur. "Yep."

It would be one thing if Cruz could skip this piece of the cipher and go back for it later. But they all knew that was impossible. In her journal, his mother had said he could unlock the third clue only when she had confirmed the second piece of the cipher was genuine, and so on. He had to go in order. And without specific instructions from Cruz on where to go next, Captain Iskandar had no choice but to resume their original course. *Orion* was now navigating southwest through the Norwegian Sea to Iceland, leaving Svalbard, and maybe even the second piece of the cipher, behind.

Cruz looked at his friends, scrolling through names on their tablets.

Emmett could have been working on Lumagine and Sailor could have been harvesting veggies in the garden, but instead, both were spending their Saturday double-checking the population databases for Freyja Skloke. Lani was nibbling on her knuckle the way she always did when she was deep in thought. They all looked as stressed as Cruz felt. He laid the feather on his nightstand. "Lani, thanks for the care package."

"Huh? Oh yeah ... you're welcome."

"Everything was great." Well, what little he'd gotten of it. His friends had helped themselves.

"The jelly was yummy," said Sailor.

"Banana bread is my favorite," added Emmett.

"Sure is," snorted Cruz. "I think I got one slice—"

"Sorry the cookies were burned," said Lani.

"Were they? I didn't notice." Cruz's white lie got an eye roll from Emmett.

"Really? 'Cause Haych said they were a little on the crispy side—" He stiffened. "Haych?"

"I had some extras I couldn't fit in the box, so ..."

"You gave them to your boyfriend." It was out before he could stop it.

"Cruz!"

He knew he sounded jealous, but he wasn't. Okay, maybe he was, but not because he wanted to be Lani's boyfriend. It went deeper than that. Beyond a crush. Haych got to see Lani at school every day. He got to go horseback riding with her and discuss robotics and eat her charred cookies. He got to be her friend. And maybe, soon, the new kid with the new name would get to be her *best* friend. Cruz knew he wasn't helping anything by snapping at her. "Sorry, Lani. I didn't mean it."

She flicked back the lock of Moondust hair and smiled. "It's all right."

Cruz's communications pin sounded a ping. "Fanchon to Cruz Coronado."

He sat up. "Cruz here."

"Can I see you in the tech lab?"

"Sure. When do y—"

"Now. If you can."

"I'll be right up." Cruz glanced at his roommate, who was giving him a pleading look. "Can I bring Emmett and Sailor?"

"Uh...yes, but no one else, please."

"O-okay." He glanced at Lani. "Cruz, out."

"That was pretty mysterious," said Lani. "I wonder what she wants?"

"We'll let you know." Cruz reached for the feather and slid it into a front pocket of his uniform. "Let's go."

It took less than five minutes for the trio to get to the tech lab on the fourth deck. Sidril met them in her usual crisp white lab coat, a tablet tucked into the crook of her arm.

"What's up?" asked Cruz.

"Some rather interesting developments. I'll let Fanchon fill you in." Sidril turned toward the vast canyon of cubicles. "Fanchon! They're here!"

An arm appeared from the center of the labyrinth. "Helloooo!"

Cruz, Emmett, and Sailor wove their way to her. Entering the small station, Cruz saw his UCC helmet sitting on a workbench. It was hooked up to a black triangular computer. "Thanks for coming so quickly," said Fanchon. She was wearing a leopard-print head scarf, a black kimono with red poppies over jeans, and a pair of black flip-flops. "I've been running diagnostics, trying to pinpoint the cause of the helmet failure. It's taken me a while but I've traced it to a bug in my program that allowed for code injection into the UCC. Malware was uploaded, directing the UCC to disable the onboard rebreathing system shortly after the translation protocol had been disengaged."

Cruz wrinkled his brow. "So you're saying...?"

"Sabotage."

The hair on Cruz's arms stood up.

"I knew it," hissed Emmett.

Sailor clasped her hands. "You're sure?"

"Positive," said the tech lab chief. "Whoever did this was no amateur. It's taken us days to find the malware. It was well hidden."

And meant for me, Cruz thought.

"It's bad enough to deliberately damage my work, but to jeopardize an explorer in the process? That's unacceptable and unforgivable." Fanchon's voice shook with emotion. "I'm so sorry, Cruz."

Cruz wanted to tell her that she had it all wrong. That someone was out to get him and she had gotten caught in the middle, but then he'd have to explain why. "It's okay, Fanchon," he said. "It wasn't your fault."

"I should have caught it. That's my job. I should have—"

"You couldn't have known." Cruz had been the victim of a hacker, too, and it had nearly cost him his spot at the Academy. Like Fanchon, he had blamed himself, as if somehow he could have prevented Renshaw McKittrick from targeting him.

"I'll be making a preliminary report to the captain and Dr. Hightower," said Fanchon. "While Sidril and I continue to investigate, I would appreciate your cooperation in keeping it quiet. The saboteur may be on board *Orion*, and I don't want to tip my hand."

Cruz, Sailor, and Emmett nodded.

Going up on his toes, Cruz looked around at the lab filled with flammable chemicals, fragile experiments, and heavy equipment. He wanted to warn Fanchon that poking around where Nebula was concerned could be fatal, but again, he kept quiet. The more he revealed, the more he'd have to explain. Plus, the more Fanchon knew, the more danger she would be in.

Cruz put his hand on the helmet. "You can repair the UCC, though, can't you?"

"I can, but"—Fanchon pursed her lips—"I don't know if I should. If adding the UCC to the rebreather's computer system makes it more vulnerable to hacking maybe I need to rethink the technology—"

"You *have* to fix it. If only you could have been there in the bay when I talked to the whales, you would have seen how well the translator worked. It was the most amazing thing that's ever happened to me. I'm even thinking about cetacean conservation as a career."

"That's wonderful, Cruz. Truly, it is. But..."

The word hung in the air like an arrow in slow motion. Cruz hated that word: "but." Rarely did anything good ever follow it.

"Fanchon?" Cruz swallowed hard. "Are you giving up on the UCC?"

She shook her head, but only once, and Cruz could tell by her pinched face that she was torn. Fanchon Quills was considering abandoning the most important work she'd ever done—might ever do—and it was because of him. Naturally, Cruz couldn't tell her that. He could say nothing to the brilliant scientist whom he liked and admired and who, with her remarkable invention, had changed his life, possibly his future.

And it was pure torture.

"**A**RE YOU *TRYING* TO PUNCH A HOLE** in the hull, mate? For the second time, that's the aft robotic arm, not the port fore camera."

Cruz drew back his hand. "Sorry, Tripp. I guess my mind is somewhere else."

"I'll say." From *Ridley*'s copilot's seat, Tripp tapped his computer screen. "We have covered quite a bit of material. How about disengaging the charger and we'll call it a day?"

Wiping sweat from his brow, Cruz turned to check the gauges. They indicated the sub's solar batteries were fully charged. He shut off the charging unit. When he spun back, Tripp was staring at him, his arms folded across his chest. "You wanna talk about it?"

"Talk about... the robotics?"

Tripp stroked his chin. "I meant, talk about what's bothering you."

"Nothing's bothering me."

"Come on. What is it? Schoolwork? Friends?" He wiggled his eyebrows. "A sheila?"

Cruz felt his cheeks flush. It wasn't a girl. "No!"

"Then what's the trouble?"

"I don't know … It's just that …" Cruz wanted to share his troubles with Tripp, yet something held him back. Maybe Aunt Marisol was right and Tripp was one of those people on board *Orion* who wanted to help him, but still, he had to be careful. He supposed he could try to tell Tripp without actually telling him. "Something … unexpected happened. A big disappointment. I feel like a failure."

"Ah." A head of messy brown hair nodded. "Been there myself, sad to say. Sorry."

It was a small comfort to know someone as accomplished as Tripp had also had his share of letdowns.

"This … disappointment," probed Tripp, "is there anything you can do about it?"

"I don't think so. At least, not now."

Tripp jutted out his lower lip. "Seems to me, if you can't change it, there's no point in worrying about it."

He made it sound so simple. Of course, the easygoing sub pilot had no idea how serious Cruz's problem was or how much depended on it. "I guess," said Cruz. "If only I hadn't let everybody down. They were all counting on me … my dad, my aunt, Dr. Hightower …"

"But not your mum."

"Huh?"

"You didn't mention your mum."

Cruz felt prickly. "Well, that's because—"

"Because you can't disappoint your mum. No child can. No matter what you do, she'll always love you."

But would she? Would his mother understand if he never found her cipher? It was as if all the air had been sucked out of the mini submarine.

"You okay, mate?" Tripp was peering at him. "Did I say something wrong?"

"No … no, I'm fine." Cruz stood up. Everything inside the shell was starting to spin. He took a couple of deep breaths. "I'd … I'd better go.

It's…uh…Funday, and I'm due in the conference room in twenty minutes."

"Sure. See you next week."

"You mean, I can come back? I didn't screw up too badly?"

"No worries. You'll be a fine pilot, Cruz, if you can remember to keep your mind on the here and now, on what has to be done. Distractions only…distract you." He laughed. "Don't quote me on that. Hooroo."

"Hooroo."

On his way back to his cabin, Cruz paused in front of Taryn's door. He was tired and not exactly in a Funday mood. Maybe if he begged a little, she would let him out of whatever activity she'd planned. Probably not, but it was worth a try. He knocked.

"Come in!"

Cruz stuck his head in. Taryn was standing near her desk, holding her tablet. Hubbard bounded toward him. Cruz reached to scratch the Westie behind the ear.

"I was about to call you," said Taryn. "Your Open Sesame band alerted me to your fever."

Cruz lifted his wrist to check his band. "I have a fever?"

"Uh-huh—99.8."

"I don't feel sick. It's probably a false alarm. My OS band must be broken."

Striding across the room, she put a hand to his forehead. "Feels like 99.8 to me."

He laughed. There was no possible way she could know that. "I was in the sub bay. It's hot down there—"

"Sore throat?"

"No."

"Congestion?"

"No."

"Headache?"

"No." He felt a tingly tightness across his forehead. "Maybe a small one."

"I'm ordering Chef's special green juice for you. It'll knock down whatever germ you're battling."

"Green juice?" He made a face. "Taryn, I don't think—"

"To bed, explorer." She turned him toward the door. "Take Hubbard with you. He's a good nurse. I'll keep a watch on your vitals and bring you dinner later. If you feel worse, you're to call me or sick bay immediately."

"I'm sure it's nothing—"

"That's not a request."

Too weary to argue, Cruz slapped his thigh. "Come on, Hub." The little white dog eagerly trotted with him into the hallway.

Back in his room, Cruz got into his pajamas. Slipping under his comforter, he patted the left side of his mattress. Hubbard jumped up and, instead of snuggling beside Cruz's waist, took most of the pillow. Before heading off to Taryn's Funday activity, Emmett mumbled something about bringing back some green juice for Cruz. Great. Two big glasses of green goo to drink!

Through the porthole, Cruz could see the sky was a peachy pink. The sun was setting. He closed his eyes, and although he was exhausted and his head was swimming, sleep wouldn't come. Tripp's words haunted him. *You can't disappoint your mum. No child can. No matter what you do, she'll always love you.* He was right. Cruz knew his mother wouldn't blame him if he couldn't find her formula. Yet, somehow, knowing that only made it worse. She had sacrificed everything for the serum. And the one thing she had asked of Cruz, the only thing she had asked of him, he could not do.

Cruz curled his fingers around the fragment of black marble resting on his chest. He knew every curve and hollow by heart. He wondered if it was the only piece he would ever find.

145

"Music," he said to his tablet on his nightstand. "Play 'Here Comes the Sun.'"

It was the first song his mother always requested their car's computer play on their way to wherever they were going. They would sing at the top of their lungs. She'd tap her fingers against the steering wheel in time to the music while Cruz bounced in his car seat. It was a brilliant move to label the seed packet with the song title. It was something only Cruz and his father would know. But the falcon's feather . . .

That was different. Cruz didn't know what it meant. Might never know.

Darkness was settling over the ship. As it swallowed him, Cruz turned his head to rest a cheek against Hubbard's back. He felt achy. Helpless. Confused. They would be leaving Norway soon, and he had no idea where he was supposed to go.

The song ended. Beneath his head, Cruz felt the gentle rise and fall of the dog's breathing. In the stillness, with all the other explorers gone, he was grateful the little Westie was with him. To be alone would have been more than he could bear. "I wish you could help me, Mom," he whimpered into the soft cushion of Hubbard's fur. "I'm so lost. What do I do?"

But no answer came.

16

REYKJAVÍK,
ICELAND

DENMARK
STRAIT

ICELAND
SEA

ICELAND

ATLANTIC
OCEAN

ATLANTIC
OCEAN

OVER the next couple of days, Cruz did his best to follow Tripp's advice. He tried to keep his mind focused on the here and now, on what had to be done. And what had to be done was schoolwork. In Monsieur Legrand's fitness and survival class, Cruz hiked across his first glacier. Sort of. Their instructor had programmed the mini CAVE to replicate Vatnajökull, the largest glacier in Iceland. In the simulator, the explorers practiced walking on the ice with crampons, probing the snow with their ice axes for cracks and snow bridges, and tying butter-fly knots to rope themselves together.

In Aunt Marisol's anthropology class, Cruz learned how to use PANDA, the Portable Artifact Notation and Data Analyzer. Another one of Fanchon's inventions, the unit, which looked like a pear sliced in half from top to bottom, could tell you the type, origin, and age of any artifact in the world. That lesson was fun, too. Until Dugan, waving his PANDA unit, stood up and blurted, "Professor Coronado, if we're going to use these gizmos from now on, why did we have to learn all that junk about stratigraphy and dendrochronology?" That earned them a stern lecture on the value of explorers knowing the fundamentals of the great and glorious study of the human record known as archaeology. It lasted 14 minutes. Zane timed it.

By Wednesday, the rubbery aftertaste of the green juice Taryn and Emmett had made Cruz drink on Sunday was nearly gone. That, along with the prospect of seeing Iceland, had him almost feeling like his old self again. Almost. Cruz wasn't the only one looking forward to reaching port. That afternoon, Professor Benedict practically flew into class. "Did you hear? We'll be in Reykjavík tomorrow! I hope everyone is as pumped as I am for your first real journalism assignment!"

Manatee classroom erupted in applause. Cruz tried to join in because he *was* excited, too. Yet he couldn't help worrying he was getting farther away from the next piece of the cipher.

"Your homework for today was to prepare background research on Iceland," said their journalism teacher. "Let's hear what you discovered. Femi, why don't you start us off?"

Clearing her throat, Femi lifted her tablet. "Reykjavík is the world's northernmost capital and is located on the southwestern coast of Iceland. Settled by the Vikings in the ninth century, Iceland is about a hundred thousand square kilometers, making it a little smaller than the state of Kentucky. Iceland is called the land of fire and ice due to its numerous geysers, hot springs, lava fields, volcanoes, and glaciers. It is powered almost entirely by renewable energy sources, such as geothermal and hydropower ..."

"It's just funny," Emmett whispered to Cruz.

"What is?"

"I keep going over it in my head, the way your mom said, 'If you run into trouble, go to Freyja Skloke.'"

"What about it?"

"She didn't say go *see* Freyja Skloke or go *look up* Freyja Skloke. She said go *to* Freyja Skloke." Emmett tapped his fingernail against his teeth. "I'm probably reading too much into it."

"No, I think I see what you're getting at." Cruz sat up. "You go to a place."

"Exactly."

"Do you think Freyja Skloke could be a street?"

"Or a park or a store or a restaurant. It could be *anyplace*."

"It would help if one of us spoke Icelandic."

Emmett tipped his head toward the fair-haired girl seated in front of them. "We could ask Bryndis."

"I don't think that's a good—"

"Ask me what?" Bryndis had turned in her chair.

Cruz hadn't realized they'd been talking so loudly. "Never mind—"

"It's okay. Really. I love Norse mythology."

Emmett frowned. "What makes you think we were talking about Norse mythology?"

"You said Freyja Skloke, so I figured—"

"Freyja Skloke is a Norse god?" asked Cruz.

"Goddess." She giggled. "And not the 'cloak'—just Freyja."

"Huh?"

Bryndis held up a finger to signal for them to wait. A minute later, she held her tablet out to Cruz. On the screen was an illustration of a tall, beautiful woman with a long blond braid. She wore a flowing white gown, a gold necklace with an amber jewel in the center, and a cape made of feathers. Below the image the caption read: *Freyja, the Norse goddess of love and beauty, is able to fly by transforming herself into a bird with her magical cloak of falcon feathers.*

Emmett and Cruz looked at each other. Cruz's mom hadn't meant "Freyja Skloke." She had meant "Freyja's cloak." They slowly smiled.

"Cruz?" Professor Benedict was calling on him.

He grimaced. "Sorry, I... I didn't hear."

"I'm not surprised." Her jaw was tight. "Why don't you tell us something you discovered about Iceland that we haven't yet heard? Stand, please."

"Um... sure..." His mind still reeling, Cruz got to his feet. "I... uh... thought the best way to learn about the country was to talk to someone who lives there, so I interviewed Bryndis." Seeing Professor Benedict's chilly expression thaw a bit, Cruz continued. "Her parents own a surfing and eco-adventure tour business in Reykjavík. You wouldn't think surfing would be big in a place as cold as Iceland, but it is. People come from all over the world to surf. And by the way, it's not *that* cold. Oh, and Bryndis told me in the summers she helps her uncle make rye bread for the tourists. It bakes in the ground, you know, because Iceland has geothermal hot springs. See, they dig a hole on the shore of the lake, bury a pot full of dough, and the hot water in the ground bakes the bread! I mean, it takes a while to cook, a day or so, because the water is only about two hundred degrees. It's called … um …" He glanced down at Bryndis for help.

"*Rúgbrauð,*" she prompted.

"*Rúgbrauð,*" he echoed. "Also, most people in Iceland don't have surnames. Instead, your last name is your dad's first name plus the Icelandic word for either 'daughter' or 'son,' depending on if you're a girl or a boy. Bryndis Jónsdóttir means Bryndis is the daughter of Jón. Her brother has a different last name. He's Jón's son so his last name is Jónsson. Bryndis says most everybody uses first names, no titles or anything, like 'Mr.' or 'Mrs.' Even students call their teachers by their first names. How great is that …" He paused. Nope. He'd better not chance it. "… Professor Benedict?"

"Pretty great." She grinned. "Thank you, Cruz."

Before taking his seat, Cruz raised his eyebrows at Bryndis to ask, *How did I do?* She gave him a nod. "*Vel gert!*"

"Now that you have a bit of background on Iceland," said their instructor, "your team mission once we reach port is to choose a news story that reflects an issue facing Iceland. It can be cultural, economic, environmental—whatever you like; however, you will tell that story as photojournalists. That means you'll use only your mind-control cameras. No text. Just photos and videos. Yes, Zane?"

"How many pictures and videos do we have to turn in?"

"As many as it takes to tell the story. No more. No less."

With class winding down, Cruz typed *Freyja's cloak* into the search engine of his tablet.

"Already did it," whispered Emmett. He tipped his tablet so Cruz could read the screen: FREYJA'S CLOAK WILDLIFE RESCUE CENTER.

Cruz's breath caught when he saw the logo. It was a gyrfalcon.

The map on the site showed that the center was only a few kilometers west of Reykjavík. He could hardly believe it!

"Are you going to email them?" asked Emmett.

"No, I should go in person. You're coming with me, aren't you?"

Emmett's glasses had become a yellow, lime, and pink pinwheel. "Like you have to ask."

"I'll let my aunt know what we've found. Can you fill Sailor in?"

"Yep."

"Emmett, could you do me another favor?"

"Double yep."

"The next time my mom gives me a clue? Remind me to ask her to spell it."

The snort was out before Emmett could clamp a hand over his mouth.

THE NEXT AFTERNOON, Cruz was beside Emmett once again. This time, they were on their veranda, with Sailor standing between them, as *Orion* sailed into Reykjavík harbor. Elbow to elbow at the rail in their heavy jackets, the trio got their first look at the bustling northernmost capital of the world. The water and mountains surrounding the city were reflected in the glass-walled condos and skyscraper windows. White church steeples poked above perfect rows of square buildings even more colorful than those of Svalbard. Their bright yellow, red, orange, and blue roofs reminded Cruz of freshly painted dollhouses. Across the bay and far in the distance were the snow-covered trapezoidal hills they had grown accustomed to seeing in the north.

Emmett pointed to a 200-foot, stair-stepped gray spire rising above the sprawling city. "That has to be Hallgrímskirkja church."

"Say that ten times fast," joked Sailor.

Emmett grinned. "It's one of the tallest buildings in Iceland."

"I believe you." She raised her hands in surrender. Good thing. Cruz did not need a repeat of their argument from Taryn's scavenger hunt.

"Bryndis must be excited to be home," said Cruz. "Uh ... where is she anyway?"

"With Taryn," answered Sailor. "They're planning our dinner out tonight. Her family is going to meet us at Svartur Köttur."

"Smarta who?" Cruz asked.

"Not Smarta. Svartur. Köttur," Sailor explained. "I think it means 'Black Cat.' Anyway, just one of the local restaurants here."

"Oh, got it," Cruz replied.

Everything was falling into place. Once the ship docked, Cruz, Emmett, and Sailor would head to Freyja's Cloak to recover the cipher, then return for dinner and a good night's sleep so they would be ready for tomorrow's mission.

Team Cousteau had already decided what they were going to do for

their photojournalism assignment. "Glaciers are melting all around the world," Bryndis had told them. "In Iceland, we lose about eleven billion tons of ice a year. Skaftafellsjökull, one of my family's favorite places to hike, is melting so fast it will be gone soon..."

"That's awful!" Sailor expressed what they were all thinking.

"We have something like two hundred and fifty glaciers, and it's hard to imagine they could all disappear in a few centuries." A shadow crossed her face. "To Icelanders, losing our glaciers is to lose a part of who we are."

"Let's do the story," said Cruz.

Emmett and Sailor agreed.

"How?" grunted Dugan. "It's not like we can watch a glacier melt."

"What if we got some old videos and photos and put them side by side with the ones we take up on the glaciers—you know, to compare then with now?" suggested Emmett.

"My cousin works at the national museum in Reykjavík," said Bryndis. "I'm sure she could help us locate some historical images."

It was settled. Team Cousteau would tell the story, in pictures, of an Iceland without ice.

Emmett was nudging Cruz. *Orion* had reached the pier. Crews were tying down the lines and lowering the gangway. Grabbing their gloves and scarves, the trio rushed out of the cabin and down the passage without a word. Cruz wanted to get off the ship before anyone started asking questions. He led the charge down the gangway and onto the dock. Tapping his GPS Earth pin, Cruz said, "Locate self-driving car rental service within walking distance of—"

"Where do you think you're going?"

"Aunt Marisol!" She was blocking his path, her hands on her hips. Shutting off his GPS, Cruz glanced back at the ship. "How did you—"

"Know you were going to make a dash for it without waiting for me? Gee, I don't know." She tapped her chin. "Lucky guess?"

She knew him too well.

"Come on," she said. "I've got a car waiting."

They piled into the small automated vehicle parked at the harbor entrance.

"Freyja's Cloak Wildlife Rescue Center, please," Cruz said to the computer, and they were off. The compact car navigated the angular streets of Reykjavík, packed with the colorful hotels, shops, and homes Cruz had seen from the harbor. As they reached the outskirts of the city, the roads became wider, the buildings more modern. They traveled through an industrial area, then followed the rocky coastline for several kilometers before turning off the highway. A long, narrow driveway led them to a barnlike building painted sage green with white trim. Above the door was a carved oval wooden sign with a gyrfalcon. Cradled in its massive wings were the words FREYJA'S CLOAK WILDLIFE RESCUE CENTER.

Cruz was the first one out of the car. He rushed up the steps and into the building.

"*Góðan daginn,*" said a young woman behind the front desk when they entered. Her blond hair was pulled back into two short pigtails behind her ears. She wore a blue flannel shirt and jeans. At another desk was a thin, dark-haired college-age guy in an olive jungle jacket wearing a fishing hat covered in enamel flags-of-the-world pins.

"Hello." Cruz's hand went to the stone over his heart. He was so anxious he could barely think, let alone speak. "We ... uh ... we were hoping you could help us."

"Ah! Americans?" When Cruz nodded, the young woman grinned, revealing a space between her front teeth. "What can I do for you?"

"My name is Cruz Coronado, and I'm looking for someone who might have known my mother. Her name was Petra Coronado. I know it sounds weird, but she told me to come here and show you this." He took the falcon's feather from his pocket.

The young woman stared at it for a bit, clearly puzzled, then turned to the guy in the fishing hat. Sniffling, he shrugged.

"Maybe our director knows." She went for the open door behind her. Five minutes later, she reappeared, followed by a man about Cruz's dad's age with straight, shoulder-length, dark blond hair.

Several inches above six feet, he was too thin for his height. He wore a wrinkled khaki jacket with holes in the front pockets, and the buttons that weren't missing were clinging by their threads. A long blue-and-white-striped knitted scarf was wrapped several times around his neck. He had bright topaz blue eyes that matched the blue in his scarf. When he smiled, the creases at their corners helped to soften his pointed jaw. "I'm Nóri. How do you do?"

Cruz cleared his throat. "Hi, I'm Cruz, and I'm looking for anyone who might have known my mother. Her name was Dr. Petra Coronado, and she was a scientist with the Society."

"The Society, huh?" Nóri's forehead crinkled. "I did work for them once. Many years ago. We collaborated on some research. Puffins, I think"—he glanced at Cruz's feather—"or maybe falcons."

Cruz lifted the plume. "Falcons?"

Nóri looked at Aunt Marisol, Emmett, and Sailor, then the two people on his staff, then back at Cruz. "Now that I think about it, it was puffins. I'm sorry, I wish I could help you, but I don't recall anyone by that name."

"I'm Petra's sister-in-law and Cruz's aunt, Dr. Marisol Coronado." Cruz's aunt extended her hand and the director shook it. "Maybe one of your employees or volunteers might have known her? It would have been some time ago, say, seven to ten years back."

"That long ago?" He shook his head. "So many people have come and gone in that time, I'm afraid . . ."

"I know it's a long shot," pleaded Aunt Marisol. "But we'd appreciate any help you could provide. It's extremely important."

"Leave your contact info with Elin here, and we'll get in touch if we find anyone who knew . . . what did you say . . . ?"

"Petra. Coronado." Cruz was starting to get irritated.

"Thank you, Nóri." Aunt Marisol put a hand on Cruz's arm. "We're traveling on the Academy's ship *Orion,* and we'll be in Reykjavík harbor until Monday morning."

He nodded. "I'd give you a tour of the facility, but we're in the process of remodeling. All our rescues have been moved off-site."

"That's okay," said Aunt Marisol. "You've been more than kind. We should be getting back to the harbor anyway."

Nóri gave them a guarded grin. "Have a pleasant stay in Iceland. *Bless.*"

Cruz was stunned. That was it? He—they—had come all this way only for a few polite words and a rushed goodbye? Why was Nóri in such a hurry to get rid of them anyway? Steaming, Cruz scribbled down his phone number on the scrap of paper the girl—Elin—slid toward him. Cruz didn't want to leave Freyja's Cloak. Not yet. Not without the cipher that he was certain was here somewhere, but Aunt Marisol had him by the elbow. She was dragging him to the door.

"Get in the car, Cruz," snapped his aunt when he loitered on the front steps.

He obeyed. Reluctantly.

As they drove away, Cruz saw Elin at the front door. She was locking it. Strange. It was only 10 after four, and the sign said they were open until five. Why would she be closing now? Plus, if they really were remodeling, where were the construction workers? Where was their equipment and building materials? Cruz didn't see a single Dumpster. "There's something odd about this whole thing," he whispered to Emmett, who was quick to agree.

TWO HOURS LATER, Cruz was sitting down in an elegant restaurant somewhere in the middle of Reykjavík with the rest of the explorers. Over tall crystal glasses filled with ice water and tall crystal vases filled with silk blue poppies, they studied their menus as they waited for Bryndis's family to arrive.

Seated next to him, Sailor lowered her menu. "Cruz, are you okay?" she said softly.

"I guess."

Her forehead wrinkled. "You're not giving up, are you?"

"No. It may take me a while to figure it all out, as in the rest of my life, but I'll do it. I have to. It's örlög."

"What-log?"

"Örlög. Bryndis says it means 'destiny.'"

"Oh. Good." The lines on her head began to smooth. "Because if you *were* thinking of giving up, I was going to talk you out of it. But since you aren't, what are you going to order? Bryndis says we should try the licorice mousse. It's a dessert, right? Because if it's a real moose, there is no way ..."

Cruz laughed. "I'm pretty sure it's a dessert."

His phone was vibrating. It was probably Dad or Lani. Sliding the rectangle from his pocket, he opened the text message.

I knew your mother. I have what you seek.

Meet me tomorrow at 9 a.m. at the geyser Strokkur.

Come alone.

17

WAS CRUZ CRAZY, going to the geyser by himself? Probably. Still, it wasn't like he had much choice.

Come alone, the text said.

Cruz barely slept. He got up before the alarm went off, shut off Emmett's security system, and quietly dressed. Tiptoeing out of the cabin in his socks so he didn't wake Emmett, Cruz put his shoes on in the hall. He mumbled something about going for breakfast to Officer Dover, who was drowsing in a chair by the elevator. However, instead of turning right at the end of the passage and going up the grand staircase, Cruz darted to his left and trotted down the gangway. He zipped down the pier and, when he was out of sight of the ship, used his GPS system to find the nearest self-driving car rental office. Yes! Autonomous Auto was just four blocks from the harbor. Fifteen minutes later, Cruz was on the road to the geyser.

"It is ninety-nine kilometers, or sixty-two miles, to the Strokkur geyser," said the male voice of the onboard computer system. "It will take approximately one hour and twenty minutes to reach your destination. Thank you for choosing Auto Auto and enjoy your ride."

It wasn't long before the car left the city behind for the farms, pastures, and rolling lowlands of the valley. Cruz laid his head back against his seat cushion and drifted off to sleep. When he awoke, he was on a narrow road with a name he couldn't pronounce, moving toward the mountains. And it was starting to snow.

It had been a long time since Cruz had seen a snowfall. In Washington, D.C., their town house had a long driveway his dad used to shovel in winter. Cruz would follow behind with his own little plastic shovel and fling chunks of the hard white powder aside. He'd loved everything about winter—soggy mittens, marshmallows oozing into hot chocolate, his mom pulling him down the sidewalk on a sled. If only he hadn't been five when she'd died. If only he'd been six. Think of it! Twelve more months. Four more seasons. One more sled ride.

Cruz leaned forward to watch the white wisps tap the windshield.

"Emmett Lu to Cruz Coronado."

Cruz jumped. The map on the computer indicated he was 94 kilometers from Reykjavík. His communications pin should have been well out of range of *Orion* by now. Fanchon! She had said the range could be boosted if necessary. Emmett must have gone to her for help. Cruz shook his head. Why hadn't he left his pin behind?

"Emmett to Cruz. Come in, *please!*"

The tone was desperate. Cruz groaned. He couldn't ignore it. "Cruz here," he said as if he hadn't a care in the world.

"Cruz? Is that you? Where are you?"

"Uh . . . well . . ." Should he lie?

"Is Bryndis with you?"

Bryndis? Why would she be with him? "No."

"Did you guys forget? We were going to eat breakfast together and then go ashore to start our photojournalism assignment for Professor Benedict."

"Yeah, about that . . . you guys go on. I'm going to be a little late."

"Late? Why?"

"Cruz, what's going on?" That was Sailor. "Where are you?"

There was no point in keeping it a secret. "I'm on my way to the Strokkur geyser."

"*What?*" Emmett again.

"I got a text. The message instructed me to go to the Strokkur geyser this morning. Nóri must have found whoever's got the second piece of my mom's cipher. I'm to meet him … or her … there."

"Stay there. We're on our way. Emmett out."

"No!" shouted Cruz. "I'm supposed to go alone. Emmett?" He collapsed against the seat. Oh well. With any luck, Cruz would have the cipher piece long before they arrived.

Passing a row of bare trees, Cruz saw plumes of steam rising from the mudflats. He was here! His car pulled into a parking lot next to a long wooden building with a red roof: the visitor center. The vehicle came to a stop near a pair of red flags, each displaying a spewing white geyser on a background of orange.

"You have arrived at your destination," said the onboard computer. "Would you like this vehicle to wait for your return trip?"

"Yes," answered Cruz. Getting out of the car, Cruz stretched, then joined the stream of people heading down a wide redbrick pathway. He paused to read a sign:

YOU ARE
HERE AT YOUR
OWN RISK

NEVER STAND ON
THE EDGES OR CLOSE
TO THE HOT SPRING.

REMEMBER THAT THE
WATER IS 80-90°C (176-194°F)
& CAN CAUSE SERIOUS BURNS!
THE NEAREST HOSPITAL
IS 62 KM AWAY.

Whoosh!

Several hundred yards to his left, a spray of water shot 60 feet into the air. The ring of people surrounding the vent clapped. His hands in his pockets, Cruz strolled toward the geyser. He wasn't sure where to go but figured it was wise to stay in plain sight. He'd let his contact find him.

"*Hjálp, hjálp!*" A woman in a pink jacket and black leggings was running toward him. Cruz activated his com pin translator. "*Er einhver hér læknir?*" A second later, it translated her frantic words: "Is anyone here a doctor?"

"What happened?" someone asked.

"A man fell into one of the hot pools."

A chill went through Cruz. How horrible!

"We've called one-one-two," said the woman. "An ambulance is coming, but we could use a doctor now ... and police."

"Try the hotel. There's probably a doctor there," said a man as the woman rushed past. "Why the police?" asked another man.

"Someone said he was pushed ... I don't know ... I didn't see."

Pushed? Cruz didn't like the sound of that. He hurried down the trail the way the woman in pink had come. Rounding a bend, he saw a cluster of people on the wrong side of the markers. Cruz elbowed his way through the crowd. Someone was lying on the ground. Cruz spotted a khaki jacket ... a tattered pocket ... blue and white stripes ... *No!*

"Nóri!" Cruz fell to his knees.

"Don't touch him." Opposite him, a man was bending to drape his coat over the wildlife rescuer. "He's badly burned."

From the chest down, Nóri was wet and violently shivering. A trembling red hand reached out for him. "Cruz?"

"I'm here, Nóri. Help is coming. Hold on."

"I wanted to talk to you yesterday ... couldn't ... too many people."

"I understand." His heart racing, Cruz clasped his hands around Nóri's. "Don't worry. It's all right. We'll talk later."

"No. Now. The piece ... Someone was asking ... questions. I took it ... and left ... I left ..."

"You left the falcon's feather." Cruz filled in the blanks. "That's what you were trying to hint to me yesterday. You knew about Mom's clue. You knew I would try to find you."

"Yes ... Langjökull ... caves ... laughing dragon ..." Nóri cried out in pain.

Cruz looked around frantically. Where was the ambulance? What was taking so long? The man on the other side of Nóri was slowly shaking his head.

"She was a good friend ... your mom." Nóri gasped. "I could always count on her ... She'd be proud of you. She said you would come. And you did. Don't forget. Langjökull ... laughing dragon ..."

Cruz felt the bony fingers in his suddenly relax. "Nóri? *Nóri?*"

Vivid topaz blue eyes stared up into the falling snow.

After that, things began to swirl around Cruz. There were busy paramedics and questioning police officers and gawking tourists. So many people, so much activity, yet nobody could do anything. Long after the paramedics had taken Nóri's body away, long after the last onlooker had walked away, Cruz stayed. He stared hypnotically into the boiling mud pit, as if somehow he could turn back time. If only he had gotten up earlier, had gotten here sooner ...

Cruz had never seen anyone die before. He had never seen a last breath or heard a final word. *Don't forget,* Nóri had said.

"Ling-something," Cruz said out loud so he could hear it again. "No, it was more like Long. Lowng-joe ..."

"Langjökull?"

Cruz's neck snapped. "Bryndis? What are you doing here?"

She lifted a shoulder. "You're not the only one who gets up early."

"You followed me?"

"Are you mad?"

He shook his head. Cruz was actually a little relieved. He was glad not to be alone.

"I told the girl at the car rental office that we were teammates and my car was supposed to follow yours. I guess since we were wearing the same camouflage jacket and were about the same age, she figured I was telling the truth." Bryndis gave a shy grin. "I … uh … would have been here sooner but my Auto Auto had problems problems."

"You could get in trouble, you know. You're not supposed to leave the ship without permission."

"Neither are you." She came toward him. "Cruz, what's going on? Why are you here? Does it have anything to do with that man who fell into the hot spring?"

He wasn't sure how much he should tell her. "His name is Nóri. He was a friend of my mom's."

"Oh dear!" She put a hand to her lips. "I'm so sorry."

Cruz dipped his head and swallowed past the knot in his throat.

"What you were saying before about Langjökull—does that have something to do with him, too?"

"Just before he died, Nóri said Langjökull. Is it a town?"

"It's a glacier."

"Nóri said something else, too, about caves and a dragon."

Bryndis's eyebrows went up. "The laughing dragon?"

"Yes!"

"Hlæjandi Dreki. It's a rock formation at the ice caves at Langjökull."

"I have to get there, Bryndis, and I can't tell you why."

She licked her lips. "I'll take you and I won't ask. It's only about fifty kilometers from here, but …"

"What?"

"It could be too dangerous to go inside the caves. It's awfully early in the season, and the ice isn't stable. If you could wait a month, when it's colder—"

"I can't," broke in Cruz. "It has to be now. I might never get this chance again."

"Okay, then … let's go." She started to back away.

"Well, I do have to wait a little longer." He put up a hand. "For Sailor and Emmett, I mean. They're on their way. They should be here in about a half hour."

"Oh." She bit her lip. "I see."

Bryndis had that look you get when you realize everyone has been invited to a party except you. He had hurt her feelings.

"I wish I could tell you more," said Cruz. "I want to tell you, but . . ."

"It's okay," she said, but she kept looking at her boots.

They took their time walking back toward the visitor center, then sat on a bench near Cruz's car. The flurries were turning to snowflakes.

"You warm enough?" Cruz asked. "'Cause we could go inside if you're cold."

"I'm not cold." Bryndis shook her head, setting her firefly earrings in motion. The tiny snowflakes that had attached themselves to her hair floated around her like fairy dust.

Any other time, watching fountains of water shoot up into a snowy sky alongside his crush would have been fun. But this wasn't any other time. Cruz had seen too much. All he could think about was getting away from here. The sooner the better.

"**WHAT DOES SHE KNOW?**" Emmett whispered to Cruz. He nodded toward Bryndis, who was in the front seat of Cruz's self-driving car next to Sailor. Emmett and Cruz were in the back.

"Nothing," answered Cruz in a hushed voice. "I told her I needed her help getting to the glacier, but I couldn't tell her why. I asked her to trust me."

Emmett squished in his lips. "I knew it."

"What?"

"She likes you."

Cruz grunted like that was the craziest idea in the world. Still, he couldn't keep from grinning.

Bryndis directed the car to stop at a large cabin near the base of the glacier with a sign that read OLVIRSSON OUTFITTERS. "We'll need climbing supplies," she said, opening her door. "Come on."

Inside the shop, Bryndis spoke to an elderly couple in Icelandic. The husband and wife began stacking items on the counter—ice axes, helmets, crampons, snow probes, ropes, headlamps, flashlights. Bryndis turned to the other explorers. "I explained we were with Explorer Academy and doing our school project on the melting glaciers. They offered to let us use some of their rental equipment free of charge."

"That's so nice," said Cruz.

"How do we say thank you?" asked Sailor.

"*Takk fyrir,*" she answered.

"*Takk fyrir!*" said the explorers, gathering up the supplies and heading for the car.

After bouncing along an uneven gravel road for several kilometers, the autonomous car pulled into a small lot, parking between two other vehicles. "You have arrived at your destination," said the onboard computer as everyone piled out. "Would you like this vehicle to wait for your return trip?"

"Yes, wait, please," instructed Cruz. The last one out of the car, he took a moment to look up at the glacier. It was huge! Two outcrops jutted upward from the snow like thrashing bear claws, their brown tips rounded by time and weather. A massive river of snow cascaded between the two peaks, as if someone had tipped over a giant carton of vanilla ice cream to watch it melt. They were going up that?

Cruz helped Bryndis get the equipment out of the trunk and pass it out. He snapped a pair of crampons on his feet and his mind-control camera and a helmet on his head. An icy gust of wind chilling him, Cruz popped his big hood up and over the helmet. He zipped his jacket, then grabbed a rope and an ice ax.

"On the other side of the glacier, there are man-made caves." Bryndis led the way across the rocky moonscape. "They drill into the ice to make tunnels for the tourists. They're popular but not nearly as beautiful as natural ice caves. Be careful where you step as we go up. It's still pretty warm. You don't want to fall through a snow bridge or into a crevasse."

"Where is the cave?" wondered Cruz.

Bryndis had put on her GPS sunglasses. She pointed. "Below the outcrop on the right."

Cruz figured it was about a 15-minute hike. An hour later, they were *still* climbing.

"It sure looked a lot closer from the car," sighed Sailor, reading his mind.

Approaching the bear claws, Cruz saw a curved opening. A row of glistening icicles lined the four-foot archway like the teeth of a monster.

"Stay here," ordered Bryndis. "I'm going in first to make sure it's safe for us to go in. Back in five." Hunching, she went under the icicles.

"I don't know about this, Cruz," said Emmett when she was gone. "Would Nóri really have come all this way to hide the cipher?"

"I hope so. It's the last thing he said to me and my only clue."

Emmett frowned. "What if it's not here?"

"What if it's a trap?" Sailor gulped.

Cruz didn't want to think about either possibility.

Bryndis was back and waving them in. "Watch it," she said as, one by one, they crouched to go under the line of icicle daggers. The explorers had to crawl in single file over shards of black ash and rock for about 20 feet before the tunnel widened enough for them to stand. Gazing up, Cruz's jaw fell. It was as if they'd entered an alien dream world. The walls and ceiling of the cave were covered with thick swells of translucent, peacock blue ice. Animated by sunlight from the surface, the ripples above their heads glowed blue. It reminded Cruz of surfing, of being inside the barrel of a wave with the sea curling over him. Except this wave was frozen, as if time had stopped.

Sailor was gaping, too. "I feel like I'm inside a giant blue crystal bowl."

"They *are* called the Crystal Caves," said Bryndis.

"Nature's artwork." Cruz reached to touch a warped, glassy wall.

Stepping around a pool of water, Bryndis gazed up. "Let's keep moving, guys."

Cruz snapped as many photos as he could on their trek through the blue cavern. He had never seen anything like this before and doubted he ever would again. Rounding a bend, they found themselves in a wide, oval chamber. Ahead, Cruz spotted a towering black pillar with stony ridges, open wings, and a curved tail. The huge, dark head was tipped back, its long snout partially open. It could be only one thing—the laughing dragon!

"Hlæjandi Dreki," confirmed Bryndis.

Cruz circled the base of the rock, looking for an opening. He didn't see one. "I'm going to climb up," he said to Emmett, taking off his gloves and handing them to his friend.

Finding a toehold in a crack, Cruz hoisted himself up onto the wide base.

"Be careful," warned Emmett. "You don't know what's up there."

"Or *on* there," added Bryndis, a half second before Cruz's toe caught ice and slid off.

Pedaling rapidly, he regained his footing. Cruz surveyed his route, spotted his next hold, and continued up. Even with the ice, this was easier than the rock wall in the Augmented Reality Challenge back at the Academy—no rockslide! He pulled himself level with the creature's body and did a quick inspection. The only opening he could find was the dragon's mouth. The split was just big enough to fit a hand inside. Naturally.

Clinging to the rock, Cruz hesitated. Stone or not, he really did not want to stick his hand inside those massive jaws.

Cruz heard something snap. It sounded like a tree branch. He looked up. A chunk of ice was falling straight for him! Grabbing the dragon, Cruz swung out to his left, and the shard whizzed past his right shoulder. He heard it hit the ground and splinter apart. That was close. So much for no falling objects!

"Is everyone okay down there?" he called.

"Yes, but hurry!" hissed Bryndis. "And don't yell."

Leaning back in, Cruz shut his eyes, took a breath, and plunged his hand into the dragon's mouth. He felt something slimy. *Ick!* His first impulse was to snatch his hand back, but he resisted. Grimacing, he latched on to the slippery object and pulled. When he opened his eyes, he was holding a small clear plastic bag.

"Cruz?" Bryndis's voice floated up to him.

"Coming." Yanking apart the zip top, he pulled out a dark green fleece cloth from inside. His heart had doubled in speed. Cruz flung back one corner of the cloth, then another, and another...

There it was: the second piece of his mother's cipher! Cruz nudged the little pie-shaped piece of marble with his finger. At last! So much effort, so much sacrifice, for something so tiny. Cruz couldn't help but think of the man who had lost his life for it.

Thank you, Nóri.

Lowering the zipper on his coat, Cruz reached for the lanyard around his neck. His fingers fumbled as he tried to attach the second piece of the cipher to the first. Should it go on the right side or the left? Clockwise was right. A flood of fear went through him. What if it was broken? What if it didn't fit? What if it was the wrong—

Cruz felt the pieces snap together. *Yes!*

"Uh...Cruz?" It was Emmett. "You might want to get down here."

He tucked the cord back into his shirt, closed his uniform jacket, and slid up the zipper of his outer jacket. Cruz began his descent. Feeling for the same toeholds he'd used going up, he made it down much faster and without his crampon slipping once. "Glad that's over," he said, feeling solid ground under his feet again. He turned. "Let's get out of here before—"

Cruz was facing two men. One was Officer Wardicorn. The other was Tripp Scarlatos. Both were holding guns.

18

▶ **"WHAT'S YOUR** hurry, mate?"

"Tripp?" Cruz could hardly believe his eyes. "What are you—"

"Just do as I tell ya and don't upset Wardicorn. He's a bit on the jittery side."

"You?" Sailor scowled at the security officer. "You're supposed to protect us."

"Pretty sure that ship has sailed," mumbled Bryndis.

"Come on. Time's wastin'." The sub pilot held out his free arm toward Cruz, palm up, and wiggled his fingers. "Hand it over."

Cruz didn't move. How did Tripp know he had come here for the cipher? And who was he working for? The Society? Nebula? Someone else?

"You heard me." There was an edge to Tripp's voice Cruz had not heard before. "Give me the journal."

Ah! So that was what he was after.

"J-journal? I don't know what you're talking about."

Wardicorn took aim at Bryndis and cocked his weapon.

"Okay, okay!" cried Cruz, putting up his hands. "I've got it, but it's useless to you, Tripp, I swear it is. It's an expanding digital holo-journal that only I can access."

"A holo-journal?" Tripp eyed him with suspicion. "Paper, plastic, or metal?"

"Paper."

Tripp sauntered toward him. "Let's see it."

Cruz obeyed.

"That can't be it," grumbled Wardicorn, watching Lani's protective sleeve transfer ownership.

"Oh yes it can." Tripp turned the journal over in his hands. "Smart. No wonder we couldn't find it."

So they were the ones! They had ransacked Emmett and Cruz's cabin! Cruz tried to make eye contact with his roommate, but Emmett had tiptoed behind the laughing dragon. He hoped his friend wasn't going to try any heroics.

"You won't be needing this anymore." Tripp flung the journal to the ground and stomped on it.

"No!" shrieked Sailor as Tripp smashed his heel into the center of the journal. Seeing his mother's journal being destroyed, it took every ounce of Cruz's energy not to swoop in and save it. Instead, he bit his lip. And tasted blood.

They heard what sounded like glass cracking.

"Quiet!" hissed Bryndis.

For a moment, everyone stood completely still, their eyes glued to the wavy blue ceiling. Nothing fell.

"So why are we here, Cruz?" The sub pilot was shuffling toward the laughing dragon. "Looking for something special?"

Cruz set his jaw. He wasn't about to tell Tripp Scarlatos anything.

"Our spies had a feeling you were looking for something at the seed vault, too," explained Tripp. "Nóri filled in the blanks."

Cruz shuddered. "Nóri?"

"He told us what we needed to know."

Cruz didn't believe it. Tripp was lying. If Nóri had said something about the cipher, Tripp would be demanding that right now, too.

"Such a tragedy." The corners of Tripp's lips curled upward, and Cruz knew the awful truth.

It was Tripp. He had pushed Nóri into the hot spring. Cruz stared at the sub pilot in horror. This was his mentor, someone he had learned from, looked up to, even confided in. Now to discover the aquatics director was capable of such a thing was more than a blow. It was a betrayal. Not only of Cruz, but of Explorer Academy and everything it stood for. There could be only one explanation.

"You're working for Nebula, aren't you?" accused Cruz.

Tripp tapped his chin, pretending to think. "Could be. Could be."

"Jerk," muttered Sailor.

"Well, it's been fun spelunking, but we have to be leaving," cackled Tripp. "You guys are gonna stay right here and pretend you're ice sculptures for the next twenty minutes, yes?"

Team Cousteau gave vigorous nods.

Wardicorn and Tripp began stepping backward over the bed of

chunky black rocks. The hair on the back of Cruz's neck went up.
Something wasn't right. Wardicorn and Tripp were going to simply walk
away? Leaving them here? *Alive?*

Once the men reached the bend in the cave leading out of the chamber, Wardicorn stuck his gun into his waistband. Tripp did the same. Cruz
exhaled. Maybe everything *was* going to be okay. Tripp had destroyed
the journal and any hope Cruz had of finding his mother's formula. Was
it possible that was enough for him? Still, once the explorers got out of
the cave, Tripp had to know they would tell the authorities what happened, but maybe by then Tripp and Wardicorn would be long gone.

"Sure is beautiful here," sang Tripp, his eyes traveling over the soaring ribbons of blue ice above them. "I can think of worse places to die."

"Hey, weren't there four of them?" asked Wardicorn.

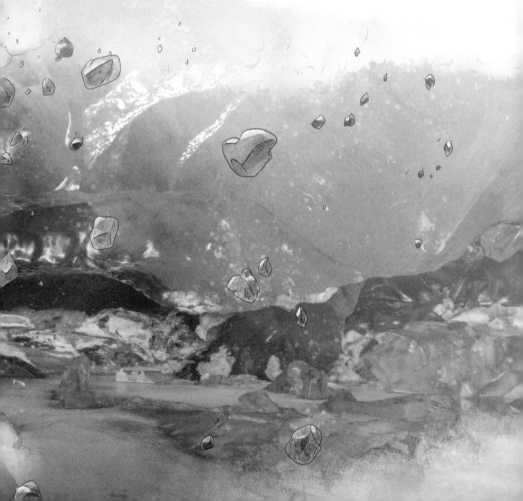

"Not anymore." Taking his hand from his pocket, Tripp tossed something round and green into the air.

It took Cruz a second to realize it was no apple. Grabbing Bryndis's wrist in one hand and Sailor with the other, he brought them to the ground with him. "Emmett, down!" he shouted a second before a massive boom rocked the cave. Ice began raining. Cruz could feel the sting of hundreds of shards pelting his head, neck, shoulders, and back. The storm seemed to last forever. Cruz waited another half minute before lifting his head. "Is everyone okay?"

"Yeah," said Sailor, rolling up on her knees. She had ice in her hair.

"Me too," coughed Bryndis.

Untangling themselves, they slowly got up. "Emmett?" Cruz called softly.

No answer.

"Emmett?" Sailor cried louder.

"Shhh!" whispered Bryndis, lifting her eyes. "We don't need a complete cave-in."

"Sorry. Look." She nodded to the mountain of ice and rock in front of them: 15 feet of debris blocked the exit.

Cruz turned to Bryndis. "Is there another way out?"

"I don't think so. The tunnel on the other side of the dragon leads deeper into the cave."

"I'm sure we can find a way out of here, but first let's find Emmett." Cruz knelt by a slab of ice. "Sailor, grab that end."

The three of them worked swiftly to lift several large hunks of ice. Those that were too big to move they got down on their stomachs to peer under. The trio covered the entire chamber but didn't find Emmett.

Cruz went to stand beside Sailor, who was staring at the pile of rock and ice blocking the tunnel. He put a hand on her shoulder.

"Maybe he made it out?" Her tone was meek. Fearful.

"Maybe," he said, but he knew it wasn't likely. Emmett had probably tried to make a break for it and had been crushed in the explosion. His eyes welling, Cruz stubbed his toe into the ground. He couldn't let himself think about his friend or he'd lose it. He needed to stay strong to help his teammates find a way to escape. Brushing his hand across his eyes, he tapped his EA communications pin. "Cruz to Marisol Coronado." Getting his transmitter to work inside a glacier was a long shot, but he had to try.

No response.

"Cruz to anyone on *Orion* or anyone within range? This is an emergency."

Still nothing.

Sailor was swiping her phone screen. "No phone, either."

Hitting her GPS in vain, Bryndis sighed. "We're too deep in the cave to get a signal in or out."

Next to the debris pile, Cruz went on his tiptoes. He carefully swept a few pebbles aside, then moved a few bits of ice. He could see light!

Bryndis was watching him. "Good effort," she said, "but I doubt we can make a hole big enough for us to safely climb through."

"It's not for us," he answered with a grin.

"Huh?"

"Bryndis and Sailor, get behind me." Cruz waved. "We're going to take a selfie."

Sailor made a face. "A selfie? Now?"

Cruz opened the lower-right pocket of his uniform and tapped the honeycomb pin attached to the lapel. "Mell, on."

From inside his pocket, two gold eyes flashed at him.

"Mell, fly to eye level, please. Camera on. Record entry."

The honeybee drone complied. With Mell hovering in front of him, Cruz cleared his throat. "The date is October twenty-third, and I'm Cruz Coronado, a first-year student with Explorer Academy. My teammates are here, too: Bryndis Jónsdóttir and Sailor York. One other team member, Emmett Lu, was with us but is missing. We're stuck in the Langjökull caves near the laughing dragon rock. Tripp Scarlatos and Officer Wardicorn deliberately set off an explosion to trap us here. The cave-in most likely killed Emmett. My aunt, Marisol Coronado, is a professor on *Orion,* our ship that's docked in Reykjavík harbor. Please contact her. Please send help." He glanced around their icy prison. "And please hurry. Mell, end recording."

Catching the drone, Cruz placed her near the opening he'd made. "Mell, fly to Olvirsson Outfitters at the base of the mountain and play my last recording for the couple that owns the place. You should be able to get GPS coordinates for the climbing shop once you have cleared the cave. Confirm, please?"

The bee winked at him twice to indicate she understood.

"Mell, go."

The three of them watched as the MAV zipped through the small gap. They stood there for a few minutes after the bee was gone.

"I hope she can do it." Bryndis didn't sound confident.

"She'll do it," Cruz assured her. "She's saved me more than once." His stomach chose that moment to let out a vicious gurgle, a reminder that he'd eaten nothing all day.

The girls grinned.

Cruz opened his insulated water bottle. It was only half full. He had forgotten to fill it before leaving the geyser. Knowing he would need to make it last, he took only a small sip.

Bryndis was digging in her pockets. "I've got some pretzel bread I brought home from dinner last night."

Cruz checked his pockets, too, but all he had was Lani's mini surfboard key chain, his time capsule, and half a pack of gum. He should have thought to bring food.

"I've got a couple of protein bars," said Sailor.

"We'd better save those." Bryndis was tearing her small loaf into three pieces.

They ate the bread slowly.

Cruz was swallowing the last of his bread when, out of the corner of his eye, he spotted something poking out of the rubble. Lani's journal sleeve! Scooping it up, he brushed off the dirt and Tripp's footprints.

Gingerly, he slipped the journal out of the envelope.

"It's not even bent," said Sailor.

Could it have survived? Maybe, but he couldn't find out here—not in front of Bryndis. He slid the holo-journal back into Lani's envelope, then placed it in his uniform pocket. He sat down at the base of the laughing dragon next to the girls. Bryndis was tracing around a curve of the rock with her gloved finger. She glanced up, craning her neck this way and that, as if studying the pillar from every angle.

Cruz looked at Sailor. A question passed between them—one that was asked by Cruz's eyebrows and answered by Sailor's nod.

Trust was a funny thing. Easy to ask for. Hard to give.

Lifting his chin, Cruz brought out the rope that hung from his neck.

"Ohhh!" Sailor zeroed in for a closer inspection of the two interlocking pieces of black marble. "The second piece! And look how well they fit together."

Bryndis tipped her head. "What is it?"

"What Tripp and Wardicorn are after. Sort of. I'll explain later," he said to her, tucking the cipher back into his shirt.

Sailor squeezed his arm. "You did it, Cruz. You really did it."

"*We* did it," he insisted. "I couldn't have made it this far without the two of you, and Lani and Emmett."

Emmett. Cruz felt a pain slice through him. He couldn't imagine an Academy without his friend. How could he continue traveling the world with the rest of the explorers without Emmett? It was unthinkable. Unbearable.

Bzzzz. Bzzzz. Bzz.

"Mell!" Cruz sat up. His honeybee drone was back. "Mell, show flight stats and new videos, please."

"That didn't take long," cried Sailor. "What's it been—two hours?"

"Thirty-seven minutes," said Bryndis drily.

Sailor rubbed her gloves together. "I'm just glad a rescue crew is on the way."

"It could be a while before they get here," cautioned Bryndis.

"But they're coming—that's all that matters."

Cruz was reading the data Mell was projecting in front of him. "Uh ... I hate to burst your bubble."

Sailor slid closer. "What's the matter?"

"Mell's flight stats show she's only gone three hundred and seventy-six feet."

"So?"

"So, we walked at least a half mile into the cave—that's about, what, twenty-five hundred feet? According to this, she didn't even make it to the cave entrance. Not even close."

"She must be malfunctioning," said Bryndis. "Could the cold have affected her circuitry?"

"Maybe, but I doubt it," replied Cruz. "The self-diagnostic shows everything is working fine. Besides, she's built to withstand air temps from fifty below zero to a hundred and fifty degrees Fahrenheit."

"We must have sent her into an air pocket," reasoned Sailor. "And she's been flying around all this time trying to find an escape route to complete her mission."

"That's what I think, too." Cruz was still scanning the readouts. "It looks like Mel tried to get a signal out for a GPS lock but couldn't. She even tried to send the message I recorded, as a last resort. Bryndis is right. No signals are getting in or out. Mell, stats off. Nice try. Thanks anyway."

She tilted her head, almost apologetically.

"Why don't we check Mell's video memory?" suggested Bryndis. "If the weather did affect her analytics, we could be missing a message that someone sent back to us—"

"I already did." Cruz shook his head to indicate there was nothing. "Mell, off."

Two tiny golden eyes went dark.

Sailor shivered. "Cruz, are you saying ...?"

Cruz looked up from the little drone perched on his thumb. "Nobody's coming for us."

19

SAILOR gave a toaster-size chunk of ice to Bryndis, who handed it off to Cruz, who gently set it on the small pile of rubble near the cave wall. They were trying to clear the exit tunnel. It was painstaking work. The explosion had destabilized the roof of the cave, and every now and then, a clump of ice would snap off and hurtle toward them like a frozen missile. They'd have to scurry under the black wing of the laughing dragon rock for cover, wait for the dust to settle, then try again. In the past two hours, more new stuff had fallen than they had cleared; however, nobody wanted to admit that they were engaged in a pointless mission.

As Sailor reached for another block of ice, a crack echoed through the cavern.

"*Run!*" called Cruz.

They made it under the laughing dragon pillar a second before a shower of ice fell on the spot where they'd been standing.

"Great," moaned Sailor. "What are we going to do? We can't go, and we can't stay."

"She's right." Bryndis looked at Cruz. "If we keep this up, we could trigger another avalanche. But if we don't . . ."

Cruz's eyes followed the curve of the dragon's extended wing as it vanished into the blue crystalline ceiling. Daylight was beginning to fade. His body was warm, thanks to his hide-and-seek jacket, but his hands were white with cold. Emmett still had his gloves. Plus, he was starving. There had to be a way out of here. But how?

Think. Think!

Cruz dug his frozen hands deeper into his pockets. His knuckle hit something hard—his time capsule. He brought it out, tipping his palm to watch it roll from one side of his hand to the other. It had been a couple of weeks since Team Cousteau had won Taryn's scavenger hunt and he had yet to give his capsule a single memory. Cruz knew what he wanted to put into the memory keeper, but he'd been too busy . . .

He had plenty of time now.

Taking a shallow breath, Cruz shut his eyes. When he felt the capsule tremble, his mind returned to a place he never wanted to forget. He listened again to a long, sad wail echoing through the Bay of Fundy and the words that followed from Fanchon's translator. "Struggle. Tired. Pain." Through the silent haze of an aqua sea, Cruz watched his teammates work together to cut away the fishing gear that trapped the right whales. He saw the flick of a free tail and a long rope unwinding and a delighted calf rolling toward its mother. "Help. Gratitude. Love." Only after the pod breached the whitecapped surface and frolicked, the sun gleaming on their shiny gray backs, did Cruz open his eyes.

He uncurled his fingers. In his palm, the capsule glowed purple. It was done. His memory had been saved. But would anyone besides him ever get the chance to experience it?

It was pretty, the way the purple capsule lit up his hand and the ice wall next to him. It reminded him of the artwork on the seed vault at Svalbard. You could see it for miles, thanks to the reflection off the snow, and even more so at night.

Cruz glanced up at the cave ceiling, then back at the capsule in his palm. Ceiling. Capsule. Ceiling. Capsule. Was it possible? Cruz spun toward the girls. "I think I know a way out, or at least a way for us to send a signal that we're here."

"How?" asked Bryndis and Sailor in unison.

Cruz pointed up. "If we can see the sunlight through the ice down here during the day, then maybe it can work the other way, too."

Sailor followed his gaze. "You mean...?"

"Maybe someone on the surface can see the light we send up at night."

Bryndis pursed her lips. "Do you realize how thick that ice is?"

"I know, but Tripp already gave us a head start. That explosion blew away a good chunk of the roof," reasoned Cruz. "If we gather everything we brought with us that emits light—flashlights, cell phones, tablets—and spread them out on the ground under the thinnest part of the roof, someone might just spot it."

"That's a big 'might,'" said Bryndis.

"Not necessarily," argued Sailor. "Someone driving up the glacier or flying overhead might see it. We can use our body heat charges to fully charge our gear first."

"Good idea," said Cruz.

Bryndis took off her helmet and started undoing the strap on the headlamp.

While their electronics were charging, they went through their pockets and packs to find everything that lit up. Gathering up their haul, they tiptoed over to the mound of rubble blocking the tunnel. Each item was turned on, before being placed on the ground with the others. They had three headlamps, three flashlights, three cell phones, two tablets, one pair of flashing LED ghost socks (courtesy of Sailor), one time capsule, one light-up surfboard key chain, and ...

Cruz unzipped his jacket. "Mell, on."

One honeybee MAV.

Laying everything out, they stepped back to survey their work.

"It's probably reflecting more than we realize," said Sailor. "We're just on the wrong side of it, that's all."

"Right, and it'll glow brighter the darker it gets outside," said Cruz.

The three of them stared at the ground.

Suddenly, it got quiet. No one wanted to be the first to say it:

There wasn't enough light.

Even the fireflies dangling from Bryndis's ears were shaking their heads.

Frustrated, Cruz watched the little enamel insects swing back and forth. Wait a minute! Cruz slapped his head. How could he have forgotten? "Bryndis, your earrings!"

"Oops, sorry, I forgot to add them." She started to take them out.

"I didn't mean that. I meant..." Cruz was wriggling free of his coat. Pulling the sleeves through to reverse it from camouflage to gray, he pressed the button on the top inside of the collar. Suddenly, thousands of twinkling blue and green lights appeared. "This! Remember, the seek side of our coats is bioluminescent!"

"That's right!"

Sailor and Bryndis hurried to copy him.

"They look like Emmett's glasses," giggled Sailor as their coats flickered and pulsed with light.

"Or the art on the Svalbard Doomsday Vault," said Cruz.

"Or the milky seas," added Bryndis.

"What's that?" asked Sailor.

"Bioluminescent bacteria that floats on the ocean. It's so bright, satellites can see it from space."

The trio looked at each other. This might actually work!

They spread Cruz's and Sailor's coats flat on the ground with the other lights, but kept Bryndis's. They needed at least one heat source to stay warm. Sitting against the base of the dragon rock, the explorers huddled together under Bryndis's coat. Cruz and Bryndis, who were on either end, each put one arm in a sleeve.

As night fell, the three of them watched and waited.

Sailor yawned. "I'd love to see the milky seas from space. I wonder why it glows?"

"I read an article about it," said Cruz. "The bacteria glows to attract fish so it'll get eaten."

"On purpose?"

"Uh-huh. See, it gets gobbled up and survives on the nutrients in the belly of the fish as the fish swims along. That way, the bacteria can travel a thousand times farther than it ever could on its own."

"So, in a weird way, bacteria are explorers, like us."

He chuckled. "I guess so."

"Bioluminescence only works if someone sees it." Bryndis's voice was barely a whisper. "What if nobody is … you know … out there?"

Aunt Marisol's face flashed in Cruz's mind. "They're out there."

But were they? Cruz hadn't told anyone where he was going—not even his aunt—and Bryndis, Emmett, and Sailor probably hadn't, either. The only thing Taryn and everyone else on board *Orion* knew was that four students were missing. They would have no idea where to begin searching for them. And if, by some miracle, they tracked them down to Langjökull and found their rental car, then what? How would they know to enter the cave? How would they know the explorers were trapped? Cruz couldn't feel his fingers anymore. His face was cold, too.

He must have drifted off, because the next thing he knew he was being poked on the forehead. "Ouch." He squinted. His honeybee drone zipped left, then right. "What is it, Mell? Oh, sure. You need to be charged again. Hold on." Cruz sat up, rubbing away the crick in his neck.

The drone was blinking her eyes at him.

"I know, I know. Give me a sec, Mell, I have to get the charging—"

Wait! Was that what he thought it was? Mell circled and blinked at him again. Three short flashes. Three long ones. Then another three short flashes. It was! Mell was displaying the international SOS signal. Either someone had just broken into his cabin back on *Orion* or …

"Sailor, Bryndis, wake up!"

"I'm up, I'm up," moaned Sailor, her eyelids fluttering.

"What is it?" Bryndis's head appeared from beneath the coat. Her hair was sticking up. "Did we reel in a fish?"

"Yep!" crowed Cruz. "The biggest one ever."

Emmett.

20

▶ **"WHAT DO YOU** mean you can't tell me?" groaned Cruz.

Emmett did not turn from his desk. "I promised Sailor and Bryndis I'd wait and tell them, too. They're helping Taryn. They'll be here in half an hour."

Cruz fell backward onto his bed. It was good to be back on the ship, even if Emmett was keeping Cruz in suspense about how he'd made it out of the cave without so much as a scratch.

"Fine," surrendered Cruz. "And while we're waiting you can tell me about the Archive."

He saw his roommate stiffen.

"Come on," urged Cruz. "You said you'd explain later. It's later."

"Okay, but if I do—"

"Yeah, yeah, yeah, sworn to secrecy. Spill it."

Emmett came over to take a seat at the end of Cruz's bed. "The Archive is a top secret, highly secure climate-controlled megavault located beneath the Academy. Inside is where the world's most important documents, discoveries, treasures, and mysteries are kept."

"A super-secret vault?" Cruz snorted. "In the basement of the Academy? You're joking, right?"

Emmett let out an impatient sigh. "Ask yourself, do you really think humanity, as a whole, can be trusted to keep valuables like, say, the

Hope diamond or the 'Mona Lisa' safe?"

"I...I don't know. I've never thought about it."

"Well, think about it. We're one earthquake, one nuclear disaster, one war away from losing everything. In the same way the Doomsday Vault was created to safeguard our food supply, the Archive was designed to protect our culture." Emmett's circular glasses were flashing a bright fuchsia pink, which meant he was being honest. "Galileo's original telescope, the Gettysburg Address, the formula for Coke, the truth about space aliens—it's all within the walls of the Archive!"

Goose bumps rippling up his arms, Cruz slowly sat up. "You *are* serious."

"Deadly."

Cruz tried to wrap his mind around what his roommate was telling him. "They couldn't...They didn't...Would they...?"

Emmett smirked.

"So how did *you* find out about it?"

His friend wagged a finger. "One secret at a time."

"No wonder Aunt Marisol wanted me to forget it."

"It's pretty hush-hush; even more top secret than the Synthesis."

"Fanchon to Emmett Lu."

They both jumped at the sound of Fanchon's voice blaring through Emmett's comm pin.

Emmett pressed his pin. "Emmett here."

"It's ready."

"Be right there!" Emmett hopped to his feet. "Come on, Cruz."

"But Sailor and Bryndis—"

"We'll catch up with them later."

As they passed Ali and Zane in the passage, Cruz nudged Emmett. "Do the rest of the explorers know what happened on the glacier?"

"Everybody thinks it was an accident," he said out of the side of his mouth. "We were taking photos for our glacier melt story for Professor Benedict's assignment when the ice cave collapsed."

"What about Tripp and Wardicorn?"

"Nobody's seen them. There are lots of rumors going around, of course. I don't think they'll dare show their faces here again."

Cruz wasn't so sure about that.

They had barely set foot in the tech lab when Fanchon slapped something on each of their uniforms. Cruz glanced down at the two-by-four-inch sticker on his chest. It was covered with small silver squares. When he moved, the squares shimmered a rainbow of colors like a hologram, yet no picture appeared. A hologram without an image? Cruz looked to her for an explanation.

"You are the proud wearer of a Lumagine Shadow Badge," said Fanchon, pushing a pair of safety glasses up over her zebra-print head scarf. "Tap it twice with two fingers and the badge releases a bio-net of Lumagine that engulfs you and syncs with the circuitry of nerve fibers in your brain—your white matter, if you will. You can then use your thoughts to alter the color, pattern, and texture of whatever you're wearing: shirt, pants, shoes, even your underwear, if you want. You can do what Emmett did in the ice cave and camouflage your outfit, or you can go the opposite way and make yourself stand out—the choice is up to you."

His jaw dropping, Cruz punched Emmett. "*That's* how you did it! That's how you got out of the cave without anyone seeing you!"

Emmett drew himself taller. "I used my uniform jacket for the first trial—that was when you saw the sleeve turn red. For the second trial, I sprayed my hide-and-seek jacket, but I didn't get to try it out until—"

Fanchon raised an eyebrow and gave them an understanding smile. "I'll let you boys talk," she said, busying herself in another part of the lab.

"Until Tripp and Wardicorn showed up in the cave," finished Cruz. "You blended in with the ice walls and walked right out of there without anybody, including us, knowing it!"

"Except things didn't go exactly as I'd expected." Emmett winced. "I didn't know Tripp was planning to seal us in the cave. I figured Wardicorn would start shooting. So when the two of them moved toward the tunnel, I slipped in behind them to grab their guns, but before I knew it they'd set off the blast and you guys were sealed in. I ran out of there as quickly as I could to get help."

"Brilliant, Emmett." Cruz patted his shoulder. "Brilliant."

"Okay!" Fanchon called from across the room. "Ready to give your badges a try?"

Cruz motioned to Emmett, who motioned right back. "You do it," said Emmett. "I want you to be the first person to officially use it."

Cruz tapped his sticker twice. Now, what to change his uniform jacket into? The first thing that came to his mind was Hubbard's red-and-gray-plaid dog bed. He watched as his jacket begin to roll like the incoming tide. Seconds later, it flickered silver, then morphed into the familiar tartan pattern of the Westie's dog bed. Cruz held out his arms. "It really works!"

"Of course it works," said Fanchon. "However, it's not permanent. Its staying power depends on the material you're originally wearing. We've found it seems to last longer on cotton, silk, and wool—you know, natural fabrics. With those you have about four hours of coverage. On man-made fibers, aka your rayon, nylon, acrylic, and poly blends, it lasts for about an hour and a half."

Cruz smelled something sweet. He sniffed the air. It smelled like home. "Is that passion fruit?"

"Good nose," laughed the tech chief. "We gave it a passion fruit scent. Emmett's idea. That way, the wearer knows it's been activated. Also, we've configured it so the bio-net won't release Lumagine onto any areas of exposed skin, but even if you were to come in contact with it—either externally or internally—it won't harm you. It's not toxic, unless you're allergic to passion fruit."

Tugging on his jacket, Emmett was trying to study his sticker upside down. "Fanchon, how many reflectin platelets did you use?"

"Sixteen. That seems to give optimum coverage."

"And what about when it gets wet?"

"The bio-net is waterproof. It's also impervious to light, including sunlight, gamma rays, ultraviolet rays, microwaves, x-rays, and radio waves..."

While Emmett continued peppering Fanchon with questions, Cruz waited patiently. Sidril popped her head out from a nearby cubicle. She gave his red-and-gray-tartan wool coat the once-over. "Is it me or are you wearing Hubbard's dog bed?"

"Not exactly." Cruz felt his cheeks flush. "I hope Fanchon is right about that four-hour time frame for Lumagine to wear off, because if she isn't, I'm not sure I know how to turn my jacket back."

"She's right." Sidril gave him a crooked grin. "She's always right. I'm going to go grab a bite. See you later." As the tech assistant left her work area, Cruz caught a glimpse of something round and black behind her.

His heart lurched. It was the UCC helmet.

Keeping an eye on Fanchon and Emmett, who had moved their discussion to a computer station, Cruz inched toward the cubicle Sidril had just left. Once he heard the tech lab door shut, he slipped into the unit. His UCC dive helmet sat on the table next to a computer. Sidril had left a program window on the laptop open. It was the UCC helmet log, scrolled to the last few entries.

10/16
STATUS
UCC helmet is nonfunctioning
Diagnostic test results: catastrophic failure caused by
unauthorized infiltration of onboard computer system.
Perpetrator unknown.

NOTES
Sidril, please run my Hacker Tracker software to see if we can
get a fix on where the hack came from. Also, send the UCC
helmet diagnostic report to Dr. Hightower, all *Orion* faculty,
Tripp Scarlatos, and Captain Iskandar. I will speak personally
with Cruz.
FQ

10/22
NOTES
I've been running the tracker program nonstop for a week
but hit a wall in identifying the hacker. He/she covered their
tracks well. It is my opinion that it is unlikely we will ever
determine who the infiltrator was or how they gained access
to the system.
SV

10/23
STATUS
UCC helmet is functioning
Diagnostic test results: onboard computer system,
rebreathing unit, and translator are all operating within normal
parameters.

NOTES
Sidril, I've repaired the UCC helmet, but I'm concerned we have
had no success in exposing the hacker or his/her method of
infiltrating the system. I have decided to halt further development of the Universal Cetacean Communicator until such time
as I can improve security. Please archive the helmet, including
all research logs and notes.
FQ

No!

Cruz almost screamed it right there in the middle of the lab. Fanchon couldn't give up on the UCC. She just couldn't! He was certain she'd eventually hit on a solution to the helmet's security issue. If only Fanchon could have seen her invention in action in the Bay of Fundy, then she'd know how truly incredible it was—

"Cruz?" It was Fanchon. "Are you still here?"

"Here!" He rushed out of the cubicle.

"I've got something else I want to show you," she said, waving for him to follow her to a corner of the lab. "I think you'll like this one."

Cruz looked at Emmett, who shrugged.

"Put these on." She handed each of them a pair of safety goggles before sliding down her own pair. She punched a code into a gray box on one of the shelves, then put her eye up to the screen for an iris scan. The door of the box opened and Fanchon brought out a black ball about the size of a jumbo jawbreaker. Several hollow blue circles covered the ball like mini doughnuts. Holding it up, Fanchon smiled. "This is an octopod. Say you need to make a quick getaway from an attacker. One press and the octopod releases a spray that paralyzes the central nervous system of your assailant. Pssst!"

Cruz and Emmett both took a large step back.

"Relax, I didn't really spray it. Besides, it's temporary."

"What's in it?" queried Cruz.

"It's a proprietary blend of plants and minerals, along with a single drop of venom from the blue-ringed octopus."

"The blue-ringed? I've read about that one!" exclaimed Emmett, backing up even farther. "It's this cute little octopus that's found in Australia and is also one of the world's most venomous animals.

Its rings start to glow just before it bites."

"You are correct," said Fanchon. "Its bite can barely be felt by humans, but the tetrodotoxin it releases into the bloodstream will paralyze your diaphragm so you can't breathe without a ventilator. For those who survive, the toxin wears off in about fifteen hours. To date, there is no antidote. My octopod, however, is much safer. The paralytic wears off in fifteen minutes. And there are no lasting side effects—at least, none that I've found." She held the ball out to Cruz. "This one's for you."

He was shocked. "Me?"

"I thought it might come in handy, given recent events." She arched an eyebrow, making Cruz wonder if she knew the reason why Tripp and Wardicorn had tried to hurt them. "Plus, it's based on your mother's research."

That got Cruz's attention. "What do you mean?"

"I told you I've read everything she's ever written. This was one of her ideas that she never got to develop. We didn't have the technology to do it nine years ago." She smiled. "But we do now."

Cruz bent for a closer look.

"See the tiny yellow beak? That's the sprayer." Fanchon gently placed the orb in his hand. "Aim the beak toward your attacker, put your thumb in the middle of the blue ring on the side, and hold it down. The rings will glow five seconds, then send out a two-second burst of the spray, which is all you'll need—believe me. This one is just for you, so please keep it in your pocket. And don't tell the other explorers or they'll all want one. I'm not sure Dugan is quite ready for this particular gadget."

"O-okay, if you're sure."

"I am."

"Thanks, Fanchon." Cruz carefully put the ball into an outer pocket, and as he did, his fingertips slid across something else. And in that split second, he had an idea. "Fanchon, I have something for you, too."

"You do? For me?"

"For her?" Emmett was puzzled.

"Hold out your hand." When she did, Cruz dropped his gift into her palm.

Fanchon stared at the glowing purple time capsule. She knew what it was, of course, because it was her invention. But she had no idea what memory it contained.

"Just watch it," begged Cruz. "And after you do, if you *still* want to give up on the UCC, well, we'll understand."

Emmett was nodding and grinning.

Giving them a skeptical look, the tech lab chief closed her eyes. And her fist. For the next few minutes, the two explorers watched as she saw Operation Cetacean Extrication through Cruz's eyes. She started moving her arms, as if swimming with Team Cousteau, which made Emmett and Cruz laugh.

"Oh!" she cried, her head tipping down toward her hip, and Cruz knew that was the moment the calf had bumped him. After that, there was a string of "aahs" and "wows!" and "oohs," and it became clear to both explorers well before she opened her eyes that Cruz had succeeded in his mission.

The UCC wasn't going to be mothballed after all.

Dr. Fanchon Quills, chief of scientific technology and innovation, had changed her mind.

21

▶ **PRESCOTT** *broke the bad news quickly.*

"Slipped through our fingers?" barked Brume. "Again?"

"I'm afraid so."

"Did you hear from Wallaby and Mongoose?"

"Right now, Wallaby is in hiding and Mongoose is . . . dead. Fell into a crevasse."

"I expected better, Cobra."

"Lion, I'm . . . I know." Prescott couldn't tell his boss he was sorry. He didn't know why but he couldn't bring himself to say the word.

In response, he heard only the crackle of fire from the other end. For this call, Brume had pointed his phone at a roaring fire inside an ornately carved cherrywood fireplace. On the front of the mantel, a curly-headed boy angel peered out at Prescott from between scrolls of fig leaves. Prescott felt weird, staring into the flames. It was like looking at one of those yule log videos that show up on television around Christmas so everyone who doesn't have a fireplace can pretend they do.

"So far, we know the kid has the journal," continued Prescott, "along with two of the eight pieces of a stone cipher his mother made. We're fairly certain she engraved the formula onto the stone, though it could also be some kind of code or map. We . . . uh . . . don't know for certain."

"Enough with the guesswork. We'll get Jaguar on it."

"Very good. Uh . . . about that, Lion. How do I reach Jaguar?"

"I don't think that's wise."

Lowering his eyes, Prescott nodded. Brume didn't trust him.

Or was losing faith in him. Or both.

"I think we've done enough chasing," said Brume. "It's time to make him come to us."

"You mean . . . ?"

"We knew it might come to this. You are still in position?"

"Well . . . yes." Rising, Prescott went toward the surfboard leaning against the wall next to the front door. The board was ice blue, painted with bold strokes of blue and green to look like crashing waves. He had thought the colors were too bright, but Marco had said it suited him. Prescott had thought he would hate surfing, but Marco had insisted that once he relaxed and let his body find its rhythm on the ocean, he would come to love it. Marco was right on both counts.

"The kid has the cipher and soon we'll have something he'll want," said Brume. "Then we'll all have ourselves a nice little trade. Or not."

Brume's fire popped. Prescott flinched. His boss wasn't an even-trade kind of guy. With Hezekiah Brume, it was all or nothing.

"I'll send Komodo and Scorpion," Brume was saying. "That should give you plenty of muscle. Please tell me you can handle this, Cobra."

Prescott ran his finger along the smooth, curved edge of his surfboard. "You can count on me, sir."

PADDLING his board into the turquoise waters of the cove, Cruz watched a wave rise behind Bryndis. As it rolled under her, she hopped up onto her surfboard and stretched out her arms. Aiming her board into the curl, she swiveled left, then right, then left again. White teeth flashed him a grin as she cruised past, riding the swell until it petered out. Bryndis was an excellent surfer! She made it look so easy. The good ones always did.

Cruz wasn't at all confident he could match her skills. Surfing in Iceland wasn't anything like in Hawaii. For one thing, the water temperature in Iceland in October was more than 20 degrees colder than the water temp in Hanalei Bay in the middle of winter! This meant that here it was vital for a surfer to cover up from head to toe. By the time Cruz put on his neoprene wet suit, hood, gloves, and surf booties, he'd added a few pounds to his weight. He felt like an uncoordinated seal. Also, unlike back home, there was no soft sandy beach leading to a gentle surf. Nope. Here, they'd had to pick their way through the giant boulders of a rocky peninsula, then jump straight into a crashing sea. Cruz was pretty sure he'd already swallowed a bathtubful of water trying to make it past the first break.

Yet all those challenges were forgotten once Cruz felt the familiar surge beneath his board. Springing upward, he firmly planted his feet and, after a few minor bobbles, somehow found his balance. Now set,

Cruz swiveled in a snakelike pattern, skimming the surface of the crest as it pushed toward the shore. He couldn't help letting out a small "whoop!" He did not want to do a major wipeout in front of Bryndis, as well as Emmett and Sailor, who were intently watching from the rocks. Only as the wave began to smooth out did Cruz dare to gaze up at the vast stretch of snow-covered anvil mountains surrounding the cove. He couldn't wait to tell Lani what it was like to surf in Iceland—*if* he ever got ahold of her.

Cruz had tried to call her last night with Sailor, Emmett, and Bryndis, as they'd planned, but she hadn't answered. It had been Saturday afternoon back in Kauai. She'd probably gone horseback riding with that Haych guy again. Cruz had seriously considered opening his mother's journal for the third clue without her. He should have, too. It would have served her right for blowing him off. Okay, he had never *seriously* considered it, but Lani could have at least texted him yesterday. Or today. When he did reach her he was going to be plenty mad. Okay, he'd be a little mad. After all, it was Lani's protective sleeve that had saved the journal from Tripp. He hoped. Cruz was still a bit nervous that the holographic book wouldn't open for him.

Cruz and Bryndis surfed for another half hour before Emmett waved them in. Cruz didn't blame Emmett for wanting to go home to *Orion*. It had to be cold sitting there on the rocks. Emmett and Sailor had wanted to surf, too, but Bryndis hadn't recommended it. Now, after wrestling with the awkward suit, unpredictable waves, and wild crosswinds, Cruz understood why she'd discouraged the pair. This was no place for a beginner.

Dropping onto his belly, Cruz began stroking his board toward shore. It was their last day before the ship sailed. He hadn't expected to surf again until he went home for a visit, so this was a perfect way to end his time in Iceland. *Orion* was leaving port tomorrow. Cruz was going to miss the land of fire and ice, but he was ready to search for the next piece of his mother's cipher. As he neared the rocks, Cruz stood, picked up his surfboard, and followed Bryndis out of the water.

Navigating carefully through the wet boulders toward his friends, he saw that Emmett was on the phone. Sailor handed them each a towel. "It's Lani," she said.

"Finally!" Cruz wiped his face and took the phone Emmett was holding out to him. "Lani, where have you—"

"I've been trying to get ahold of you all day . . ." She was breathless.

"*You've* been trying to reach *me*?" He laughed. "We've been surfing. You should see the waves here, Lani—"

"Are you all right?"

"Uh-huh." His dad must have told her about the cave-in.

"And your dad? Is he on his way to see you?"

"My dad? Coming to Iceland? No."

"So you haven't heard from him?"

"I talked to him yesterday, if that's what you mean."

"But not since?"

"No. What's with the third degree?"

"Your dad . . . he's . . . well, he's missing."

Cruz froze. "Missing?"

"I stopped by the Goofy Foot after my piano lesson yesterday and he wasn't there."

"He probably went to the beach or for a hike—"

"Without locking up the store? Or telling Tiko?"

A pang of fear sliced through him. His dad had left the shop open? And his assistant manager, who was also Lani's brother, had no idea where he was? "No, he would never have done that," said Cruz.

"Mom and I thought maybe you had an emergency."

"Not me. Maybe someone else did? One of my cousins or a friend?"

"I bet that's it," Lani said, but Cruz could tell she wasn't convinced.

"Let's hang up. I'll call him right now," said Cruz.

"Okay. If you find out anything, text me."

"You do the same."

"I will. Don't worry, Cruz. I'm sure he'll turn up. He's probably helping out a friend or one of your relatives, like you said."

"Yeah," said Cruz, though his stomach was churning. "Talk later. Bye."

He tried to call his father, but Cruz was so upset, he couldn't get his cold fingers to work. Bryndis had to dial for him. When his dad didn't pick up, Cruz called Aunt Marisol.

"Come back to the ship," she instructed. "I'll look into things from here."

For the next six hours, Cruz dialed his dad's number every 20 minutes, 18 times in all—and 18 times his call went to voice mail. He texted dozens of messages, too. All went unanswered. Aunt Marisol got in contact with their relatives, friends, and former Goofy Foot employees, but nobody had seen or heard from Cruz's dad in more than 24 hours. She even called the local police and hospital in Kauai, but there had been no car or boat accidents, drownings, or unidentified injury victims. It was as if Marco Coronado had simply vanished from the face of the Earth.

Early the next morning, *Orion* sailed from Reykjavík harbor. Cruz stood on the deck of his veranda as the ship left the fishing boats and colorful roofs and tabletop mountains behind. Spinning Nóri's gyrfalcon feather between his thumb and index finger, he wondered: Was Nebula behind his dad's disappearance? Or was it something else? Could his dad have taken a wrong turn on a hike? Maybe he'd lost his footing on a trail, slid down a hill, and was stuck on an outcrop waiting to be rescued? So many possibilities. None of them good.

Cruz leaned over the rail, keeping land in sight as long as he could. He straightened only when the island of Iceland was merely a dark outline against a periwinkle sky. Cruz turned toward the horizon. He saw nothing in front of him but the white-tipped waves of a cold gray ocean.

Cruz let the falcon's feather go. He watched it swirl on the north wind, curling this way and that, before touching down on the dark sea.

"Dad," he whispered, "where *are* you?"

THE TRUTH BEHIND THE FICTION

magine swimming alongside a pod of right whales to capture a photograph, piloting a submersible to the depths of the ocean to discover new bioluminescent species, or trekking to Iceland to measure glaciers. These are some of the adventures undertaken by the real explorers of National Geographic, whose commitment to protecting the planet served as inspiration for this book.

ERIKA BERGMAN

Cruz's adventures aboard *Ridley* might not have turned out as expected, but Erika Bergman, a deep-sea submersible pilot, knows the thrill Cruz must have felt when he took his first step into the tiny submarine. "Every single dive—it doesn't matter if you've been to the spot a hundred times—is completely different. There are so many things that we don't know about the ocean. Every single time you dive you see something new and unexpected."

BRIAN SKERRY

Underwater photographer and explorer Brian Skerry knows a thing or two about getting up close with whales. In fact, in the photo illustration on pp. 108–109, Cruz's figure was drawn in place of Skerry's assistant in a real-life photo! While marine scientists aren't able to "speak whale" yet, they are unlocking some of the mysteries of cetacean language. They have discovered that the moans, grunts, knocks, chirps, and whistles of the North Atlantic right whale and other baleen whales may travel for hundreds of miles underwater. Researchers believe these social creatures use sound to identify one another, find food, and communicate. Different pods have even been found to have unique dialects! Scientists are also using such sounds to help save this endangered species. In the crowded shipping lanes of Massachusetts Bay, a chain of smart buoys listens for right whales 24/7. When the network picks up the call of a right whale, it alerts the Cornell Lab of Ornithology, which then relays the information to ships in the area so they can slow down and watch for whales.

▶ THE TRUTH BEHIND THE FICTION

DINO MARTINS

The Svalbard seed vault where Cruz discovers the feather in the seed packet that his mother left for him is a very real place. Located deep inside a mountain halfway

M JACKSON

The future, however, may not be as bright for our planet's glaciers. Glaciers are more than massive chunks of ice. They are a vital part of our environment, providing water, creating local weather, building landscapes, and revealing important clues about our changing climate. National Geographic explorer M Jackson has spent years studying the effects of climate change on glaciers in Iceland and around the world. She believes glaciers mean much more to humanity beyond their direct effects: "They have been witnessed, recorded, and represented by countless human beings throughout time. My research finds that glaciers inspire, hold memory, directly connect cultures to landscapes, provide spiritual fulfillment, and link people to greater forces at plan across the planet." Langjökull glacier, one of the settings in this book, is the second largest glacier in Iceland. Geoscientists have found that Langjökull is retreating, or getting smaller, due to rising global temperatures. Statistics show that if things continue at their present rate, Langjökull and most of Iceland's more than 250 glaciers will be completely gone in less than two centuries.

between Norway and the North Pole, the structure is built to withstand natural disasters and catastrophic events. Inside the facility is the largest collection of crop diversity in the world—a safety net to avoid the extinction of global plant and food sources. Explorer Dino Martins may never have been to the seed vault itself, but he understands the delicate balance between ecosystem and biodiversity, and how much care it takes to make sure everything remains in balance so our crops can thrive. Martins's main focus is conservation of pollinators—bees (the real-life Mells!) and other insects that are responsible for ensuring a lasting future for our plant species.

DAVID GRUBER

Just as whales use sound to survive, other creatures use the sense of sight to their benefit. The bioluminescent jackets of the students at Explorer Academy may be fictional, but many animals, such as fireflies, jellyfish, and sharks, rely on this biochemical reaction for survival. It aids in warding off predators, attracting prey, and finding mates. Scientists and explorers, like David Gruber, are also studying how people may benefit from bioluminescence. Gruber discovered that some of the proteins found in bioluminescent creatures can be used to track cancer cells and illuminate parts of the brain to help doctors diagnose diseases. Perhaps, one day, we'll also see bioluminescent trees naturally lighting up our roads, reducing the need to use electricity to power streetlights, or bioluminescent plants that would glow to tell farmers when they needed watering or nutrients.

To learn more about these topics and the passionate explorers who study them, check them out at the Explorer Academy website!

exploreracademy.com

EXPLORER ACADEMY

BOOK 3:
THE DOUBLE HELIX

30.3285° N   I   35.4444° E

"Cruz!" Fanchon was stalking toward him in her red flip-flops. She was wearing a purple apron over a white sparkly tee and pink jeans. The front of her apron read, *Forget Princess, Be a Scientist*. "What's up?"

"I ... uh ... was wondering if I could borrow a PANDA unit to ... uh ... analyze a cool fossil I found in Barcelona."

"Hmmm." She swished her mouth from side to side as if it were filled with mouthwash. "I'm not supposed to check them out without faculty approval, but I guess it would be okay to let you use it in here."

"H-here?" Cruz felt his skin go prickly. He had planned to take the device back to his cabin, where he could analyze the cipher away from security cameras and prying eyes.

Fanchon went along the wall of cabinets, stopping about halfway down the row. Bending, she unlocked a door, reached in, and took a PANDA device out of a box. "Come on. I'll set you up where you won't be disturbed." Cruz followed her to one of the back cubicles. It was empty. She set the unit on the desk. "Will you be okay?"

"I do have a question," said Cruz. "I know I can upload the analytics to my tablet, but if I find any DNA on the ... uh, fossil ... can I upload the holo results, too? You know, to watch later."

"Absolutely. Once your analysis is complete, hit stop. Select 'holo-video file,' then find your name and hit send and it'll upload everything to your tablet, including DNA recovery info, which will allow you to project the hologram anywhere, anytime."

"Great."

"Let me know if you have any more questions."

"Actually … uh … I do have one, but it doesn't have anything to do with the PANDA."

"Shoot."

Cruz glanced down at her flip-flops and asked a question he had been dying to ask since he'd first met the tech lab chief. "Isn't it kind of dangerous to wear those in here? What if you spill a chemical or something on your feet?"

Fanchon let out a tiny snort. Reaching into a cubicle, she grabbed a pair of lab gloves and goggles. She tossed them to Cruz. While he put them on, she opened a nearby cabinet. Fanchon brought out a beaker of a ruby red liquid and held it out to him.

"What is it?"

"A combination of jalapeño pepper extract, fire ant venom, and a few other spicy chemicals." She held out her foot. "Pour it on my toes."

"Are you kidding?"

"Trust me. It'll be okay."

Cruz was defiant. "Nope. Nuh-uh. No way."

"Oh, great globs of goat cheese." She took the beaker and, as he watched in horror, tipped it. The bright red liquid streamed out, but instead of hitting her toes, it rolled off her foot, as if she were wearing a glass boot.

Cruz's jaw fell. "How did you—?"

"Force field." She winked. "And that's all I'm saying. If you need me, I'll be on the other side of the lab in the cubicle. It's the one right behind the dinosaur eggs."

"Okay." Reaching for the PANDA, Cruz's head snapped around. Dinosaur eggs?

Too late to ask about it; the *splick-splack* sound of her flip-flops was fading away.

Cruz took the cipher from his pocket and held it in his cupped hand. He didn't want a security camera to get a look at it. Hunching over, he turned on the PANDA unit and pressed the blue ID button. When the screen read SCAN NOW, he slowly swept it across all three pieces of stone. A minute later the results came up:

Item: non-foliated metamorphic limestone
Composition: calcium carbonate (CaCo$_3$), quartz (SiO$_2$),
graphite (C), pyrite (FeS$_2$)
Common Name: black marble
Origin: Mexico
Age: 729 million years old

Cruz's finger hovered over the yellow button, the one that checked for DNA. His heart jumped. His mom's DNA could still be on the cipher. He didn't know why that scared him, but it did. It wouldn't mean anything if it was. It wouldn't change anything. So why was he so nervous to find out the truth? Cruz hesitated, then forced himself to push the yellow button. He waited for the "go" signal and slid the unit across the marble stones one more time. He heard a soft tone.

It was there! The unit had found DNA on the cipher.

What was he getting so excited about? Of course it had. Cruz had handled the stones. So had Lani, Sailor, Emmett, and Aunt Marisol. The device had probably identified all of their DNA. But what if there was more? Cruz knew he had 15 seconds before the unit began producing images of the life-forms the DNA belonged to. Actually, he was probably down to five seconds now. Four . . . three . . . two . . .

Cruz punched STOP.

Read a longer excerpt from *The Double Helix* at exploreracademy.com.

EXPLORER ACADEMY

BOOK 4:
THE STAR DUNES

24.7681° S | 15.2959° E

Getting on all fours, Cruz began to crawl around the perimeter of the cave. There *had* to be a way out.

"Or not." He grimaced, gently rolling a skull out of his path.

Ten minutes later, Cruz was huffing and about to take a break, when he realized his shoes were wet. If water was getting in, it had to come from somewhere. This could be a way out!

The grotto was quickly beginning to fill. Cruz had to get to higher ground.

Fortunately, *Orion*'s science tech lab chief, Fanchon Quills, had designed their uniforms to be waterproof, but Cruz had a feeling Fanchon hadn't expected he would have to swim in the thing. In another few minutes, however, that's exactly what he was going to have to do.

Closing the collar of his uniform, Cruz felt something scrape the back of his neck. He reached behind him, his fingers closing around a metal tab. That's right! Every explorer's jacket was equipped with two critical survival items: a parachute, which wouldn't help him here, and a flotation device, which most definitely would! Except Cruz wasn't sure how to inflate the thing. He could almost hear his adviser, Taryn Secliff, say, *You'd know what to do if you hadn't glossed over the uniform instruction manual.*

"I know, Taryn, I know..." Cruz yanked open his belt and unzipped his jacket. Wrestling free of the sleeves, he whipped the coat inside out. He found a small plastic tab near the collar. It was engraved with a *P*—for "parachute," no doubt. Okay, so where was the one to the float? Frantically, he went down the lining, searching for an *F* tab. He didn't find one. Cruz moaned. "How in the world am I supposed to activate this dumb flotation device?"

"Personal flotation device deployment confirmed." The calm female voice startled him. It was Fanchon!

"Cruz Coronado, please prepare for PFD deployment," said Fanchon. Her instructions were coming from his OS band! Smart. He should have known that when all else failed, he could count on his OS band for help.

"Please fully secure jacket, pockets, and cuffs. Beginning ten-second countdown sequence now. Ten ... nine ... eight..."

"Hold on!" Cruz threw his jacket over his shoulders and shoved his arms into his sleeves. The water was edging up past his knees. A current was beginning to form. He had to take a wider stance to remain upright in the swirling water.

"Six ... five ..."

Cruz yanked the buckles tight on the bottom of each sleeve, then jerked the zipper on the front of his jacket up so hard he was sure he'd broken it.

"Two ... one," said Fanchon. "PFD activation commencing."

The hem of Cruz's jacket tightened against his hips. His cuffs and collar were sealing, too. A sudden rush of air down his back sent a chill through him. Cruz watched his sleeves slowly swell. As they did, his arms rose from his sides. His chest was puffing up, too. His jacket took less than 15 seconds to fully inflate. He felt like a giant marshmallow.

The water was still rising ... up to his hips ... his stomach ... his ribs ...

Once the water level reached his chest, Cruz lifted his feet to test if the float could hold him. It did! He was buoyant. As the floodwaters inched upward, they took Cruz with them. It was strange to be going back up the very hole that had brought him down here, but at least he was moving in a better direction. Cruz wasn't sure how far he had fallen into the shaft. He strained, looking for the gap in the rock he had fallen through.

Uh-oh. Trouble ahead. Cruz was heading for an opening on the opposite side of the cave wall. No! He needed to go up, not down. Kicking, he thrashed his arms to steer away from the hole, but the current was too strong. He was going in! The force of the tide spun him through the opening, tipping him to one side. Water went up his nose and down his throat. Cruz came up coughing, trying to spit out water while gulping in air.

When he could see again, Cruz realized he was riding the rapids through a narrow tunnel. Of course! This must be a lava tube. Once the water had risen to the level of the tube, he'd been dumped into the passage like a helpless spider down a bathtub drain. The river was powerful and choppy. It was like rafting on the wildest white water imaginable, except *Cruz* was the raft. The swift flow tossed him from one side of the tube to the other.

Bouncing from wall to wall, Cruz quickly saw he wasn't out of the woods yet. About 30 yards ahead, there was a fork in the tube. The river was propelling him straight toward the wall of rock between the two paths. Which way should he go? Cruz kicked hard with his right foot and tried to row with his right arm, shooting for the left fork. This was going to be close!

Read a longer excerpt from *The Star Dunes* at exploreracademy.com.

ABOUT THE CONTRIBUTORS

TRUDI TRUEIT imagined a career as a novelist ever since she wrote, directed, and starred in her first play in the fourth grade. A shy and quiet kid, she found that when she wrote, she could say what she wanted and people would pay attention and listen. A former television news reporter and weather forecaster, she's published more than 100 fiction and nonfiction books for young readers, including *My Top Secret Dares & Don'ts, The Sister Solution,* and the Secrets of a Lab Rat series (Aladdin). Her expertise in nonfiction for kids comes through in books about history, weather, wildlife, and earth science.

Each book in the Explorer Academy series took her about six months to write, and included a great deal of brainstorming and imagining how the fictionalized world, and the characters who inhabited it, would look. In order to develop characters for the series, like Cruz and his friends Lani, Emmett, and Sailor, Trudi often doodled to visualize who the people were and the places that they would go. When she thought about what kind of cool and innovative technology these young explorers could use during their training missions, she was largely inspired by the groundbreaking projects and inventions of real National Geographic explorers. A lover of photography, she says that if she had her own high-tech honeybee drone like Mell, she would have it take photos of incredible places and phenomena, like the northern lights or snow leopards in Nepal.

When she's not busy writing, Trudi can be found in the Pacific Northwest, where she was born and raised. She makes her home in Everett, Washington, with her husband, Bill, and her cats. She loves science fiction, weather books, and all things chocolate. **Visit her website at www.truditrueit.com.**

SCOTT PLUMBE, an illustrator, designer, and fine artist, grew up in a house at the edge of a vast forest in Vancouver, Canada. Scott and his family have been walking in the woods, painting, reading books, and making things for as long as he can remember. As a student, he studied design and illustration and has worked with words and pictures ever since. His creative childhood and schooling led him to create the inside illustrations for *Explorer Academy: The Falcon's Feather*. In addition to making illustrations for books, magazines, and games for clients around the world, he regularly contributes to conceptualizing interpretive centers, museum exhibits, and more. He is especially known for his realistic renderings of people, wildlife, and detailed adventure scenes. **See his work at www.scottplumbe.com.**

DR. GARETH MOORE is the code master for the Explorer Academy franchise, having created all of the exciting and mind-boggling codes and puzzles throughout the book. He is the author of over 100 best-selling international puzzle and brain-training titles from a wide range of publishers. His content can also be found in various newspapers, magazines, newsletters, and corporate publications. Furthermore, he is the producer of "Brained Up," a cutting-edge brain-training site offering scientifically designed daily sessions, and is on the board of the World Puzzle Federation. He lives in London, England, with his wife and son. **Find him online at www.drgarethmoore.com.**

Cuban-born illustrator, graphic designer, and graphic novel artist **ANTONIO JAVIER CAPARO** created the dramatic cover illustration for *Explorer Academy: The Falcon's Feather*. Passionate about animation and comics, his realistic illustrations regularly appear in magazines and books in the United States, Europe, and South America. Although he started his career in graphic design, his passion for worlds and magical characters soon led him to focus on illustration, creating intense and conceptual pieces. He is a graduate of the Superior Institute of Design in Havana, Cuba, and currently lives in Montreal, Canada.

As the vice president of visual identity at National Geographic Kids, **EVA ABSHER-SCHANTZ** oversees the designers, illustrators, and photographers who create the stunning art found in the Explorer Academy book series. Bringing to life the amazing fictionalized world author Trudi Trueit had imagined and written about was no small feat. The process included surveying kids to find out how much art, and what kind of art, they wanted to see in the series, deciding which key moments in the book to illustrate, inserting hidden clues for readers to discover in certain scenes, and brainstorming ways to make sure readers felt like they were a part of the action. The unique, hybrid art that she ultimately decided on for the series combines photography and illustration. In order to celebrate and represent National Geographic's longstanding history of beautiful photography from around the world, she included real-life photography of places and animals and overlaid it with fictional art to make the world of Cruz and his companions both realistic and fantastical.

ILLUSTRATION CREDITS

Cover illustration by Antonio Javier Caparo. Interior illustrations by Scott Plumbe unless otherwise noted below. All maps created by NG Maps.

11 (postcard), paladin13/iStockphoto/Getty Images; 11 (stamp), Susana Guzm/ iStockphoto/Getty Images; 61 (paper), Davor Ratkovic/Shutterstock; 62 (sand), Anna Kucherova/Shutterstock; 62 (figures), Zaur Rahimoff/Shutterstock; 62 (whisk), Ingram; 62 (clothes), urfin/Shutterstock; 62 (gold), teena137/ Shutterstock; 62 (den), Chris Philpotts; 85, Brian J. Skerry/National Geographic Image Collection; 108-109 (photograph), Brian J. Skerry/National Geographic Image Collection; 130-131 (photograph), Jim Richardson/National Geographic Image Collection; 152, Kay Dulay/Moment RF/Getty Images; 172-173 (photograph), Caios Campos/iStockphoto/Getty Images; 181 (photograph), Caios Campos/iStockphoto/Getty Images; 196 (photograph), Chris Burkard/Massif; 202 (UP), Barry B. Brown/National Geographic Image Collection; 202 (LO), Mike Parmalee/National Geographic Image Collection; 203 (UP), Brian J. Skerry/ National Geographic Image Collection; 203 (LO), Brian J. Skerry/National Geographic Image Collection; 204 (UP), Cecilia Lewis/National Geographic Image Collection; 204 (CTR LE), Eric Kruszewski/National Geographic Image Collection; 204 (CTR RT), Randall Scott/National Geographic Image Collection; 205 (UP), Kat Keene Hogue/National Geographic Image Collection; 205 (LO), Cengage/National Geographic Image Collection; throughout (feather illustration), Oldesign/Shutterstock; throughout (abstract technology background), Rabbit_Photo/Shutterstock; throughout (abstract watercolor background), happykanppy/Shutterstock; throughout (abstract curved framework background), Digital_Art/Shutterstock; 212 (UP), Bill Trueit; 212 (LO), Matt Leaf; 213 (UP), Simon Annand; 213 (CTR), Adriana Garcia Cruz; 213 (LO), Mark Thiessen/ National Geographic Staff

ACKNOWLEDGMENTS

I am blessed to have the *best* team in children's publishing behind me. Thank you to Becky Baines, Erica Green, Jennifer Rees, Jennifer Emmett, Eva Absher-Schantz, Scott Plumbe, Ruth Chamblee, Caitlin Holbrook, Holly Saunders, and everyone at National Geographic who left a piece of their heart in the pages of this book. You are a class act, through and through. Thanks also to my agent, Rosemary Stimola, who nurtured my career from the beginning, always with grace and humor. I am grateful to the amazing National Geographic explorers, who inspire me each and every day. Special thanks to Gemina Garland-Lewis, Nizar Ibrahim, and Zoltan Takacs, for going the extra mile in support of this project. I am indebted to Karen Wadsworth and Tracey Daniels, for so expertly and cheerfully handling my travels and all the little emergencies that come with them (like broken shoes)! I am so appreciative of the Seattle-area independent booksellers, who allow local authors the opportunity to shine. Special thanks to Suzanne Perry from Secret Garden Books, René Kirkpatrick from University Books, and Annie Carl from the Neverending Bookshop. I am also grateful to Barbara Stolzenburg and Valerie Stein, extraordinary librarians and dear friends. To every educator who invited me to share my love of books and writing with their students— thank you! Finally, thanks to my friends and family, my husband, Bill, and especially my dad, who saw the writer in me early on and urged me to follow my dream. Because, after all, what is life without passion?

There's MORE to EXPLORE!

The adventure continues with more books in the thrilling seven-book series, along with fun activity books that feature the characters and themes of Explorer Academy.

Watch videos, play a codebreaking game, and discover more at ExplorerAcademy.com

UNDER THE *Stars*

NATIONAL GEOGRAPHIC

AVAILABLE WHEREVER BOOKS ARE SOLD

© 2019 National Geographic Partners, LLC

Illustration Credits

AKG London: Figs. 5, 11, 20, 23, 27, 28.

Corbis U.K.: Figs. 8, 13, 14, 16, 29, 30.

Mary Evans Picture Library, London: Figs. 1, 3, 4, 6, 9, 10, 12, 15, 17, 19, 21, 22, 26.

National Portrait Gallery, London: Figs. 2, 18, 24, 25, 31.

Royal Horticultural Society, London: Fig. 32.

Royal Photographic Society, U.K.: Fig. 7.

About the Author

———————— ✖ ————————

James Burke, a noted authority on the history of technology and science, is the bestselling author of *Connections*, *The Day the Universe Changed* and *The Pinball Effect* and, with Robert Ornstein, of *The Axemaker's Gift*. He also hosts the highly rated documentary television series *Connections*. He lives in London, England.

ALSO BY JAMES BURKE

Connections

The Day the Universe Changed

The Axemaker's Gift
(with Robert Ornstein)

The Pinball Effect

The
Knowledge
Web

From Electronic Agents to Stonehenge
and Back—and Other Journeys
Through Knowledge

⋈

JAMES
BURKE

Simon & Schuster

SIMON & SCHUSTER
Rockefeller Center
1230 Avenue of the Americas
New York, NY 10020

Copyright © 1999 by London Writers
All rights reserved,
including the right of reproduction
in whole or in part in any form.

SIMON & SCHUSTER and colophon are registered trademarks
of Simon & Schuster Inc.

Designed by Pagesetters

Manufactured in the United States of America

10 9 8 7 6 5 4 3 2 1

Library of Congress Cataloging-in-Publication Data

Burke, James, 1936–
The knowledge web : from electronic agents to Stonehenge and back—
and other journeys through knowledge / James Burke.
    p.   cm.
Includes bibliographical references and index.
1. Technology—History. I. Title.
    T15.B763   1999
609—dc21   99-24539
                                        CIP

ISBN 0-684-85934-3

To Madeline

Acknowledgements

✖

I should like to thank Carolyn Doree and Jay Hornsby for their extremely valuable assistance in research.

Contents

Introduction

⊠

Change comes so fast these days that the reaction of the average person recalls the depressive who takes some time off work and heads for the beach. A couple of days later his psychiatrist gets a postcard from him. The message on the card reads: "Having a wonderful time. Why?"

Innovation is so often surprising and unexpected because the process by which new ideas emerge is serendipitous and interactive. Even those directly involved may be unaware of the outcome of their work. How, for instance, could a nineteenth-century perfume-spray manufacturer and the chemist who discovered how to crack gasoline from oil have foreseen that their products would come together to create the carburetor? In the 1880s, without the accidental spillage of some of the recently invented artificial colorant onto a petri-dish culture that revealed to a German researcher named Ehrlich that the dye preferentially killed certain bacilli, would Ehrlich have become the first chemotherapist? If the Romantic movement's concept of "nature-philosophy" had not suggested that nature evolves through the reconciliation of opposing forces, would Oersted have sought to "reconcile" electricity and magnetism and discovered the electromagnetic force that made possible modern telecommunications?

Small wonder, then, that the man and woman in the street are left behind in all this, if the researchers themselves don't get the point. But given the conditions under which science and technology work, how else could it be? At last count there were more than twenty

thousand different disciplines, each of them staffed by researchers straining to replace what they produced yesterday.

These noodling world-changers are spurred on by at least two powerful motivators. The first is that you are more likely to achieve recognition if you make your particular research niche so specialist that there's only room in it for you. So the aim of most scientists is to know more and more about less and less, and to describe what it is they know in terms of such precision as to be virtually incomprehensible to their colleagues, let alone the general public.

The second motivator is the CEO. Corporations survive in a changing world only by encouraging their specialists to generate change before somebody else does. Winning in the marketplace means catching the competition by surprise. Not surprisingly, this process also surprises the consumer, and nowhere so frequently today as in the world of electronics, where by the time the user gets around to reading the manual, the gizmo to which it refers is obsolete.

We live in this permanently off-balance manner because of the way knowledge has been generated and disseminated for the last 120,000 years. In early Neolithic times the requirement to teach the highly precise, sequential skills of stone-tool manufacture demanded a similarly precise, sequential use of sounds and is thought to have given rise to language. The sequential nature of language facilitated description of the world in similarly precise terms, and in due course a process originally developed for chipping pieces off stone became a tool for chipping pieces off the universe. This reduction of reality to its constituent parts is at the root of the view of knowledge known as "reductionism," from which science sprang in the seventeenth-century West. Simply put, scientific knowledge comes as the result of taking things apart to see how they work.

Over millennia, this way of doing things has tended to subdivide knowledge into smaller and more specialist segments. For example, in the past hundred years or so, the ancient discipline of botany has fragmented and diversified to become biology, organic chemistry, histology, embryology, evolutionary biology, physiology, cytology,

pathology, bacteriology, urology, ecology, population genetics and zo-
ology.

There is no reason to suppose that this process of proliferation and
fragmentation will lessen or cease. It is at the heart of what, since
Darwin's time, has been called "progress." If we live today in the best
of all possible materialist worlds, it is because of the tremendous
strides made by specialist research that have given us everything
from more absorbent diapers to linear accelerators. We in the tech-
nologically advanced nations are healthier, wealthier, more mobile,
better-informed individuals than ever before in history, thanks to
myriad specialists and the products of their pencil-chewing efforts.

However, the corollary to a small minority knowing more and
more about less and less is a large majority knowing less and less
about more and more. In the past this has been a relatively unimportant matter principally because for most of history the illiterate majority (hard-pressed enough just to survive) has been unaware that
the problem existed at all. Technology was in such limited supply
that there was only enough to share it among a few elite decision-
makers.

It is true that over time, as the technology diversified, knowledge
slowly diffused outward into the community via information media
such as the alphabet, paper, the printing press and telecommunications. But at the same time these systems also served to increase the
overall amount of specialist knowledge. What reached the general
public was usually either out-of-date or no longer vital to the interests of the elite. And as specialist knowledge expanded, so did the
gulf between those who had information and those who did not.

Each time there was a major advance in the ability to generate,
store or disseminate knowledge, it was followed by an "information
surge" and with it a sudden acceleration in the level of innovation
that dramatically enhanced the power of the elites. But sooner or
later the same technology reached enough people to undermine the
status quo. The arrival of paper in thirteenth-century Europe
strengthened the hand of church and throne, but at the same time
created a merchant class that would ultimately question their author-

ity. The printing press gave Rome the means to enforce obedience and conformity, then Luther used it to wage a propaganda war that ended with the emergence of Protestantism. In the late nineteenth century, when military technology made possible conflicts in which hundreds of thousands died, and manufacturing technology generated untenable working and living conditions for millions of factory workers, radicals and reformers were aided in their efforts by new printing techniques cheap enough to spread their message of protest in newspapers and pamphlets.

By the mid twentieth century scientific and technological knowledge far outstripped the ability of most people, even the averagely well-informed, to comprehend it. The stimulus of the Cold War brought advances in computer technology that seemed likely to place unprecedented power in the hands of economic and political power blocs. There was talk of "Big Brother" government, rule by multinational corporations, the central databases that would hold personal files on every individual, and the creeping homogenization of the human race into one giant "global village." Unchecked state and corporate industrialization finally began to generate the first visible signs of global warming, runaway pollution decimated the animal population and the tropical forests went down before fire and axe at an alarming rate.

However, at the same time, the falling cost of computer and telecommunications technology also began to make it possible for these developments to be discussed in an unprecedentedly large public forum. And the more we learned about the world through television and radio, the more it became clear that urgent measures were needed to preserve its fragile ecosystems and its even more fragile cultural diversity. At the end of the twentieth century the emergence of the ubiquitous Internet and affordable wireless technology offered the opportunity for millions of individuals to think of becoming involved.

However, the culture of scarcity with which we have lived for millennia has not prepared us well for the responsibilities technology will force on us in the next few decades. Reductionism, representative democracy and the division of labor have tended to leave such

14

matters in the hands of specialists who are, increasingly, no more aware of the ramifications of their work than anybody else.

The result is that national and international institutions are coming under unprecedented stress as they try to apply their obsolete mechanisms to twenty-first-century problems. In Britain recently a case was brought against an individual which rested on the fifteenth-century meaning of the word "obscene." Medical etiquette has changed little since 1800. In some places science and religion are in conflict over the definition of life.

Western institutions function as if the world had not changed since they were established to deal with the specific problems of the time. Fifteenth-century nation-states, emerging into a world without telecommunications, developed representative democracy; seventeenth-century explorers in need of financial backing invented the stock market; in the eleventh century the influx of Arab knowledge triggered the invention of universities to process the new data for student priests.

In the coming decades it is likely that many social institutions will attempt to adapt by becoming virtual, bringing their services directly to the individual much in the way that banks have already begun to. But their new accessibility will in turn likely subject them to proliferating and diversifying demands that will change how they work and make them redefine their purpose. In education, the old reductionist reliance on specialism and testing by repetition will have to give way to a much more flexible definition of ability. As machines increasingly take over the tasks that once occupied a human lifetime, specialist skills may take on a merely antiquarian value. New ways will have to be found to assess intelligence in a world in which memory and experience seem no longer of value (again, this is nothing new: the alphabet and later the printing press both presented the same perceived threat).

When a corporate workforce becomes scattered across the country, or the globe, in thousands of individual homes or groups, and deals direct with millions of customers, the value of communication skills is likely to outweigh that of most others. Such ability may be pos-

sessed by people who would previously have been thought unqualified to work for the corporation, because in the old world they would have been too young, or too old, or too distant, for example. A virtual education system will have to deal with problems such as a multicultural global student body bringing very diverse experience, attitudes and aims to the class. In terms of international law, recent cases involving copyright or pornography reveal how complex such legal problems are likely to become.

This book does not attempt directly to address any of these problems. Rather, it suggests an approach to knowledge perhaps more attuned to the needs of the twenty-first century as described above. Some readers will no doubt see this approach as more evidence of the "dumbing-down" of recent years. But the same was said about the first printing press, newspapers, calculators and the removal of mandatory Latin from the curriculum.

In its fully developed form, the "webbed" knowledge system introduced here would be inclusive, not exclusive. Modern interactive networked communications systems married to astronomically large data storage capability ought to ensure that at times of change nothing need be lost. No subject or skill will be too arcane for its practitioners to pursue when the marketplace for their skills is planetwide.

Also, no external memory device from alphabet to laptop seems to have degraded human mental abilities by its introduction. Rather these abilities have been augmented each time by the new tools. Some skills, such as rote memory, become less widely used, but there seems to be no evidence that the capability for them disappears. In many cases machines also take over routine work, freeing individuals to use their skills at higher levels.

The latest interactive, semi-intelligent technologies seem likely to make this possible on an unprecedented scale. They also bring to an end a period of history in which the human brain was constrained by limited technology to operate in a less-than-optimal way, since the brain appears not to be designed to work best in the linear, discrete way promoted by reductionism. The average healthy brain has more than a hundred billion neurons, each communicating with others via thousands of dendrites. The number of potential ways for signals to

go in the system is said to be greater than the number of atoms in the universe. In matters as fundamental as recognition it seems that the brain uses some of its massive interconnectedness to call on many different processes at once to deal with events in the outside world, so as quickly to identify a potentially dangerous pattern of inputs.

It is this pattern-recognition capability that might prove to be the most useful attribute of a webbed knowledge system driven by the semi-intelligent interactive systems now being developed. As this book hopes to show, learning to identify the pattern of connections between ideas, people and events is the first step toward understanding the context and relevance of information. So the social implications of webbed knowledge systems are exciting, since they will make it easier for the average citizen to become informed of the relative value of innovation. After all, it is not necessary to understand the mathematics of radioactive decay to make a decision about where to site a nuclear power plant. As I hope you will see, this approach to knowledge may be one way to enfranchise those millions who lack what used to be called formal education and to move us toward more participatory forms of government.

I would not pretend that what follows is more than a first exercise, a number of linked storylines intended to introduce the reader to the kind of information infrastructures we may begin to use in the next few decades. But I hope they will introduce the reader to a new, more relevant way of looking at the world, because in one way or another, we're all connected.

JAMES BURKE
London 1999

How to Use
This Book

⊠

*T*he *Knowledge Web* takes ten different journeys across the great web of change. There are many different ways to read this book, just as there are many different ways to travel on a web. The simplest way is to read from start to finish, in the manner unchanged since the appearance of alphabetic writing thirty-five hundred years ago. Or you can read the book the way your teacher once told you not to. You can do this at many points throughout the book, when the timeline of a particular journey reaches a "gateway" on the web, where it crosses with the timeline of another, different journey. At such a gateway, you'll see the coordinates for the location of that other place.

Using the coordinates you may, if you choose, jump backward or forward (through literary subspace) to the other gateway, pick up the new timeline and continue your journey on the web, until you reach yet another gateway, when you may, if you choose, jump once again. The coordinates that identify a gateway appear in the text like this:

> This was the ducal seat of the Hamilton family and leased by Dr. John Roebuck,[17] a successful entrepreneur and ex-pupil of Black's.   **17** 36 *68*

In the text, "Roebuck,[17]" is the site of the seventeenth gateway so far. In the margin, "36 *68*" is the gateway you'll jump to (the thirty-sixth gateway, located on page 68).

Sometimes, there'll be multiple gateways you can jump to, at busy moments in history, where several pathways of change meet. Good luck!

Since there are 142 gateways here that cross, then in one sense, that means this book could conceivably be read at least 142 different ways. Though I don't suggest you try it, doing so would give you a rather visceral feeling for the way change happens.

And it happens that way to all of us, all the time. It's happening to you now, though you may not know it yet.

CHAPTER 1

⬡

Feedback

This book takes a journey across the vast, interconnected web of knowledge to offer a glimpse of what a learning experience might be like in the twenty-first century once we have solved the problem of information overload.

In the past when technology generated information overload the contemporary reaction was much the same as it is today. On the first appearance of paper in the medieval West, the English bishop Samson of St. Alban's complained that because paper would be cheaper than animal-skin parchment people would use paper to write too many words of too little value, and since paper was not as durable as parchment, paper-based knowledge would in the long run decay and be lost. When the printing press was developed in the fifteenth century it was said that printed books would make reading and writing "the infatuation of people who have no business reading and writing." Samuel Morse's development of the telegraph promised to link places as far apart as Maine and Texas, triggering the reaction: "What have Maine and Texas to say to each other?" The twentieth-century proliferation of television channels has led to concerns about "dumbing-down."

The past perception that new information technologies would have a destabilizing social effect led to the imposition of controls on their use. Only a few ancient Egyptian administrators were permitted to learn the skills of penmanship. Medieval European paper manu-

facture was strictly licensed. The output of sixteenth-century printing presses was subject to official censorship by both church and
state. The new seventeenth-century libraries were not open to the
public. Nineteenth-century European telegraphs and telephones
came under the control of government ministries.

The problem of past information overload has generally been of
concern only to a small number of literate administrators and their
semiliterate masters. In contrast, twenty-first-century petabyte lap-
tops and virtually free access to the Internet may bring destabilizing
effects of information overload that will operate on a scale and at a
rate well beyond anything that has happened before. In the next few
decades hundreds of millions of new users will have no experience in
searching the immense amount of available data and very little training in what to do with it. Information abundance will stress society
in ways for which it has not been prepared and damage centralized
social systems designed to function in a nineteenth-century world.

Part of the answer to the problem may be an information-filtering
system customized to suit the individual. The most promising of the
systems now being developed will guide users through the complex
and exciting world of information without their getting lost. This
book provides an opportunity for the reader to take a practice run on
such a journey. The journey (the book) begins and ends with the in-
1 142 262 vention of the guidance system itself—the semi-intelligent agent.[1]

There are several types of agent in existence acting like personal
secretaries in a variety of simple ways: filtering genuine e-mail from
spam, running a diary, paying bills and selecting entertainment. In
the near future agents will organize and conduct almost every aspect
of the individual's life. Above all they will journey across the knowledge webs to retrieve information, then process and present it in
ways customized to suit the user. In time they will act on behalf of
their user because they will have learned his or her preferences by
learning from the user's daily requirements.

In the search to develop semi-intelligent agents, one of the most
promising systems (and the one which starts this journey) may be
the neural network. Such a network consists of a number of cells
each reacting to signals from a number of other cells that in turn fire

22

their signals in reaction to input from yet other cells. If input signals cause one cell to fire more frequently than others, its input to the next cell in the series will be given greater weighting. Since cells are programmed to react preferentially to input from cells that fire frequently rather than from those that fire rarely, the system "learns" from experience. This is thought to be similar to the way learning operates in the human brain, where the repetition of a signal generated in response to a specific experience can cause enlargement in the brain cell's synapses.

The synapse is the part of the cell that releases transmitter chemicals that cross the gap to the next cell. If sufficient chemicals arrive on the other side, they generate an impulse. If enough of these signals are generated in the target cell, they cause its synapses to release chemicals in turn, and "pass the message on." A cell with larger synapses, releasing larger amounts of chemical, is therefore more likely to cause another cell to fire. Networks of such frequently firing cells may constitute the building blocks of memory.

This theory of neuronal interaction was first proposed in 1943 by two American researchers, Walter Pitts and Warren McCulloch, who also suggested that such a feedback process might result in purposive behavior when linking the senses with the brain and muscles if the result of the interaction were to cause the muscles to act to reduce the difference between a condition in the real world as perceived by the senses and the condition as desired by the brain.

Pitts and McCulloch belonged to a small group of researchers calling itself the "Teleological Society," another of whose members was the man who invented the name for this neural feedback process. He was Norbert Wiener, and he was the first to see the way in which feedback might work in a machine, during his research on antiaircraft artillery systems during World War II. Wiener was a rotund, irascible, cigar-chomping MIT professor of math who prowled what he described as the "frontier areas" between the scientific disciplines. Between biology and engineering Wiener developed a new discipline to deal with feedback processes. He called the new discipline "cyber- [2] 141 262 netics."[2] Wiener recognized that feedback devices are information-processing systems receiving information and acting upon it. When

applied to the brain this new information-oriented view was a fundamental shift away from the entirely biological paradigm that had ruled neurophysiology since Freud, and it was to affect all artificial-intelligence work from then on.

Wiener first applied his feedback theory early in World War II, when he and a young engineer named Julian Bigelow were asked to improve the artillery hit rate. At the beginning of the war the problem facing antiaircraft gunners was that as the speed of targets increased (thanks to advances in engine and airframe technology) it became necessary to be able to fire a shell some distance ahead of a fast-moving target in order to hit it. Automating this process involved a large number of variables: wind, temperature, humidity, gunpowder charge, length of gun barrel, speed and height of target, and many others. Wiener used continuous input from radar tracking systems to establish the recent path of the target and use that path to predict what the target's likely position would be in the immediate future. This information would then be fed to the gun-moving mechanisms so that aiming-off was continually updated.

The system had its most outstanding successes in 1944, when British and American gunners shot down German flying bombs with fewer than one hundred rounds per hit. This was an extraordinary advance over previous performance, estimated at one hit per twenty-five hundred rounds. In 1944, during the last four weeks of German V-1 missile attacks on England, the success rate improved dramatically. In the first week, 24 percent of targets were destroyed; in the second, 46 percent; in the third, 67 percent; and in the fourth, 79 percent. The last day on which a large number of V-1s were launched at Britain, 104 of the missiles were detected by early-warning radar, but only four reached London. Antiaircraft artillery destroyed sixty-eight of them.

Early in his work on the artillery project Wiener had frequent discussions with a young physiologist named Arturo Rosenbleuth, who was interested in human feedback mechanisms that act to ensure precision in bodily movement. For the previous fifteen years Rosenbleuth had worked closely with Walter Cannon, professor of physiology at Harvard. Earlier in the century Cannon had invented the

barium meal, which was opaque to X-rays. When ingested by a goose the barium revealed the peristaltic waves that occurred in the bird's stomach when it was hungry. Cannon observed that hunger seemed to precipitate the onset of these waves. He then observed that when a hungry animal was frightened the waves stopped.

This led to Cannon's ground-breaking studies of the physical effects of emotion. He discovered that when an animal was disturbed its sympathetic nervous system secreted into the bloodstream a chemical that Cannon named "sympathin." This chemical counteracted the effects of the disturbance and returned the animal's body systems to a state of balance. Cannon named the balancing process "homeostasis." In 1915 Cannon discovered that the principal body changes affected by the sympathetic system were those involved in fight, sexual activity or flight. In such situations sugar flowed from the liver to provide emergency energy and blood shifted from the abdomen to the heart, lungs and limbs. If the body were wounded, blood clotting occurred more rapidly than usual. In 1932 Cannon published a full-scale account of his research titled *The Wisdom of the Body*.

What had initially triggered Cannon's interest in homeostatic mechanisms was the work of the man to whom Cannon dedicated the French edition of his book. He was an unprepossessing but eminent French physiologist named Claude Bernard, who had started his working life as a pharmacist's assistant in Beaujolais, where his father owned a small vineyard. After being forced to give up his early schooling for lack of funds, Bernard took up writing plays. He produced first a comedy and then a five-act play, which he took to Paris in 1834 with the intention of making a career in the theater. Fortunately for the future health of humankind Bernard was introduced to an eminent theatrical critic, Saint-Marc Girardin, who read the play and advised Bernard to take up medicine.

At first Bernard planned to be a surgeon, but becoming dissatisfied with the general lack of physiological data he began to gather his own data by experimenting on animals. By 1839 his dexterity in dissection had brought him to the attention of the great physiologist François Magendie, who appointed him as assistant. One winter

morning in 1846 some rabbits were brought to Magendie's lab for dissection and Bernard noticed that their urine was clear and acidic. As every nineteenth-century French winemaker knew, the urine of rabbits is usually turbid and alkaline. Bernard realized that the rabbits had not been fed and theorized that since the urine of carnivores is clear, the hungry, herbivorous rabbits must have been living on their fat. When he fed grass to the rabbits their urine returned to its normal alkaline turbidity. He double-checked with an experiment on himself. After twenty-four hours subsisting only on potatoes, cauliflower, carrots, green peas, salad, and fruit, Bernard's own urine went turbid and alkaline. Bernard then starved the rabbits, fed them boiled beef and dissected them to find out what had happened. He saw a milklike substance (he took it to be emulsified fat) that had formed at the point where the rabbit's pancreatic juice was pouring into the stomach. There was clearly some link between the juice and the emulsification of the fats.

Two years later he discovered the glycogenic function of the liver, which injects glucose into the blood. It was this discovery that led to Bernard's greatest contribution to the sum of human knowledge, because he saw that the function of the liver and the pancreas (and perhaps other systems, too) was to maintain the body's equilibrium. He summed up his research: "All the vital mechanisms, however varied they may be, have only one object, that of preserving constant the conditions of life in the inner environment." Follow-up research on the pancreas led an English researcher, William Bayliss, to coin the phrase that Cannon would use as his book title: "the wisdom of the body."

Not everybody was happy with Bernard's work, especially when he designed an oven in which to cook animals alive. An American doctor, Francis Donaldson, who attended Bernard's lectures in 1851, wrote: "It was curious to see walking about the amphitheater of the College of France dogs and rabbits, unconscious contributors to science, with five or six orifices in their bodies from which at a moment's warning, there could be produced any secretion of the body, including that of the several salivary glands, the stomach, the liver, and the pancreas."

Bernard was well aware of public opposition to vivisection but defended it: "The science of life is like a superb salon resplendent with light which one can enter only through a long and ghastly kitchen." Alas, Bernard's wife was unable to take the heat. After leaving him in 1869 she went in search of the antivivisection activists to whom she had been sending regular contributions.

She did not have far to go. In Paris a fanatical young vegetarian Englishwoman named Anna Kingsford, the owner of the *Lady's Own Paper*, had come to France to study medicine. Kingsford became well-known at the medical school for refusing to let her professors vivisect during the lessons she attended and for demonstrating against the practice. Kingsford's lecture halls were close to Bernard's labs, and she became so obsessed by his work that she set about directing all her energies toward killing him with thought waves. Bernard died only few weeks after she had begun to concentrate her mental energies on him, convincing her that she had been the instrument of divine will. Kingsford also claimed to have been responsible for the death of another vivisector, Paul Bert. However her efforts to do the same to Louis Pasteur[3] failed.

Legislation to protect animals from ill treatment took a long time to reach the statute books, even in England, where the first such laws were passed. In 1800 the first bill to outlaw bull-baiting had ignominiously failed in its passage though the Houses of Parliament, opposed by George Canning (later prime minister), who claimed that bull-baiting "inspired courage and produced a nobleness of sentiment and elevation of mind. . . . Putting a stop to bull-baiting was legislating against the spirit and genius of almost every country and age." However, in 1821 Dick Martin, MP for Galway, forced through a bill to protect horses and cattle against ill treatment. It was the first law of its kind in any country. In 1824 the Society for the Prevention of Cruelty to Animals was formed at the unfortunately named Old Slaughter Coffee House in London. The publication in 1859 of Darwin's[4] *Origin of Species* seemed to strengthen the relationship between humans and animals and support the animal-defense argument. In 1876 the Victoria Street Society against Vivisection was formed with Lord Shaftesbury as chairman. The same year a bill was

3 54 *114*
3 125 *235*

4 72 *143*
4 74 *145*

passed to prevent the vivisection of dogs, cats, mules, horses and asses. By the late nineteenth century the animal-defense movement had spread throughout the Western world and given birth to hundreds of local groups known as Humane Societies, in spite of the fact that the name more properly belonged to earlier humanitarian work of an entirely different nature.

5 133 251   The Royal Humane Society[5] was founded in London in 1774 largely as the result of the efforts of Dr. William Hawes to promote knowledge of artificial-respiration techniques. Hawes based his ideas on the translation of a paper by the Amsterdam Society for the Recovery of the Apparently Drowned. The society had been founded in 1767 after several cases of successful resuscitation had been reported in Switzerland. In the nineteenth century interest in drowning became acute with the spectacular increase in cargo tonnage and passenger traffic on the high seas following the spread of industrialization. As the number of ships rose so did the number of shipwrecks and deaths.

From time to time the Royal Humane Society awarded a gold medallion for outstanding feats of bravery, and in 1838 the recipient hit the front pages because she was a slightly built, twenty-two-year-old woman. On the night of February 6, a paddle steamer, the *Forfarshire*, battling through a gale en route from Hull to Dundee with a full cargo and sixty-three passengers, sprang a leak in her boiler. The captain decided to take shelter among the Farne Islands off the coast of Northumberland. During this maneuver the ship hit the rocks and broke in two, and all but thirteen passengers and crew were drowned. The survivors, exposed to the full force of the storm, included a mother and two children. Overnight the two children and an adult died. At five o'clock the next morning Grace Darling, daughter of the local lighthouse keeper, caught sight of the wreck and the survivors clinging to the rocks. Grace and her father rowed to the rescue, struggling through mountainous sea in a small open boat. The drama was reported in the newspapers and Grace became an instant national hero. Alas, she was to die four years later from tuberculosis. Meantime she had inspired the public to offer massive fi-

Fig. 1: *Henry Greathead's "Original," in 1890 the first purpose-built, oars-only lifeboat designed without a rudder to be steered either way.*

nancial and political support for the eventual establishment of the Royal National Lifeboat Institution, in 1854.

That same year came another highly publicized loss at sea. The USS *San Francisco*, an American troopship carrying hundreds of soldiers, foundered in an Atlantic hurricane. The secretary of the navy sent for Matthew Maury,[6] the only man in America who would be able to tell where to look for survivors. After studying his wind and current charts, Maury pinpointed the spot and the survivors were found in the water.

6 31 63

Maury was the fourth son of a Huguenot-English family long settled in Virginia (his grandfather had taught Thomas Jefferson), and he had joined the U.S. Navy in 1825. It was during a voyage to South America that Maury became interested in finding faster ways to cross the ocean. On his return in 1834 he took leave and wrote his first work on navigation. In 1839 Maury published a series of articles in the *Southern Literary Messenger,* one of which advocated the establishment of a naval school. It would become the U.S. Naval Academy at Annapolis.

In 1847 Maury issued the first of several charts and then, in 1851, *Explanations and Sailing Directions to Accompany the Wind and Current Charts.* At the instigation of the U.S. government, copies of the

charts and *Sailing Directions* were distributed free to all masters of vessels on the understanding that they would keep a full log of journeys and forward these logs to Maury, in Washington. Logs were to include temperature of air and water, direction of wind and currents, and air pressure. Captains were also required to throw overboard (at given intervals) a bottle containing a piece of paper carrying the ship's position and the date. They were also to pick up any such bottles they came across and note all details in their logs. In return for these services masters would receive free copies of Maury's further work. Over eight years Maury collected and processed data on many millions of observations, as a result of which he was able to identify faster sailing routes. One ship's master following Maury's suggested route from New York to Rio de Janeiro halved the usual journey time. It was reckoned that Maury's "Path-of-Minimum-Time" routes saved American shipping forty million dollars a year.

In 1853 Maury crowned his career when he persuaded sixteen countries (among them the United States, Britain, Belgium, Holland, 7 28 57 Russia, France, Norway, Denmark and Portugal) to meet in Brussels[7] for the first International Meteorological Congress "to plan an uniform system of meteorological observation at sea, and to agree a plan for the observation of the winds and currents of the oceans with a view to improving navigation and to enrich our knowledge of the laws which govern those elements." Not long after he had returned from Brussels, Maury received a letter from a retired paper- 8 31 63 manufacturing millionaire named Cyrus W. Field,[8] who was seeking advice on the ideal route for a transatlantic submarine telegraph cable.

Submarine cables had already been laid successfully in the relatively shallow waters between England and Holland, Scotland and Ireland, but the Atlantic represented a formidable challenge. Field had managed to get a favorable charter from the British government for a fifty-year monopoly on any cable laid between Newfoundland and Ireland. The British also offered to provide a cable-laying ship as well as a generous advance on income from telegraph messages. Field then spent two years laying a cable between Newfoundland and the North American mainland (stockholders in the company in-

Feedback

cluded such luminaries as Lady Byron and Thackeray). When the link was completed Field wrote to Maury to solicit his views on the best route out of Newfoundland toward Europe.

Maury reported that soundings revealed a shallow "telegraph plateau" across much of the North Atlantic, and in 1857 work began on laying the cable. After a few hundred miles had been laid the cable snapped. Three more attempts were made and on August 5, 1858, 1,850 miles of copper wire connected Valencia, Ireland, with Trinity Bay, Newfoundland, and traffic began with an inaugural message from Queen Victoria to President Buchanan. At the celebration dinner in New York Field said modestly: "Maury furnished the brains, England gave the money, and I did the work." Then the cable failed again. In 1865 they found the parted ends, spliced them and the work was done. The U.S. Congress voted Field a gold medal.

Field had also written to the man whose work had inspired the whole venture: Samuel Morse,[9] inventor of the most successful form of telegraph. Morse's advantages over other telegraphers were his key and the Morse Code, which he demonstrated before Congress in 1844. The idea had come to him in the autumn of 1832 during a voyage back to the United States from France. Morse first learned what he needed to know about the principles of electricity and one of his friends, Alfred Vail, provided the finance and hardware (Vail's father had a machine shop in New Jersey). Vail also suggested what would later become known as the Morse Code.

At this time Morse was a well-known artist, professor of art at New York University, and had just spent three years in Europe studying and painting. Morse was a strange man given to apocalyptic patriotic views. He had been brought up as a strict Calvinist by his father Jedidiah, America's foremost geography scholar, who had earlier led the Old Calvinist "Great Awakening" crusade against liberal theology. Like his father, Morse looked forward to the triumph of American culture and believed that only an elite could lead the country to salvation. Morse was also extremely xenophobic. At one point he painted a picture of the pope conspiring to arm American Catholics, provoke disorder, rig elections and elect foreigners to public office. Morse also helped publish a book about Maria Monk, a woman who

9 32 64

31

claimed to have been a nun in Montreal, where she also claimed to have witnessed unnatural sexual acts performed by clergy and to have seen crypts filled with the corpses of illegitimate children. In the end it was revealed that Monk (rumored to have had a romantic affair with Morse) had escaped from a mental institution.

Morse believed that art was a tool placed in his hands by God to be used to save Protestant America. He believed that the millennium was imminent, and that when it came America would carry the empire of peace to the world. It was therefore essential to prepare American art for the great day. Morse founded the National Academy of Arts and Design in 1826 and was its president until 1845. The aim of the academy was to foster American artistic talent so that American genius could take its rightful place in the world and inculcate true Protestant virtues in other Americans.

In 1829 Morse decided to visit Europe to study artistic masterworks in preparation for what he hoped would be his greatest triumph, the commission to paint the four remaining murals for the Rotunda of the Capitol Building in Washington D.C. To this end, while in Paris in 1831, he painted the giant *Gallery of the Louvre*. The painting reproduced in miniature thirty-eight Louvre masterpieces. Morse's aim was to show that while the classical past was worthy of study it should not be the subject of slavish emulation by American artists, who, like the artist shown in the *Louvre* painting (Morse himself), could learn from the Old Masters and then develop their own distinctively American style. On his return the *Louvre* painting was put on exhibition in New York and was a disastrous flop. The commission for the Rotunda murals went to other artists. Morse turned to the telegraph as an alternative tool with which to make Protestant America great. Communications technology would be an instrument of Divine Will, redeeming America by transmitting messages of peace and love. At his demonstration in Congress in 1844 Morse's first transmitted message echoed these beliefs: "What hath God wrought!"

Morse had learned his art at the feet of Washington Allston, the most completely Romantic American painter, whom he had met in Boston in 1810 and with whom he became life-long friends. Only a

year after their meeting Allston inspired Morse to attempt the first of his grand historical American scenes, *Landing of the Pilgrims at Plymouth*. That same year Morse joined Allston and his wife on his first trip to Europe. Allston was a good-looking Harvard-educated gentleman from South Carolina who on the death of his step-father in 1801 had sold the family property to finance a career in painting. On his earlier visit to London Allston had studied with Benjamin West, the president of the Royal Academy, and then in 1804 moved on via Paris to Rome. There he met Washington Irving, who later wrote: "I do not think I have ever been more completely captivated on a first acquaintance. He was of a light and graceful form, with large blue eyes, and black, silken hair waving and curling around a pale, expressive countenance. A young man's intimacy took place immediately between us, and we were much together during my brief sojourn at Rome. . . . We visited together some of the finest collections of paintings, and he taught me how to visit them to the most advantage, guiding me always to the masterpieces, and passing by the others without notice." Allston's *Italian Landscape* shows the profound effect of Italy on his work. His fresh New England eye was overwhelmed by the light, the color, the ancient ruins, the landscape dotted with hilltop villages, the rich mingling of Renaissance, medieval and classical architecture and the pastoral nature of Italian peasant life.

In 1805 Allston met and painted the English Romantic poet Samuel Taylor Coleridge, whom he would later recognize as his greatest intellectual mentor. At the time of their meeting Coleridge was suffering the aftereffects of his failure to give up opium. Aged thirty-three, with "Kubla Khan" and the "Ancient Mariner" poems behind him, Coleridge was already famous. He was also an alcoholic, deeply in debt, unhappily married with three children, had failed in a venture to set up a utopian settlement on the banks of the Susquehanna in Pennsylvania, and was extremely hypochondriac (he coined the word "psychosomatic").

It was partly to try to wean himself from opium (and his penchant for taking it in brandy), and partly to get away from his wife, that in 1804 Coleridge had run away to Malta. There, thanks to an influential acquaintance, he landed the job of secretary to the British civil

commissioner, Alexander Ball. The post also included free food and accommodation in the commissioner's palace in Valetta, the island's capital. Coleridge's workload was light and consisted principally of rewriting Ball's dispatches to London. Although Coleridge complained incessantly about his health, the nightmare of withdrawal symptoms, the dull company and his inability to write new poems, he enjoyed the climate and the countryside and managed to produce some of his best prose. He also began to feel the first stirrings of mortality: "I had felt the Truth; but never saw it before clearly; it came upon me at Malta, under the melancholy dreadful feeling of finding myself to be Man, by a distinct division from Boyhood, Youth, 'Young Man.' Dreadful was the feeling—before that, life had flown on so that I had always been a Boy, as it were—and this sensation had blended in all my conduct." When his friends William and Mary Wordsworth saw him on his return to England, they were to remark that he had changed for the worse.

Coleridge saw from the dispatches he was editing that he had arrived in Malta at a critical time. Ball was arguing the strategic importance of the island now that Napoleon[10] had given up Louisiana,[11] lost Santo Domingo and would inevitably turn his attention to the Mediterranean. Ball also suggested to the British government that Algiers, Tunis and Tripoli were ripe for colonization and "they are capable of growing all our colonial produce." He also argued that though both Russia and France wanted Malta they should not be allowed to take it. At the time, the island was a hotbed of intrigue. The Maltese were agitating for independence, Russian and French spies were imagined to be everywhere and there was an American naval squadron on station commanded by Commodore Edward Preble. Among Preble's officers was the young Stephen Decatur,[12] leader of the daring and successful 1804 raid on Tripoli harbor to destroy the American frigate *Philadelphia,* which had run aground and been captured during the American-Tripolitanian War. During a brief trip to Sicily Coleridge met and dined with both intrepid Americans, and for years later regaled friends with tales of their exploits.

Coleridge's employer, Rear Admiral Alexander Ball, had joined the British Navy at the age of twelve. This event, he told Coleridge, had

10 43 78
10 59 120
10 112 212
11 67 139

12 61 123

been inspired by reading *Robinson Crusoe*. Ball had the air more of an academic than a sailor, bookish and thoughtful. After serving in the Caribbean, America and Newfoundland, in 1783 he took a year off and went to France to study the language. At one point there, during a visit to St. Omer, he met another young captain with whom his fate was to be bound up, in spite of the fact that on this occasion each expected the other to make the required formal call, so neither did so. Ball then served in the English Channel, went again to Newfoundland, was stationed off the French Coast and in 1798 was posted to the Mediterranean where he was to meet the young captain with whom he had failed to exchange courtesies in St. Omer. At this time Britain was expecting to be invaded by Napoleon, and much of the British fleet was patrolling outside French harbors in the English Channel and on the French Atlantic coast. Hearing a rumor that Napoleon was assembling a Mediterranean fleet in Toulon, the British also sent a fleet to blockade that port.

In April the Toulon blockade fleet fleet was joined by a small squadron under the command of the man Ball had met in France, Captain (by now Admiral) Horatio Nelson, the fastest-rising star in the British Navy. No sooner had Nelson's squadron arrived off Toulon than it was blown south and scattered by a ferocious gale. Off the coast of Sardinia Nelson's flagship lost its mainmast as well as much of its rigging and was being driven by mountainous seas toward a rocky coast. At the last minute Ball brought his own ship alongside, took Nelson's flagship in tow in spite of Nelson's orders to the contrary and saved the day. The captain of the flagship later reported that Ball used his speaking trumpet to call "with great solemnity and without the least disturbance of temper . . . 'I feel confident that I can bring you in safe. I therefore must not, and by the help of Almighty God will not leave you.'" After the rescue Ball was mentioned in dispatches and the two men remained close friends for the rest of Nelson's brief life.

Meanwhile Napoleon's fleet had taken advantage of the situation to slip out of Toulon and head for Egypt. On the way there Napoleon sent a detachment to capture Malta. Ball was now dispatched (with Nelson's influential approval) to retake the island. After a two-year

35

Fig. 2: *The great British hero Admiral Lord Nelson, who was killed by a French sniper at the Battle of Trafalgar, aged forty-seven.*

siege he did so and was appointed commissioner. Nelson himself caught up with Napoleon at the Battle of the Nile, where he defeated the French, and then sailed back to Naples for repairs. In Naples Nelson would fall in love for the fifth time (after the daughter of Quebec's provost marshal, a clergyman's daughter, the wife of the commissioner of Antigua, and Fanny Nisbet, niece of the president of the St. Nevis Council). In 1787, Fanny had become Nelson's wife, to the chagrin of his colleagues, one of whom remarked that Fanny had two remarkable attributes: her good complexion and a "remarkable absence of intellectual endowment."

Ten years after the marriage the heroic Nelson arrived in Naples. He was Europe's unlikeliest heart-throb: he was thirty-eight, short, plump, white-haired, with a squeaky voice and Norfolk accent, blind in the right eye and with a stump for a left arm. He was in the habit

of introducing himself: "I am Lord Nelson and this [gesturing to his good arm] is his fin."

The object of Nelson's Neapolitan infatuation (and later, while her husband was still alive, his mistress and later still mother of his two children) was a thirty-three-year-old married Englishwoman with a hidden past and the habit of wearing no underwear. Lady Emma Hamilton was the wife of Sir William Hamilton,[13] the sixty-seven-year-old English minister to the Court of Naples. In 1785 Hamilton had, so to speak, taken Emma over from his impecunious nephew Greville to clear the decks for the latter's impending marriage into a rich family. Emma was not told of the arrangement, merely that she would be living in Naples for six months until Greville could return for her. Nine months later, realizing that Greville was not coming, Emma gave in to the widower Hamilton and they became lovers.

To please Emma, Hamilton arranged singing and music lessons, trips to the newly excavated ruins of Pompeii and Herculaneum, rides up Vesuvius and a series of *conversazioni* at which Emma was introduced to the local nobility and the Neapolitan royal family. Soon she had become famous for her "entertainments," in which she posed, diapahanously dressed, in various classical tableaux: Agrippina scattering the ashes of Germanicus, Orestes sacrificing his sister, Oedipus blinded, and (very popular) the Bacchante "surprised while bathing." In 1791 Hamilton returned briefly to England to marry Emma. The couple then returned to Naples where Hamilton continued "collecting" antiques from archeological sites to sell in London, where his Greek and Roman vases would inspire the potter Josiah Wedgwood and help kick off the Neoclassical[14] movement.

In the light of Emma's past, her marriage to Hamilton made quite a furor. Emma had begun life as Emma Lyon, daughter of a humble smith. Brought up in Wales, at the age of twelve she was already employed as a nursemaid. A year later Emma was in London, maid to Mrs. Kelly, a well-known madame, and soon thereafter became one of Mrs. Kelly's "girls." By the age of sixteen she was living with a "protector," Harry Featherstonehaugh, who then passed her on to William Hamilton's nephew, Greville.

In London Emma was also rumored to have been employed as a "maiden" at Dr. James Graham's wildly fashionable Temple of Health, where patrons, including the duchess of Devonshire, were given electric shocks and served by transparently dressed "attendants." Graham's Temple was an elaborately decorated Adam house in The Adelphi, London. The fencing master to George IV later recalled "carriages drawing up next to the door of this modern Paphos, with crowds of gaping sparks on either side, to discover who were the visitors, but the ladies' faces were covered, all going incognito. At the door stood two gigantic porters, with each a long staff, with ornamental silver head, like those borne by parish beadles, and wearing superb liveries, with large, gold-laced cocked hats, each was near seven feet in height, and retained to keep the entrance clear." Entering under an enormous gold star, Graham's clients found themselves in lavishly decorated rooms with stained-glass windows. Music played and perfume drifted on the air. In these salubrious surroundings the elite were treated with medications including Nervous Aetherial Balsam, Electrical Aether and Imperial Pills. The star of the show had been made for Graham by an expert tinsmith. It was the Magnetico-Electrico Celestial Bed, on which childless couples would receive electrical shocks while coupling. The shocks were said to ensure immediate conception.

15 134 251 Graham may have derived his interest in electricity from conversations with Benjamin Franklin[15] in Paris in 1779 when he met Franklin during the latter's time as U.S. minister to France. Electricity was the subject of much speculative experimentation at the time. In 1720 the Englishman Stephen Grey had electrified a small, suspended boy. In 1743 Johann Kruger, professor at Helmstadt University, had suggested that passing an "effluvium" of electricity through the body might be good for the health. Christian Ratzenstein claimed electric shocks raised the pulse rate and increased the circulation of the blood. Samuel Quellmaltz said he had used electricity to cure paralysis of the hand well enough for his patient to play the klavier. Even such respectable persons as John Wesley recommended electric treatment for nervous disorders. In 1777 an electrical machine was

ordered for St Bartholemew's Hospital in London. Graham is often described as a quack, but in an age when much medicine was still guesswork and mumbo-jumbo, he may have been no worse than anybody else. Besides, he had received his training at Edinburgh University, site of the best medical school in Britain, where he attended lectures by the great Joseph Black.

Black was a high-flier who had made his international reputation by the age of twenty-seven, when in 1755 he published a paper on an experiment in which he had heated limestone and caused it to become caustic quicklime. The value of this particular bit of research was that all contemporary treatments for kidney stone, common at the time, involved caustics. Up to then it had been thought that quicklime acquired its causticity from the fire. Black proved otherwise and changed the course of chemistry. He found that quicklime was made when a gas in the limestone was driven out by the heat; and that this gas could be recombined with quicklime to form limestone once again. Moreover, this combining and recombining process could be continued without limit. Each time the volume and weight of the relevant components were exactly the same.

The other world-changing discovery by Black came as a result of his investigation into the process of distillation. The Scottish whisky manufacturers' market had expanded rapidly since the union of Scotland with England in 1707, and distillers were keen to find ways of getting more whisky for less cost, so Black was concentrating his researches on finding ways to save fuel. His experiments on the amount of heat required to boil off liquids revealed the existence of latent heat, which explained the extremely high temperature of steam and why the distillers needed such copious quantities of cold water to condense it.

The latent heat discovery also showed James Watt[16] (who worked at the University of Glasgow when Black was teaching there) why the Newcomen steam-driven pump was so inefficient. In the pump (one of which Watt was repairing at the time) steam entered a cylinder kept ice-cold with a water jacket. This caused the steam entering the cylinder immediately to condense, creating a partial vacuum and al-

16 37 *68*
16 139 *259*

lowing air pressure to force the cylinder piston down. The piston rod was attached to one end of a pivoted beam set above the cylinder. As the piston moved down the other end of the beam moved up, lifting a rod attached to a suction pump. The problem was that the high temperature of the steam was heating the cylinder too much and weakening the subsequent condensing process on each stroke until the cylinder became so hot that no condensation would take place and the pumping action would stop. Black showed Watt that the cylinder would have to be linked to a separate, chilled condensing chamber (immersed in cold water) so that the scaldingly hot steam could condense there and not heat the cylinder while doing so. This separate condenser was the secret of Watt's success.

Through his association with Black in 1769 Watt was able to carry out some of his key experiments at Kinneil House, outside Edinburgh. This was the ducal seat of the Hamilton family and leased **17** 36 *68* by Dr. John Roebuck,[17] a successful entrepreneur and ex-pupil of Black's. Roebuck owned a coal mine that supplied his Carron ironworks, and since the coal mine was subject to flooding, his hope was that a successful Watt pump might save it. In the event the mine flooded early and drove Roebuck to bankruptcy, but not before he had helped finance Watt's research by paying off his debts in exchange for a percentage of Watt's patent rights on the steam pump. When bankruptcy intervened in 1772 Roebuck sold his share of **18** 38 *68* Watt's patent to Matthew Boulton,[18] a shoe-buckle manufacturer in **18** 97 *178* Birmingham, and Watt finally met the partner he needed. Together Boulton and Watt turned the steam pump into the engine of the Industrial Revolution.

Meanwhile, Roebuck had already made his own contribution to industry with a new process for the manufacture of sulphuric acid. Not long after graduation he had invented an improvement in refining precious metals. This process used sulphuric acid, and in 1749 Roebuck set up a new sulphuric acid manufacturing facility at Prestonpans, near Edinburgh. The earlier manufacturing technique had involved burning sulphur and niter over water and condensing the acid from the fumes in glass globes. Roebuck replaced the glass

globes with small lead chambers and quartered the manufacturing costs.

The market for sulphuric acid was growing steadily as the textile industry became more mechanized. By 1760 John Kay's flying shuttle was in general use, doubling the output of weft threads. Nearly ten years later James Hargreaves's spinning jenny multiplied the number of weft thread spindles that could be worked by one spinner. Richard Arkwright's 1769 water frame drew out the weft thread on mechanically rotating cylinders, and in 1779 Samuel Crompton's mule combined the jenny and the frame to complete the mechanization of the entire process. The mule produced thread fine enough for the best muslin cottons. By this time the market for cotton was booming, quadrupling raw cotton imports between 1791 and 1800.

The growth of cotton manufacture triggered a consequent rise in the demand for bleach. Before Roebuck's new system traditional bleaching of cloth (to rid it of its natural gray-yellow color) had been done in bleachfields. Between March and September the cloth to be bleached was stretched out, doused with fermented milk and left for six weeks to whiten. Roebuck's cheap, diluted sulphuric acid would do the same job in twenty-four hours. In 1785 the French chemist C. L. Berthollet had discovered that chlorine gas was a powerful bleaching agent, and James Watt introduced its use in Scotland. Cloth to be bleached was hung in gas-filled rooms, where bleachers sometimes died from the effects of breathing the gas. Then in 1799 Charles Tennant passed the gas over slaked lime and produced the first safe, cheap bleaching powder.

As an almost immediate result white paper became common. Before this, as can be seen from the gray tinge of English paper and the muddy color of early American documents, the color of paper depended on the rags from which it was made. Paper was made by pounding rags to a pulp, leaving them in water to ferment, pounding them again, then straining out the water on a vibrating wire mesh belt, and finally drying it by rolling the pulp between felt cloths and

heated rollers. The first version of this process was invented by a Frenchman, Louis Robert, in 1799. The width of the paper made by his machine was that required for wallpaper, the fastest-growing furnishing accessory in Europe at the time. The Paris *Journal des Inventions* reported: "For the view, the cleanliness, the freshness and the elegance, these papers are preferable to the rich materials of the past; they do not allow any access to insects, and when they are varnished, they retain all the vivacity and charm of their colours for a long time. Finally, they can be changed very frequently . . . making us thus inclined to renovate our homes, cleaning them more often and making them gayer and more attractive."

When Robert's paper-making venture failed for lack of financial support in France he sold the patent to his erstwhile employer, Didot Leger. Didot's English brother-in-law John Gamble[19] then took it to Britain, where the paper-making brothers Fourdrinier set up the first fully operational version of Robert's process at their mill in Frogmore, near London, in 1808. In 1836, when the British government repealed the high wallpaper tax, mass production began. In 1839 Harold Potter of the Darwen wallpaper factory perfected a power-driven roller printer. By 1850 machines were able to print perfectly registered patterns in eight colors on fifty-four thousand feet of paper a day. The effect on the wallpaper industry between 1834 and 1860 was to increase output from a million to nine million yards. Prices dropped like a stone. What had been a luxury item was now available to all but the very poor.

An Englishman named William Morris used the new manufacturing and printing techniques to put wallpaper into the homes of the industrial middle class for the first time. Morris was a well-off Oxford graduate influenced like others of his age by the social conditions of industrial-age Britain. In the mid nineteenth century government surveys were beginning to reveal the scale of social problems that had been created by the rapid industrialization of the previous decades and exacerbated by overcrowded living conditions and the widening gulf between the rich factory owners and their disfranchised, poverty-stricken workers. Morris and his friends turned away

19 113 *213*

from the horrors of the cities to medieval art and architecture. For them the Middle Ages represented an age of innocence when the craftsman had been an independent, creative spirit, free to take his skills wherever he chose, protected from exploitation by professional guilds.

Morris led the new Arts and Crafts movement dedicated to bringing this medieval sweetness and light to urban homes. From 1877 his company showrooms in Oxford Street displayed "traditional" furniture, tapestries and wallpaper with simple floral patterns based on medieval designs. The style revolutionized public taste. One social commentator wrote: "It may be questioned whether the decorative treatment of the walls should give place to pictures in rooms which are occupied from day to day. If we imagine the tired man of business returning to his suburban home . . . it can hardly be supposed that he will be in a position to make the special mental effort involved in inspecting his pictures; but supposing him to be the happy possessor of a harmoniously decorated room, he will at once be soothed and charmed by its very atmosphere."

Morris took his artistic views into his political life. The utopian spirit of his art was mirrored by socialist beliefs that drove him to what he called "holy warfare" against capitalism. From 1877 he gave a series of lectures to working men in which he attacked the values of Victorian society. In 1883 he joined the Democratic Federation, inspired by Marx's views on the alienation of industrial workers. Morris sold the federation's weekly paper, *Justice,* on the streets, and joined its executive committee together with Marx's daughter, Eleanor. In 1884 he broke with the federation (when it proposed to become an orthodox political party) and set up the Socialist League. When this in turn was infiltrated by anarchists he broke away again and founded his own Socialist Society in Hammersmith, London.

At the Society's musical evenings, where socialist songs were sung under the direction of composer Gustav Holst, two society members played piano duets. One of them was a twenty-seven-year-old would-be journalist named George Bernard Shaw, his ragged cuffs trimmed with scissors, wearing shabby, cracked boots and an ancient coat and

Fig. 3: *Annie Besant, free-thinker, social reformer and hygienist, who played piano duets with George Bernard Shaw.*

sporting a red beard and an Irish brogue. The other, one of Morris's ex-colleagues on the Democratic Federation executive, was the equally charismatic Annie Besant.

Besant was by this time a well-known activist, having been involved fifteen years earlier in one of the most widely publicized trials of the nineteenth century. In 1877 she and the national Secular Society's Charles Bradlaugh had been sentenced to six months in prison and a fine for republishing a forty-year-old pamphlet by an American author, Charles Knowlton,[20] titled "Fruits of Philosophy." The pamphlet contained detailed instructions on contraception for young married couples. During the trial (for obscene publication), Besant and Bradlaugh spoke out eloquently about the new threat of over-

population that would result from slowly improving living conditions and sanitation; on the overcrowded conditions in slums, rife with immorality and incest; on the effects of pauperism that led to a death rate of one in three infants; and on the need for freedom from prosecution for those publicizing the facts about contraception. The sentence passed on Besant and Bradlaugh was quashed by the judge before the two defendants had left the dock. Besant had become the first woman ever to speak out publicly to advocate contraception and get away with it.

In 1889 Besant became a Theosophist, and by 1891 she was effectively running the Theosophist Society. Theosophists rejected material things, encouraged vegetarianism, sought to bring the universal brotherhood of all races, investigated latent psychic powers and studied ancient and modern religions and philosophies. In pursuit of all these aims, in 1893 Besant visited India and set up the Central Hindu College for the Study of Comparative Religion in Benares. Earlier that same year she had visited the Chicago Exposition[21] and 21 24 49 together with Indian Theosophists had participated in meetings of the "Parliament of Religions." They took the meetings by storm, with four thousand attendees turning up at the last session to hear them. The Theosophists' vegetarian message was greeted sympathetically in the United States. The first vegetarian society had been formed in Philadelphia in 1850. In 1858 Dr. Caleb Jackson founded a health center at Danville, New York, based on vegetarian principles and including cold water treatments.

In 1865 Danville was visited by a Seventh Day Adventist named Ellen White. Two years earlier she had had a vision in which she was told to eat only two meals a day, avoid meats, cake, lard or spices, and consume only bread, fruits, vegetables and water. In Danville Mrs. White had a further vision. This time the message she received was to set up another Danville. A year later she and her Adventist colleagues bought a farm on seven acres of land just outside a small Michigan town and opened their health center.

The center's rules were strict: no levity, no playing checkers, lots

of oatmeal pudding and religion and cold water cures. The diet excluded tea and tobacco. Soon after the center opened it was in financial difficulties. The Adventists looked around for a new superintendent. They chose a young man who lived in the same Michigan town and had at the age of fourteen begun typesetting for the Adventist printing house. The church elders sponsored him through a course at Bellevue Medical College in New York, and in 1875 he graduated and took over what was now known as the Western Health Reform Institute. The first thing he did was to rename it the Medical and Surgical Sanitarium. The new superintendent had a natural eye for publicity. He dressed entirely in white, seemed to need no sleep, and was seen frequently with a cockatoo perched on his shoulder. He fostered vegetarian diets and set up the Three-Quarter-of-a-Century Club (healthy eating promoted longevity) and, in 1914, the Race Betterment Foundation. At the sanitarium he developed courses in nursing, physical education and home economics. For the patients he introduced room service, a gymnasium, a string orchestra in the dining room and wheelchair social events on the front lawn.

There was one aspect of the diet that still troubled him: "the half-cooked, pasty, dyspepsia-producing breakfast mush." To this end he began experiments in the sanitarium kitchen. Some time in 1894 he boiled and steamed wheat into a paste, flattened it between rollers, scraped the pieces emerging from the rollers and baked them crisp. In March 1895 at the General Conference of Adventists he presented his invention. It changed life in the Adventist community and then the world. The Superintendent of the Battle Creek Sanitarium was named John H. Kellogg, and his invention was named "cornflakes."

CHAPTER 2

✖

What's in a Name?

There used to be as many different kinds of breakfast as there were different cultures to eat them. The few still served around the world include corn pancakes and curry (India), blood pudding and fried potatoes (England), waffles and maple syrup (America), cold ham and cheese (Germany) and meat-and-cabbage soup (Colombia). However, these quaint local anachronisms are gradually disappearing before the onslaught of television advertising campaigns that exhort viewers to "eat healthy." The breakfast-food marketplace is now global. Today in almost any store anywhere in the world you can buy breakfast cereals.

For every hundred kilograms of grain used to make cornflakes, eighteen kilograms of used corncob are left. This vegetable detritus has had a varied career. Early in the twentieth century it was used to increase the water-holding capacity of mulch and soil, as well as for landfill in swampy ground. Corncobs have also been used for animal and poultry feed, as poultry litter, as a mild abrasive to clean car windscreens, and in soft-grit blast-cleaning of metals in aero engines.

However, it was the work of a nineteenth-century German chemist named Wolfgang Dobreiner that turned corncobs into a world-changing product. Dobreiner rose from obscure beginnings to become an unqualified journeyman chemical manufacturer, and at the age of thirty had the good fortune to befriend Johann Wolfgang von Goethe,[22] chief administrator of the technical college in the Univer-

22 69 141
22 71 142
22 82 153

sity of Jena, Germany. The college patron, Grand Duke Carl August of Saxony-Weimar, probably approved Dobreiner's hire in the hope that he would produce potentially profit-making inventions. Whatever the reason, in 1810 the unqualified Dobreiner was given a doctorate and a place on the faculty. Twenty-two years later he found a use for corncobs.

Dobreiner processed corncobs (it is not known how, or why) and produced an amber-colored chemical he named "furfurol." Little or no use was made of this discovery until the 1920s, when the growing petroleum industry had begun to make inroads into the chemicals market. Up to this point most chemicals had been derived from plants, so the change was bad news for the agricultural industry. Quaker Oats looked around for more ways to make money from their products and found that pressing, boiling, steaming and acidifying oat husks (and other forms of bagasse, such as corncobs) would yield the almost-forgotten furfurol. It was then discovered that furfurol could be processed to make a solvent for use in oil refining, in the manufacture of synthetic rubber and the development of nylon. It also found uses in carbuncle ointment, antibacterial medicine, acid-resistant containers, molds for the metal industry, insecticides, charcoal for barbecues, herbicides and antiseptics.

Furfurol was also used as an adhesive resin that would bond abrasives to a grinding wheel. Up to the end of the nineteenth century the abrasives (emery or sandstone) wore out quickly. Then in 1891 a young American, Edward Goodrich Acheson, made an accidental discovery that changed grinding and illumination. Acheson had previously worked as timekeeper, railroad ticket agent, assistant surveyor and railroad engineer and oil-tank gauger. In 1880 he was inspired by an article in *Scientific American* to seek employment with

23 75 147   Thomas Edison[23] at Menlo Park, where for four years he worked on electric lamps. In 1888 he set up his own small electric plant in Monongahela, Pennsylvania. Three years later he was using an electric-arc furnace to pass an extremely powerful electric current

through a mixture of clay and powdered coke (he may have been seeking to make artificial diamonds), when he noticed a few bright specks in the fused mass. Putting one speck on the end of a pencil-lead he drew it across a window pane and saw that it cut the glass. Using a furfurol derivative Acheson stuck many of these abrasive specks on a small wheel, took it to New York and sold it to a diamond cutter. Fliers posted to twelve thousand dentists brought enough response to finance a booth at the 1893 Chicago Exposition, and it was there that Acheson's grinding wheel came to enlighten the general public.

The Chicago Exposition[24] was the biggest of its kind ever staged. Between May and October of that year over twenty-one million visitors would attend. Tenders had been requested for the Exposition's illumination, and General Electric put in a bid for lights at $13.98 each. There was also a bid from Charles F. Locksteadt of the Chicago South Side Machine and Metal Works for $5.25 a light. Locksteadt got the contract and approached Charles Westinghouse[25] with a request for 250,000 lamps. Since Edison owned the patent to the incandescent light bulb, Westinghouse designed a new type of bulb. Edison's patent was for a one-piece bulb, so Westinghouse designed a bulb that came in two pieces: the glass bulb and a separate, airtight glass plug, fitting into the end of the bulb and carrying the power leads and filament. The plug was airtight because it was in the form of a ground-glass stopper. The 250,000 glass stoppers for the Exposition were ground by sixty thousand small Acheson abrasive wheels.

Acheson called his new abrasive "carborundum." Today it is better known by its chemical name: silicon carbide. The material (and its sister product boron carbide) came into international prominence following the development of armor-piercing shells and bullets. Both carbides are the hardest-known ceramics and the hardest materials in existence after diamond. When either of the carbides is used as armor, when a bullet strikes it a cone-shaped depression is formed in the carbide. This is then pushed by the bullet into the softer, backing

24 21 45

25 76 147

material of the armor. The area of the cone is wider than the cross-section of the bullet so the energy of impact is absorbed by the armor over a much bigger area, attenuating the force. At the same time the carbide pulverizes the bullet and spreads the impact energy even further. These characteristics made body armor popular when it reached its most refined stage of development in the 1960s Vietnam War, where it was used to protect Air Cavalry helicopter crews and ground forces. Aircrew armor reduced wounds 27 percent and fatalities 53 percent. On the ground, in hand-to-hand combat troops could throw hand grenades as close as thirty feet and absorb in their flak jackets the grenade blast that killed the enemy.

The need for armor-piercing weapons first emerged when navies began to switch from wooden ships to ironclads. In the 1860s, when the first of the new French ironclads was launched to the accompaniment of belligerent noises from the French Emperor, Napoleon III,[26] the British responded by building their own. In the first ironclad-to-ironclad encounters cast-iron cannonballs fired against two feet of wrought-iron cladding backed by a foot or more of solid teak proved ineffectual. It was a Captain Palliser of the British Eighteenth Hussars who first came up with the idea of a pointed shell with a hard nose. During the Chile-Peru war of 1879 a Palliser shell, aimed at the Peruvian ship *Huescar,* penetrated five and one-half inches of wrought-iron armor, then thirteen inches of teak and finally a half-inch of steel.

In the 1880s an American researcher made a major discovery. Charles E. Munroe had been working on gun cotton and found that if he exploded a slab of it against a slab of steel the words "U.S. Navy" incised on the gun cotton slab were reproduced by the blast in the surface of the steel. Early in World War I a German experimenter, J. Neuman, found that if the incision were lined with metal the impression on the steel was greatly deepened. In its final form the "Munroe effect" was achieved with ammunition holding a charge of high explosive in a cavity lined with copper plate. When the explosive was detonated at the end farthest from the cavity it collapsed the liner and created a focused blast in the form of a fine jet of hot gas and molten metal that punched through steel with ease.

26 117 220
26 127 244
26 129 246

What's in a Name?

World War I gave added impetus to the search for effective armor-piercing systems because of an entirely new battlefield development. It was an invention so secret that during the early stages of its manufacture by the British it was officially described as a water cistern being made for Russian factories. Because of this it became known as a "tank." The tank was initially developed because of two other inventions that had recently appeared on the battlefield: barbed wire and the machine gun. Because of the large number of casualties caused by machine guns when infantry were entangled by barbed wire, it was essential to find a way of breaking rapidly through the wire. The tank was developed to fulfill this function.

On November 20, 1918, at the battle of Cambrai, the first use of the tank changed the face of war. Behind a rolling artillery barrage 358 Allied tanks crept forward toward German positions heavily fortified with barbed wire. The tanks attacked in what became known as the "unicorn" formation: groups of three tanks, one central and leading the other two flanking it on either side, each protecting infantry advancing behind it. The tanks could also carry fascines (bundles of brushwood), which were dropped to fill trenches. The Cambrai at-

Fig. 4: *The terror weapon of World War I. Note the machine gun set in the swiveling sponson at the side.*

tack was a total success. Along a front stretching thirteen thousand yards, protected by the tanks the infantry advanced ten thousand yards in ten hours. Eight thousand prisoners and one hundred artillery pieces were captured. Allied casualties were minimal. The future of the tank was assured.

Part of the reason for the tank's success was its versatility. Mounted on two caterpillar tracks it could cross ditches and plowed ground or climb over banks, walls, hedges and fences. It could knock over small trees, cross streams over a foot deep, climb a slippery slope, handle a six-foot wall and survive a sheer drop of fifteen feet. It would do all this at a speed of three miles per hour. By the end of the war, the Mark V tank speed had increased to five miles per hour and it could turn in seventy-five feet. Only fifty of the Mark Vs were ready, but they made all the difference. In 1918 fifty-nine British divisions defeated ninety-nine German divisions because the British had the tanks and the Germans only had what had become known in German as "tank terror."

When the first tank (codenamed "Mother") was produced in 1915 it owed its existence to a friend of Major General Sir Earnest Swinton who had written to him about the new American tractor the British army was already using to haul supplies. A total of twelve hundred of these machines had already been bought by the Allies. They were tracked vehicles that would traverse almost any ground and had originally been developed near Stockton, in the San Joaquin Valley of California, where the rich, damp bottom land (which would not support a horse) convinced lumber merchants Benjamin and Charles Holt of the need for a haulage vehicle capable of working in such conditions. The advantage of a tracked vehicle was that whereas in a conventional vehicle with a wheel diameter of six feet four inches. the area of each wheel's contact with the soil (on which the weight of the vehicle rests) is only twenty-three inches, a track spreads the weight over an area more than three times larger. On November 24, 1904, while the Holts were testing their first steam-driven "crawler," a photographer friend, Charles Clements, remarked that it looked like a caterpillar. In 1910, when the firm was incorporated in Illinois, its name was the Holt Caterpillar Company.

The version sold to the Allies in Europe was gasoline-powered and was relatively maneuverable, with each track driven independently. In 1917 a new 120-horsepower version was produced. Then in 1925 came the first field trials of a new four-cylinder version with a radically different engine. This was the brainchild of a German who had already sold his engines to eleven countries. In Russia they were being used in power stations. In France they powered canal barges and submarines. The British installed them in battleships, the Dutch in passenger ships and the Germans in locomotives. The new engine had numerous advantages: it was more fuel-efficient, it was compact, it started cold, and it used cheap fuel. The engine's inventor was named Rudolf Diesel.

Born in 1858 the son of a bookbinder in Paris, Diesel attended the Munich Polytechnic where he was taught by Carl von Linde,[27] the inventor of the refrigerator. Graduating with the best exam results ever, Diesel then worked for the Sulzer refrigerator factory in Winterthur, Switzerland, and then sold the fridges, first in Paris and then in Berlin. By 1890 Diesel was well known as an inventor with an obsession: to replace the steam engine. His aim was to make an engine thermodynamically efficient and capable of using a wide range of fuels. In February 1892 he filed the patent for his new engine (which he had wanted to call "Delta" or "Beta" but finally, at his wife's insistence, named after himself). The diesel engine was an internal combustion engine in which the fuel was injected into the cylinder where the air had been compressed so that its temperature rose to eight hundred degrees Centigrade, the fuel's spontaneous ignition point. Since there was no spark that might ignite the fuel at the wrong time in the piston cycle, the system was highly efficient.

The main attraction of the engine for Europeans was that it could run on fuels other than gasoline. In the early part of the twentieth century few European countries had their own oil supplies, and the cost of the fuel was considerable. Diesel engines would run on liquid fuels of many types: whale oil, tallow, paraffin oil, shale oil, naphtha, even peanut oil. Diesel mentioned the most attractive fuel of all in a speech at Kassel in 1897, when he said that the engine would reach its real potential only when it used common hard coal. This may

27 55 115

have been the reason Diesel won a contract with Heinrich Buz's Augsburg engine factory. Buz's partner in the deal with Diesel was the coal king of Germany: Alfred Krupp.

The Krupp family had come to Essen in the sixteenth century, married into a local gun-making family, and became gunsmiths themselves. For the following three hundred years they were active in trade and in public office. Unlike all the other great German mercantile families, no Krupp ever took up a profession. In 1811 Friedrich Krupp left the spice trade and founded an iron and steel works in Essen. The city was ideally situated for foundries, located as it was among over a hundred local coal mines. In 1826 Friedrich's son Alfred (in charge of the company at the time of the Diesel deal) took over at the age of fourteen after his father had left family finances near rock bottom. For twenty years Alfred endured "perpetual grind and near-gloom" to make a success of the enterprise. He was aided by the 1834 German Customs Union, which created a single market of twenty-five million people. In 1851 Alfred exhibited a steel six-pounder gun at the Crystal Palace Exhibition in London and caused a sensation. At the same exhibition Krupp also showed the world's biggest steel casing, which weighed a staggering forty-three hundred pounds. The Exhibition made Krupp famous overnight and, more important, attracted the attention of Prince William, who later would become Kaiser and decorate Alfred with the Order of the Red Eagle with Oak Leaves, an honor usually reserved for victorious Prussian generals. Krupp went on to build the core of the new German navy: nine battleships, five light cruisers, thirty-three destroyers and ten submarines. By the early 1860s Krupp was already Europe's biggest cast-steel manufacturer, with representatives in every major city. He had built a fully integrated business that included iron-ore mines, collieries, iron- and steel-making foundries and railroads.

By 1890 Alfred was employing seventy thousand workers and facing the social problems that went with a large workforce in a country going through political turbulence. Alfred was a first-class organizer, saying once: "As pants the hart for cooling streams, so do I for regulation." He held his company together with the introduction of spe-

cially designed uniforms for the workers to wear at home, a sick fund, a burial fund and a pension fund. He built company housing, hostels, schools, hospitals, canteens, stores, bars, skittle alleys, baths, a church and a cemetery. Alfred was virulently anti-Marxist and regarded his unprecedented welfare schemes as a way of countering the revolutionary message of socialism. On one occasion, when some workers attempted to form cooperative food shops, he bought the shops and incorporated them into his own company stores, saying: "We must make certain that every worker's immediate thought is of the firm, and the interests of the factory, and that he is not tempted to mull over speculations in coffee, tobacco, sugar and raisins." The Krupp empire was a state within a state. Workers joined for life.

The Krupp technique for dealing with political radicalism inspired the most influential man in Germany at the time, Otto von Bismarck, who became prime minister of Prussia in 1862. Two years later both men met in Essen when Bismarck was returning to Berlin after negotiations in Paris. They discovered a mutual attraction to horses, guns, trees and misanthropy (Bismarck once wrote to his wife: "I have more to tell myself when I am with trees than when I am with men"). Both men suffered from megalomania and both were tyrannical and unscrupulous. Bismarck was concerned with preserving the Junker class against the revolutionaries, and he believed that guns were the final argument of kings. The two men were made for each other.

In 1883 Bismarck gave Germany his version of the Krupp welfare program with a National Health Insurance Scheme, which provided medical treatment and up to thirteen weeks' sick pay for three million low-paid workers and their families. Employees paid two-thirds of each premium and their employers paid the rest. A worker who was permanently disabled or sick for longer than thirteen weeks was given protection by the Accident Insurance Bill, which followed in 1884. In 1889 Bismarck introduced the world's first state pension for retired persons over seventy, and disablement pensions for adults of any age. As he said, the legislation was aimed at neutralizing the effect of socialism: "Whoever has a pension assured to him for his old age is more contented and easier to manage than a man who has none," and, "We must carry out what seems justified in the socialist

Fig. 5: *The Iron Chancellor,*
Otto von Bismarck. For him
great national issues were to
be solved with "blood and
iron."

programme and can be realised within the present framework of
state and society." At the same time Bismarck curbed the Socialists
with draconian legislation that outlawed strikes and jailed party activists.

To aid him with the introduction and administration of these
major acts of social policy Bismarck ordered comprehensive data to
be collected on the population at large. Over the previous two centuries growth in trade and industrialization had generated an increasing number of population surveys. In the seventeenth century
data was often arrived at by crude methods, e.g. estimating the age
and sex distribution of a community by multiplying an assumed average family size by the number of chimney pots. Another method
was to analyze data on births and deaths found in the baptismal and
burial records of parish churches. By Bismarck's time statistics had
introduced a measure of certainty into the analysis of the data. Be-

cause of their potential military value to an enemy population figures were now a matter of national security.

The entire study of social statistics was to be changed by a man who profoundly influenced Bismarck's chief of statistics, Ernst Engel. This was the Belgian astronomer Adolphe Quetelet. Quetelet was born in Ghent in 1796 to a family of modest means. On the early death of his father he became a math teacher in a local school. By the time he was twenty-four his remarkable talents had gained him the chair of mathematics at the Brussels Athenaeum and membership of the Belgian Royal Academy of Science. Over the next fifty years he was to dominate the country's science. In 1820 Quetelet led the movement to build an observatory in Brussels and traveled widely so as to learn all he could about astronomy. By 1842 the observatory was in place and he became its resident astronomer for the next forty-two years. Meanwhile, he had already carried out observations on the regularity of meteor showers, sunspots and tides and begun the collection of hourly meteorological observations. It was this work that brought the first international meteorological conference to Brussels[28] in 1853.

28 7 30

Quetelet extended his observations to periodicity in a wide variety of phenomena, including daily mean temperatures, times of foliation and leaf fall and the blooming of flowers (he noted that the common lilac flowers when the sum of the squares of the mean daily temperatures, counted from the last frost of the previous winter, adds up to 4,262 degrees Centigrade). Quetelet's ambition was to discover the order that lay behind the apparently random natural world.

In all this he was informed by his experiences in astronomy, where techniques of measurement and observation were perhaps more developed than in any other science. One particular mathematical tool used by astronomers was extremely valuable when dealing with data that had been derived from separate observations of a heavenly object and that revealed apparent irregularities in its behavior. The "law of least squares" (a technique for smoothing out extremes of difference in data) was originally applied in astronomy to calculate the most likely position of a planet or meteor whose movement had been

observed too infrequently to provide continuous data. Using the least-squares technique Friedrich Gauss had been able to predict where a newly discovered asteroid, Ceres, would be found when only three measurements of its movement had been made before observers lost sight of it.

In 1826 Quetelet became regional correspondent for Belgium's statistical bureau and began the work for which he is now best remembered. His greatest contribution to statistics was the concept of the "average person." Quetelet believed that if such a person could be reproduced mathematically then a new science of social physics would reveal the natural laws governing human behavior, making possible the identification of deviation from the norm. This would remove the element of guesswork from all social planning. "Chance," said Quetelet, "that mysterious, much abused word, should be considered only a veil for our ignorance." In 1831 he published *The Growth of Man*, a statistical survey of human physical data, and *Criminal Tendencies*, a study of the individual's propensity to commit crime. In 1835 came Quetelet's greatest work: *Social Physics: Man and the Development of His Faculties*.[29] The book contained a rigorous analysis of almost every aspect of human behavior, and it effectively founded modern social science.

In 1832 Quetelet was invited to Cambridge, England, to attend the third meeting of the new British Association for the Advancement of Science. At a meeting of a small group of scientists and mathematicians interested in statistics, discussion of Quetelet's work on suicide and crime led to the proposition that the BAAS should set up a statistics section. Not everybody in the association shared the enthusiasm for such an idea. The association president, Adam Sedgwick, warned in his concluding address that the new statistics section would have to follow strict rules: "For if we transgress our proper boundaries, go into provinces not belonging to us, and open a door of communication to the dreary world of politics, that instant will the foul Demon of discord find his way into our Eden of philosophy."

In spite of this and other objections, the precursor of the Royal Statistical Society was founded in 1834. Seldom can a new science have come at a more opportune moment. Following on the heels of

the Industrial Revolution, rapid urbanization had brought hundreds of thousands of workers into the city factories. Their living conditions were unspeakably filthy and degrading. Thousands lived in tenement blocks surrounding courtyards filled with sewage. Families often found themselves living in cellars ankle-deep in water, crammed ten to a room. Prostitution and incest were the inevitable result. By the 1830s social discontent was rife. The middle classes were becoming alarmed at the possibility of revolution and turned for help to statistics.

Surveys were carried out less with the the aim of improving the lot of factory workers and their families than of finding out the causes of the moral decay that rendered them disobedient to authority. Mathematics might provide the means with which to control the masses. To this end attempts were made to discover how many women could knit, or sing a jolly song, how many owned books and were literate, how many had insurance, or hung improving prints on their walls. Surveys sought to discover the workers' religious persuasions, the number of "amatory" pictures in their possession, how many of them cultivated flowers and how often they had their hair cut.

Hairdressers changed the life of the president of the new British Statistical Society, one of the members of Quetelet's Cambridge discussion group. He was Charles Babbage, at this time already one of the most famous figures in British science. Even for Victorian times Babbage was an extraordinary polymath. He was an inventor, mathematician, philosopher, scientist, outspoken critic of the scientific establishment, raconteur, political economist, socialite, visionary and prolific writer. He designed a recorder for monitoring the condition of railway tracks, lights for communication with ships, an ophthalmoscope, a pen with rotating discs for drawing dotted lines on maps, a system for delivering messages via aerial cables and footwear for walking on water. He also suggested designs for a tugboat, as well as for submarines propelled by compressed air, diving bells, an altimeter, a seismograph, a hydrofoil, a coronagraph to make artificial eclipses, a release-coupling for railway carriages, speaking tubes to link London and Liverpool and two kinds of cow-catcher for use on locomotives.

In 1819, during a visit to France, Babbage heard that the Baron De Prony had been commissioned to produce a new set of logarithmic and trigonometric tables for the recently introduced metric system. The Baron had brought together a group of "computers" to do the thousands of additions and subtractions required for the tables. In the new Republic complicated aristocratic hair styles were no longer fashionable, so many of these "computers" were out-of-work hairdressers. Babbage was stuck by the "division of mental labor" manifested in this French exercise, and this may have given him the idea of trying to automate such work. With the growth of commerce new surveys and tables were being produced every day, and they were subject to human error, which could cost money. In 1834 the science writer Dionysius Lardner wrote that a random selection of forty volumes of numerical tables revealed no fewer than thirty-seven hundred errors. Babbage himself reckoned that mistakes of this kind were costing the government up to 3 million pounds a year.

In 1834 his answer to the problem was to build an automatic calculating machine that would add and subtract. He also designed a more advanced, multiplying-and-dividing version (the "Analytical Engine"), which would foreshadow the modern computer. The core of this machine was a set of rods on each of which was mounted a series of independently rotating toothed wheels. Each wheel, with the numbers zero to nine marked on its edge, represented a numerical decade. The wheels interacted through complex sets of interlocking rods and cams, to produce addition, subtraction, multiplication and division. Sums were indicated by the number appearing in a small window set alongside each wheel in the outer casing. The Analytical Engine was also capable of carrying out complex calculations by means of stored programs. Addition or subtraction took a few seconds, multiplication and division a few minutes.

The operation was controlled by punched cards. A constant could be introduced into the machine's calculations by a "number-card." A "variable-card" defined the rod on which a number was to be placed or entered into the "mill" (the unit holding the stored programs for addition, subtraction, multiplication and division). A third type of card, the "operation-card," controlled which stored program was to

be used. Babbage's use of the cards solicited a poetic description from his backer and colleague Lady Ada Lovelace (Byron's[30] daughter): "We may see most aptly that the Analytical Engine weaves algebraic patterns just as the Jacquard loom weaves flowers and leaves." 30 60 122 30 132 249

Lady Lovelace was referring to the punched-card system originally developed for the French-designed Jacquard silk-loom, in which sprung hooks were pressed up against one of a series of cards held on a belt above the loom. When a particular thread or set of threads was required to be lifted during weaving the relevant control card presented a set of holes through which the necessary hooks could pass and lift the threads, thus automating the patterning process. In the late nineteenth century the same cards would be used (with electrified wires instead of hooks) to automate the American census. The engineer who developed the system, Herman Hollerith, set up a business that would eventually become known as IBM.

Meanwhile, in Babbage's time others were using the same cards for very different purposes. In 1844 the British Parliament decided to open a rail link to run through Wales to the port of Holyhead on the Irish Sea. This meant crossing the Menai Straits, a rocky channel about three quarters of a mile wide. The Admiralty insisted that its tall-masted ships be able to go under the bridge, and on these grounds vetoed the use of a cast-iron arch. Several suspension bridges had recently fallen down and were considered unsuitable. The contract went to Robert Stephenson, a locomotive engineer and bridge-builder who had spent most of his life working on the railroads, and he decided on a revolutionary new scheme.

His fifteen-hundred-foot-long Britannia Bridge over the straits consisted of two gigantic wrought-iron tubes, each made up of four shorter tubes riveted together. The tubes would each carry one railroad trackbed and be large enough for a train to pass through. The tubes would be supported by three masonry towers and held on an abutment at each end. Since the longest wrought-iron bridge span built to this date was thirty-one feet, Britannia was totally unprecedented in both design and scale. The other new record to be set by the bridge was the number of rivets it required: 2,190,000. Such an amount of riveting could not possibly be completed by hand in time,

and it fell to a Welsh tool-maker named Richard Roberts to solve the problem. Roberts produced an automatic, card-controlled device that would gang-punch holes through a wrought-iron plate as it passed through the machine. The punching machines could be thrown out of gear when not required. Those needed for a particular pattern of holes would be engaged via control rods operated by punched cards.

One of Stephenson's friends was another engineer, Isambard Kingdom Brunel, who was on site when the great iron tubes were floated into position below the bridge. He knew that all the tube stress-testing had been done by William Fairbairn, a prominent ironmaster and shipbuilder, who said at one point: "Provided we regard a vessel simply as a huge hollow beam or girder, we shall then be able to apply with approximate truth the simple formulae used in computing the strengths of the Britannia . . . and other tubular bridges."

These words were music to the ears of Brunel, who was about to begin work on the largest ship ever built, the *Great Eastern*. The idea for the ship was born of the Australian gold strike of 1851, which boosted emigration from Britain and added to the general growth in commerce between the two countries. Sailing ships completed the voyage in up to four months but were at the mercy of the winds. Australia was beyond the range of existing steamships because of the absence of sufficient bunkering facilities en route. A ship capable of doing the journey nonstop at an average speed of fourteen knots would take seventy days round trip and burn an average of 182 tons of coal per day. The ship would have to be capable of carrying twelve thousand tons of coal. The newly formed Royal Australian Steamship Company commissioned Brunel to build two such ships. Several factors combined to influence the design.

It was known that the larger a vessel, the less onboard space was needed to carry coal and the more room there would be for fare-paying passengers. In 1839 naval architect John Scott Russell had discovered that turbulence and wave-making were a major cause of energy loss. Wave-making could be reduced by giving the ship hollow, sinusoidal lines at the bow and cycloidal lines in the rest of the hull. The length of the bow section (called the "entrance") related to the wave of the required speed. The higher the speed the longer this

section and therefore the longer the entire hull had to be. This calculation gave rise to what was known as Russell's "wave-line" principle.
So *Great Eastern* was going to be long. At 692 feet length and 82 feet
beam, and displacing 32,160 tons, she turned out to be six times
larger than any ship built so far. The clear danger of such a design
was that in heavy seas when balanced on a single wave amidships or
supported by only one wave at bow and one astern a ship of this
length might break her back. Brunel dealt with this eventuality by
using Stephenson's tubular Britannia Bridge construction. He sand-
wiched the ship's longitudinal tubes between the inner and outer
hulls and linked them with transverse tubes so that the ship resembled a giant box girder. The ship's three million rivet holes were
punched out by Roberts's machine.

On January 31, 1858, the sixth attempt to launch *Great Eastern*
succeeded. The costs of launch, estimated at £14,000, had risen to
£100,000. Other costs had also spiraled and there was talk of auc-
tioning the ship off before her maiden voyage. So far the ship had
cost the astronomical sum of £640,000, the owners were already
£90,000 in debt, and the ship was only partially engined and still to
be fitted out. Then the Indian Mutiny of 1858 disrupted Eastern
trade, so an alternative, Atlantic run began to look more attractive.
Costs continued to spiral as the elaborate fitting-out took place.
Shares in the vessel were now a fifth of face value, debt was mount-
ing and on her maiden voyage *Great Eastern* sailed with forty-six passengers instead of the possible three hundred. She returned with
only seventy-two. By 1863 the company directors decided to cease
operations. A year later, after failing to meet the reserve price at auc-
tion, the ship was sold. In the words of one of the buyers: "Mr Barber
went down to Liverpool to attend the sale when, strange to state, a
ship that had cost a million of money and was worth £100,000 for
the materials in her, was sold to us for £25,000."

Great Eastern now began a new career, thanks to a thirty-four-year-
old American self-made millionaire named Cyrus Field,[31] who had   31 8 30
amassed a fortune in paper-making. In 1858 he had succeeded in
linking Newfoundland and England with a transatlantic telegraph
cable, when on the very day the cable was opened for the first mes-

Fig. 6: *The* Great Eastern, *laying cable over the stern. The ship would end up as a floating music hall and bar.*

sage traffic, it mysteriously failed. Examination showed that manufacture of the earlier cable had been incorrectly done, allowing the copper cable core to protrude through the insulation and come into contact with seawater. New and more accurate measures were suggested for the amount of insulation needed. This left the matter of finding a ship capable of carrying the new two-thousand-mile cable as well as all the necessary equipment for laying it, as well as 120 sheep, 10 oxen, 20 pigs and scores of chickens. Only one ship was big enough: *Great Eastern*. On her first attempt, about one thousand miles out the cable snapped. The final attempt started in July 1866. The ship had been refitted with improved engines and she set off with 2,400 miles of new-design cable weighing only 5,000 tons, as well as 8,500 tons of coal fuel, 500 tons of equipment and assorted farmyard supplies as before. This time the laying was successful. On July 26 the first Morse[32] Code message was transmitted.

Key to the entire effort was a new kind of cable insulation discovered in Singapore by a surgeon named William Montgomerie. The material was called "gutta percha," which was produced by evaporating the milky latex of the gutta percha tree into a firm, inelastic ma-

32 9 31

terial that could be softened and molded in hot water. In cold, high-pressure environments the material became hard but not brittle, so it was ideal for the deep ocean. Gutta was also later used to make rowing boats for Arctic explorers, and in ear trumpets, stethoscopes, domestic telegraphs and speaking-tubes, artificial teeth and fillings, chemical apparatus and machinery drive belts. It was employed as decorative and fine-art material in inkstands, pen-trays, baskets and vases. It also became a substitute for leather, papier-mâché, cardboard, wood, millboard, paper and metal.

Gutta percha was also found to be the ideal material for golf balls. The first golf club was formed in 1744, in Leith, Scotland. In 1754 another club opened at St. Andrew's, and it was here that the eighteen-hole course would be developed. Before this, courses ranged from five to twenty-five holes. At St. Andrew's the course ran alongside the shore: eleven holes out and the same number back. In due course these were reduced to eighteen and this became standard. By the early seventeenth century leather balls filled with feathers had replaced those made of boxwood. However the "featheries" easily became waterlogged and were rarely perfectly spherical. So when gutta percha balls became available they caused a sensation. At first they flew badly, but then it was noticed that after the ball had been hit a few times flight improved. Balls were then beaten with a small hammer to produce the effect deliberately. Today we call this "dimpling." In 1850 the new gutta balls were so much cheaper and long-lasting than their predecessors they created a boom in Scottish golfing.

This was a time of general expansion in Scottish leisure-time activities, following the country's rapid industrial development and the spread of the railroads. Economic growth had accelerated late in the previous century, when manufacturers began to take advantage of Scotland's ideal position for the rapidly growing transatlantic trade. Scotland became the center for tobacco exports, sugar and cotton. Trade generated an infrastructure of banks, warehouses and ports. These in turn facilitated further industrial development, particularly after the 1801 discovery by David Mushet (an assayer at the Calder Iron Works) of large deposits of blackband ironstone throughout the

western counties of Scotland. These deposits were rich in iron mixed with coal but required an unprofitable amount of heat to use for smelting.

In 1816 a new gasworks was built in Glasgow. The manager of the works was James Beaumont Neilson, who had previously worked as an engine-wright at John Roebuck's Boroughstounness colliery. Neilson would radically change the face of Scottish industry by making it easy and profitable to use blackband ironstone. In 1820 he became interested in finding a way to sell gas to iron foundries. For years it had been thought that because foundries produced more iron in winter, refrigeration of the foundry air blast should increase output. This proved not to be the case. Experiments convinced Neilson that production would be increased with a hot-air blast. This could be done by first passing the air through a tube surrounding a gas burner, thus adding heat to the fire and saving fuel. Neilson entered into partnership with a local industrialist, Charles Macintosh, and the apparatus was built. The air passed through tubes placed over a gas grate and was heated to 600 degrees Fahrenheit. The hot blast tripled production. More important, the heat was now sufficient to make use of the plentiful blackband ironstone, and since the rock contained both iron and coal, extra fuel was not required for smelting.

In 1830, 40,000 tons of Scottish pig-iron were produced. Only ten years later the use of ironstone increased annual output to a quarter of a million tons. By 1848 Lanarkshire alone had fifteen ironworks and ninety-two furnaces and Scotland was producing half a million tons of iron a year. Cheap iron also launched the Scottish shipbuilding industry. In 1835 5 percent of British shipping was built on the Clyde. Between 1851 and 1870 this rose to 70 percent.

[33] 114 214   Charles Macintosh,[33] Neilson's partner in the hot-blast venture, had also signed another deal with the Glasgow gasworks. Two of the by-products of the gas-making process (which involved baking coal to collect the gas it gave off) were coal tar and ammoniac liquid, both of which were dumped in rivers and quarries. Since 1777 Charles Macintosh's father, George, had been manufacturing a dye known as "cudbear." Cudbear gave a violet/purple color to wool and silk, but could with the use of acids also produce red. Alkali would return the

color to purple or blue. Cudbear was also used by paper stainers, who knew it as "litmus." The chief ingredients for the dye were lichen and ammonia. Previously the ammonia had been provided from the urine of friends and workers. From 1819 the ammonia was obtained from coal tar. Further treatment of the coal tar also produced naphtha, used by Charles Macintosh to liquefy rubber, which he spread between sheets of cotton to produce the first raincoat (which still bears his name in Britain today).

Earlier George Macintosh had formed a partnership with David Dale to set up a works producing another dye, Turkey Red, but the venture failed and the factory was sold off in 1805. Dale (one of Scotland's foremost textile manufacturers and the founder of the country's first cotton mill) then set up a mill on the River Clyde at New Lanark, and by 1799 it was the largest in Scotland, employing over thirteen hundred workers. That year Dale sold the mill to a Manchester company, which installed a manager named Robert Owen, who then married Dale's daughter. Owen's enlightened social attitude brought new and liberal conditions of work for the employees in New Lanark, where he provided education and medical services for workers and their children. In 1824, when Owen had become a leading light in what would eventually be the socialist movement, he moved to America and set up the utopian commune of New Harmony, Indiana. By 1827 the venture had failed and Owen returned to the United Kingdom.

His four sons remained behind in the United States and became citizens. The eldest, Robert Dale Owen,[34] went on to follow in his father's liberal footsteps, first in the Indiana legislature and then in Washington D.C., championing causes such as contraception and the emancipation of women. A pamphlet he wrote on birth control, titled "Moral Physiology," was published in 1830 and provided much (unacknowledged) material for "The Fruits of Philosophy" by Charles Knowlton[35] which, when it was republished by Annie Besant in England, led to her trial for obscenity.

In 1846 Representative Owen introduced a bill to the U.S. Congress to authorize acceptance of a large foreign bequest to America. In the curious way history works, the bequest linked Owen through

[34] 20 44
[34] 130 248

[35] 20 44

his father-in-law, David Dale, to the Glasgow gasworks manager James Neilson. Neilson's employer at one time had been the entre-
³⁶ 17 40 preneur John Roebuck,[36] whose interest in coal mines had led him to
³⁷ 16 39 become acquainted with James Watt,[37] who was working on ways to
³⁷ 139 259 make the Newcomen steam pump (used primarily for draining mines) more efficient. Roebuck offered Watt a cottage in the grounds of his house near Edinburgh so that Watt could experiment further. He also took over Watt's debts in exchange for a two-thirds share of any profits that might come out of the experiments. In 1772 Roebuck
³⁸ 18 40 sold his share to Matthew Boulton,[38] a metal manufacturer of Bir-
³⁸ 97 178 mingham who would in 1774 become Watt's engine-maker.

Nearly ten years later, and by now rich enough to indulge in scientific work of a more theoretical nature, Watt wrote a paper about his experiments on the composition of water. This brought him into conflict with Lord Henry Cavendish, who claimed to have made the same discovery (that water was made up of two parts hydrogen and one part oxygen) before Watt. The argument for priority rested on a number of mistakes made by the Royal Society regarding the date of publication of various documents and the dates on which various letters had been received. In the long run in 1785 when Watt became a fellow of the Royal Society he met Cavendish and the two men resolved the issue amicably, realizing that they had both been working on the same problem independently.

The previous year Cavendish had been on a geology field trip to Fingal's Cave in Scotland together with a young assistant named James Macie. Macie was the illegitimate son of the duke of Northumberland and an avid amateur scientist. On Macie's graduation from Oxford in 1786 Cavendish proposed him for membership in the Royal Society, and Macie began a career whose high points were the discovery of a flintlike substance in the joints of bamboo, the discovery of a new way of making coffee (that foreshadowed the modern vacuum method), the study of tears, and the identification of a type of calamine.

Macie's illegitimacy severely curtailed his activities, as witnessed by the British document of naturalization granted when he was born in France: He "shall not be hereby enabled to be of the Privy Council

or a member of either House of Parliament or to take any office or place of trust either civil or military or to have any grant of lands, tenements or hereditaments any inheritable property from the Crown to him or to any person or persons in trust for him anything herein contained to the contrary notwithstanding." The document may have been instrumental in establishing one of the greatest scientific institutions in the world, because in the event that no blood relative surviving him should have heirs Macie's will left his entire fortune (equal to 104,960 gold sovereigns) to the United States of America. This bequest was the subject of Robert Dale Owen's bill of 1846.

The gold had arrived earlier in 1838 when it had been recoined as over half a million gold American dollars (approximately two billion dollars in modern money). Then, in one of the more complex and devious financial deals in the history of America nearly $550,000 of the funds were almost immediately invested in the Real Estate Bank of Arkansas (which delivered a low rate of return) to be redeemed only in 1860. Subsequent investigations in 1845 revealed that the bank had grossly overvalued its real estate, was in serious danger of foundering and had in the meantime not paid any of the interest due on the invested sum. After heated discussions on Capitol Hill it was agreed that the Treasury would guarantee the missing bank interest. The way was clear for Owen's bill of acceptance.

Only now could the bequest be used for the purpose Macie had originally intended in his will of 1826: the foundation in Washington of "an establishment for the increase and diffusion of knowledge among men." The will also stipulated that the institution be named after Macie himself. Since on his father's death Macie had been given permission to take on the family name of the dukes of Northumberland (Smithson) the new American institution was duly named The Smithsonian.

CHAPTER 3

⊠

Drop the Apple

The Smithsonian Institution has well exceeded James Smithson's hopes. It has been at the forefront of scientific research since its foundation over 150 years ago. Today it includes sixteen museums and galleries and the National Zoo. It operates facilities in eight U.S. states and in Panama and has research teams in the field all over the world. One of the Institution's galleries contains an unparallelled collection of crystals, including the one investigated by the Institution's founder in 1801. Smithson described and classified the three separate substances known as calamine: carbonate of zinc, hydrous silicate of zinc and zinc oxide. In honor of his work, in 1832 the carbonate form was given the name "smithsonite." Then in 1852 the name was applied instead to the silicate. Today it is also used for the zinc oxide. But whatever its composition, calamine is now best known for use in lotion, sunburn cream, cosmetics, mineral supplements and in some cases as a treatment for chickenpox. It is also used in ceramics, as a rubber reinforcer, in semiconductors and as a photoconductor in photocopying machines.

What is less commonly known about calamine is something that was first noticed in 1703 by an unknown Dutch jeweler who reported that after heating the crystal tourmaline on coal embers, as it cooled small particles stuck to it as they would to a magnet. Tourmaline became known as the "electric stone." In the early nineteenth century the French researcher René-Just Haüy discovered that the

crystal behaved like this because it carried an electric charge strongest at each pole and that if tourmaline were smashed, each fragment would exhibit the same bipolar characteristics. Haüy also discovered the same "pyro-electric" features in other crystals, including calamine. Then it was discovered that the phenomenon was associated with a change in the crystal shape during heating and cooling.

In 1880, two French scientists, Pierre and Jacques Curie, found that pressure on the crystal would produce the electric charge, and that the charge was proportional to the amount of pressure. They named this phenomenon "piezo-electricity" (Greek: *piezen*, to press). A year later, using both quartz and tourmaline, they proved the reverse: an electric charge changed the crystal shape. The Curies went on to design an instrument for measuring very small electrical charges by the amount of shape-change the charges caused in a crystal. The crystal they used was quartz, and the instrument became known as a piezoelectric quartz balance. The device was the subject of Jacques's doctoral dissertation in 1889.

In 1894 Pierre Curie met a twenty-seven-year-old Polish physicist who would use the balance to extraordinary effect. Her name was Marie Sklodowska, and a year later she and Pierre married and began the work that was to change the world. By late 1897 Pierre was teaching an electricity course at the Paris Municipal College of Physics and Chemistry. Two years earlier Wilhelm Roentgen had discovered X-rays, and a few weeks after that French research Henri Becquerel attended a meeting at the French Academy of Sciences and heard that the new rays caused phosphorescence on the glass wall of a vacuum tube. Since Becquerel's father had done research on phosphorescence, Becquerel began to investigate the possibility that the X-rays Roentgen had discovered might be caused by phosphorescent materials.

At one point in his experiments Becquerel used powdery white uranium salts: potassium uranyl disulfate. After wrapping a photographic plate in thick black paper to keep out the light, he laid a saucer on which some of the salts had been placed on top of the paper and then left everything exposed to sunlight for several hours. When he developed the photographic plate the outline of the salts

was clearly visible, together with the outline of any object placed between the salts and the paper wrapping. Assuming the sunlight was causing the salts to fluoresce and generate the image, Becquerel prepared another experiment. For a number of cloudy days without sun the package (the wrapped plate, a copper cross and the salts) remained in a closed cupboard awaiting better weather. At one point Becquerel decided not to wait any longer and developed the photographic plate. To his surprise the cross was clearly visible in the picture even though there had been no exposure to sunlight. In May 1896 Becquerel announced the news and dropped the matter.

Nine months later Pierre and Marie Curie's quartz balance identified a small electrical charge in the air above the same uranium salts. Intrigued, Marie set out to discover if any other substances behaved the same way. On February 17, 1898, she tested a sample of pitchblende and discovered the charge it produced was much greater than that from the uranium salts. The Curies began boiling down and distilling the pitchblende to find out what was causing the charge. By late June their highly concentrated sample was giving off a very large charge. The Curies described the substance as "400 times as *active*" as uranium, and in July, coined the term "radio-active." It was this radioactivity that had been causing the image on the photographic plate. In December 1898 they named their new substance "radium."

One of the Curies' close friends (so close that after Pierre's death he would briefly become Marie's lover) was Paul Langevin, a brilliant physicist. Pierre had been Langevin's lab supervisor at the Municipal College and Langevin had been present at the start of the Curies' radioactivity work. In 1914, at the start of World War I, Langevin was working on ballistics when he was asked to look into the problem of submarine detection. Langevin turned to the old Curie quartz balance. In less than three years he produced what his lab team referred to as the "Langevin sandwich": two three-centimeter layers of steel sandwiching a four-millimeter layer of quartz crystal.

When an electric charge of the right frequency was applied to the quartz it caused the crystal to change shape and eventually to oscillate at its own resonant frequency. This in turn caused the steel plate

to vibrate. When the "sandwich" was set into the hull of a ship the vibrating steel would send out high-frequency pulses into the surrounding water. If these vibrations hit an object, they would bounce back and be picked up by a receiver, which would apply the returning vibrations to another quartz plate. The effect of these vibrations would cause the quartz to emit electrical signals that could be processed to show the range and size of the object. In 1918 the system identified a submarine from 600 meters away, even when the submarine was stationary on the seabed. British and American researchers took the technology (now known as sonar) to the same stage, then the war came to an end before ship-fitting could be begun, and in the 1920s all three powers dropped the matter.

In World War II German U-boat activity brought sonar to the fore again. By the end of May 1940 the wolfpacks had sunk 241 ships totalling 853,000 tons. In June the total was 58 ships, in July 38, August 56, September 59 and October 63. In the same period the Germans had lost only six of their 57 U-boats. Sonar was rapidly deployed, and it helped the Allies win the Battle of the Atlantic. By the end of World War II U-boats had sunk a total of 23,351 Allied ships, and 782 U-boats had been destroyed.

In the early years of the war, before America joined, U-boats were sinking ships faster than British yards could build them. In February 1941, President Roosevelt announced an emergency shipbuilding program. He described the new ships to be built as "dreadful looking objects." Each was to be just over seven thousand tons, and the aim was to produce them quickly and cheaply. Many of the ships were launched with no radio direction finders, fire detection equipment, emergency generators or lifeboat radios. Some went to sea with only one anchor. A total of 2,710 of these "instant" ships were built.

The first one, the *Patrick Henry*, was launched on September 27, 1941, to the president's ringing words: "Each new ship strikes a blow at the menace to the nation and for the liberty of the free peoples of the world." The ships became known as "Liberty Ships." Their rate of manufacture was phenomenal. By September 1942, American shipyards were launching three ships a day. The *Robert E. Peary* was

launched on November 12, 1942, only four days, fifteen and one-half hours after her keel had been laid. Liberty yards assembled each ship from thirty thousand components that had been mass-produced at thousands of factories in more than thirty-two states. In those places without slipways the yards simply flooded the dock and the ship floated out. Component parts were consumed virtually nonstop and it was quite commonplace to see complete deckhouses erected upside-down on a wheeled trolley and then inverted and placed in position. Stockpiles of double-bottom hull sections, with piping already installed, waited to be dropped complete onto the keels.

One reason for such a high rate of production was the early decision to make Liberties virtually all-welded. Oxyacetylene welding was a simple "fusion-welding" process. Both pieces of metal were heated to 3,100 degrees Centigrade, at which point they melted and flowed together once filler material had been placed in the gap between them. Acetylene[39] gas had originally been discovered in 1836 by Edmund Davy, cousin of Sir Humphrey. The technique for producing it on a commercial scale was discovered by accident. In December 1892 a French researcher named Henri Moissan (the man who provided Marie Curie with uranium salts during her early experiments) was attempting to make artificial diamonds in an electric-arc furnace in which two blocks of lime held a crucible, heated when the spark between two carbon electrodes caused them to burn incandescent and produce extremely high temperatures. Moissan failed to make diamonds but went on to other experiments, out of which came a material second in hardness only to diamonds: calcium carbide. Pouring water on calcium carbide produced considerable quantities of acetylene gas.

Moissan had developed his electric-arc furnace from lighting technology. In 1809 Humphry Davy had made the first arclight by attaching a charcoal rod to each terminal of a Volta battery, bringing the ends of the rods close together and producing a brilliant white light as the current jumped the gap between them and the rod tips burned away. From 1845 onward determined efforts were made to establish arclight on a commercial basis. However, the arclight required a con-

39 57 119
39 127 244

stant supply of electricity, and that required the development of a generator.

In one of those related-yet-unrelated incidents with which history is replete, other people were trying to find ways of generating large quantities of hydrogen to burn in the limelight apparatus used by lighthouses. One way of doing this was to disassociate hydrogen molecules from water with an electric charge. This led to the requirement for a constant supply of electricity, which in 1870 led to the development of the Gramme dynamo. The dynamo was exactly what arclight makers needed, and the arclight soon became commonplace in railroad stations and lighthouses.

The other obstacle to arclight production was the need for a regulator to advance the carbon rods toward each other at a precise rate so that they were always the optimum distance apart. If the rods came too close, they burned out too quickly; if they were too far apart the light level was insufficient. An English electrical engineer, W. E. Staite, developed a clockwork regulator. His carbon rods were placed vertically, one above the other. A wound-up, weight-loaded gear train was released (by the expansion of a copper wire heated by the arc), and it engaged with rackwork to raise the lower carbon rod gradually as both rods burned away. In 1849 a French scientist, Leon Foucault,[40] developed an improved regulator, which worked well enough for arclights to make their historic entry to the theater (where they replaced limelight).

40 119 221

Foucault's interest in the regulation of motion stimulated his most spectacular invention. In 1851 he hit the headlines when in the Paris Pantheon he hung a two-hundred-foot steel piano wire pendulum to which he attached a sixty-two-pound cannonball with a stylus fixed to its underside. He pulled the ball to one side and tied it off with a thick thread. When he set fire to the thread it parted and the pendulum was released unaffected by any influence. As the ball swung back and forth, the stylus traced out a line in sand on the floor. At the end of an hour the stylus had traced a line that had gradually turned through 11 degrees 18 minutes. Foucault's pendulum was the first demonstration of inertial motion, in which the pendulum swung un-

affected by the rotation of the Earth beneath it (as shown by the stylus). This was the first physical proof that Copernicus had been right.

Following his inertial work, in 1867 Foucault produced a heliostat and siderostat, two mechanisms designed to operate by clockwork so as to keep a telescope pointed at the sun or a star. Earlier, in 1845, Foucault had become interested in this aspect of astronomy following the announcement of a new photographic technique by Daguerre, and had taken the first daguerreotype picture of the sun, confirming the existence of limb-darkening as well as revealing several sunspots and their penumbrae. A daguerreotype taken during an eclipse in 1850 also revealed solar prominences and the sun's corona.

By 1819 Louis-Jacques-Mandé Daguerre was a well-known stage designer at the Paris Royal Academy of Music, and in 1822 he began to present spectacular dioramas, complex visual shows that included effects produced by the sequential illumination of scenes painted on multiple semitransparent backdrops, so that the scenes "dissolved" from one to the other. Dioramas were the rage of Paris and London, and it was probably during the drawing and painting involved in preparing the backdrops that Daguerre became acquainted with the painter's standard tool: the camera obscura.[41] In a camera obscura, light entering a pinhole in a darkened box would show an image of the outside world, upside down, on the opposite side of the box. The technique had been in use since the seventeenth century when it had aided accuracy of reproduction by artists such as Dürer and by astronomers such as Kepler,[42] who used one to make drawings during a partial solar eclipse in 1600. Daguerre decided to use the camera obscura to develop a photographic process.

In 1831 he learned from the earlier work of Joseph Niepce that iodide of silver would very slightly darken in the presence of light. He exposed a silvered copper plate to a camera obscura image and then placed the plate in iodine vapor. The image it created was too faint to see. One day in 1835 Daguerre put away an exposed plate in a cupboard full of various chemicals, intending at some point to polish the plate and use it again. A few days later he opened the cupboard and to his amazement found the plate now carried a distinct picture. By process of elimination he discovered that the image had developed

Fig. 7: *An early daguerreotype. The subject is the son of astronomer Sir John Herschel.*

because of the presence in the cupboard of a few drops of spilled mercury.

By 1839 he felt confident enough to make his new photographic technique public. The photographic plate was a thin film of polished silver on a copper base, sensitized by being placed face down in a vessel containing a few particles of iodine whose vapors formed a yellow layer of silver iodide less than a micron thick on the silver surface. After subsequent exposure for a suitable length of time in the camera obscura the plate carrying the latent image was developed by a vapor of mercury heated to 75 degrees centigrade. The mercury vapor stuck to the parts of the plate carrying an image while leaving untouched the unexposed parts. The image was then fixed by immersion in a solution of hyposulphite, which dissolved the unused silver iodide. Finally the plate was rinsed with hot distilled

water. The final image was seen immediately as a positive, when examined at such an angle that a dark background appeared reflected in the undeveloped parts of the plate.

The iodine Daguerre used had originally been discovered by another Frenchman as the result of another accident. During the Napoleonic Wars at the beginning of the nineteenth century the Allies imposed a total trade blockade[43] on all French ports. In consequence, one of the imports France could no longer obtain from abroad was saltpeter. This was unfortunate during a war since saltpeter was an essential ingredient of gunpowder, which was made from 75 percent saltpeter, 15 percent charcoal and 10 percent sulphur. Previously France had imported saltpeter from India and North Africa, where climatic conditions (hot and wet, followed by hot and dry) favored its production. Saltpeter was the product of a process in which organic materials, principal of which were human and animal waste products, decayed in the soil. This decay formed nitrates, which, when combined with potassium compounds, produced potassium nitrate in solution. In the dry season this solution rose to the surface and evaporated, leaving behind a deposit of potassium nitrate salts (saltpeter).

Denied imports by the blockade, Napoleon's scientists set up niter beds all over France and began to produce nitrates artificially by mixing urine and dung with powdered limestone. This made calcium nitrate through the oxidation of the ammonia produced by the breakdown of the organic materials. Turning calcium nitrate into saltpeter involved dissolving the nitrate in water and boiling it in a vat containing potassium carbonate derived from wood ashes. The only problem with this method was that the wood for the wood ash was ruinously expensive. It was also extremely difficult to obtain, since severe government restrictions limited the use of forests to shipbuilding.

In 1811 Bernard Courtois, a French chemist who operated niter beds near Paris, hit on the idea of producing ash by burning a type of seaweed known as "kelp." Before it could be used the kelp underwent an intermediate process to extract sodium carbonate for use in the soap industry. This took place in copper vats in which the

43 10 34
43 59 120
43 112 212

sodium carbonate extraction process left a thick insoluble deposit. On one occasion when Courtois was cleaning the deposit out with sulphuric acid he used too much acid and saw violet vapors rising from the vat. Then he found crystallized violet deposits on the inside. He passed these crystals to a couple of chemist friends and in due course in 1814 the crystals were identified as a new element and given a name based on the Greek word for violet (*iode*): iodine. Unfortunately for Courtois, in 1815 the war and the blockade ended, France returned to importing cheap foreign gunpowder, and his business went bust.

The kelp Courtois used had been harvested along the coastline of northwestern France. A much larger kelping industry had already developed in Britain, in response to earlier industrialization. Most of the British kelping industry was concentrated on the western coast of Scotland, where villagers raked the seaweed off rocks and burned it in circular pits about five feet across and one foot deep. A fire was then lit with dry kelp in the center of the pit and wet kelp heaped on top. The dense white smoke given off by pits could sometimes be seen miles away at sea and kelp-producing islands often gave the appearance of volcanoes. As the kelp burned it solidified and was beaten flat with shovels, and flat stones were placed on top to press it down. After two days the burned kelp had fused into a single large piece of slag, which was then broken up into smaller stones and ground down. So great was the demand for kelp ash that Scottish landowners made fortunes. Since the Union with England in 1707 the Scottish aristocracy wanted money to maintain a fashionable presence in London or Brighton. The second Lord Macdonald of the Isles had an annual kelp income of twenty thousand pounds. Macdonald of Clanranald (who moved villagers' homes if they spoiled his view) made eighteen thousand pounds. These sums were extremely large at the time, and much of the money went on a luxury lifestyle and the construction of pseudo-Gothic castles, which can still be seen today.

The demand for kelp was widespread. Although it was not known at the time, kelp contains as much nitrogen as animal manure, and it was prized as a local fertilizer. Industrial uses for kelp were more

profitable and demand grew steadily through the mid- and late-eighteenth century. The earliest commercial demand for kelp ash had come from glassmakers, denied (by the same shipbuilding constraints) the wood ash they had traditionally used to make "frit," an essential ingredient in their product. Kelp made the greatest contribution to British economic advance in the textile industry. When kelp ash was dissolved in water to which quicklime was added, the alkaline solution could be used as the first stage in bleaching cloth. It could also be mixed with fatty substances to make soap (to be used in washing grease out of raw wool before it was woven). Muriate of potash could also be extracted from the mixture and used in the dyeing industry. The greatest demand for kelp ash was, however, generated by the extraordinary rise in demand for cotton.

Middle Eastern cotton was brought to England in 1601, probably by Dutch immigrants. At first it was used to make fustian, a linen-cotton mix. Around 1730 cotton stockings became popular. At the same time the printed calicoes (cotton products named after Calcutta, the Indian port of export) and chintzes being brought into Europe by the Dutch East India[44] Company were creating an insatiable market. These imports were met with some opposition by local English manufacturers who described the new cloth as "a tawdry, pie-spotted, flabby, low-priced thing called Callico . . . made by a parcel of Heathens and Pagans that worship the devil and work for a halfpenny a day." Cotton was durable and comfortable to wear, it washed and ironed well, and it could be dyed and worked with ease. As the standard of living rose cotton became popular for aristocrats' underwear and workers' shirts. The exceptionally good weather and bumper harvests in the first decades of the eighteenth century had brought a fall in the price of food and a rise in the value of wages. In consequence the birth rate rose and the market for household goods and clothing expanded rapidly. Since England ruled India at the time regular cotton supplies seemed assured. The requirement only remained for technology that would enable cotton manufacture to keep up with demand.

In 1753 a woolen manufacturer named John Kay invented a "flying shuttle" that could be tugged back and forward across the loom

44 66 137
44 109 208

on small wheels. It doubled the weaver's output. The new loom worked faster than thread-spinners could keep up so in 1764 weaver James Hargreaves developed the "spinning jenny" with which one spinner could spin thread onto a number of spindles at the same time. In 1779 an inventive wigmaker named Richard Arkwright automated the thread-spinning process. Sets of rollers moving at different speeds pulled the thread from the mass of raw cotton, then automatically twisted it and wound it onto spindles. Arkwright drove his machine by water power and took cloth production forever out of the cottage and into the factory. In his first textile mill the machinery, filling six floors, was run by belt drives set on shafts turned via gearing by one huge waterwheel. Arkwright called his device a "water frame." This met all the demand for coarse cloth, but for finer fabrics the manufacturer had still to use the older (and now slower) jenny.

In 1779 Samuel Crompton combined the principles of the jenny and the water frame in one hybrid machine, which he aptly named the "mule." The thread was wound onto bobbins in the same way as on the water frame, but the spindle-mounting moved away and back, stretching the thread as it was twisted. This resulted in a much thinner thread, making possible the production of fine muslin cloth that was washable and now cheap. By 1785 the *Annals of Commerce* wrote: "Women of all ranks from the highest to the lowest, are clothed in British manufactures of cotton, from the muslin cap on the crown of the head, to the cotton stocking under the sole of the foot . . . with the gentlemen, cotton stuffs for waistcoats have almost superseded woolen clothes . . . cotton stockings have also become very general for summer wear."

In 1787 there were 119 cotton mills in Britain. By 1837, 1,791 mills employed a quarter of a million people. In the same period, cotton output rose from one to ten million pounds a year. Then in the latter part of the eighteenth century war in India began to interrupt cotton supplies. Indian sources had always been unreliable. Thanks to the dreadful state of the roads, loads often arrived at ports too late for shipment. As the British consumer became more sophisticated, the short-staple coarse Indian fibers lost their appeal. Shortage of In-

dian producer capital also drove down quality, and with most growers incurring debts to be paid off by their children and grandchildren there was no money to spare for better husbandry. By 1792 the situation had reached crisis point. Some more reliable source of cheap, good-quality cotton had to be found.

That year a young Yale graduate named Eli Whitney, on board ship from New York to Georgia, fell in with a fellow passenger who happened to be the wealthy widow of a Revolutionary War general, Nathaniel Greene. She invited him to visit her on his way to Savannah. At her Mulberry Plantation he met many of Widow Greene's friends and heard constant talk about the problems associated with removing seeds from the green-seed cotton grown all over the South. It took one man one day to clean the seeds from one pound. Whitney said he thought he might be able to design something to deal with this problem. Mrs. Greene promptly offered him room and board, and he stayed on.

The following year Whitney applied for a patent for his new cotton gin. It was a simple apparatus consisting of a wooden cylinder with wire teeth set in transverse rows around it. When the cylinder was turned the wire teeth picked up raw cotton from a hopper and pulled it through a wire screen that separated lint from seed. At this point a revolving brush removed the seeded lint from the wire teeth. Whitney's gin was able to seed cotton a hundred times faster than a man, and it would one day be a major contributing factor in the outbreak of the Civil War, because the gin made cotton profitable enough to sustain the social system that believed in slavery. By 1807 U.S. cotton exports had risen from 190,000 pounds in 1791 to over 66 million pounds. By 1825, with the British market avid for every pound of cotton it could buy, thousands of slaves were cultivating cotton on hundreds of thousands of acres throughout the South. In Britain 450,000 factory workers were processing and weaving the raw import. By 1859 two-thirds of the world's cotton was American, and Senator Hammond of South Carolina was uttering the immortal words: "Cotton is King!"

Unfortunately, all this did little for Whitney's fortunes. Pirated copies of his gin appeared everywhere and redress was virtually im-

possible. As he said: "I have a set of the most depraved villains to combat and I might almost as well go to Hell in search of Happiness as to apply to a Georgia Court of Justice." Whitney got out of the ginning business and took up making muskets with interchangeable parts. In January 1798, back in New Haven, Connecticut, he won a contract with the U.S. government to deliver four thousand guns within twenty months and another six thousand the following year. In the end it would take him nine years to fulfil the contract. In the course of this Whitney invented the milling machine, which enabled workmen to cut metal to standard patterns, so as to make the interchangeable parts from which every musket was to be made. Another Connecticut Yankee, Eli Terry, was doing the same thing with clocks. There are suggestions that the two men met, but it is more probable that word of Whitney's techniques had gotten around. After all, he had been copied before.

Terry started by making his wooden clock parts with a hand-operated wheel and pinion-cutting engine, but by 1806 he had signed a contract for six thousand clock movements and needed to move on to mass production. By 1820 thirty workmen were using templates to make twenty-five thousand identical wooden clocks a year and Terry was rich. In 1816 he was joined by a young cabinet-maker named Chauncey Jerome, who had been hired to make Terry's clockcases. When his contract with Terry was ended Jerome sold Terry his house in Plymouth for a hundred completely fitted mantle-clock movements, made 114 more, encased them all, sold these 214 complete clocks for a house, a barn and seventeen acres in Bristol, Connecticut, and set up in business.

In 1838 Jerome (or his brother) invented the brass clock. The advantage of brass was that it did not need seasoning as did wood, so no delays were involved in going from raw material to finished product. In 1844 Jerome moved to New Haven to make cases, while in his Bristol factory three workmen continued to turn out all the wheels for 500 clocks per day. A single machine using three cutters performed three sequential operations: simple cutting, rounding off teeth and finishing. By 1850 Jerome had two factories in New Haven turning out 280,000 clocks a year. During its operational life the firm

exported millions of clocks to Europe, Asia, South America, Australia and the Middle East. However, in 1855 Jerome found himself in financial difficulties. It was at this point he met an extraordinary character named Phineas T. Barnum and was persuaded to go into business with him.

Barnum had begun life as a store clerk, and then set up his own fruit and confectionery shop in Bethel, Connecticut, where he also ran a local lottery. In 1831 he began publication of a weekly newspaper, *The Herald of Freedom*, which he edited for three years until forced to resign after libeling a deacon of the local church. In 1834 Barnum moved to New York and began his show-business career, exhibiting freaks and curiosities all over the country. In 1842 he discovered a two-foot, one-inch midget in Bridgeport, Connecticut, dubbed him "Tom Thumb" and made a fortune showing him off to European royalty and American audiences, who thought the midget a sensation. In 1851 Barnum bought a museum in New York and, in his own words, "scoured America for industrious fleas, automations, jugglers, ventriloquists, living statuary, tableaux, gypsies, albinos, fat boys, giants, dwarfs, rope dancers, dioramas, panoramas, models of Niagara, Dublin, Paris and Jerusalem, Punch and Judy, fancy glass-blowing, knitting machines, dissolving views, and American Indians." Barnum would eventually go into the history books with the "Greatest Show on Earth" circus he started in 1876.

Meanwhile, in 1847 he returned from a trip to Europe, decided it was time to become respectable and built a mansion in Bridgeport. Called "Iranistan," the house was modeled on the Royal Pavilion in Brighton, England: a turreted Oriental palace surrounded by gardens and fountains. By 1849 his New York Museum was staging plays and other cultural events, and Barnum was giving lectures on the value of temperance. In this new mood of sobriety he hit upon another way to make a fortune. He would invite the new Swedish soprano Jenny Lind to tour America.

At the time Lind was twenty-nine and already the toast of Europe. Although no beauty, she had tremendous personality and the voice of an angel. As Barnum said to a reporter: "It is a mistake to say that the fame of Jenny Lind rests solely upon her ability to sing. She is a

woman who would have been adored if she had had the voice of a crow."

After a few years' training in Paris Lind had returned to Stockholm in 1842 to sing Norma. People cried at the sound of her voice. Hans Christian Andersen fell madly in love with her but his feelings were not reciprocated. In 1844 Lind sang Norma in Berlin. It was her first role outside Sweden. She was an immediate sensation and over the next six years became famous everywhere. Her concerts were booked out weeks in advance. Mendelssohn idolized her. She was waited on hand and foot by princes and empresses. In 1847, at her London debut, Queen Victoria dropped her bouquet at Lind's feet. Her voice was superb, able to manage crescendos better than any other singer alive and capable of expressing magnificent emotional intensity.

When Lind received Barnum's offer to tour the States she was wary. His reputation for showmanship and extravagant public relations tricks was already well established. However, Lind accepted because

Fig. 8: *A typical piece of P. T. Barnum pizzazz: the daring spectacle of an all-woman band in the streets of New York.*

Barnum had converted everything he possessed to cash, taken out mortgages on his property and obtained loans from friends so as to be able to give Lind an advance of $187,500 (today, the equivalent of over $2 million).

Lind arrived at the dockside in America to a Barnum-orchestrated welcome. Flags and triumphal arches decked the port, and thanks to thousands of publicity handouts twenty thousand fans waited outside her hotel. After a rapturous opening night in New York Lind toured the American East Coast and then moved on to California. The general public went crazy. One man offered to pay a thousand dollars to touch her shoulder "and see where the wings began." Another paid $650 for a ticket even though he could not attend the concert. The American tour made Lind rich enough to buy herself out of the contract with Barnum after ten months and return to Europe.

Earlier in 1847, Lind's first triumphant performance at Her Majesty's Theater in London had brought her into contact with another musical megastar, Giuseppe Verdi, who had written the opera for that occasion. The work was *I Masnadieri,* based on a work by Schiller. Lind sang the leading role of Amalia and Verdi himself conducted the first two (of only four) performances. In the event Verdi and his star did not get on. Verdi's amanuensis Muzio (who accompanied him to London where they both complained about the weather, the food, and the English audiences) wrote : (Lind) "is inclined to err in using excessive *fioriture,* turns and trills, things which were liked in the last century but not in 1847." Verdi had accepted the commission to write *I Masnadieri* because he could earn four or five times as much writing for foreign opera houses as he could writing for La Scala in Milan.

The theme of the London opera was for Verdi a typical story of the fight against cruel authority and the triumph of heroism against all odds. Living in Italy under Austrian occupation, Verdi risked life and limb with operas whose themes tended toward thinly disguised nationalist propaganda. *Nabucco* was about Hebrews captive under the Egyptian yoke, and at its first performance had set off a near-riot. *The Battle of Legnano* featured Barbarossa defeating the Lombard League

(opening chorus: "Long live Italy!"). *A Masked Ball* had been intended as the story of the assassination of King Gustav III of Sweden, but under pressure from the censor the story was eventually set in pre-Independence Boston.

It may have been these nationalistic themes that first brought Verdi to the attention of the khedive of Egypt, Ismail Pasha, whose country was part of the Ottoman Empire at the time and who was looking for ways to loosen the Turkish grip. Ismail invited Verdi to write an opera to be performed at the Cairo Opera House in celebration of an event the khedive had arranged, which was intended to be Egypt's greatest contribution to civilization since the Pyramids. The financial offer for the opera (over seven times the standard rate at La Scala) was too good to refuse, and Verdi dutifully obliged with what turned out to be his greatest and most successful work: *Aida* (sure enough, set to another nationalist theme). In the event *Aida* was not ready in time for the pasha's great event in 1869: the opening of the Suez Canal.

Since Roman times there had been several attempts at building a canal to link the Mediterranean with the Red Sea. In the eighth century the Arabs had given up because of the risk of opening their seas to the Byzantine navy. In the fourteenth century the Venetians decided the enterprise would cost too much. The English were against the idea because the route around Africa was "comprehensive, safe, bold, truly English." Nonetheless a Suez Canal was attractive because it would save the four-thousand-mile journey around Africa. In 1800 Napoleon stimulated new interest in the canal when his engineers surveyed a possible route during his brief occupation of Egypt. With Napoleon's defeat the idea went back on the shelf until renewed French interest (and their rivalry with the British) was expressed by a young diplomat named Ferdinand de Lesseps,[45] French [45 92 164] vice-consul in Egypt in 1832, after he read the original report prepared for Napoleon. De Lesseps proposed the idea to the Egyptian ruler Mohammed Ali and received a concession to build. This was due almost entirely to the fact that it had been De Lesseps's father who at the behest of Napoleon had put Mohammed (an illiterate but

charismatic soldier) on the Egyptian throne. The De Lesseps family were royal favorites. The fact that De Lesseps was related to the French empress Eugénie[46] also helped.

46 120 223

By the time Ferdinand finally began work on the project in 1856 Mohammed's son (and Ferdinand's personal friend) Said Pasha was on the throne. The construction of the canal eventually took twenty-four years, employed twenty-five thousand laborers and used the new mechanical dredgers. The opening in 1869 was attended by dignitaries from all over Europe and America. They included crowned heads, artists and writers, ambassadors and aristocrats. Eight thousand guests sat down to dinner on the night of the opening. As it happened the guests were celebrating something that already belonged to them rather than to Egypt since the expenditure involved in building the canal had bankrupted Said Pasha and obliged him to sell all his shares to the English prime minister, Benjamin Disraeli.

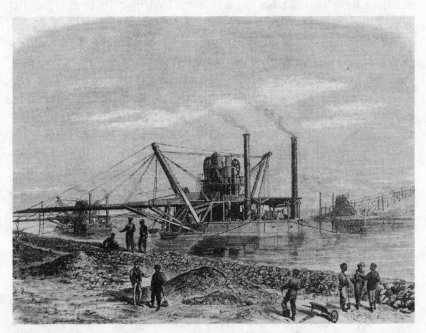

Fig. 9: *Building the Suez Canal. The final breakthrough to the Red Sea was made on August 11, 1869.*

The rest of the shares had already been sold to Switzerland, Italy, Spain, Holland, Denmark and France.

There were one or two among the French guests who might have thought De Lesseps had unfairly taken all the credit for the great achievement. Back in 1833, a year after obtaining the original concession, De Lesseps had met (and helped to keep out of jail) a strange French individual named Prosper Enfantin, who was on a visit to Egypt looking for a wife. Enfantin was a banker and the head of a religious sect known as "New Christians." This quasi-communist, free-love group preached a new kind of social religion and had already set up a number of churches throughout France. Although in the end Enfantin would go to jail for advocating free love in 1833 he and his followers were still active and trying to find him a bride from the East so as to achieve the mystic union between East and West that was part of the sect's attempts to unite all peoples in a brotherhood of love and equality. Enfantin later claimed that part of this union would involve the building of a Suez Canal.

Enfantin's interest in canals had been stimulated by the man who also inspired him to become leader of the New Christians: Henri de Saint Simon. At the age of nineteen Saint Simon had fought on the American side during the War of Independence. Of his presence at the siege of Yorktown he said later: "I contributed in a rather important manner to the capture of General Cornwallis and his army. So I may regard myself as one of the founders of the liberty of the United States." Saint Simon also claimed that in 1783 while in Mexico he had proposed a precursor to the Panama Canal. In 1787 he went to Spain to outline his plan for a canal from Madrid to the Mediterranean. Later he developed plans to unite the Danube and Rhine rivers and to link the Rhine with the Baltic Sea. After a period in 1795 when he became one of the leading financial figures in Paris, by 1797 Saint Simon had failed in several business ventures and was practically destitute. It was at this time he decided to become a philosopher.

Living in increasingly dire circumstances, often penniless and relying on the charity of friends, Saint Simon began to conceive of a

grand new social order. In 1817 he started publication of *L'Industrie*, a periodical in which he expounded his new theory: that society depended entirely on industry; that it was industrial "producers" who maintained society; and that political power should rest in the hands of financiers and industrialists. By 1821 he included spiritual values: all men were brothers, and spiritual power must spring from a scientific understanding of the world. Not surprisingly, the new view gained adherents among businessmen, bankers and engineers. The "positive" scientific view of the value of human knowledge in ameliorating the condition of society and the importance of applying scientific analysis to how society functioned has since earned Saint Simon the title of "father of sociology." In 1823, aged sixty-two and once again destitute and depressed, he fired seven bullets at his head. He lost an eye from one of the bullets. The rest missed and Saint Simon survived. Two years later he had founded New Christianity, and shortly thereafter was dead.

Among those attending the funeral was Auguste Comte, whom Saint Simon had met in 1817 and who had briefly been his secretary.

Comte's major contribution to the sum of knowledge might be said to have sprung from a single remark by Saint Simon, which informed Comte's view of the world: "The only absolute is that everything is relative." Comte drew on Saint Simon's positivist view of human society to develop his own philosophy, today known as "positivism." He held that human history was divided into three stages: the theological, when men believed in gods and demons; the metaphysical, when descriptions were sought for "forces" in nature; and the scientific. Humanity must therefore apply scientific principles in government.

The only means of assuring order was to place social rule on a positive or scientific basis. There could be no world harmony while some people explained the world in terms of theology and metaphysics.

To this end the primary study of science should be the nature of
47 29 58 Man and the development of what Comte called Social Physics,[47] through which laws of behavior could be applied to the study of society. All perception and understanding of the world came from the

brain and the senses and from this Comte deduced that the development of human knowledge was, as Simon had said, a matter of what people knew at any time. This was affected by their historical context. In this sense all knowledge of the world was relative. By 1850 Comte was an examiner at the Paris Polytechnic and known throughout Europe. Such eminent men as John Stuart Mill considered him an intellectual guide and moral mentor.

In the 1860s a physics professor in Prague looked more closely at Comte's concept of the relative nature of perception in a series of experiments, including one in which subjects were placed on a rotating chair with a paper bag over their heads. The experiment revealed that the subjects were able to perceive rotation only during the phases of acceleration and deceleration. When the chair rotated at a constant speed neither movement nor direction could be identified in the absence of external cues. The same phenomenon also occurred during linear motion. The physics professor, Ernst Mach, theorized that these perceptions were controlled by messages to the brain from the liquid in the ear's semicircular canals.

By the time Mach returned to Vienna (where he had qualified), he was famous for his crowded public lectures on subjects such as "The Role of Accident in Invention and Discovery." By this time he had extended his relativist view of perception to all aspects of scientific investigation. In one lecture he stated: "When we say the acceleration of a freely falling body is 9.810 meters per second, we mean the velocity of the body with respect to the center of the earth is 9.810 meters greater when the Earth has performed an additional 864,000th part of its rotation—a fact which itself can be determined only by the Earth's relation to other heavenly bodies. . . . The aim of research is the discovery of the equations which subsist between the elements of phenomena." In this sense, for example, science could only refer events to the passage of the hands of a clock around its face and never to absolute time.

The essence of Mach's thinking rested in a concept he himself never articulated but which was referred to by his most famous disciple as the "Mach Principle." In simple terms it stated that Newton was wrong in postulating absolute space as a frame of reference, be-

cause it could not be observed. All mass and motion in the universe could only be relative to the observer's frame of reference, which was relative to other masses and motions, which in turn could only be described in terms of yet further phenomena. So there could be no such thing as an isolated or detached element of experience. As Newton's apple fell, attracted by the Earth, the Earth was also attracted by the apple.

The German physicist who coined the term "Mach Principle" was introduced to Mach's ideas by a friend and once said: "Even those who think of themselves as Mach's opponents hardly know how much of Mach's views they have, as it were, imbibed with their mother's milk." He came into contact with Mach's ideas thanks to a thought experiment he conducted regarding light. At the time light was considered to travel in a "luminiferous," invisible, intangible, elastic medium that permeated the whole of existence and was called "ether." Unfortunately, nobody had succeeded in finding "ether," so the matter of how light traveled was still in question. In the course of· thinking about this the German physicist imagined himelf traveling on a beam of light. As Mach had pointed out, this meant that to the traveler the light beam was, in effect, stationary. So since the light was not traveling with respect to the observer, if he held up a mirror, the light carrying his image would not travel to the mirror and therefore he would see nothing in the mirror. It was at this point that a friend referred to Mach's work regarding the nonexistence of absolute space and motion. According to Mach, within the local frame of reference of the light-rider light would still move as it should and reach the mirror to be reflected, no matter how the light might be perceived from outside the light-rider's frame of reference. It was this which led the German physicist, Albert Einstein, to the realization that the speed of light must be the only constant property in the universe.

Another Machian idea about light presented intriguing possibilities. If everything in the universe were affected by everything else, then light should also be affected. Developing this concept, in 1916 Einstein presented an idea that shook classical physics to its foundations. He theorized that light ought to be affected by gravity as if

light had mass. Light ought to be affected by a gravitational field. In 1919 came an opportunity to test the theory, thanks to an eclipse of the Sun. On May 29 that year a group of bright stars in the Hyades was expected to form the starfield around the sun (that is, they were directly beyond it in space at the time).

The eclipse track was due to pass just off the coast of West Africa and run through the island of Principe. Photographs were taken of the Hyades starfield several months earlier when the sun was nowhere near them in the sky. Then on May 8, a British expedition headed by Sir Arthur Eddington, Director of the Cambridge Observatory, set out for Principe. On the day of the eclipse sixteen photographic plates were exposed. On July 5, after taking further comparison pictures, the expedition left the island, returning to the Royal Observatory in Greenwich on August 25. Of the sixteen plates taken only two had reliable images. These plates revealed that the light from the stars indeed had been deflected, by 1.75 seconds of arc, as it passed through the sun's gravitational field. Eddington send Einstein a telegram confirming his theory.

One of Einstein's students, noting his unruffled reaction to the news, asked him how he would have felt had the observations not confirmed his predictions. Einstein replied: "I should have been sorry for Eddington. The theory is correct."

CHAPTER 4

—————— ✕ ——————

An Invisible Object

Not long after Einstein predicted that light was affected by gravity (a prediction confirmed by the eclipse in 1919), the German astronomer Karl Schwartzchild theorized that there could be objects in space so massive they would attract and hold light. The objects would of course be invisible since no light from them could escape to be seen. Such an object would be like a hole into which light "vanished." For this reason the theoretical phenomenon became known as a "black hole."

In 1992 the presence of massive black holes (in galaxy M-87) was confirmed by an instrument named after the astronomer who, like Einstein, revolutionized the modern view of the cosmos. His name was Edwin Hubble, and in the 1920s at the Mount Wilson observatory near Los Angeles, he began a study of extragalactic nebulae, clusters of stars that look like clouds (Latin: *nebulae,* cloud). In attempting to gauge the distance of these nebulae Hubble used a new law described ten years earlier by Harvard astronomer Henrietta Swan Leavitt. She had observed that the brightness of a group of stars named Cepheids waxed and waned regularly. The length of time between the brightest and dimmest state indicated the true brightness of the stars. The magnitude of brightness of a star indicates how far away it is (the brightness diminishes inversely with distance, so a star twice as far away is one quarter as bright). Hubble found varying Cephids in Messier 321, the great star-cloud in the Andromeda con-

stellation. Their magnitude and period of variation revealed them to be 750,000 light years away. This caused astronomers to double the previously accepted size of the universe. In 1929, using the same magnitude test, Hubble observed stars in the Virgo cluster and discovered them to be 250 million light years away.

It was also at this time that he began to measure stellar red shift known as the Doppler[48] effect, which is caused by the way in which light waves from a receding source will arrive at the observer's eyes less frequently (the waves having been "stretched out" by the movement of their source). This shift makes the light redder (low-frequency light is redder). Hubble found that the red shift increased with the distance to the stars and from this observation formulated Hubble's Law: At double the distance, the star is receding twice as fast. This astonishing discovery led to a total revision of scientific understanding of the cosmos that was as fundamental as the change in thinking brought about by Copernicus four hundred years earlier. The red shift was observable everywhere and indicated that the entire universe was expanding. By plotting this expansion backward it was possible to arrive at a point in the past when the universe had begun in an immensely dense concentration of matter that had exploded. Hubble's red shift generated the Big Bang theory.

According to this theory the farther out into space telescopes can see the farther back in time they look, since the most distant objects will be those which have been moving away longest. To search out such objects was one of the goals of the astronomical intrument that also confirmed the existence of black holes: the Hubble Space Telescope. The telescope was able to give an unprecedented view of the universe primarily because of its position six hundred kilometers above the Earth and free of the distorting effects of the atmosphere. Hubble was taken to orbit April 25, 1990, by the crew of Shuttle Mission STS-31 and was operated by the Johns Hopkins Space Telescope Science Institute on behalf of NASA and the European Space Agency. Although initially the Space Telescope was due to be returned to Earth at intervals for servicing, not long after it had begun to work NASA decided that maintenance would be better accomplished in orbit.

48 118 221

On both the delivery and later maintenance missions the 121-foot, 4.5-million-pound shuttle, a craft the size of a DC-9 and with a wingspan of 78 feet, maneuvered into the exact position for the telescope's initial release or (on maintenance missions) close enough to the orbiting telescope to grapple it. The delicacy of these maneuvers shows the extreme accuracy with which the shuttle can be flown, thanks to its reaction control system (RCS). The RCS consists of forty-four small nozzles set on the nose and the aft fuselage near the main engines. Thirty-eight of the thrusters each produce 870 pounds of thrust and six of them each produce 25 pounds. The larger engines are designed to be able to do fifty thousand firings, the smaller five hundred thousand. The RCS enables the pilot to position the shuttle to within half a degree and burns nitrogen textroxide and monomethyl hydrazine. Hydrazine is an extremely powerful fuel (first used as a fuel during World War II by the German rocket-powered ME 163 fighter) and provides more bang for the buck (greater specific impulse) than any other fuel except hydrogen. Hydrazine has other less explosive uses: in pharmaceuticals, for corrosion control in water-heating systems, in photography, photocopying, dyes and metal-plating. It is also used in fungicides.

The first fungicide was developed in reaction to the greatest disaster France has ever experienced: the great downy mildew plague that struck French vineyards in 1878. The irony was that the fungus had been introduced on American vine stock brought to France to solve an earlier wine crisis: the great phylloxera epidemic of 1865, which by the time downy mildew appeared had already decimated French wine production.

Toward the end of October 1882 the Bordeaux University professor of botany, Pierre Millardet, was strolling among the vineyards and noticed that some of the vines were a strange greenish-blue color. They were also healthy. Inquiries revealed that it had long been the custom among local growers to spatter their vines with a mixture of copper sulphate and lime to deter would-be thieves. Millardet had been looking for an antifungus chemical with which to coat vine leaves at the point in the year when downy mildew fungus was most vulnerable to chemical attack. By the time of the next harvest Mil-

lardet had produced the "Bordeaux Mixture" of copper sulphate, quicklime and water. It was the world's first chemical fungicide.

The wine plagues had halved French output. Since wine accounted for a quarter of the country's agricultural income and provided a living for over six million people, the government was keen to prevent such a disaster from happening again. In 1878 an international quarantine conference took place in Bern, Switzerland, where regulations were agreed on the transfer of plants across frontiers. Unfortunately, the delegates seemed to ignore the fact that phylloxera had been caused by an aphid and that aphids can fly.

Other problems related to the crossing of frontiers were exercising the minds of Swiss conference delegates around the same time. In 1874 twenty-one countries met at a Bern Postal Conference to regulate the delivery of international mail[49] and in particular to establish agreed charges and categories. Four years later members of the International Postal Union added a Money Orders Agreement. In 1882 an American organization started the first Express Money Order with a tamper-proof order form. The purchaser tore off a row of figures, printed at the side of the form, down to the required amount. This made it impossible for anyone to increase the sum to be cashed at the receiving end. The company, American Express, also guaranteed against loss or forgery.

American Express began in 1850 with the amalgamation of three express services. The impetus to merge had come from the discovery of gold in California two years earlier. The attraction for American Express was the $60 million worth of gold being shipped East in one year alone and the growing demand by the gold miners and businesses in California for faster deliveries from suppliers on the East Coast. To facilitate these deliveries American Express also invented the "Cash On Delivery" system. Then, in 1860, seventy-five thousand Californians signed a petition to Congress demanding a regular and efficient postal service to link them with the families they had left behind. In 1858 gold had been found in Colorado and Kansas. These factors combined to stimulate interest in closing the last gap left in overland communications. It lay between St. Joseph, Missouri, and Sacramento, California.

49 78 *149*

Fig. 10: *A romantic view of the Pony Express. Most riders did not carry guns, trusting to outride their attackers.*

On April 7, 1860, the first Pony Express rider left St. Joseph carrying mail for California. The route was hazardous in the extreme, crossing nearly two thousand miles of the worst terrain on the continent, inhabited by hostile native Americans and bandits. Riders were recruited for their ability to withstand severe hardship and fatigue. Some were as young as fourteen. Orphans were preferred. One hundred thirty-eight stations lined their route. Every hundred-odd miles came a "home" station where riders rested briefly. At every other home station a new rider took over. At twenty-mile intervals between home stations smaller stations provided fresh horses. Schedules were tight, allowing only two minutes for a change of rider. The Pony Express never went slower than at the gallop and company policy was

that whatever the conditions or dangers "the mail must go through."
The system lasted less than two years, after which the railroads pushing from East and West joined and made the Pony Express obsolete.

American Express bought the Pony Express for the last few
months of its existence and during that time hired an extraordinary
rider. He eventually became known as "Buffalo Bill," thanks to his
prowess in shooting the animals (sixty-nine in one day) when he was
working as a meat-supplier to the Kansas Pacific railroad construction gangs in 1868. William "Buffalo Bill" Cody was a legend before
his twenty-eighth birthday, in 1872. That year, having worked for the
Pony Express, the railroads, the Army, and as a scout he appeared on
the Chicago stage playing the lead role in *Scouts of the Prairies*. After
his stage career had begun, periodic returns to spectacular adventures on the prairies added to his reputation. In 1883 he brought the
frontier to the city with his Wild West Show. The spectacle acted out
a mainly fictitious history of the West, with buffalo hunts, Indian attacks, Pony Express riders, cavalry rescues, sharpshooters, wagon
trains, trappers and scouts, and starred Cody as master of cere-
monies. By 1913, when Cody went bankrupt, the show had toured a
dozen countries and performed before fifty million people in a thousand cities.

The only competition Cody's show faced in America was from another new kind of entertainment, known as "vaudeville." By the end
of the nineteenth century the standard vaudeville program consisted
of nine ten-minute acts, including a ventriloquist, a dance routine, a
comedy and pantomime, a short play and a spectacular finish, often
a trapeze artiste. One of the first vaudeville shows had appeared in
San Francisco in 1850, billed as a racy "Parisian" entertainment. The
link with France is obvious from the genre name, the original French
version of which was *Vau de Vire* (River Vire valley). The Vire valley
is in Normandy, where the first vaudeville appears to have been invented by a fifteenth-century songwriter named Olivier Basselin. Not
much is known about Basselin except that he probably started as a
cloth fuller. Most of his musical output consisted of drinking songs
with titles like "Fun at the Table," "Drinking Produces Good Verse,"
and "Let's Have Another Glass!"

The period when Basselin was writing coincided with the gradual loss of Normandy by the English, who had occupied the country for over two hundred years. In 1450 at the Battle of Formigny (the last conflict before the final defeat and withdrawal of the English) Basselin was killed. Formigny was the first engagement in which the French used the new small cannon known as "culverins." Their use was to prove decisive. Traditionally, English tactics were to choose a defensive position, draw up their longbowmen, stick stakes point-up in the ground in front of them and wait for the French to come forward. This would be encouraged with volleys of arrows aimed at galling the mounted French knights into charging. The knights would then be halted by the stakes, and English infantry would move in to finish them off.

At Formigny this plan failed. The French set their culverins to fire along the English front and provoke their archers into action. Some of the archers broke ranks and rushed out to capture the culverins. They were dragging them back to the English side when French reinforcements turned up, saw the break in English lines and attacked. Of the 4,500 English soldiers, 3,774 perished. One further English defeat would mark the end of England's control of Normandy.

The tide had been turning against the English for over twenty years thanks to an illiterate young girl who in 1428 had turned up at the castle of Vaucouleurs in Burgundy demanding audience with Robert de Baudricourt, captain of the town. The girl claimed to have come at the urging of the voices of St. Margaret, St. Catherine and St. Michael. Wearing a "poor, thin" red dress, she announced her sacred mission: to expel the English from France and put the dauphin Charles (heir to the crown) on the throne. Swayed by her piety, De Baudricourt took her to visit Duke Charles of Lorraine, whom she persuaded to lead a less dissolute life. In return for this advice the duke gave her a horse. De Baudricourt added a sword and took her to see the dauphin at Chinon. To test her miraculous powers the dauphin wore ordinary clothes and hid among his courtiers. The girl went straight to him and they talked. Later it was said that she had told him things only he and his confessor knew. Next the clergy

questioned her about her heavenly voices, and doctors confirmed that she was also in a rare and mystic state: virginity. When she had passed all the tests the dauphin equipped her with armor, lance and standard and gave her command over his armies, much to the discomfiture of his feuding aristocrats, who resented obeying a commoner.

In 1429 victory over the English at the Battle of Orleans made her name. Henceforth she would be known as Joan of Arc, the Maid of Orleans. In battle after battle she routed the English, and finally on July 17, 1429, she led the dauphin to his coronation in Rheims. Once Charles was safely crowned he regarded Joan's mission as complete and disbanded the army the following September. He reckoned without Joan's promise to remove the English from France. Deprived of the dauphin's army, Joan turned freelance and things started to go wrong. After a series of defeats, on May 24, 1430, Joan rode out of Compiègne to attack the English and their Burgundian allies. After being caught in a pincer movement she returned to the city only to find that the gates were closed and the drawbridge raised. Within hours she was prisoner of the Burgundians.

A year later she was before a court of the Inquisition.[50] The verdict: "Having weighed the aim, manner and matter of [Joan's] revelations, the quality of her person, and the place and other circumstances, they [her voices] are either lies of the imagination, corrupt and pernicious, or the said apparitions and revelations are conjured up and proceed from malign and diabolical spirits, Belial, Satan, Behemoth." In September 1430 the Burgundians sold her to the English and on May 24, 1431, she was burned to death on a scaffold too high for the executioner to give her the customary *coup de grace*. Left to the flames, Joan died a terrible and lingering death.

The Inquisition that condemned Joan had originally been established two hundred years earlier to combat the heretical Cathars,[51] a sect that believed in poverty and free love and advocated the renunciation by the church of all material possessions. A young Spanish cleric, Domingo de Guzman, suggested that the only way to combat the growing disaffection (with a bloated church hierarchy that flaunted its wealth and indulged in gambling and fornication) was by

50 104 *197*

51 103 *196*

meeting the Cathars on their own ground. His tactic of mendicant preaching failed, and the pope launched the crusade that would by 1209 bring about the massacre of thousands of Cathars. In 1215 Pope Innocent III placed Domingo at the head of a new "Dominican" Order whose only task would be to seek out and combat heresy.

Some time between 1227 and 1233 the problem of heresy had become widespread enough for Pope Gregory IX to take further steps. By the time Joan of Arc was being interrogated the Dominican Inquisition had been set up. With the authority of the Papal Bull *Ad Extirpanda* ("those who must be wiped out"), inquisitors outranked the secular authorities and were empowered to imprison suspects without trial and submit them to torture, to confiscate the property of any suspected person, and in the final analysis to put heretics to death by fire. However, the atrocities of the Inquisition must be viewed in the light of general practices of the day. Torture was common. Punishment for treason in France involved hanging the guilty party until he was almost unconscious, then opening his abdomen and drawing out the entrails, and finally cutting his body into four pieces. Castration was an optional extra. It was also virtually impossible to survive the process of inquisition without confessing. Charges were never specified, and the names of witnesses for the prosecution were withheld. Plaintiffs were asked to imagine which crime might have led to their arrest and then to confess to that crime. They were also promised lighter sentences if they named other heretics. In the fifteenth century the Spanish Inquisition was set up to deal with people easier to identify than scattered groups of heretics: the Jews. The purpose of the new Inquisition was ostensibly to check and confirm the true conversion of Jews. In reality its task was to solve the "Jewish problem" by identifying *conversos* who still secretly professed their faith and dispossessing the richest Jews of their property and position.

The Iberian Jewish population had been in Spain and Portugal since before the eighth century, when the first Muslim invaders had taken the city of Cordova. Muslims regarded Jews as "people of the Book" who worshiped the same God and treated them as a protected minority. Jews were permitted to observe their own religion, were ex-

empt from military service and were allowed their own forms of government. While it was true that in courts of law their testimony carried less weight than that of a Muslim, they could not marry a Muslim, and they were not allowed to bear arms, nonetheless their condition compared favorably with that of Jews in Christian countries. Iberian Jews often reached high public office and were active in trade and finance. Jewish scholars were held in high esteem and played a significant role in the cultural life of the Spanish Muslim states.

After 1100 Muslim Spain began to contract as the Christian "reconquest" moved south, capturing Leon, Asturias, Aragon, Navarre, Catalonia and Castile. The last Muslim states to fall were those of Seville, Saragossa and, in 1492, Granada. Muslim tolerance of the Jews was now to be replaced by Christian repression. Jews were gathered into ghettos, forbidden to leave their homes at night and subjected to taxation that bankrupted them. In 1281 all Jews in Castile had been imprisoned and only freed on payment of a huge ransom. In the fourteenth century the synagogues of Madrid, Burgos, Cordova, Toledo and Barcelona were attacked and destroyed. The Dominicans worked tirelessly to convert Jews to Christianity. Faced with the terrifying alternative thousands of Jews became Christians. Many of these *conversos* rose to positions of power and influence, because after centuries of living in the sophisticated Muslim world they possessed skills such as numeracy and literacy that their new Christian masters lacked.

In 1474 the charismatic Dominican prior of Segovia became confessor to Queen Isabella of Castile, and in 1482 Isabella and her husband, King Ferdinand, installed him as inspector general of the Spanish Inquisition. Tomas de Torquemada's name would become synonymous with the worst excesses of the institution. On January 20, 1492, the capture of Granada, the last Muslim stronghold on the peninsula, brought 781 years of Islamic rule in Spain to an end and doomed Iberian Jews. On March 31 that year Ferdinand and Isabella confirmed the decree expelling Jews from Spain. They were given four months to prepare for their departure and forbidden on pain of death to return to Spain. All their property was to be confiscated;

they were not permitted to take gold, silver or minted coins with them; and anyone giving help, food or shelter to a Jew after July 1, 1492, would be severely punished. The Edict of Expulsion was a disaster for the Jews, most of whom could not realize their worth in the time available. Houses in the ghetto were valueless, and Christians made a fortune by buying Jewish assets at giveaway prices. Best estimates are that 250,000 Jews were driven out.

Iberian Jews scattered throughout Europe, many of them to Eastern Europe, Holland and Portugal, but most returned to the Islamic community that had treated them with understanding and sympathy for so long. The vast majority of these headed for Istanbul, ruled at the time by Sultan Bajazet, who remarked that Ferdinand was a poor statesman, since by expelling the country's most intelligent and industrious members he had impoverished his own kingdom to benefit his rivals.

It was not long before the Jews were performing valuable services in their new home. The year 1520 saw the start of the forty-six-year reign of Bajazet's great-grandson Suleyman the Magnificent, who would take the Ottoman Empire to its cultural apogee and extend its rule over three continents. The Jews were of particular value to Suleyman because their knowledge of European banking systems and their development of a sophisticated system of bills of exchange with other Jewish bankers throughout Europe made them able to transfer funds more efficiently than their Christian and Turkish competitors. Their contacts with Jewish colleagues in the European marketplace, their flair for languages and their ability to keep accounts and write commercial letters and contracts combined to make them critically important to the Turkish exchequer. Jews became indispensable wherever they developed a monopoly, as they did in the trading of sugar, coffee and spices. In 1552 one of these high-placed Jews, Moshe Amon, petitioned the Turkish government to secure the transfer to Istanbul of funds belonging to a Portuguese Jewish banker, Dona Gracia Mendes. This formidable lady had recently renounced her conversion to Christianity and expressed the wish to emigrate to Istanbul together with her nephew Joseph Nasi.

Joseph had spent time in the Mendes family bank in Antwerp and had become a personal friend of the Emperor Charles V. Gracia and Joseph's wealth soon bought them power and influence in Turkey. Gracia became a confidante of Roxelane, Suleyman's favorite wife. By the early 1560s Joseph was fabulously wealthy and was in all but name Turkish foreign minister, in one instance mediating an agreement between Selim (Suleyman's successor) and Charles IX of France. Joseph was extremely ambitious, once styling himself "King of the Jews," although the highest rank conferred on him by the Turks was the dukedom of the Greek island of Naxos.

In 1564, not long after Joseph had gained Suleyman's ear, the sultan's council discussed the possibility of an attack on Malta. The island was the headquarters of the Knights of Malta, a Christian Order Suleyman had expelled from their previous base on the island of Rhodes several decades earlier. Voices at the council were raised against the scheme, arguing that Turkish expansion should be to the north and east, beyond Hungary. In the end the council decided to capture Malta and use it as a base from which to attack Spain, Italy and southern Europe. By this time the Knights of Malta, positioned in the channel between Sicily and North Africa, were indulging in what would best be described as organized piracy, one act of which decided Suleyman on his course of action. The Knights captured a merchant ship belonging to Kustir-Aga, chief eunuch of the sultan's seraglio. The ship carried a cargo of eighty thousand ducats and was loaded with Venetian merchandise in which the principal ladies of the imperial harem had taken shares. Suleyman was therefore under pressure by members of his immediate family to capture Malta, retrieve the goods and free Muslim prisoners (now being used ignominiously as galley slaves on ships fighting the Turks).

On Friday, May 18, 1565, the first Turkish ships were sighted by the Maltese defenders. They were the vanguard of a massive invasion fleet consisting of 181 ships carrying 30,000 men, 6,000 barrels of gunpowder, 1,300 cannonballs, 80,000 rounds of small-arms shot and provisions. Malta's defenders numbered 9,000 fighting men, 5,000 of whom were native islanders. The Knights were superb,

highly trained soldiers with a Crusader tradition of courage. So strong was their fear of capture by the Turks that Malta's defenders were prepared to fight to the end. Their leader, Jean Parisot de la Valette, grand master for seven years, had an extraordinary grasp of military tactics and inspired his men by example. He had already spent months preparing the ground, erecting fortifications and razing buildings that offered cover to the attackers. In the long run the tenacity of the defenders and the rifts in the Turkish command, coupled with their total lack of tactical planning, finally led to the attackers' withdrawal and the lifting of the siege.

After the Turks had left almost every major building in Malta was in need of repair or replacement. It was decided by the European powers (which had come too late to the aid of the island) that Malta should be heavily fortified for the key strategic role she was now to play. In December 1565 Francesco Laparelli, a military engineer, arrived to start building. It was decided to erect a fortified capital city to be called Valetta. The new city was the last word in Renaissance design. A rectangular pattern of streets and open spaces was surrounded by walls and bastions. Every house was connected to the town sewers and contained cisterns for collecting rainwater. A uniform style of building was required.

The outstanding new construction in the new city was the hospital, which opened in 1575. The Knights of Malta had begun as a nursing order founded in Jerusalem in 1048 to care for wounded Crusaders, so they were also known as "Knights Hospitallers." The hospital director, known as the grand hospitaller, ranked with the highest officials of the order. The Valetta hospital incorporated many radically new ideas. There were separate wards for different types of disease: one for the treatment of kidney stones, one for venereal and skin diseases, one for hot-bath treatment of syphilis, one for the terminally ill, one for contagious diseases, one for dysentery and most unusual of all, one for mentally ill patients. Another outstanding feature was the provision of single beds, each of which was made up every evening. If necessary sheets were changed several times a day.

Treatment was limited. Anesthesia was administered with a narcotic sponge soaked in belladonna and mandrake and held over the

patient's mouth, or by the use of a hammer with which the physician struck a wooden helmet worn by the patient to knock him out. Wounds were usually washed with salt water. Splints and traction were employed. Severed blood vessels were ligatured and wounds in soft tissue were stitched. The corps of physicians operating in the hospital were required to be "learned and experienced" and to swear on oath that they would do their best for the sick. They were also required to base their practice of medicine on that of the "most approved physicians."

The most approved physician of the time was a doctor whose father had been pharmacist to the imperial house of Hapsburg and who himself had been physician to Emperor Charles V. Andreas Vesalius had qualified in Paris and then at Padua, where in 1537 his demonstration of dissection techniques was so impressive he was immediately made professor of surgery at the age of twenty-three. In 1543 he stunned the medical world with a publication entitled *De Humanis Corporis Fabrica* (On the Structure of the Human Body). The book was the first truly modern anatomy text with illustrations taken from life. Vesalius dispensed with the authority of ancient Greek and Roman medical texts and presented what he saw: everything from skeleton to nerves, organs, muscles and skin. Vesalius also described his dissection methods well enough for a practicing reader to follow. The *De Corporis* illustrations were woodcuts carved in pear, sawn with the grain and then rubbed with hot linseed oil to give the surface greater elasticity. The identity of the cutter is unknown but there is little doubt that the extraordinary drawings from which he worked were done in the studio of the great Venetian painter Titian.

Tiziano Vecelli was born of aristocratic parents in northern Italy in 1488 and already at the age of eight showed such a talent for art that he was sent with his brother to be apprentice to a master in Venice. The Most Serene Republic of Venice was the richest seaport in Europe and known for conspicuous consumption. Art offered profitable career opportunities, as Giovanni Bellini, the leading Venetian painter when Titian arrived, had found out. His contract with the government provided him with a life-long pension in return for

painting one portrait of each doge as he was elected. It was to the studio of Giovanni's brother Gentile that Titian and his brother were sent.

After a short stay with Gentile Titian left to work for Giorgione da Castelfranco, who had just shocked the Venetian art world with an altarpiece in which he had painted the Madonna standing in a landscape instead of a church. It was Giorgione ("Big George") who for the first time began to use the shading of colors to suggest shape and volume. His innovative idea of using canvas and oils flouted tradition and introduced a realist style that Titian was quick to adopt. In 1526 Titian produced an altarpiece for the Church of the Friars that is reckoned to be the first example of his personal style. It shows a shapely Madonna being lifted to heaven by a host of angels. The radical thing about the painting is that the Madonna looks heavy. The Friars were said to be "shocked" the first time they saw it. Titian's full-blooded realism caught on like wildfire. Titian's women were so realistic because he was a master of flesh tones, the skill that had made the illustrations in Vesalius's book so powerful.

By 1530 Titian was everybody's favorite artist, and he began to paint portraits of the great: the queen of Cyprus, the duke of Ferrara, a Medici cardinal, the king of France. In 1545 he went to Rome and was welcomed by the pope like a prince. His portrait of Paul III was so realistic it is said that when he put it out on a terrace to dry passers-by doffed their hats. The Holy Roman Emperor Charles V thought highly enough of Titian to create him a count palatine and knight of the Golden Spur, with right of entry to the imperial court. This was an honor not normally granted to painters.

Perhaps the most famous of Titian's many portraits of Charles was painted while the emperor was in Germany in 1548. For a number of years Charles had been attempting to find common ground between the Catholic church and the new breakaway German Protestants, who had been led to schism in 1521 by Martin Luther. By 1545 the Protestant princes had formed a league, had refused to attend the upcoming Council of Trent (whose mandate was a sweeping reform of the Catholic church in response to the Protestant movement) and had rejected every attempt at compromise. The emperor had no re-

Fig. 11: *Titian's portrait of Paul III. In 1545 the pope welcomed the painter to Rome "like a Prince."*

sort but to force. In the spring of 1547 at the Battle of Muhlberg, Bavaria, the Protestants were routed, and one of their leaders, the elector of Saxony, was taken prisoner. Titian painted him. Then in nearby Augsburg he painted a portrait of Charles astride his horse in full parade armor, dressed as he had been for the battle.

Charles V's armor had been made in Augsburg because the city was famous for its metalworkers and lay close to a major mining area producing gold, silver and iron. The suit Charles wears in the Muhlberg painting features one of the other things for which Augsburg was famous: a screw. The screw principle had been known since Classical times when it was used in olive presses and to lift water, but it was only in the Renaissance that metal screws were developed, and one of their uses was in armor. Part of the armor, known as a *manteau d'armes* (a rigid shield fixed to the left breast and shoulder and used in tilting) was attached by means of a square-headed bolt tightened with a spanner. The *manteau* was often also a feature of the kind of parade armor Charles wore at Muhlberg.

It is probable that the metal screw was originally developed in Augsburg by jewelers or goldsmiths whose expertise in precious metal work also led to the development of a new method of coinage. At some time around 1550, thanks to the enthusiastic recommendation of the French ambassador to Augsburg, a goldsmith named Max Schwab was invited by Henry II of France to bring one of his new balance presses to Paris. Schwab's press was turned by means of a long transverse wooden handle, weighted at each end. When the handle was turned to screw the press down, the weights on the handle exerted a balanced pressure so that the die held in the press was forced evenly onto the metal and created an unusually sharp impression.

Henry II was keen to reform his coinage because he suffered from a problem common to all heads of state at the time: Bills were settled in cash, of which there was a very limited amount available. In 1530 Charles V had held the sons of the French king Francis I to a 2 million gold ecu ransom. Since there were not enough gold ecus in France to pay the ransom, Francis was obliged to buy foreign coin, melt it down and turn it into ecus. The cost of wars and the mercenaries who fought them frequently obliged kings and princes to borrow money. When Max Schwab arrived in France, Henry II owed the Lyons bankers almost his entire annual income. The situation was complicated by the presence of large amounts of counterfeit coins and the fact that all coinage was easily debased through shaving down. Henry's idea was to create new coins to replace the debased currency. The ecu was to be renamed the "henri" and given a lower gold content. In order better to manage the recoinage (and the currency in general) Henry set up a royal treasury in the Louvre to house money chests to which only Henry and his chancellor held the keys.

One of the major demands on Henry's purse was the expenditures of his wife, Catherine de Médicis, renowned for her love of luxury. On her accession she had doubled the size of the queen's traditional personal retinue to 100. Catherine lived a life of ostentation during the royal progresses round the kingdom. She also personally owned nine chateaux and palaces, one of which (La Tournelle, on the banks

of the Seine) she demolished to make way for the Tuileries. She also built a new wing on the Louvre, two new chateaux (Monceau and Chaillot, both near Paris) and added a gallery to the Chateau de Chenonceaux. Her personal apartments were filled with Indian tables, Turkish carpets, hangings of gold and silver cloth, vases of jasper, cabinets inlaid with silver, mother-of-pearl tables, enamel, porcelain, glass, tapestries and hundreds of portraits. It is also said she introduced much of Italian cuisine to France and popularized the idea of restaurants.

Catherine held grand fetes, called *magnificences,* to show off the royal family to diplomats and ambassadors. At one of these occasions she developed one of her famous migraines and retired to take her new medicine. In 1559 the first examples of the newly discovered tobacco plant had arrived in Iberia, and the French ambassador, Jean Nicot, sent Catherine some leaves he grew from seeds given him by a Dutch explorer. Later the great Swedish taxonomist Carl von Linne would coin the term "nicotine" from Nicot's name.

Catherine may have been the first European to take snuff but she was not alone for long. In 1560 Nicot wrote to the cardinal of Lorraine that tobacco had healed an ulcer and eliminated a fistula pronounced incurable by physicians. Over the next twenty years tobacco would be prescribed as an antiseptic, an emetic, and a cure for flatulence, toothache, a heavy cough (inhale smoke deeply), pregnancy pains, halitosis, rabies, gangrene and itching. By 1610 there were few ailments that it was not reputed to cure.

For rulers everywhere the problem with the rapidly growing craving for tobacco was the amount of money leaving their countries to pay for it. Elizabeth of England issued a decree against "misuse" of tobacco. The Turkish sultan Murad IV made snuff-taking a capital offense. Pope Urban III issued an interdict on the taking of snuff in places of worship. None of these measures worked. In London courses in how to smoke were being given by "professors in the art of whiffing." By the mid-seventeenth century the French, Spanish and English governments had awakened to the possibility of turning the situation to fiscal advantage by setting up tobacco-growing colonies in America and state tobacco monopolies at home.

The English colony of Maryland was established almost exclusively for the purpose of producing tobacco. Maryland was one of the three points on the great trade "triangle": English ships would take slaves to the Caribbean, exchange them there for sugar, spices and rum, then deliver these to the American colonists in exchange for tobacco, brought to England. Growing tobacco in the Colony was a night-and-day endeavor, involving thirty-six separate operations, including stirring the ground, transplanting, covering with oak leaves, "hilling," picking off worms, pinching to prevent flowering, cutting, drying, curing, stripping and packing. When the cured tobacco was ready, four-hundred-pound hogsheads were packed tightly with leaves and rolled to the nearest jetty for loading. Some of the roads used for this purpose are still referred to as "rolling" roads. Maryland was an attractive location for tobacco-growing because with hundreds of creeks and inlets around the Chesapeake Bay plantations would rarely be more than a few miles from water.

Early plantations were poor affairs. The majority of Maryland immigrants were single young men, because after the mid-seventeenth century the Barbados plantation owners wanted only black slaves, and New England's foreign exchange shortage limited immigrants to those with skills or capital. Maryland immigrants were granted a piece of land once they had worked off a five-year service agreement. It would then take a further five years to make enough money to get married. Tobacco-growing required few tools: an axe to clear land and a hoe. Most planters lived in one-room frame houses with planks laid across the rafters to make sleeping lofts. The houses were often made of green wood and required frequent repairs, becoming virtually uninhabitable after a decade, when owners simply moved on and built again. This "throwaway house" was a feature of the Maryland countryside that struck most visitors.

The explosive growth of tobacco imports to Europe coincided with a general and rapid increase in international trade as the new European nation-states established colonies and began the exploration of Africa and the East. The opportunity for governments to raise revenue from imports was too good to miss. By the end of the first quarter of the seventeenth century most European countries had

updated and extended their excise departments. In 1643 the English government had introduced the first excise duty, initially a levy on home-produced goods such as beer and ale, liquor, cider, soap, meat, salt, leather and cloth. The tax was tremendously unpopular because it was extended beyond the promised single year of collection (and never repealed), and also because a tax on the necessities of life hit the poor hardest. As the number of taxed commodities increased so too did the complexity of administration. The calculation of excise taxes was exacerbated by the fact that different measures were applied to different commodities such as glass, salt, windows, bottles, leather, wood and tobacco. As trade flourished and the marketplace grew more varied the calculations involved in taxation grew ever more complex.

In the early part of the seventeenth century a radically new method of calculation had emerged that would lighten the burden of tax collectors. In 1614 a Scots mathematician named John Napier published a book detailing his new "logarithmic" calculation system. Four years later it had the attention of scientists and mathematicians throughout Europe. In essence Napier made it possible to carry out complex arithmetic calculations through simple addition and subtraction. For example, using a base of 10, 100 can be also written as 10^2 (10×10), and 1,000 as 10^3 ($10 \times 10 \times 10$). Multiplication of the two numbers can be done by adding their logarithms (the small superscript numbers). So $10 \times 1,000 = 10^4$. Division involves subtracting the logs: $1,000 \div 100$ $(10^3 - 10^2) = 10$. Using a base of 2, multiplying 8 (2^3, or $2 \times 2 \times 2$) by 32 (2^5, or $2 \times 2 \times 2 \times 2 \times 2$) means adding their logs ($3 + 5 = 8$), and looking up the number for log 8 ($2^8 = 256$). Finding the square of 32 means doubling its log (2^5). The result, 2^{10}, is the log of 1,024 (the square of 32). To find square roots, halve the log: the square root of 256 is half its log (2^8), that is, 2^4, which is 16 (the square root of 256). Large and detailed tables were worked out to provide the logs of all numbers, so as to make possible quick calculation of the largest and most complex sums.

The discovery of logarithms soon led to the development of an instrument that would make the work even easier. Some time after 1622 William Oughtred, a Cambridge mathematician, produced a

circular brass table carrying two joined pointers that "slid" around scales to perform calculations of any logarithm. Oughtred's slide rule was almost certainly made by Elias Allen, one of the most famous instrument-makers of the day. Allen was one of the first masters of the new London Clockmakers' Company, established by royal charter in 1631 to protect the craft against immigrant foreigners (all clockmakers in London at the time were foreign). The company was given regulatory powers over all clockmaking in England.

One of the foremost London clockmaking firms of the day was run by the Dutch Fromanteel family. In 1658 one of them advertised an amazing new kind of clock: "There is lately a way found out for making Clocks that go exact and keep equaller time than any now made without this Regulator . . . and are not subject to alter by change of weather as others are, and may be made to go a week, or a month, or a year, with once winding up, as well as those that are wound up every day, and keep time as well." Fromanteel was referring to the development by his friend and fellow-Dutchman Christiaan Huygens,[52] who a year earlier had invented the pendulum clock capable of measuring time accurately to within ten seconds a day.

Huygens had spent time at the Paris Royal Academy of Science, where his assistant was a Protestant Frenchman named Denis Papin, an extremely skilful mechanic and instrument-maker who also had a degree in medicine. In 1675 Papin turned up in London, possibly as the result of religious persecution in France, took employment with Robert Boyle[53] and began a series of vacuum-related experiments. In 1679 Boyle's instrument-maker Robert Hooke introduced Papin to the Royal Society, and Papin showed them his new "digester." This was an apparatus for boiling food under pressure in a closed iron pot fitted with a safety valve.

Papin's digester was to find use as a sterilizer of hospital instruments three hundred years later, following the work of a French scientist named Louis Pasteur.[54] In 1854 Pasteur took over the Faculty of Science at Lille University and began to investigate recent problems related to sugar beet alcohol, which was inexplicably turning sour. Pasteur discovered that tiny organisms were present in the sour solution. Further experiments with meat juice revealed that similar

Fig. 12: *Louis Pasteur, whose work inspired the Carlsberg brewery to open the first fermentation research lab.*

organisms were present and could be killed by boiling. If a flask of the boiled juices was sealed, a short time after the flask was cracked open again live organisms appeared once more. Pasteur concluded these "germs" came from the air. He then went on to discover the presence of microbes in sour wine. Heating the wine to fifty-five degrees Centigrade would kill the bacteria while not damaging the wine. The same turned out to be true of milk. In a spirited attempt to make French beer as good as its German counterpart Pasteur carried out the same type of research at breweries, with the same results. Pasteur's process became known as "pasteurizing" and was eventually used to sterilize medical instruments in a latter-day version of Papin's digester known as an autoclave.

In the 1870s the German beer-makers, against whose efforts Pasteur's brewery work had originally been aimed, commissioned a locomotive engineer, Carl von Linde,[55] to find ways to keep their beer **55** 27 53

cool in summer so as to permit year-round production. Linde responded by developing the first successful compressed-ammonia refrigerator. At around the same time a Scottish engineer named James Harrison was perfecting a similar system in Australia in response to the near-catastrophic food shortage in England, where the rapidly rising population of industrializing towns was fast outstripping the country's ability to feed them.

In the event others than Harrison succeeded in producing techniques for chilling Australian meat, which was delivered by refrigerated ship,[56] and saved England from famine in the 1870s. However, at one point in the previous decade Harrison returned to London and set up a refrigeration plant that would chill paraffin into paraffin wax, ideal for candles. A little later, with the development of novel ways of machine-folding cardboard, paraffin-waxed card containers made possible the introduction of fast foods. In 1906 came the first waxed-card milk containers and the paper cups that would become so familiar as to be invisible at every coffee dispenser in the Western world.

56 77 149

CHAPTER 5

⊠

Life Is No Picnic

Instant coffee is a perfect example of modern convenience food. It came into existence in the 1930s when due to good weather Brazil and the other South American coffee-producing countries found themselves with massive coffee-bean surpluses. Various methods of turning this excess into a saleable commodity were tried, and in 1938 Dr. Hans Morgenthaler of the Nestle Company came up with the answer. Coffee was brewed in a gigantic percolator two stories high. The ready brew was then pumped to the top of a tower from which it was sprayed into a drying chamber. As the coffee fell it was blasted with hot air. By the time it reached ground level all the water in the coffee had evaporated, leaving only the fine grounds.

At the time there was no obvious market for the new coffee. Then came World War II and the instant coffee market was instantly created. American quartermasters (and soldiers) were keen to reduce the weight of rations to a minimum so as to keep the size of the ration package small and make the ingredients palatable but not easily spoiled. Eventually, "K" rations became standard throughout the American military. They consisted of three small boxes, each one including a can for each meal (meat, meat and egg, or processed cheese), biscuits, crackers, dextrose tablets, a fruit bar, a chocolate bar, bouillon, lemon juice crystals, sugar tablets, a stick of chewing gum, four cigarettes and instant coffee. The package provided thirty-four hundred calories a day and was easily delivered. This was par-

ticularly important in the extremely mobile conditions of World War II when armies were unprecedentedly mechanized. By the end of the war America had over eight million troops in the field, using tanks, trucks and Jeeps. The soldiers were giving quartermasters night-mares because of the speed with which their position changed almost daily. Logistics were extremely complex and large-scale. When fifty thousand American troops went ashore on D-day they were backed up by five hundred thousand quartermasters, medical personnel, ordnance suppliers and signal and transportation corps.

What made the gigantic wartime supply task possible was an ex-traordinary vehicle specially developed for the purpose: the Jeep. The original specification was for a four-by-four truck, weighing thirteen hundred pounds empty, seating four people including the driver, with minimum ground clearance of six and a half inches, an operating speed range from three to fifty miles per hour and room to carry a 0.30mm machine gun. The manufacturer was to deliver one prototype within forty-nine days and a further seventy vehicles within seventy-five days. The Willys Overland vehicle company won the contract and in the end came in within seven ounces of the all-up specifications because they weighed the paint. The Jeep became the most versatile war machine ever. It was used variously as a command vehicle, weapons carrier, ambulance, cargo carrier, personnel carrier, ammo carrier (with a trailer) and mobile control tower. Above all it was a Jeep that did the final run each day, to deliver rations and sup-plies to front-line troops. Of the twenty-seven pounds of supplies each American soldier needed to stay fighting no fewer than fifteen pounds of it was gasoline.

Ironically, as the Jeep raced across the battlefields it was using up this precious and limited resource but at the same time riding on tires developed as part of the solution to the fuel shortage. Gasoline was produced by a process developed well before the war and known as "cracking." This involved pumping crude oil through pipes lining a large, white-hot brick furnace, which heated the oil to about eight hundred degrees Centigrade. At this temperature the oil was released into the bottom of a tall steel cylinder known as the "fractionating tower," where all but the heaviest constituents flashed into vapor and

Fig. 13: *The amazing "can-do" World War II Jeep. Names like Peep and Puddle Jumper were also suggested.*

rose up the cylinder. At various levels perforated trays heated to a different specific temperature caused different parts of the rising vapors to condense, the lighter the higher. The last two fractions condensing at the highest levels were kerosene and gasoline. At the top of the tower the final product of this entire process escaped in the form of methane gas.

The Jeep tires were developed because acetylene[57] gas can be derived from methane. Acetylene had been around since the late nineteenth century, when it was discovered almost by accident when water was dropped on calcium carbide, which gave off the gas. The Notre Dame University professor of chemistry, Julius Nieuwland,[58] began investigating the properties of acetylene. In 1925 he read a paper to the American Chemical Society about his success in using acetylene to derive an unusual compound: chloroprene. DuPont became interested enough to take the work to the next stage, which

57 39 74
57 127 244

58 115 216

119

was to polymerize the chloroprene to produce neoprene. Polymerization consists of attaching certain molecules to the ends of other molecules in order to produce gigantically long molecular chains (polymers), which exhibit elasticity and sensitivity to heat. For this reason the generic name for the product of this process is "thermoplastics." The product of this early polymerization, neoprene, was artificial rubber, and the first neoprene tires came off the production lines in 1940 just in time for the Jeep.

The chemist at DuPont who had worked on neoprene was Wallace Carothers. By 1935 Carothers had developed a polymer he named "66" because both of its linked molecules contained six carbon atoms. The "66" was extruded in filaments that could be stretched up to seven times their length when cold and woven into extraordinarily strong fibers that exhibited both elasticity and high tensile strength. The fibers were also sheer, creaseproof, and waterproof. When DuPont released the new fiber onto the market in 1940 in the form of women's stockings, they named it "nylon." When the war was over and nylon could once again be used for civilian purposes it caused a revolution in all kinds of fashion wear.

Nylon stockings were knitted on "Cotton" stocking machines virtually unchanged since 1864, when the stocking-frame machine had reached its final stage of development at the hands of William Cotton, in Loughborough, England. Stocking-frame machines knitted stockings in two pieces, determining the shape of each side of the leg by the number of stitches used in any particular row. The two pieces were then joined with a seam running up the back of the leg.

The early stocking-frame was responsible for one of the most violent episodes in the history of the early Industrial Revolution. In 1812 the trade blockade[59] during the war with Napoleon caused a slump in commerce because it cut England off from her markets abroad. Stagnant trade brought soaring prices and the war brought high taxation. Average wages fell by one-third. Bad harvests between 1809 and 1811 meant that a four-pound loaf cost almost one-fifth of a worker's weekly income. Profiteering was rife. As the war continued and small manufacturing firms went broke unemployment rose. In the county of Nottingham, the home of stocking manufacture,

59 10 34
59 43 78
59 112 212

piecework weavers usually rented stocking-frames from master hosiers and wove at home (the long windows to catch the best light longest through the day can still be seen in their cottages). As the economic crisis worsened, hosiers began to cut back, reducing wages and increasing rentals.

To all this was added one final, unexpected twist: a change in fashion. Around 1790 people had begun to reject knee breeches and stockings in favor of the new long trousers. Nobody cared about what kind of stockings they wore under their trousers, so manufacturers began to cut stockings out from large pieces woven on ordinary looms. The stocking weavers faced ruin. On March 11, 1811, a weavers' demonstration in the city of Nottingham was broken up by a company of dragoons. The crowd moved on to the nearby village of Arnold, where the rioters broke into cottages and smashed sixty frames. Over the next few weeks the pattern was repeated all over the county. Soon proclamations and pamphlets began to appear, written by the rioters' leader, who called himself General Ned Ludd. It was at this time that the word for machine breaker, "Luddite," entered the language.

The rioters became better organized and began to wear masks and scarves to hide their identity. The movement spread rapidly to the textile manufacturing towns of Yorkshire. Curfews were imposed and 3,000 troops mustered. The country suddenly recalled the riots and violence of the recent French Revolution and the government overreacted. In February 1812 the Home Secretary introduced a bill enacting the death penalty for frame breaking. The same month, in Nottingham, nine men charged with frame breaking (two of them sixteen-year-old boys) were transported to Australia for between seven and fourteen years. The outcry was immediate: Their sentences had been too lenient. As a result, people were transported merely for administering the Luddite oath. In January 1813 at York fourteen men were executed. They were young, hardworking and deeply religious. They sang hymns on the gallows and the crowd joined in.

As the death penalty bill was being debated in Parliament the Luddites found support from an unexpected quarter. A young, unknown

60 30 *61*
60 132 249

aristocrat[60] rose to give an impassioned speech in the House of Lords. It was his maiden speech and in it he spoke of men "convicted of the capital crime of poverty. . . . Are not their capital punishments enough in your statutes? Is there not blood enough upon your penal code that more must be forced forth to ascend to Heaven and testify against you? Are these the remedies for a starving and desperate populace? Will the famished wretch who has braved your bayonets be appalled by your gibbets? When death is a relief (and the only relief, it appears, you will afford him) will he be dragooned into tranquillity?"

A few weeks later with the publication of his epic poem *Childe Harold* the young speaker, Lord Byron, was a household name. He said, "I awoke one morning and found myself famous." Five hundred copies of the poem were sold in the first few days, five thousand by the end of the month. The poem had everything: a call to liberty, a hint of libertinism, Eastern mystery, doom-and-gloom forebodings, the tale of a hero outcast for unnamed sins. Women swooned at Byron's feet, seeing the poem as a love letter written for them alone.

At the time of his defense of the Luddites in 1812 Byron had just returned from the journey during which he had written *Childe Harold*. The trip had been financed by a friend who raised a loan on a gambling win. Byron's journey to the mysterious East was in part inspired by the tradition that rich young aristocrats with a passion for culture had for the previous seventy-five years or so been obliged to take the Grand Tour of Europe. Initially in the mid-eighteenth century this had been triggered by growing interest in such archeological discoveries as Pompeii and Herculaneum. By Byron's time the emphasis had shifted, now that the Greek Revival phase of the Romantic Movement was in full swing. The focus was now on the struggle to free Greece from the yoke of the Turk. Byron's was a fact-finding mission, initially to Turkey and then to Greece and Albania, both under Turkish control. During the trip Byron did everything a young Romantic was supposed to: he dressed in Albanian costume, drank wildly, danced Greek dances, fell in love every day (with women and men), sat up all night around campfires plotting revolution, swam the Hellespont and visited Troy.

At one point on the trip Byron was spotted in the Gibraltar garrison library by a Scotsman named John Galt, who had traveled out from England on the same ship. The initial reason for Galt's journey was to set up a Gibraltar branch of the Glasgow textile manufacturing firm Kirkman Finlay. Galt also had a plan to find a way around the Napoleonic War blockade that had caused such problems for the stocking-weavers and virtually ended all import-export in Britain. For a newly industrialized country this was little short of disaster, and British manufacturers were desperate to find ways around the problem.

Galt's mandate from Kirkman Finlay was to find a route into central European markets through the back door. For Galt this meant moving the goods (a hundred bales of cotton) across the Mediterranean into Turkey and then into Europe over the Turkish-Hungarian border. In the long run the plan came adrift when Galt found himself on the Turkish-Hungarian border with the goods, forty-five camels and a no-show contact. Galt was obliged to get rid of the goods at cost to a local Turk. After this he returned to England, married and became a journalist. Success finally came when he published his *Life of Byron* in 1830.

Meanwhile one other side effect of the Anglo-French blockade was causing trouble elsewhere. In answer to wartime needs for more sailors the British navy had for some decades resorted to press-ganging. By 1806 the navy had eight hundred ships and keeping them staffed required up to 150,000 men. Press-ganging usually involved sending raiding parties ashore to find and drag unwilling men off to sea. The practice became an international issue when the British started doing it to American ships. The Americans saw this as a direct violation of their sovereignty, but the British argued that the American merchant marine included thousands of British deserters who had obtained false certificates of American citizenship.

Things came to a head in Norfolk, Virginia, in 1807 when the USS *Chesapeake* was being readied for a Mediterranean cruise. The British consul in Norfolk officially complained to the yard commander, Captain Stephen Decatur,[61] that the ship was carrying four British deserters. Decatur refused to accept this and the *Chesapeake* set sail. At

61 12 34

123

Fig. 14: *The end of the USS* Chesapeake, *in 1813, off Boston, being boarded by the victorious British ship* Shannon.

3:00 P.M. as the ship was clearing the area and the crew were still busy stowing provisions and cargo, the *Chesapeake* was approached by the British warship *Leopard* with a request that she heave to so that *Leopard* could put aboard dispatches destined for England. Instead of dispatches, however, *Leopard* delivered a demand for the release of the four "deserters." When the *Chesapeake*'s captain, Commodore James Barron, refused, the *Leopard* opened fire, killing three American sailors and wounding eighteen. A British party then boarded the *Chesapeake,* took the four deserters and left. In reaction to this act of violence President Jefferson imposed a blockade on all British trade with America. The blockade would ultimately lead to the War of 1812.

In August 1814, after burning the White House, the Capitol and all other Washington buildings except the Patent Office, the British army attacked Baltimore. Their immediate target was Fort McHenry, which commanded all sea approaches to the city. On the afternoon of September 13 the British arrived and found the fort well-nigh im-

pregnable from land. It was decided to soften up the city with a bombardment from the sea. The British "bomb" ships *Terror, Metero, Aetna, Devastation* and *Volcano* were brought to within two miles of the fort and the bombardment began. It lasted for twenty-five hours (from 6:00 P.M. on the thirteenth until 7:00 A.M. on the fourteenth). Up to one thousand eight hundred shells and Congreve rockets were fired into the fort, the aim being to cause the defenders to panic and desert. During the attack a young American lawyer who had earlier been attempting to arrange the release of an American civilian found himself negotiating on board the British admiral's flagship when news came of the British plan of attack. The American's release was postponed and they were returned to their truce boat, manned by Americans, from which they were able to observe the entire bombardment.

The last view of the fort they had on the evening of the thirteenth was of the American flag pierced by British shells. One of their British guards told them to take a long look at it, since by morning it would no longer be flying once the defenders had deserted the fort. In the gray light of dawn as the bombardment ceased they looked toward the fort. The flag still flew. The attack had failed. The young lawyer, Francis Scott Key, was so overcome by the situation he dashed off a song that would one day become the country's national anthem. He called it "The Star Spangled Banner." The song first appeared as "The Defense of Fort McHenry," published in the *Baltimore Patriot and Evening Advertiser* on September 20, the first day the paper recommended publication after the war had caused its temporary closure.

The irony was that this most patriotic of all American songs had been written to an English tune titled "To Anacreon in Heaven." At the time the music was already well-known in England, having been written in 1766 by John Stafford Smith, perhaps the first English musicologist, who had risen to prominence in the 1750s when he wrote a number of very popular catches and glees (short, amusing songs). In 1766 the Anacreontic Society was formed in London and Smith wrote the music to a poem with the same title, which had been written by the Society's first President, Ralph Tomlinson.

Society members were well-heeled men who met once every two weeks to have dinner, sing songs, drink and read poetry. The Society primarily existed to write and recite "anacreontics," a relatively obscure form of verse first written by a sixth century B.C.E. Greek writer named Anacreon. Born in 570 B.C.E. at Teos, an Ionian city of Asia Minor, Anacreon flowered in Athens, where he wrote erotic poetry about the pleasures of love and wine. Anacreon's work had been rediscovered in 1554 by a French publisher named Henri Estienne, who came across the poems in a neglected manuscript at the library of the Dutch University of Louvain while he was on one of his usual hunts for Classical manuscripts. Henri was the third in a line of family publishers, who had started business in 1502 when the grandfather, also named Henri, established himself in the Paris University book trade. After he died in 1520, his son Robert began to make a name with Greek editions. Because of religious difficulties (Robert was Protestant) in 1550 he and his family left for Calvinist Geneva where Robert became a Genevan citizen and opened a printing house. It was Robert's eldest son, Henri, who would introduce Anacreon to Europe.

Young Henri had been brought up in a cosmopolitan printing house atmosphere, where a staff of ten different nationalities each dealt with texts in their mother tongue. Much of the time Henri was obliged to speak Latin, the *lingua franca* among scholars. By the time he was fourteen, Henri already also knew Greek. Two years later he left for Italy on the pursuit that occupied all intellectuals at the time, the search for classical Greek and Latin manuscripts. The late sixteenth century was the time of the great discoveries of "lost" ancient manuscripts in almost every field of classical scholarship: botany, pneumatics, physics, chemistry, medicine, geography, philosophy, metallurgy and literature. Continual discoveries of ancient classical manuscripts amazed and enlightened Renaissance thinkers. The manuscripts naturally required glosses—analyses of what the ancients had meant by their use of terms. This exercise attracted scholars in every discipline. Each time a new manuscript became available for analysis, editors would first collate all earlier manuscripts already written on the same subject and produce a definitive version. This

process of analysis and synthesis laid the basis for what would become the scientific revolution of the early seventeenth century. The editorial intellectual fallout also generated new scientific disciplines and put old ones on a firmer footing.

It was Henri Estienne's son-in-law Isaac Casaubon who would lead the field in these endeavors, because it was he who turned the art of glossing into an analytical technique that could be applied to any text regardless of subject matter. Casaubon was another Genevan Greek scholar, born nine years after Estienne's father had arrived in Geneva, whose Protestant family had also fled persecution in France. In 1578, aged nineteen, Casaubon was sent to the Geneva Academy that Calvin had founded and by the age of twenty-three was appointed professor of Greek. By 1591 his reputation as a Greek scholar was established throughout Europe. In 1586 Casaubon married Estienne's daughter Florence who then bore him eighteen children.

Casaubon importuned anybody he could find to collect manuscripts for him. In many cases he received copies of originals, penned for him by traveling friends and colleagues. When somebody died and his collection was being sold Casaubon would make sure one of his contacts was there to bid. Sometimes publishers would send him copies of their new editions. Often, at a time before the invention of the publisher's catalogue, the only way to find out what was coming onto the market was to go as Casaubon did to the twice-yearly book fairs in Frankfurt.

In 1596, irritated by the niggardly Genevan authorities who refused to provide him with either books or adequate recompense, Casaubon accepted an invitation to teach at the University of Montpellier in France, where at last his worth was recognized. By now he was the leading Greek scholar on the continent, except for another Huguenot refugee from France who had settled in Holland at the University of Leiden. His name was Joseph Justus Scaliger, and in 1593 when the thirty-four-year-old Casaubon first made contact with him Scaliger was already a grand old man of scholarship at the age of fifty-three. The friendship began when Casaubon plucked up courage to send a letter of greeting. He received no reply. Then an

English friend wrote to say Scaliger had recently read Casaubon's new edition of a classic text and was much impressed. Two letters then arrived direct from the great man (who was not noted for his open and friendly disposition), and a correspondence began which lasted until Scaliger's death in 1609. In that time Casaubon wrote Scaliger over twelve hundred letters. Later Casaubon would say of the man he regarded as a mentor that he was "a man who, by the indefatigable devotion of a stupendous genius to the acquisition of knowledge has garnered up vast stores of uncommon lore. And his memory had such a happy readiness that whenever the occasion called for it, whether it were in conversation or whether he were consulted by letter, he was ready to bestow with lavish hand what had been gathered by him in the sweat of his brow."

Like many of his contemporaries Scaliger was a traveling scholar who moved from place to place (including at one point the court of Mary Queen of Scots)[62] to avoid wars and persecution. Like many of his contemporaries he settled finally in Holland, the most tolerant country in seventeenth-century Europe. By this time Scaliger had already produced his greatest contribution to scholarship, in the form of a new chronological system that became known as the "Julian period." The work was intended to address the problem exacerbated by each newly discovered ancient manuscript. The text would often contain references to dates that did little to help place the manuscript historically, since the dates tended to refer to local events such as a battle, or a siege, or the birth of a child, or the appearance of some heavenly sign. Most often dates related in some way to the in-house chronology of the institution in which the manuscript had been originally copied. These varied dating systems bedeviled textual analysis, since it was often essential to know the date of a manuscript to know whether it had been written before or after others.

Scaliger decided to produce a foolproof chronological system in which all events could be dated with complete accuracy. To do so he took as a base three time-cycles: the twenty-eight-year solar cycle (ending each time the days of the week in the Julian calendar repeated on the same date), the nineteen-year lunar cycle (ending when the phases of the moon recurred on the same days of the

62 106 204

128

week), and the fifteen-year period of the Diocletian tax census. Calculating backward, Scaliger was able to say that the first time all three cycles had started on the same day was in the year 4713 B.C.E., so he called this "Year One" of his new system. Starting at this point, and running all three cycles simultaneously, any historical date could be identified by three reference points. Twenty-nine years after Year One, for instance (4684 B.C.E.) would be Year 2 in the latest solar cycle, Year 10 in the latest lunar cycle, and Year 14 in the latest taxation cycle. Scaliger would have referred to 4684 B.C.E. as "2:10:14." Since the overall triple cycle would only repeat every $28 \times 19 \times 15$ (7,980) years Scaliger reckoned his system would serve its purpose for the foreseeable future.

Unfortunately for Scaliger, in 1582, a few months before the publication of the great work (which he called *A Treatise on the Correction of Chronology*) Pope Gregory decreed the switch from the old Julian calendar (on which Scaliger had based all his work) to the new Gregorian calendar, thus rendering Scaliger's work virtually useless at a stroke.

In the last few years of Scaliger's life at Leiden he had established himself as a leading humanist scholar and became a welcome guest at the court of the Dutch ruler, Prince Maurice of Nassau, who from time to time would ask Scaliger to handle problems like the translation of an Arabic letter the prince had received from a Muslim king. Scaliger and other scholars found refuge in Holland primarily because the country had thrown off the yoke of Spanish rule and, with it, severe constraints on intellectual freedom. The leading player in the gradual removal of the Spaniards from Holland[63] was Prince **63** 122 230 Maurice himself, who gradually recovered all Dutch territory north of the Rhine and the Meuse. In 1596 the independence of the new Dutch republic was recognized by England and France.

Maurice's other great success was his reorganization of the army. He always claimed that his military reforms sprang from his interest in ancient Roman military tactics, but much more likely is the way Maurice's thinking was influenced by developments in battlefield technology. For the previous three hundred years war had been dominated by cavalry and pikemen. Large formations of as many as three

thousand men (known as phalanxes or squares) carrying twelve-foot-long pikes could either form impregnable defensive "hedgehog" formations with pikes lowered all round, or crush opposition by sheer weight of numbers. In the years before Maurice's reforms these pikemen had also begun to act as a defensive wall around the new, slow-firing muskets. In the 1590s Maurice realized there was a way to improve the rate of musket fire by drawing musketeers up in ten ranks so that the front rank could fire and then retire to the rear to reload while the second rank fired and then did the same, giving way to the third rank and so on. In this way an almost continuous volley of fire was maintained. However, this arrangement also exposed large numbers of men to enemy fire and made discipline and concerted movement more important than ever before. This in turn required elements of standardization in both movement and weaponry.

In 1599 Maurice equipped the entire army with weapons of the same size and caliber, and his brother John began work on a new tool for training: the drill manual. John analyzed all the separate movements associated with the use of pike and musket and gave them numbers. In 1607 a book was published by Jacob de Gheyn and soon translated into English (as *The Book of Arms*), French, Danish and German. It contained detailed illustrations for the sequence of movements to be followed by soldiers, dividing up the use of pikes into thirty-two different positions and the loading and firing of muskets into forty-two separate movements. In 1616 John opened a military academy at Siegen where young gentlemen were trained in the use of weapons, armor, maps and terrain models. Several training manuals were also produced, all based explicitly on Dutch military practice. The presence of numerous foreign units, including English, French, Scottish and German troops, ensured that Maurice's ideas would soon spread. Unfortunately, Maurice's new tactics were never tested in a full-scale pitched battle.

It was only a quarter of a century after their introduction that the reforms were to show their true potential at the hands of the Swedish king Gustavus Adolphus. Thanks to constant drilling and practice Gustavus was able to increase his musketeers' rate of fire enough to

Fig. 15: *From Jacob de Gheyn's "weapon-handling" manual, four illustrations for loading the musket before discharge.*

maintain volleys from only six ranks. Firepower was also greatly enhanced by Gustavus's introduction of standard-caliber field guns,
some even supplied with cartridges and capable of a rate of fire of
twenty rounds an hour, which was not much slower than muskets.
Gustavus's critical improvement on Dutch practice was to make his
musketeers advance ten paces before firing, then stand where they
were to reload, while the following ranks passed them by to fire and
so on. In this way not only was a constant volley maintained but it
also advanced toward the enemy. The superiority of the technique
was devastatingly demonstrated at the Battle of Breitenfeld, just outside Leipzig, on September 17, 1631, when Gustavus beat a Catholic
imperial army that outnumbered him three to two. The victory
briefly made Sweden a world power. Small wonder that Gustavus
earned the title: "Captain of Kings and King of Captains."

When Gustavus died in battle in 1632, his heir was a six-year-old
girl, Christina. On February 1, 1633, Christina was proclaimed king
of Sweden (all Swedish monarchs were kings; only the wife of a
monarch was a queen), and for the next thirteen years the country
was run by a regent, Axel Oxenstierna. In 1644 Christina came of age
and set about the greatest achievement of her brief reign: bringing to
an end the bloody war against Denmark. Christina was extraordinarily gifted and fluent in German, Greek, Latin, French, Spanish and
Italian. She was obsessed by her "ugliness," never taking longer than
fifteen minutes to wash and dress, throwing on whatever clothes
happened to be at hand, heedless of her appearance. Visitors to the
Royal Palace in Stockholm were struck by her habit of wearing men's
shoes. She also had a passion for culture and learning, and because of
her ready wit became known as the "Minerva of the North."

After being formally crowned king in 1650, her abdication four
years later stunned Europe and especially her own countrymen. She
chose as successor her cousin Charles. He was crowned on June 6,
1654, the day she abdicated. That night Christina left the country
dressed as a man, with her hair cut short. On December 23 she formally entered Rome, was greeted by cardinals and senators, processed to St. Peter's and (to the amazement of Europe) on Christmas
Day was accepted into the Catholic church by the pope himself.

Christina settled into Rome and was soon at the heart of its cultural life. Her palace contained the greatest collection of Venetian paintings ever assembled. She founded the Arcadia Academy for philosophy and literature. It was at her urging that the first public opera house was opened. She sponsored Alessandro Scarlatti and Angelo Corelli. She amassed an enormous collection of books and manuscripts and worked to protect the Jewish community in the city. She also (it is suspected) had a long-term affair with Cardinal Decio Azzolino, a leading figure in Vatican politics.

It was while she was still in Sweden that she made what was perhaps her greatest mark on the intellectual life of Europe. It was her habit to surround herself with brilliant and eminent foreign artists, scholars and musicians, and in 1649 she invited René Descartes to come and be her philosopher-in-residence. The enterprise turned out to be a disaster. Descartes was asked to write verses to accompany theatrical productions, to take part in ballets, to write a libretto and on the occasions when he gave lessons to Christina she preferred to discuss literature rather than philosophy. The worst problem was the timing of the lessons, which Christina insisted take place in her library at 5:00 A.M. Six months after arriving in Stockholm, struggling through the bitter Swedish winter dawns, on February 11, 1650, Descartes contracted pneumonia and died.

Descartes was another of the intellectual exiles who, like Scaliger, had found refuge with the Dutch. For a brief period in 1618 he joined Maurice's army as a military engineer. Before this, after graduation he had become more and more obsessed by the fact that his years of study at university had provided him with knowledge that was useless and uncertain. The study of the classics, he wrote, involved "those who are too interested in things which occurred in past centuries . . . [and who] are often remarkably ignorant of what is going on today." Literature "makes us imagine a number of events as possible which are really impossible . . . those who regulate their behavior by the examples they find in books are apt to fall into the extravagances of the knights of romances." The study of philosophy by the greatest minds had not "produced anything which is not in dispute and consequently doubtful and uncertain."

About knowledge in general Descartes concluded: "When I noticed how many different opinions learned men may hold on the same subject, despite the fact that no more than one of them can ever be right, I resolved to consider almost as false any opinion which was merely plausible. . . . From my childhood I lived in a world of books . . . taught that by their help I could gain a clear and assured understanding of everything useful in life. . . . But as soon as I had finished the course of studies which usually admits one to the ranks of the learned . . . I found myself so saddled with doubts and errors that I seemed to have gained nothing in trying to educate myself unless it was to discover more and more fully how ignorant I was."

In 1637 these thoughts led to the great *Discourse on Method* that was to lay the foundations of reductionist thought and prepare for the rigorous disciplines of modern science. Descartes's methodical doubt set the ground rules for a system of intellectual analysis that would render more reliable the discoveries of thought, prescribing as it did a systematic process for thinking things through. The route to certainty was to begin by doubting everything and then to take as axiomatic whatever survived this exercise. Descartes regarded the only certainty to be the existence of the doubting mind. He summed this view up in his axiom: *cogito, ergo sum* (I think, therefore I exist). Attacking the speculative and metaphysical nature of the scholastic modes of thought that had preceded him, Descartes turned his attention in 1633 to the nature of biological life in *Treatise on Man*. He approached the workings of the body and brain mechanistically, describing the ten principal functions of the body (digestion, circulation, growth, respiration, sleep, sensation, imagination, memory, appetites and movement) in terms of mechanical systems.

It is possible that Descartes was influenced in his thinking by the latest high-tech gadgetry in the gardens of the royal château at St. Germain-en-Laye, the principal royal residence at the time. In 1598 Tommaso Francini, a Florentine architect and mechanician, arrived to embellish a series of terraces in the gardens with grottoes and fountains. Using water from the Seine, Francini devised an extraordinary system of waterworks whose main feature was a giant fountain. Water from the fountain then descended into a large number of

reservoirs in the galleries lower down the slope. Secondary tubes from these reservoirs supplied other fountains and drove water-powered automata all around the gardens. In one area there was an animated dragon, an organ player and a Neptune. Grottoes of Hercules, Perseus and Andromeda, and Orpheus featured these mythological figures, which, when visitors stepped on hidden plates in the floors, performed complex movements. Perseus, for instance, descended from the ceiling and used his sword to slay a dragon that had arisen from the water basin. In another grotto Bacchus sat drinking from a barrel.

Descartes referred to these extravaganzas in his writings on the brain: "Truly one can well compare the nerves of the machine that I am describing to the tubes of the mechanisms of these fountains, its muscles and tendons to divers other engines and springs which serve to move these mechanisms, its animal spirits to the water which drives them, of which the heart is the spring and the brain's cavities the water main. Moreover, breathing and other such actions which are ordinary and natural to it, and which depend on the flow of the spirits, are like the movements of a clock or mill which the ordinary flow of water can render continuous."

Descartes thought the cerebrospinal fluid in the internal cavities of the brain worked like the garden water supply, flowing down through nerves to power the motion of muscles. This engineering view of the brain excited an English doctor named Thomas Willis, who in 1664 was the most successful physician in Oxford. He was also one of a group of intellectuals, including among others John Evelyn,[64] John Wilkins and Robert Boyle,[65] who met regularly at Wadham College to discuss the latest scientific discoveries and in particular the various experiments and applications triggered by Evangelista Torricelli's recent discovery of the vacuum. In 1664 Willis broke new ground with his book *The Anatomy of the Brain*. Basing his approach on Descartes's mechanistic view, Willis described in detail the central, peripheral and autonomic parts of the nervous system. Using pathological and clinical observation, Willis divided the brain into different functional areas, postulating that the cerebrum was the seat of thought while the cerebellum controlled in-

[64] 111 210
[65] 53 114
[65] 87 160

voluntary motor function. In many cases Willis's dissection methods were far from exact but his empirical methods were a considerable improvement over earlier, purely philosophical speculation.

To describe his activities Willis coined the word "neurology." While some of his ideas did not stand the test of time, the book was the most complete and accurate account of the nervous system so far and stimulated much further research. One reason for the book's extraordinary success (it became the standard textbook on the subject for 150 years) was its illustrations. These were the first properly modern views of the brain, beautifully and precisely drawn by one of Willis's colleagues at the Wadham College meetings, Christopher Wren.

Two years after the publication of Willis's book came an event that was to shape Wren's life. At the time he was Savilian Professor of Astronomy at Oxford and a classic polymath. His list of "things to think about," which he made shortly after graduating, included "hypothesis of the moon in solid; to find whether the earth moves; the weather wheel; a perspective box for surveys; several new ways of graving and etching; to weave many ribbons at once with only turning a wheel; improvements in the arts of husbandry; divers new engines for raising of water; a pavement harder, fairer and cheaper than marble; to grind glasses; a way of embroidery for beds cheap and fair; pneumatic engines; new ways of printing; new designs tending to strength, convenience and beauty in building; divers new musical instruments; a speaking organ; new ways of sailing; probable ways for making fresh water at sea; the best way for reckoning longitude and observing at sea; fabrick for a vessel at war; to build in the sea forts, moles etc.; inventions for better making and fortifying havens, for clearing sands and to sound at sea; to stay long under water; submarine navigation; easier ways of whale-fishing; new cyphers; to pierce a rock in mining; to purge or vomit or alter the mass by injections into the blood; anatomical experiments; to measure the height of a mountain only by journeying over it; a compass to play in a coach or the hand of a rider; way of rowing; to perfect coaches for ease, strength and lightness."

This unusual mind was provided with a single task large enough to engage it in 1666 with the Great Fire of London. It broke out on the night of Sunday, September 2 and burned for five days before being extinguished. The fire destroyed about 80 percent of the City of London, including the Customs House, the Guildhall, the Exchange, six prisons, eighty-seven churches and the cathedral of Old St. Paul's. The situation after the fire was particularly dire, since there was no insurance to recompense any who had lost their homes and businesses. Such people desperately needed new homes, new storehouses, new offices and a new Exchange without delay. Within days of the end of the fire Wren was one of those who offered King Charles II a plan for a new London. On September 11 the king announced that the city was to be rebuilt in brick and stone with wider streets across which a fire could not jump. He appointed six commissioners to oversee the work. One of these was Wren, who spent time on several small commissions and then in 1669 at the age of thirty-six was appointed royal surveyor and offered the commission to rebuild the cathedral. Thirty-nine years later, in October 1708, the final stone was added to the lantern on top of the great dome and the work was complete. By this time Wren had also been busy elsewhere and the London skyline was dotted with evidence of his architectural skill. Wren built a total of fifty-two churches, twenty-eight of which survive today.

In 1679 Wren became a member of the council of the Hudson's Bay Company and for five years was an active director and stockholder. Since the beginning of the seventeenth century, when the first cargoes of tea and porcelain started arriving from China and Japan on the ships of the Dutch East India Company,[66] more and more money had been invested in these speculative journeys of trade and exploration. England soon followed the Dutch example. The Eastland Company had a monopoly of Baltic trade. The Muscovy Company traded as far as Persia. The Turkey Company went to Basra, and one of their ships even reached Malacca. Most sea captains returning from these journeys were interviewed by the Reverend Richard Hakluyt, lecturer in geography at Oxford, whose collected data came to-

66 44 *80*

66 109 *208*

gether in his *Principall Navigations, Voyages and Discoveries of the English Nation,* which became required reading for those thinking to set up in the overseas trade business.

As the companies expanded their activities it became clear that the navy was unable to protect each single venturer ship, so they began to band together to organize armed fleets of their own both for protection and to help keep their prices competitive. The stock of each venturer was joined with that of the others and thus the cooperatives became known as "joint-stock companies." By the time Wren was a director of the Hudson's Bay Company the joint-stock market was a thriving concern, attracting investors who had nothing else to do with their money but bury it or buy land. At the start of the eighteenth century the urgent need was for a banking system capable of supporting and facilitating the new stock market.

In 1716 the first joint-stock bank, established to attract investment funding, was set up in Paris. It was the brainchild of John Law, a Scottish gambler and financier. Law's life was a series of extraordinary ups and downs. At some time between 1694 and 1704 he spent two years in Holland acquainting himself with the Dutch banking system. He then moved to Genoa and Venice, gambling and becoming rich. In 1703 he wrote a proposal for the introduction of paper money in Scotland (at the time paper money was in circulation only in Sweden, Genoa, Venice, Holland and England). Law's argument was that paper was more convenient than specie, the scarcity of which was seriously hampering trade. Paper backed by arable land values could be issued in sufficient quantity to release large amounts of money, which in turn would boost economic growth. The Scots, more concerned with the impending Union with England four years later, turned the idea down.

Over a number of years Law made efforts to persuade the French to take up the idea, and in 1716 he succeeded. The Banque Générale was the first private bank, John Law was its first managing director, and it issued paper money. The new money was backed by specie at a fixed rate, and it soon began to be preferred to the fluctuating value of (often counterfeit) French coinage. In 1717 a decree made legal the payment of taxes in paper money, Law began to issue loans at fa-

vorable rates and the nearly bankrupt French economy revived. Law then introduced a scheme for revitalizing French industry with a trading company that would have the monopoly of trade with French Louisiana.[67] At the time this included the entire territory drained by the Mississippi, Ohio and Missouri rivers.

67 11 34

In 1717 Law's trading company became known as the Company of the West. Law's prospectus painted a glowing picture of hardworking, welcoming natives, as well as of mountains of emeralds and gold that the locals would exchange for knives and mirrors. In 1719 Law proposed an extension of the company to include trading monopolies in Africa, Asia, India and China. This huge corporation would effectively trade with the entire world and generate enormous profits. In 1719 the Company of the West was renamed the Company of the Indes, and speculation in Company shares reached frenzied proportions. Stock worth 1,000 livres in July was worth 6,000 in September. News spread of individuals making more than 1,000 percent profit overnight.

Then came Law's greatest coup: The company was granted the right to collect French taxes and to raise money to liquidate the national debt. For this purpose 300,000 new shares were to be sold. It was now that the first cracks in the edifice began to appear.

The Banque Générale had been so successful it was taken over by the regent, who began to print money at an alarming rate, showering courtiers with extravagant salaries. In future paper money was no longer to be secured by gold, but to be redeemed against the currency of the time. Confidence in the notes began to evaporate. Louisiana stock was grossly overvalued. During the bitter winter of 1719–20 inflation exploded, accompanied by a rapid rise in prices. Devaluation was announced in May. The end had come and the bubble burst. The economy was crippled. Law was exiled and dispossessed of all he owned, including the land on which the Champs Elyses stands today.

Over the following three decades France lost ground to England as the extravagance of the French court, the chaotic state of national finances and the costs of war continued to sap the country's strength. By 1760, the idea was growing that France could only recover at the

expense of Great Britain. This anti-British faction was led by Joseph Paris-Duvernay, another financier brought in to stop the rot. In 1760, at the age of seventy-six, Paris-Duvernay met a twenty-five-year-old clockmaker who was radically to change the fortunes of Europe and America. He was Caron de Beaumarchais and at the time he was in residence in Versailles, making watches for the royal family and acting as musical director to the four young princesses. Beaumarchais was also a budding playwright, who would eventually write *The Marriage of Figaro* and *The Barber of Seville*.

In 1776 the king asked Beaumarchais to become a secret agent and go to London to suppress a lampoon being circulated about the king's mistress. In London Beaumarchais became convinced that the British wanted an easy way out of their entanglement with the American colonies and that the simplest way for France to weaken British supremacy would be by covert support for the Americans in the coming War of Independence. In the summer of 1776 a fake company was set up with the blessing of the French government and Beaumarchais began to channel massive amounts of money, arms and

Fig. 16: *Revolutionary Americans tear down the statue of King George III in New York.*

140

French "military advisers" to the American rebels. After American independence, when the financial effects of this latest adventure hit the French economy, a Swiss banker named Jacques Necker[68] was called in to help sort out the mess. In a series of famous "accounts" Necker persuaded Louis XVI that the economy was sound and that the treasury was in the black. The truth was far different. From 1776 to 1786 the state borrowed 1,250 million francs and ran an annual deficit of 115 million. The economy lurched toward disaster. Necker was fired and recalled three times. The absurdity of his stance was greeted each time by increasing invective. Finally in 1789 Necker resigned and returned to Switzerland, leaving his daughter in Paris to enjoy the Revolution that followed.

68 96 *177*

Germaine Necker had been married three years earlier to the Swedish ambassador to Paris, Eric Magnus Baron of Staël-Holstein. She was now known as Madame de Staël, and her dazzling conversation made her salon the cynosure of French intellectual life. Each morning she would greet her guests in her bedroom, diaphanously dressed and flaunting her libertarian opinions. By 1802 Napoleon was in power and these opinions were less than welcome. De Staël's writing (*On Literature Considered in Its Relations with Social Institutions* and a novel, *Delphine*) had by now made her name all over Europe. That year she traveled to Weimar, Germany, where she was greeted with delight by the grand duke and his family. She met the cream of the new German intelligentsia, including Schiller and Goethe,[69] though the latter tried to keep out of her way, saying: "She insists on explaining everything, understanding everything, measuring everything. She admits of no darkness; nothing incommensurable; and where her torch throws no light, there nothing can exist."

69 22 *47*
69 82 *153*

It was in Weimar while preparing her book *On Germany*, which would make her a household name among Romantics and establish German culture and the new Romantic movement stirring in Weimar, that De Staël met and captivated August von Schlegel, the foremost theoretician of the new movement. He led her through the Romantic maze and then fell in love with her. On April 18, 1804, when De Staël received the news of her father's illness and was obliged to leave immediately for Switzerland, Schlegel made an instant deci-

sion to leave with her and spent the rest of his life as her lapdog. Whether or not he expected the affair to turn passionate it never did. De Staël had other lovers and Schlegel was obliged to resign himself to a platonic relationship.

Earlier, in 1803, Schlegel's marriage had been dissolved and his wife had married his friend and colleague Friedrich von Schelling.[70] Schelling had spent time in Leipzig, tutoring and studying the natural sciences. Out of this came his grand concept, *naturphilosophie*, which was to inform the Romantic movement and much of science for the next forty years. In essence, Schelling's view was that Nature's constant power to evolve and transcend itself, to rise from lower to higher levels and forms, revealed a clear teleological pattern. The overall harmony of Nature was expressed in the way apparent opposites were reconciled. As an example Schelling chose the magnet, in which opposite poles attracted. The same balance could also be found in the interaction of acid and alkali, electricity and magnetism.

One of Schelling's colleagues, Johann Wolfgang von Goethe,[71] sought similar purpose and design in embryology. So did other *naturphilosophen*, one of whom was an Estonian professor of anatomy named Karl von Baer, whose aim was to find the unity in Nature expressed in the developmental stages of all organisms. To this end he became expert in the embryonic growth of chicks from the moment of conception to hatching. In 1828 von Baer published a work on the sequential development of the chick embryo, detailing the various stages through which the embryo passed. He discovered the way in which cellular growth proceeded from the general to the particular in the way that the early, homogeneous mass of chick cells separated and then specialized into wings, eyes, beak, legs, the internal organs and so on. Most important of all, von Baer theorized that embryonic development went through different stages in lower and higher life forms. A higher form might pass through early developmental stages that were equivalent to the fully developed forms of lower organisms. This idea was to have the most profound effect on the biological sciences in the latter half of the nineteenth century.

In 1846 HMS *Rattlesnake* left Britain on a voyage of exploration to the South Seas carrying a young naturalist who would take the work

of von Baer and others to the next stage. His name was Thomas Huxley, and in 1849 in the waters of Eastern Australia he began a study of jellyfish. When he published his results he noted that the Medusa, with its inner and outer membranes, seemed to be constructed on the same plan as the two primary layers von Baer had seen in the early development of vertebrate embryos. These similarities between the early stages of a higher form and the adult stages of a lower form confirmed von Baer's theory.

Once back in England Huxley would speak in defense of a man who took the implications of these embryonic relationships to their logical conclusion in a great theory of development that sought to describe the processes by which the massively heterogeneous, specialized life forms on the planet had emerged through the mechanisms described in part by von Baer and Huxley. According to the new theory, organisms either specialized to fit their habitat or died. The proponent of the sober thought that life is no picnic was Charles Darwin.[72]

72 4 27
72 74 145

CHAPTER 6

⋈

Elementary Stuff

There is a respectable body of opinion that holds that the theory of evolution ought not to be known as Darwin's but as Wallace's. Alfred Russel Wallace was a self-educated surveyor, apprentice clockmaker, teacher and beetle-collector who left school at fourteen, became a railway surveyor and developed an interest in geology. His self-improvement took the form of reading the explorer Alexander von Humboldt's[73] *Personal Narrative of Travels to the Equinoctal Regions of America,* the works of geologist Charles Lyell, the natural history of Robert Chambers, and Malthus's *Essay on Population.* Lyell's theory postulated an extremely ancient Earth, Chambers's *Vestiges of Creation* suggested that animal species were descended from other animal species, and Malthus's work put forward the notion that populations expanded at such a rate vis-à-vis the availability of food as to make survival a struggle.

Such were the ideas that triggered a wanderlust in Wallace, especially after he had met and been inspired by an entomology enthusiast named Henry Bates. Wallace and Bates would spend many afternoons on field trips collecting beetles. Afterward they would exchange letters about each other's beetle-collecting activities. Wallace saved one hundred pounds and used it to finance a trip to the Amazon with Bates in 1847. There they separated again, Bates taking the Upper Amazon and Wallace the Rio Negro. Five years later, returning with twenty cases of specimens, Wallace's ship caught fire and he lost

73 117 220

144

everything. He had, however, developed an idea that would color his work from then on.

He had noticed that from one part of the forest to another there were major changes in animal and insect life. These differences were manifest even on either side of a wide river. It became clear to Wallace that any species collection ought to be accompanied by notes of a creature's habitat. In 1854 Wallace left England again and spent the next eight years in the Malay archipelago, traveling fourteen thousand miles and building a collection of more than 125,000 different species, the greater part of which was beetles. The collection included no fewer than nine hundred species of longhorn beetle and two hundred new species of ant.

Much of Wallace's interest was taken by the way in which different locations seemed to contain minor species variants, each suited to the location in which it was found. In 1855 Wallace sent back to London a paper titled *On the Law Which Has Regulated the Introduction of New Species*. The paper was clearly influenced by Lyell's view that if geological processes had not differed through history, then immensely slow and long-term processes were at work in nature. Wallace related this idea to his observations on species change: "It would be most unphilosophical to conclude without the strongest evidence that the organic world so intimately connected with it [the inorganic world of Lyell's work] had been subject to other laws which have now ceased to act, and that the extinction and production of species and genera had at some later period suddenly ceased."

Wallace believed that a species could be divided into two or more variants, and if at some time the original species died out it left its variant behind as new species. Wallace had developed a theory of evolution. When Darwin[74] read Wallace's paper he wrote to him: "I [74 4 27] agree to the truth of almost every word of your paper; and I daresay that you will agree with me that it is very rare to find oneself agreeing pretty closely with any theoretical paper . . . I can plainly see that we have thought much alike and to a certain extent have come to similar conclusions."

Three years later Darwin (and nobody else) received Wallace's next paper, *On the Tendency for Varieties to Depart Indefinitely from the*

Original Type. Darwin said it hit him like "a bolt from the blue." Everything he had been thinking about for twenty years was in Wallace's paper. In great haste he put pen to paper to produce a work uncannily like Wallace's. On July 1, 1858, the Linnaean Society in London heard both men's papers. Wallace conceded Darwin's primacy.

In one important way Wallace differed from Darwin. For him evolution could not account for the clearly special nature of human consciousness: "Neither natural selection nor the more general theory of evolution can give any account whatever of the origin of sensational or conscious life. They may teach us how, by chemical, electrical, or higher natural laws, the organised body can be built up, can grow, can reproduce its like; but those laws and that growth cannot even be conceived as endowing the newly-arranged atoms with consciousness." Wallace, like many other eminent Victorian scientists, turned for the answer to spiritualism, becoming a leading apologist for the movement in England. Wallace accepted as valid all manifestations of the psychic world, including ghosts, haunted houses, communication with the dead, levitation, and ectoplasm. In 1882 he joined the new Society for Psychical Research, but refused the post of president.

One of his colleagues at the society was a Liverpool University professor of physics named Oliver Lodge. Like many other scientists, Lodge attempted to use scientific method to provide a philosophical or religious meaning to life and in this way mitigate the apparently godless aspects of science. In 1883 Lodge was asked to examine the case of two department-store salesgirls who appeared capable of thought transference. So as to avoid ambiguity in the test results, Lodge developed the now-well-known "telepathy" cards carrying a circle or triangle or square.

Lodge was also interested in other forms of transference. In 1889, after a number of experiments with lightning conductors and the electrical waves created by sparks, he became involved in developing a sensitive receiver for the very weak signals given out by spark transmitters. In 1889 he said he "came across a curious effect . . . whereby a couple of little knobs in ordinary light contact, not sufficient to transmit a current, became cohered or united at their junc-

tion whenever even a minute spark passed, and thus enabled the passage of a current from a weak E.M.F. [voltage] through a galvanometer, until they were broken asunder again, which a light tap sufficed to do."

Lodge noticed that the same phenomenon happened when currents passed through iron filings. Even a relatively weak signal was enough to cause the filings to stick together and pass on the signal. Lodge built a small glass tube filled with the metal particles and later added a "tapper" that would give a series of repeated blows to the glass tube when the filings had cohered, breaking them apart ready to receive the next signal. In 1891 the detector became known as the Branly-Lodge "coherer" (Edouard Branly was a French physicist who turned out to be working on the same principle, in parallel with Lodge).

It was a Canadian engineer who would take things to the next stage. The coherer had severe limitations in that it reacted only to the kinds of signal bursts given off by spark transmitters (the kind Marconi used with his new radio telegraph to send Morse Code dots and dashes). The Canadian, Reginald Fessenden, realized that to send anything more than dots and dashes required an entirely different form of radio transmission. His experience working for Edison[75] on dynamos, and then as chief electrician at the Westinghouse[76] Electrical Company was to prove useful. As part of Fessenden's involvement with power generation and electric motors he had worked with alternating current. This is a current which grows to a peak, then decreases, reverses its direction, reaches a peak, then returns to its original state. It completes this cycle thousands of times a second. Fessenden realized that he could use this process to set up continuous wave transmission at a set frequency (so a receiver could be tuned to it), and then use the wave as a carrier of smaller energy inputs from a microphone reacting to sound inputs. The signals from the microphone would modulate the carrier wave. At the receiving end, these modulations could be fed to a loudspeaker diaphragm that would vibrate in sympathy with the fluctuating input and repeat the original sound.

On Christmas Eve 1906 at Brant Rock, Massachusetts, Fessenden

75 23 48
76 25 49

described what happened when he put the theory into practice: "The program . . . was as follows: first a short speech by me saying what we were going to do, then some phonograph music, the music on the phonograph being Handel's 'Largo.' . . . finally we wound up by wishing them a Merry Christmas and then saying that we proposed to broadcast again on New Year's Eve." Those listening to this first-ever radio program were asked to write to Fessenden at Brant Rock. Several did so, including the radio-telegraph officers on board ships in the Caribbean. The ships belonged to a company whose fortunes were to be radically changed by Fessenden's work. They were the banana boats of the United Fruit Company.

Bananas had been a highly profitable commodity ever since 1870, when a Bostonian schooner master had returned from taking a party of gold prospectors to Venezuela. On his way home he stopped in Jamaica for repairs and bought 160 bunches of bananas for twenty-five cents a bunch. Later he sold them in Boston for more than ten times as much. By the time of Fessenden's Brant Rock transmission the banana business was flourishing. American banana growers owned nearly a quarter of a million acres in Costa Rica, Cuba, Honduras, Jamaica, Santo Domingo and Colombia. Many of them had considerable influence with these local governments, and the countries were becoming so dependent on the export of the fruit they were beginning to be known as "banana republics."

The reason United Fruit leaped at Fessenden's invention was simple. Bananas are so profitable because while an acre of wheat will yield thirteen hundred pounds of crop, and corn about twenty-eight hundred pounds, an acre of bananas will provide eighteen thousand pounds. Moreover, bananas can be harvested all year round and they grow extremely fast. The problem for United Fruit was that the fruit matured and rotted with equal speed, so the crop had to be dispatched as quickly as possible. Tens of thousands of banana bunches were loaded on trains in plantations and delivered to the docks with the requirement that they be loaded on board ship and dispatched within a few hours of the scheduled time. It took dozens of train-loads to fill a ship's hold, so the scale of the investment at risk was

considerable. In 1900 United Fruit (an association of twelve banana firms) owned 11 steamships, 112 miles of railroad, 17 locomotives, 12,000 cattle and 2,000 horses and mules and employed 15,000 people clearing 8,000 acres of jungle a year ready for planting.

In 1908 the value of refrigerated ships[77] was already proven, and United Fruit commissioned the construction of seventeen five-thousand-tonners. The enterprise became increasingly complex as the company began building piers, laying hundreds of miles of railroad tracks, developing dock facilities in a dozen tropical ports and, as the market continued inexorably to grow, organizing the clearance of thousands of acres of jungles for ever-more plantations. The logistical task of organizing this far-flung and fragmented commercial empire with its critical reliance on efficient and timely scheduling was made possible almost at a stroke by Fessenden's radio. **77 56 116**

During the early years of the banana trade the world authority on the fruit was a book written in 1882 by a reclusive Swiss botanist (from a family of reclusive botanists) named Alphonse Pyramide de Candolle. His book was called *The Origin of Cultivated Plants* and contained the first detailed botanical description of the banana. Candolle also wrote books on the culture of fruit trees, the age of trees and the dormancy of plants. As a member of Geneva's Grand Council Candolle also introduced the first postage stamps to the canton. In 1843 the Geneva Council voted to introduce (on the English model of only four years earlier) a single-value stamp that would prepay all local postage. Two stamps would be required for postage to another canton. In 1852 this system was extended to the whole of Switzerland.

By the 1860s the international postal situation[78] was close to chaotic. Countries applied their own rates (some as many as six) to different kinds of mail and different distances of delivery. Errors and losses were endemic. Various attempts were made to arrive at some kind of international postal consensus modeled on the highly successful Austro-Prussian Postal Union, which had been operating since 1850. Eventually, in 1874, Heinrich von Stephan, director of posts for the North German Confederation, managed to organize an **78 49 97**

International Postal Congress in Bern, Switzerland. Twenty-one countries sent delegates with the aim of "transforming the entire world into a single postal territory for the reciprocal exchange of the mails." At Bern it was agreed that where possible mail should be pre-paid by means of postage stamps and that countries of origin should keep the income from the sale of stamps on the grounds of simple reciprocity: a letter tended to elicit a reply.

One of the other congress decisions settled the cost of different classes of mail. These were to be printed materials, letters and (a new category) postcards. Postcards had first been mooted by von Stephan, who realized that letter-writing was a long-winded affair and that people might want a briefer form of correspondence. He suggested a card carrying a preprinted postage stamp, which would have no need for an envelope. The card itself would be free. This last proved a sticking point and the idea was dropped. It was revived again in 1860 in Austria with the printing of official "correspondence-cards," which proved immensely popular. Half a million were sold in the first month and several million were posted in the first year. Germany followed the example, then Britain. In 1870 cards began to carry printed Christmas greetings. In 1872 Britain authorized private printers to issue cards. In 1889, at the Paris Exhibition, the picture postcard **79** 128 244 burst on the scene. It could be mailed at the top of the Eiffel Tower.[79] One side of the card carried a lithograph of the tower, the other was left blank for address and greeting. The idea was a huge success and inspired others to follow.

By the end of the nineteenth century the first artists' cards appeared in France, principally displaying the work of poster painters like Boutet and Mucha. In 1900 illustrated cards started appearing in Britain. Here, however, the illustrations took the form of humorous cartoons and caricatures featuring the "day-tripper" at the seaside. Over the next decade the pictures became more sophisticated, particularly with the work of such artists as Phil May. May began at the age of fourteen in the Leeds Grand Theater, helping to paint backcloths. After he had painted several of the actors his talents were noticed and he began to draw for London magazines.

Fig. 17: *An early British postcard showing the usual "naughty" scene of industrial workers on holiday at the beach.*

Eventually May was hired as a cartoonist for the satirical magazine *Punch,* where his work lampooned the politically great and good. *Punch* had begun publication in 1841 at a time when Britain was suffering from the worst excesses of overrapid industrial development. The high hopes of the great Reform Bill of the previous decade had come to nought. The towns were packed with factory workers living in appalling conditions. Corruption among government officials was rife. MPs were venal and self-seeking. The disparities between rich and poor were great and widening. *Punch* entered the fray on behalf of the poor and dispossessed, mercilessly attacking those in power.

In 1843 came an opportunity too good to be missed. Queen Victoria's husband, Prince Albert (not known for his artistic abilities), joined a committee to judge a design competition for frescoes to be painted in the newly built Houses of Parliament. The committee required competition to be inspired by Classical themes or subjects from English history. The works submitted were so bad that *Punch* decided to run its own competition and present its own winning de-

signs. These included cartoons excoriating everybody from factory owners to aristocrats. Meanwhile the real competition triggered a storm of criticism when the winning designs were painted. By 1895 all but one had peeled off the walls or had been covered up. Today none is visible.

The historical subjects of the frescoes suited the style of the Parliament buildings. Ever since 1733 there had been demands for a new seat of government. At one point Buckingham Palace was offered by **80 14 37** William IV. By the end of the eighteenth century the Neoclassical[80] style of buildings like Buckingham Palace had been replaced by Neo-Gothic, which appealed more to the nationalist fervor of a country at war with France. Gothic architecture was held to be of English origin and favored by those who looked back to the golden age of Saxon liberty when the rights of free Englishmen had first been proclaimed. In 1801 the British and Irish legislatures were combined, then in the 1830s (after the Reform Bill) the number of MPs grew to over six hundred, and conditions in the old Parliament became impossible. The situation was exacerbated by the Great Fire of 1834, which destroyed the building.

It was decided that the new Houses would be Neo-Gothic. Their decoration was given to the greatest exponent of the English Gothic Revival, August Pugin. Pugin's first book stated his position unequivocally. It was titled *The True Principles of Pointed or Christian Architecture,* and it described the direct link between spirituality and design, citing the religious faith of medieval builders as the prime example. Gothic architecture for Pugin was faith writ large in stone. Pugin designed everything in Parliament, from gargoyles to ceiling moldings, woodwork, carpets, metalwork, furniture, carvings, glass and everything in the great ceremonial chambers such as the House of Lords, perhaps the greatest pseudomedieval interior ever built. Pugin's theme in the Lords stressed the medieval origins of the parliamentary system. He included bronze statues of the barons who forced King John to sign Magna Carta, angels modeled on those of the 1388 Westminster Hall, and a three-part, raised medieval throne. The whole extraordinary edifice was described by American author Nathaniel Hawthorne as "gravely gorgeous."

Ironically, given the nationalist fervor behind the British decision, the Gothic Revival had begun in Germany with the recent Romantic movement, whose aesthetic leader was an ex-medical student and writer named J. G. Herder.[81] Herder first taught at the Cathedral school in Riga, Estonia, in 1764, where he began to write about German literature. Five years later he traveled in France and Holland. In 1770, visiting Strasbourg for an eye operation, Herder met another young student who was there to complete his legal education. Johann Wolfgang von Goethe[82] was to prove a seminal influence on Herder, persuading him of his position as an important German author. Herder in turn stimulated Goethe to give up the law and concentrate on literature.

81 93 174

82 22 47
82 69 141

Herder's interest in folk-poetry and ancient languages led him to a deepening involvement with the German past and a growing understanding of the particular nature of German culture. From the German art historian Johann Winckelmann Herder borrowed the idea of the need to understand the historical context of cultural expression. Herder became known as the founder of the "historical outlook," the originator of the concept of humankind united at all times and in all conditions, and the idea that man existed as part of nature. These were the first guiding principles of what would become known as Romanticism. One of Herder's essays dealt with the development of language. In *Treatise on the Origin of Language,* published in 1770, he traced the development of language through history, describing language as a divine gift capable of expressing the most fundamental awareness of God's revelation. The value of ancient languages was that because they were archaic they were the purest, least alloyed by the effects of historical development. Herder argued that the oldest examples of language would reveal the most meaningful understanding of humanity's origins.

Not surprisingly, when a major third-century epic poem in Gaelic was discovered Herder and the other Romantics received it like revealed truth. The poem was called "Fingal, an Ancient Epic Poem in Six Books, Together with Several Other Poems Composed by Ossian the Son of Fingal." In it Herder and the other Romantics found the answer to their prayers. Here was a vivid portrait of third-century

Celtic society that revealed a culture as great as that of Rome or Greece. The poem served as a beacon to those who sought an identity and a tradition for German culture. "Ossian" was the lyrical expression of a simple peasant, living in a society before the emergence of class, wealth or any of the other destructive artificial aspects of modern Enlightenment (French) civilization. For Herder the poem was a clarion call from the noble savage to all Germans, and in his essay "Ossian and Ancient Folk-Poetry" he rallied every Romantic to the cause.

Most unfortunately the epic "Ossian" was an epic fake put together by a young, literary Gaelic-speaking Scottish Highlander named James Macpherson, who was concerned at the fact that Gaelic culture might be dying and was anxious to preserve it. Macpherson toured the Scottish Highlands and Islands collecting ancient Gaelic tales, songs and poems, and in 1761 he published them in the "Ossian" collection. Macpherson "creatively restored" the fragments he had written down, adding his own material and assembling them into an epic structure, biblical in diction and classical in style, creating a Celtic twilight zone that had never really existed, full of the supernatural, the mysterious, the heroic. A world where man was at one with nature. A world perfectly designed for the Romantic mind.

The reason for the forgery lay in the changing social conditions of Scotland early in the eighteenth century. Not long after the Union with England in 1707, resentment still smoldered north of the border, where the Scottish government had been dissolved and Scots felt themselves under-represented in London. In 1715 a Scottish rising against the English was headed by James Stuart, who claimed the English throne and united the clans against the English occupying forces. After the rebellion was savagely put down the English took pains to make sure it would never happen again. Gaelic was banned in schools. To facilitate the movement of English garrison troops military roads were built through the Scottish Highlands by Marshal Wade (in whose honor an extra verse was added to the national anthem). The Society in Scotland for Propagating Christian Knowledge did all it could to undermine the Highland Catholic faith in Scotland and replace it with Protestantism, especially in the Lowland areas

where the new Union was promoting economic growth and turning places like Glasgow into commercial entrepôts. The added effect of the industrialization of the Lowlands was to split Scotland in two and weaken further the position of the economically backward Highlands.

The Stuarts, exiled on the Continent, continued to claim the English throne. James moved to Rome, living on handouts from the Vatican and the Italian nobility. In 1719 he married the daughter of the Polish royal house and their Roman residence in Palazzo Muti became a center for Jacobite disaffection. In 1720 James's wife gave birth to a son christened Charles Edward Louis John Casimir Silvester Maria Stuart. Wrapped in the robes of the Prince of Wales and laid under a royal canopy of state, the infant was visited by hundreds of Jacobite well-wishers and treated in every way as if he really were the heir to the English throne. For the next twenty-five years Charles

Fig. 18: *The young Chevalier, Bonnie Prince Charlie, wearing the Royal Order of the Garter (to which he was not entitled).*

grew up with the myth of kingship, charming and good-looking, a natural athlete, speaking English with a foreign accent.

In 1740, with the British at war with France, the Jacobites decided (with French support) to try again. James was too old to lead so Charles was to be sent in his stead, backed by a French fleet and troopships. Bad weather scattered the fleet and Louis's support for Charles's adventure melted away. In an act of supreme folly Charles elected to go on alone, landing in the Scottish Western Isles in July 1745. Hailed by the Highlanders as their savior, "Bonnie Prince Charlie" miraculously got his rag-tag Highland army as far south as Derby, fifty miles from London, before they were turned back and chased north by the British army. The decisive battle was fought at Culloden on April 16, 1746, when one thousand badly equipped and ill-fed Highlanders wielding claymores were massacred by nine thousand disciplined British redcoats using artillery. Charlie fled back to the Islands and was soon on the run.

The systematic destruction of the Highlanders began in earnest. British soldiers went on a rampage, looting, raping, killing and burning property. Charlie escaped, returned to the Continent, and for the rest of his life moved from borrowed palace to palace, existing on charity and becoming a chronic alcoholic. Toward the end he would play Scottish airs on his cello and drink himself insensible every night, weeping at his lost greatness, eventually dying in Rome in 1788 at the age of sixty-eight.

Meanwhile in Scotland Highlanders were forbidden to carry arms, play the bagpipes or wear tartan. The estates of the fourteen most prominent Highland clan chieftains were seized by the English crown. All ancient feudal jurisdictions were abolished, and the hereditary authority of the chiefs was destroyed forever. Thirteen years later the Highlands were considered to have been subdued. A new, sentimental view of the ancient Highland world began to find expression among the English chattering classes. The king visited Scotland wearing a kilt.

Highlanders deserted Scotland in thousands. In 1775, one of the émigrés was a fifty-three-year-old woman named Flora Macdonald. As a young girl of twenty-three she had played a significant role in

the 1745 rebellion, smuggling Charlie (disguised as a maid named "Betty Burke") out from under the noses of the British troops and rowing him to safety on the island of Skye. Such was her fame for this act that many years later Samuel Johnson was to say: "Her name will be mentioned in history, and if courage and fidelity be virtues, mentioned with honor."

When Flora and her husband left Scotland[83] they followed in the footsteps of their fellow-countrymen and took ship for colonial America, the land of plenty and above all of freedom. Although British ill-treatment had been instrumental in the Highlanders' decision to leave, it is more likely that poverty was the principal factor. With the destruction of the old feudal system, in which chieftains had taken their rents in kind or in service, the new conditions encouraged landlords to charge money for rent. Many Highlanders could not pay. In the winter of 1771 and the disastrously cold and wet spring that followed much of their livestock died. Population pressure played a part, as Highland women were noted for their ability to bear as many as twenty children. The introduction of sheep also brought large-scale evictions. Wherever they went on their tour of Scotland in 1773 Boswell and Johnson found people preparing to leave. Farewell laments were being sung in every village.

83 98 *181*

By far the largest number of Highlanders went (as did Flora) to North Carolina. The land grant of fifty acres for every immigrant to the colony was an attractive prospect for people who left Scotland with virtually nothing. In spite of their past experiences the Highlanders remained Loyalist in the impending conflict between America and Britain.

For the British, North Carolina was of particular importance because it provided much of Britain's naval stores. At the beginning of the eighteenth century, when Britain had been at war, the only source of naval stores had been the monopolistic Swedish Tar Company, and it was to avoid a repetition of this situation, and as part of the general mercantilist thrust to achieve economic independence, that Britain had passed the 1705 Naval Stores Bounty Act, authorizing subsidies for all domestic production of naval stores.

"Naval stores" was a term that described materials used in various

ways to waterproof ships. Stores included tar, pitch, rosin and turpentine. Tar was used to preserve ropes, hulls were caulked with pitch, and turpentine was used to thin paint and to protect woodwork (although it was more often used as a medicine, administered orally for tapeworm, rubbed on for rheumatism and bronchitis, put on wounds as an antiseptic, or ingested as a purgative). In an era of wooden ships, naval stores were essential to maintaining naval capability, so when the first North Carolina colonists discovered the extensive areas of long-leaf pine trees on the colony's coastal plain, the area rapidly became Britain's new source. Turpentine was distilled from the rosin that flowed from a cut pine tree; tar was produced by cooking pieces of pinewood in kilns; pitch was made by boiling the tar in caldrons or open pits. By the second half of the eighteenth century 70 percent of the tar, 50 percent of the turpentine and 20 percent of the pitch imported to Britain came from North Carolina, earning for the colonists the nickname "tarheels."

When the American War of Independence ended new sources of British turpentine had to be found, not least because of the new craze for Chinese lacquered furniture. Fine lacquer work reached its zenith in 1680 at the Imperial Palace in Peking and by mid-eighteenth century was being imported to Europe by the Dutch. Lacquer was astronomically expensive and came in the form of tea tables, panels, chests, screens, snuffboxes, trinkets, even coaches. "Japanning," as the technique came to be known in England, involved covering the objects in several layers of clear varnish and then painting or gilding them and adding further coats of varnish to produce a lustrous effect. At some time around 1730 a Welshman named Thomas Allgood developed a cheap substitute. His ingredients were linseed oil, umber (brown oxide of iron) and litharge (a lead monoxide). The mixture was heated and diluted with turpentine obtained from oil shale in the hills around Pontypool where Allgood lived.

Allgood applied his new "Pontypool Japan" to metal. Wood was scarce and the use of timber was severely restricted to shipbuilding, but Pontypool was also the location of one of the best ironworks in Europe, run by John Hanbury and employing the Algood family. The works produced large quantities of rolled sheets of iron and used the

158

latest hot-rolling processes. In order to prevent rusting iron sheets were "tinned" by being dipped in molten tin. Thomas Allgood's grandfather (also named Thomas) had learned his tinning during a visit to Saxony and Bohemia, the European center of tin-making at the time. Thomas Junior applied several layers of his "Pontypool Japan" to tin plates and stoved them for hours in an oven. The finished product was then shaped into trays, tobacco boxes, candlesticks, coffeepots, tea caddies, sugar canisters, kettles, pans, basins, boxes and other household articles. The Royal Navy purchased some for use as bread containers.

A similarly naval use for tinplate was planned in France where in 1661 the new first minister, Jean-Baptiste Colbert,[84] had recently taken over an economy that was in ruins. In an attempt to set French industry on its feet Colbert began by importing foreign craftsmen to teach Frenchmen how to set up their own production units. Colbert brought cloth-makers from Holland, tar-makers from Sweden, lace- and glass-makers from Italy, goldsmiths from England, leatherworkers from Russia, sugar-refiners from Germany and hatmakers and weavers from Spain. However, attempts to persuade tin-makers from Saxony to emigrate to France under very favorable conditions (tax-free subsidies and automatic rights of French citizenship) failed.

One of Colbert's other (and more successful) economic reforms involved the navy. When Colbert took over, the French navy consisted of only eighteen warships, some over twenty years old. Six thousand French sailors were serving in foreign navies. Not a single mast could be found in France's arsenals and storehouses. Ten years later, thanks to Colbert, France possessed 190 vessels, of which 120 were fully equipped warships. Colbert bought masts in Savoy, tar in Prussia, wood in Poland, naval stores and munitions in Holland. He imported Dutch carpenters and English naval architects, built or refurbished shipyards in Brest, Toulon and Rochefort, opened schools of hydrography at Rochefort and Dieppe, and established officer training courses at Rochefort, St. Malo, Toulon and Brest. In addition he reformed conditions for enlisted men by requiring a man to serve only one year in three, and provided free education for children, homes for wounded or disabled sailors and family allowances.

[84] 138 255

In 1667 the Toulon Arsenal employed a painter named Pierre Puget as artistic director, whose prime responsibility was ship decoration. Puget's style did not appeal to Colbert, one of whose administrators said he felt they were "more relevant to the decoration of a palace than to ships." Puget specialized in carved and gilded stern-pieces, which including a remarkable variety of caryatids, atalantes and triton figures. These showed the powerful influence of the man who had been Puget's mentor (and employer) in the early years of his artistic development, the Italian master Pietro da Cortona, with whom Puget had worked in Rome and Florence.

By the time Cortona was employed by the dukes of Tuscany, in 1637, he was already successful and well-known as a painter and architect, having worked for the Sachetti and Barberini, two of the most powerful families in Rome. It was while passing through Florence with Cardinal Sachetti that Cortona was persuaded by Duke Ferdinando II[85] of Tuscany to join the many Florentine artists employed in embellishing the newly refurbished ducal residence (the Pitti Palace). Ten years later Cortona was again employed to decorate the ceilings of the ducal apartments with scenes from Greek heavenly mythology, as a result of which the apartments became known as the Planetary Rooms. On one of the ceilings Cortona artfully included references to the "Medicean" satellites, the moons of Jupiter discovered by Ferdinando's mentor Galileo[86] and named after the ducal family in recognition of its support of science. Ferdinando and his brother Leopoldo were both admirers of Galileo and had given him a formal burial when the church had forbidden him any monument. The two brothers also established a science academy, carried out their own experiments and closely followed the work of Evangelista Torricelli, Galileo's pupil, during his work on the vacuum in 1643.

The news of Torricelli's discovery took Europe by storm. Apart from anything else it stirred up a major theological row. If the vacuum was an absence of everything was God also absent from it? Scientists concentrated on more mundane aspects. In 1661 Robert Boyle[87] published Boyle's Law after he had used a vacuum pump to show that at a constant temperature the volume of a gas is inversely

proportional to its pressure. In France this became known as Mariotte's Law, after the name of the French scientist who relied heavily on Boyle's work when in 1679 he produced his own: *On the Nature of Air.* Edmé Mariotte indulged in semiplagiarism more than once, eliciting complaints from several scientists, including Christiaan Huygens,[88] the inventor of the pendulum clock. Mariotte had a similar, "symbiotic" relationship with Pierre Perrault, an ex–tax collector in Paris who had been caught with his hand in the till and who in 1674 published a book titled *The Origin of Springs.* Perrault had measured the drainage characteristics and annual rainfall in the Seine Basin, examined runoff processes in plants, and concluded that only one-sixth of the annual rainfall was necessary to sustain the Seine's flow. This was the first experiment that showed that rivers owed their flow to rainfall. Mariotte extended Perrault's findings by setting up a series of weather-reporting stations across France and published his own book, *The Movement of Waters,* in 1686.

88 52 114

Pierre Perrault came from a talented family. In 1667 his younger brother Claude designed the colonnade in the Louvre. His older brother Charles was a member of the new French Academy of Sciences and at the age of thirty-five became Jean-Baptiste Colbert's factotum, minister for culture, member of the French Academy, and adviser to poets, including Racine. He also had the unenviable task of keeping the accounts during the construction of Versailles.[89]

89 137 254

Charles Perrault goes down in history principally for having written a collection of children's stories in 1697 under the title *Tales Told by Mother Goose,* which included "Little Red Riding Hood," "Puss in Boots," "Cinderella," "Tom Thumb" and "Sleeping Beauty." The collection was later translated into English and published as *Mother Goose's Melody.* In the same year Perrault also triggered a great literary debate with the publication of a poem in which he denigrated the value of classical literature, claiming that modern writers were better and describing Plato as "boring." A furious argument broke out within the French literary establishment and then spread across the Channel to England. There, a retired statesman, Sir William Temple, rose to Perrault's defense. This was a time when recent mathematical

and scientific discoveries, economic advance and exploration were all contributing to a general rise in confidence that made such people as Temple feel that the modern age had much of value to offer. Temple reckoned without opposition from the entrenched establishment of the church and from the old guard at Oxford and Cambridge.

Fortunately, he had in his employ a young man who was to prove equal to the task of defending Temple's position. His name was Jonathan Swift[90] and in 1704, in "The Tale of a Tub," Swift employed his devastating satirical wit in an attack on pedantry and religion, referring to the clergy: "Who that sees a little paltry mortal, droning and dreaming and drivelling to a multitude, can think it agreeable to common good sense that either Heaven or Hell should be put to the trouble of influence or inspection upon what he is about?" As for officials: "If one of them be trimmed up with a gold chain and a red gown and a white rod and a great horse, it is called Lord Mayor. If certain ermines and furs be placed in a certain position we style them a judge; and so, an apt conjunction of lawn and black satin we entitle a bishop."

Not surprisingly this approach to authority lost Swift all chance of a well-paid sinecure within the church. Temple died leaving him only one hundred pounds per annum, and Swift was in dire straits until the Lord Chief Justice in Dublin, George Berkeley, took him on as chaplain. Berkeley had spent twenty-four years in Dublin at Trinity College, studying Classics, Hebrew, logic and theology. He had also traveled Europe, become dean of Derry, and married the daughter of the speaker of the Irish House of Commons. In 1728 he had gone to America, where his scheme was to establish a university in Bermuda to educate young men working in the plantations and train native Americans as missionaries. When the money for the foundation was not forthcoming Berkeley spent five years in New England, helping to found the Philosophical Society and leaving his mark on American education (several cities were named after him, including the university city in California). After leaving his books and his estate to a recently founded college in New Haven (it would become Yale), he returned to Ireland as bishop of Cloyne.

90 124 232

In 1709 at an early age Berkeley had already published *A New The-ory of Vision,* in which he developed the idea, later to be incorporated into his associationist philosophy, that light and color were merely tactile experiences to be interpreted and given meaning by the brain. This act of interpretation relied on the association of ideas, which was in turn learned through experience.

Berkeley's observations on vision were taken up at the end of the eighteenth century by Thomas Young,[91] a precocious talent who was said to have read the Bible twice by the age of four. Before he was twenty Young had learned French, Italian, Latin, Greek, Hebrew, Syr-iac, Chaldee, Samaritan, Arabic, Persian, Turkish and Ethiopian, as well as entomology, botany and philosophy. In 1793 the twenty-year-old Young entered St. Bartholomew's Hospital in London as a medical student. That same year he wrote his first important scientific paper, *Observations on Vision.* In it he stated the first modern optical theory of color vision, noting that the retina reacted to colors in terms only of variable amounts of the three primary colors: red, green and vio-let. By 1801 Young was professor of natural philosophy at the Royal Institution, where he lectured on acoustics, optics, gravitation, as-tronomy, tide, capillary attraction, electricity, hydrodynamics, mea-surement and other things.

91 140 259

In 1814 this polymath turned his attention to hieroglyphics when a friend brought back fragments of papyrus from Egypt. He then began work on the Rosetta Stone, a monument carrying inscriptions in Greek, and two forms of Egyptian (demotic and hieroglyphic). By comparing the Greek and demotic Young was able to locate the names "Alexander" and "Alexandria." He also noticed the frequent repetition of a sign that turned out to be "and." Reasoning that Egyptian scribes would use the phonetic form of foreign names and that proper names would be surrounded by a ring (forming a "car-touche"), he identified the names of Ptolemy and Cleopatra. Young's work prepared the ground for the full decipherment of hieroglyphics by Jacques-Joseph Champollion less than a decade later.

The Rosetta Stone, on which both men worked, was a slab of pol-ished black basalt three feet nine inches long and two feet four

inches wide discovered in 1799 by French soldiers repairing the ruined Fort Rashid, close to the town of Rosetta in the Nile Delta, during the Napoleonic occupation of Egypt. After the British had driven Napoleon out of Egypt, the Stone was removed and taken back to London. Other hieroglyphic source materials (including inscriptions on temples, obelisks and stele) had also become available between 1809 and 1816 with the publication by the French authorities of *The* **92** 45 87 *Description of Egypt*,[92] a giant book full of drawings, measurements and reports on the country prepared at Napoleon's command during the occupation.

The work of publication was superintended by Nicolas-Jacques Conté, who spent three years in Egypt as a kind of quartermaster, keeping the military and scientific staff supplied with everything from swords to magnifying glasses and surgical instruments. Before Conté's departure for Egypt he had been head of the new Paris Conservatory of Arts and Crafts and had made his reputation by solving the great French pencil problem. The Napoleonic Wars and the trade blockade that accompanied them had curtailed French imports, including that of pencils. Conté developed a method for refining graphite by mixing it with clay and making it smooth enough to use as pencil lead. The pencils he produced still bear Conté's name today.

At this time Conté was also known for his work at the Aerostatic Institute at Meudon, near Paris, where he helped found the new Aerostatic Corps of the Artillery Service. The Corps mission was to fly in reconnoitering balloons and observe enemy troop movements. For some reason Napoleon took against the idea, and in 1802 on his return from Egypt disbanded the force. Meanwhile others had been excited by the possibilities of flight. Benjamin Franklin had seen the original Montgolfier balloon experiments in 1783 and agitated in America for similar work to be undertaken there.

However, it was not until the beginning of the American Civil War that American aeronauts would take to the sky. At the time, they were referred to as "professors," the most famous of whom was Thaddeus Lowe. In 1859 he had built the largest-ever balloon (named *Enterprise*, it was 200 feet high and 130 feet in diameter)

Fig. 19: *1861. A Union balloon prepares to ascend. In the absence of a telegraph wire, note the white flag for signaling to the ground.*

with the intention of crossing the Atlantic. Unfortunately, the wind blew him the wrong way and he landed in South Carolina, where he was arrested as a Yankee spy. By 1862 Lowe was a real spy, working for General McClellan's Army of the Potomac, using a number of his balloons to rise to five thousand feet and report via telegraph wire to the ground the disposition and activity of Confederate forces. Lowe's most famous and successful effort was at the battle of Chickahominy, on June 1, 1862, when the *Times* of London reported that he had hovered two thousand feet above the battlefield during the whole of the engagement.

General George McClellan was well aware of the value of spying and recruited a man who had worked for him during McClellan's prewar time as president of the Illinois Central Railroad (whose legal counsel was Abraham Lincoln). Earlier, in 1849, McClellan's new employee had become Chicago's first full-time detective. In 1850 he had set up his own detective agency, whose motto was "We Never

Sleep." Allan Pinkerton's firm was successful because he collected dossiers on known criminals and was probably the first detective to develop the idea of criminal MO (modus operandi). Pinkerton was also a master of disguise, with a large collection of wigs and costumes. As soon as McClellan was appointed to his military post he brought Pinkerton to Washington, where Lincoln asked him to organize a secret service department that would gather information on the social and political activities of suspect individuals in the city.

After the Civil War ended, one of Pinkerton's greatest successes (apart from catching Butch Cassidy and the Sundance Kid) involved a group of Irish-American anarchists named the Molly Maguires. The group carried out assassinations and bombings in the Pennsylvania coalfields, where relations between mine owners and miners were at an all-time low. In 1873 the president of the Philadelphia and Reading Railroad, which had lucrative contracts to haul coal, hired Pinkerton and asked him to infiltrate the Mollies. Pinkerton chose a recent Irish immigrant named James McParlan. Over the next two years McParlan managed to gain the trust of the Mollies, to the extent that they began to ask him to carry out assassinations. In order to avoid this, McParlan pretended to have a drinking problem while continuing to write secret letters to Pinkerton reporting on the Mollies' activities. In 1875, fearing that his cover was blown, McParlan managed to escape by the skin of his teeth and Pinkerton sent him to Denver as head of the local agency there (as well as to recover his health). Meanwhile, partly because of McParlan's work, the Mollies were rounded up and thirteen of them hanged.

In 1913 William Burns (at that time America's greatest detective, with his own agency) visited London and recounted the tale of McParlan's adventures to a fellow crime enthusiast whose own detective methods were to become so well-known that in 1924 the *Illustrated London News* referred to him as the man who had "evolved and disseminated successfully the constructive method in use today in all Criminal Investigation Departments. Poisons, hand-writing, stains, dust, footprints, traces of wheels, the shape and position of wounds, and therefore the probable shape of the weapon which caused them; the theory of cryptograms, all these and many other excellent meth-

ods . . . are now part and parcel of every detective's scientific equipment."

In 1914 the English crime enthusiast wrote about McParlan in a book he titled *The Valley of Fear.* It was the last of Conan Doyle's novels in which Sherlock Holmes would say "Elementary, my dear Watson!"

CHAPTER 7

✸

A Special Place

In 1984 the job of every detective was changed when a British scientist named Alex Jeffreys began the investigation of a group of genes responsible for the production of a protein that carries oxygen into muscle tissue. He was studying DNA as part of his research into the "hypervariable regions" discovered in the United States four years earlier.

The genetic code in these regions of DNA differs markedly between individual human beings, since no two people except identical twins share the same set of hypervariable regions. The regions are short sequences of DNA repeated many times over. DNA itself consists of a long sequence made up of four bases: adenine, guanine, cytosine and thymine (abbreviated to A, G, C and T). The DNA molecule has a double, threadlike structure made up of these bases, which looks like two interlocking spiral chains (a double helix). The helix is held together by the chemical attraction between pairs of bases: adenine is attracted to thymine and cytosine to guanine. If one of the helix threads is, for instance, a sequence of bases, AATTCGTA, the matching thread sequence will be TTAAGCAT.

Long stretches of the DNA chain are the same in all humans, which accounts for the fact that we all share common features, such as two eyes, four limbs and two feet. The differing hypervariable regions appear interspersed in the DNA chain, repeated over and over again. Jeffreys discovered very short "core" base sequences, ten to fif-

teen bases long, within the hypervariable regions and common to many of them. This invariable segment within a variable sequence was in effect a genetic marker that would flag the presence of a hypervariable region. Jeffreys isolated core sequences and cloned them many times over to produce large quantities. He then labeled the marker sequences with radioactive chemicals. Since a DNA sample could be "denatured" (heated to cause the two strands of its helix to separate), the short genetic-marker sequences could then find their match (A binding with T and C with G) in one of the single strands.

The bonded bases could then be made visible by exposing a cut-up DNA strand and its attached radioactive marker sequences to a film. When the film was processed the radioactive markers showed up as dark bands. Since the markers identified hypervariable regions (different in all humans except identical twins), the dark bands on the exposed film would identify a single individual very much more specifically than a conventional fingerprint. Since a DNA sample can be derived from any human cell (for example from hair, skin, semen or blood), DNA fingerprinting has proved tremendously effective ever since its first use in 1987 in a British criminal case, when it was used to identify a rapist. Since then the technique has had a dramatic impact on the pursuit of justice.

Basic to the process of DNA fingerprinting is the way in which the pieces of DNA to be marked are separated out according to the length of the strands. This involves a technique originally developed by a Swedish scientist named Arne Tiselius, who in 1925 began separating proteins. Tiselius was assisting The Sveborg, who had developed a centrifuge that as it spun caused the lighter or smaller proteins to move out to the edge of the serum in which they were present. Tiselius noticed that proteins sorted out in this way would often be mixed up, making exact identification impossible. To get around this problem Tiselius developed a new process called "electrophoresis," which would become essential to the development of biochemistry. Tiselius put the molecules under investigation in a gel and subjected the gel to an electric charge. The effect of the charge was to repel the molecules. The lighter and smaller the molecules, the further they went. It was this work that gained Tiselius the Nobel

Prize, "For his discovery of the complex nature of molecules occurring in blood serum."

Electrophoresis separates molecules by size or weight into different bands along a glass tube containing the gel. In order to see and photograph these bands, Tiselius used a technique originally invented by a Viennese physicist named August Toepler. It was called "schlieren ['smear'] photography" and it revealed the bands of different protein concentrations because of the changes caused by the bands to the refraction of light passing through the glass tube. In the 1880s Toepler's original use of the schlieren technique had been to show the shock-wave patterns caused by explosions or created by the movement of projectiles.

It was this latter capability of schlieren photography that was to interest a Hungarian mechanical engineer and ex-artillery cadet named Theodor von Karman. Von Karman's father had been knighted by Emperor Franz Joseph for services to education, and Theodor followed in the same academic footsteps, winning a fellowship from the Hungarian Academy of Sciences to visit the German University of Gottingen, where he studied under Ludwig Prandtl. Prandtl was already famous for his work on aerodynamics and for his breakthrough discovery of the boundary layer of air passing over the surface of a wing, the study of which revealed much valuable data about drag and lift. In 1914 Prandtl also discovered the vortices formed when air curls over the tip of a wing and trails behind the aircraft, causing extra drag. Prandtl's mathematics helped wing designers minimize this vortex drag effect.

One major phenomenon was left for Theodor von Karman to explain. On occasion, when airflow broke away from a body, it formed a series of vortices known as a "vortex street." Von Karman showed that these vortices formed alternately at the top and bottom of the body into two vortex trails. If the vortices at top and bottom formed sequentially the effect was stable. If both vortices were generated in parallel the effect was to cause instability and set up cycles of vibration. Von Karman was proved spectacularly right on November 7, 1940, when the new Tacoma Narrows suspension bridge at Puget Sound collapsed after a half-hour of violent oscillations (filmed by a

passing member of the University of Washington faculty) generated by a forty-two-mile-an-hour wind. With the use of a model, von Karman showed that the collapse had been caused by a vortex street being shed by the solid sidewall of the bridge. When the oscillations of the bridge were moving in synchrony with the parallel vortices the bridge fell apart. As a result of von Karman's report all suspension bridge sidewalls were subsequently slotted to prevent pressure buildup.

Von Karman's interest in airflow also led him to the study of aerodynamics, and in 1930 he moved to the California Institute of Technology in Pasadena where he helped to set up one of the world's most advanced aerodynamics centers, the Jet Propulsion Laboratory. JPL would carry out much of the leading work on supersonic flight and the development of rockets and spacecraft over the following decades, using schlieren photography to observe the vehicles' behavior.

Earlier in his life von Karman had directed the Austro-Hungarian Air Force research laboratory, where he studied the behavior of propellers and armament. Part of his mandate was to find a method by which pilots could shoot machine guns through their propellers without hitting the revolving blades. At one point early in World War I a Dutch engineer named Anthony Fokker visited von Karman's lab, and the two of them discussed the matter. Fokker knew the answer to the problem, because in April 1915 a Morane-Saulnier monoplane piloted by French pilot Roland Garros had been forced down near Ingelmunster in Germany. On board the aircraft was a machine gun positioned to fire directly ahead and a propeller whose blades were protected by wedges of steel plate to deflect bullets. Fokker immediately devised a way by which the propeller would control the firing of the gun through an interrupter mechanism that fired a bullet only when a propeller blade was not in the way.

When the German Air Force installed Fokker's device it found itself with the world's first fighter planes. All the pilot had to do was point his aircraft at the enemy and pull the trigger. In 1916 when one of the new German fighter planes was being delivered from the factory the pilot inadvertently landed at a British airfield in France. The

British rapidly copied the interrupter mechanism and the way was clear for dogfights. By 1917 aerial combat was commonplace, and the fighter ace was catching the public imagination. In France a pilot became an ace after his fifth kill. Germany required ten. Greatest of all German daredevils was Manfred von Richthofen, the son of a cavalry officer. Manfred was a handsome young Prussian aristocrat whose favorite occupations were hunting and drinking champagne. In 1916 he was assigned to one of the new fighter squadrons and early in 1917 had his own command. Von Richthofen painted his aircraft bright red, earning himself the nickname "Red Baron." By April 1916 von Richthofen had achieved fifty-two kills (his final total would be eighty) and had become a national hero. The German propaganda ministry churned out millions of photographs of him, he received

Fig. 20: *The daredevil Red Baron at the height of his fame in 1918.*

sacks of fan mail and was obliged to make public appearances in factories to denounce communism. By now von Richthofen had a Fokker fighter and all the planes in his squadron had been painted red. Manfred and his squadron were known to their British counterparts as "von Richthofen's Flying Circus." His most famous remark was: "When I have shot down an Englishman my hunting passion is satisfied for a quarter of an hour."

Manfred's great-uncle Ferdinand was professor of geography at the University of Leipzig, and by 1883 he had spent several years as a geologist traveling in Sri Lanka, Japan, Taiwan, the Philippines, Java, California and China (about which he wrote the first definitive geographical description). Ferdinand von Richthofen was the first to bridge the gap between geology and geography. He did so by dividing geography into two fields: special geography (primarily descriptive) and general geography (primarily analytical). Von Richthofen described special geography: "Every area on the earth, no matter how small, whether a continent, a small island, or a naturally bounded inland area, an artificially bounded state, a mountain, a river basin or a sea, is examined as a grouping of smaller unit areas." The description of each of these units in an area became known as "chorography." A synthesis of special and general geography permitted von Richthofen to analyze the interaction between different elements in a geographical area. This also revealed how human presence affected the environment and took into consideration such factors as the distribution of population, races, languages, frontiers, settlements, industries, religions, trade centers, communications routes and products. This kind of study was known as "chorology."

The inclusion in chorology of historical analysis of the effects of human intervention over time was the idea of a German scholar and historian named Carl Ritter, professor of history at Berlin from 1820 until his death in 1859 and founder of the Royal Geographical Society of Berlin. Ritter proposed that the structure of a country was an important element in the development of its inhabitants. He widened the scope of geographical studies: The "science aims at nothing less than to embrace the most complete and the most cosmic view of the Earth to sum up and organise into a beautiful unity all that we know

of the globe . . . and shows the connection of this unified whole with Man and with Man's Creator." The aim for Ritter was to seek the underlying laws uniting the diversity of nature with humankind. In this he was developing the ideas that had galvanized Europe a few decades earlier, at the beginning of the Romantic movement, thanks to J. G. Herder.[93]

93 81 *153*

In *Plastic Art,* published in 1778, Herder sought a psychobiological explanation of aesthetic reactions and introduced the same relativist concepts linking humans and their environment that Ritter and von Richthofen would adopt later. For Herder sense perception was linked to environment. Greenlanders, Herder stated, had no beauty and hence no sense of beauty because their climate was not conducive to the development of beauty. He applied the same argument to history. The arts were a product of their time, defined by the contemporary environment and the physical temperament of the race. One effect of Herder's recognition that each period had unique qualities was the rehabilitation of the Gothic style. Because of this Herder virtually triggered the Gothic Revival that was to sweep Europe in the nineteenth century. For Herder the close links between humans and their location showed that humans were an intrinsic part of Nature itself.

This was the view of Johann Joachim Winckelmann, the founder of the study of art history. In 1764 Winckelmann wrote *History of Ancient Art,* a work that fundamentally influenced Herder, Schelling,[94] Goethe, Hegel and many other Romantics. Ten years earlier, after an uneventful life, at the age of thirty-eight Winckelmann had arrived in Rome, settling in the artists' quarter near Piazza di Spagna. In 1758 he entered the service of Cardinal Albani, an avid collector of antiques. Winckelmann devoted himself to a study of these *objets d'art* and in 1762 published *Observations on the Architecture of the Ancients.* This included a description of the recently unearthed city of Pompeii. Since 1748 the gradual excavation of Pompeii and Herculaneum had stupefied Europe. Every day more artifacts and buildings were revealed. Drawing on the new discoveries, in *History of Ancient Art* Winckelmann developed the argument that the ancient world and especially Greece had enjoyed a uniquely "creative" environment.

94 70 *142*

The Classical spirit had been born of a place whose natural beauty and temperate climate had fostered beauty. For Winckelmann the Greeks represented the ideal, and he painted a glowing picture of them and their artistic genius. Winckelmann's book was a comprehensive analysis of all that was known about Classical art. Winckelmann presented Greece as the origin of modern culture, and put forward the idea, so passionately taken up by the Romantics, that the only way to understand any period in history and its art was to attempt to understand what it had been to live at the time.

One of Winckelmann's friends in Rome was the artist Raphael Mengs. In 1763 Mengs introduced him to an extraordinary young woman painter recently arrived from Switzerland. She was twenty-two-year-old Angelica Kauffmann, and she had just spent time in

Fig. 21: *Winckelmann's inspiration, Pompeii, discovered by workmen digging a well for Charles III of Naples, here inspecting the excavations in 1751.*

175

Parma, Bologna and Florence, studying and copying the masters. Kauffmann had been a child prodigy, painting the bishop of Como when she was only twelve. She was beautiful, sang well and was an accomplished clavichord player. By the time she arrived in Rome she was feted wherever she went, welcomed by the highest in the land. Winckelmann taught her everything he knew. In return she painted his portrait. It was one of her best.

A year after she arrived Kauffmann visited Naples, where many of the foreign visitors were avid for her to paint them. In 1766 she met the wife of the English resident in Venice, who suggested she go to London. In 1766 she took that city by storm. She had arrived at a brilliant moment in British art. In 1768 the Royal Academy was founded and by 1770 there were so many art exhibitions in London, attracting so many viewers and buyers, that it was difficult to move easily through the streets. Horace Walpole said: "After gaming, the folly of the day is pictures." The doyen of the art world was Sir Joshua Reynolds, recently knighted by the king, at the height of his fame and the Academy's first president. The Academy had only thirty-six members, and (after only two years in London) Kauffmann became one. Part of the reason might have been her relationship with Reynolds, rumored to be more than professional. Within one year Kauffmann was the most fashionable portraitist of the day, with commissions to paint Queen Charlotte and her children, Princess Augusta, and the king of Denmark. Four of her paintings were on show at the Royal Academy's first exhibition in 1769. The only cloud in her sky was that when the RA proposed her name as one of a small group of artists offering to paint the interior of St. Paul's Cathedral, Kauffmann was turned down on the grounds of her Catholicism.

The first Kauffmann picture to be exhibited in London, even before her arrival, had been one painted during her visit to Naples. It was a portrait of David Garrick, by this time the most famous actor-manager in England. He had originally come to London with his brother and set up in the wine trade. At one point he contracted to supply the Bedford Coffeehouse, a venue for literary and theatrical people. Garrick began writing for the stage, and in 1740 his *Lethe* had a successful run at Drury Lane Theater. In 1741 his *The Lying*

Valet was staged. The wine business was languishing, so he decided to make the theater his full-time career and became an actor, first appearing anonymously in *Richard III*. His performance astonished the audiences. Garrick introduced realism to the stage for the first time. He moved around the stage naturally, using a variety of facial expressions and speaking in a conversational tone. Alexander Pope[95] said he would never be equaled. The Prince of Wales said he had not known what acting was until he saw Garrick. In both London and Dublin (where productions went at the end of the London season), Garrick was a box-office smash hit. **95** 123 232

In 1747 he became actor-manager of the Drury Lane Theater and began to introduce changes. In 1762 he enlarged the theater, doubling its capacity. He cleared the stage of members of the audience, who had previously been in the habit of talking to the actors during performances. In the 1770s he hired John Philip de Loutherbourg, who revolutionized stage settings with the use of different levels to achieve perspective effect, lush backgrounds, transparent gauzes painted with scenes that would suddenly appear when lit, as well as free-standing pieces of stage furniture and colored lights. All of this made Garrick's productions the most exciting spectacles in London.

Before Garrick candles were the only source of illumination, either set on candelabra and lowered into a scene, or in the footlights. Garrick's new acting technique required better illumination, so he put reflectors behind the candles and added lighting from the wings. In 1785, after Garrick had left, the theater introduced an extraordinary new form of illumination that won instant plaudits: "The effect of this light, which is, in a manner, a new kind of artificial light, was brilliant beyond all expectation. The flame is bright without dazzling, strong and vivid, perfectly clear and yet at the same time steady, that the eye can bear to dwell upon it not only without pain, but even with some degree of peculiar satisfaction."

The new lamp had been invented by the Swiss Aimé Argand. Early in his adult life he lectured to the French Academy of Science on the distillation of spirits of wine and attracted the attention of winemakers in the South of France. By 1778 Argand was writing to the director general of the Herault Department (Jacques Necker,[96] soon to be **96** 68 *141*

French director of finances and the father of the Romantic writer Germaine de Staël) offering information on his distillation process in return for a monopoly on the production of brandy and spirits of wine. In 1780 Argand demonstrated his technique in Montpellier to winemakers and two years later set up a large-scale distilling operation. Argand later said that it was during this period he began to think about his lamp. In 1783 he went to London to see if the lamp might have a British market. This made sense, since by now the country was in the early stages of the Industrial Revolution and factories needed better and safer illumination than candles. In his search for a manufacturer Argand went to Birmingham to the Soho works of James Watt and Matthew Boulton,[97] where a deal was struck. Boulton began production of the lamp in 1784.

The lamp itself consisted of a pedestal supporting a vase-shaped oil reservoir. Fitting on top of the reservoir was a metal structure consisting of two concentric brass tubes (pierced by ventilation slits), which held the circular wick and the wick-moving mechanism. A glass chimney rested on top of this. The advantages of the new lamp were that the entry of air through the slits past the wick and up through the open glass chimney facilitated the complete combustion of the fuel. The chimney ensured a bright, flicker-free light. In 1788, two British lighthouse towers, rebuilt on the southern tip of Portland Bill, were fitted with the new Argand lamps. By 1820 Argands were installed in some fifty British lighthouses. They would eventually be used in lighthouses all over the world. In some later versions the number of circular wicks was increased to ten. The lamp was ideal for lighthouses, since it gave off bright light and above all was less likely to cause fires (the main cause of lighthouse destruction), because there was no naked flame.

Lighthouse building reflected a growing demand for greater safety at sea following the general increase in the amount of shipping on the oceans, especially around Europe and across the Atlantic, carrying raw materials for the new Industrial Revolution factories and delivering their manufactured products. Argand's lamp had one unintended side-effect. Brighter lighthouses also made life easier for

smugglers. Throughout the eighteenth century smuggling made up at least half of all English overseas trade. Smugglers dealt in almost every major commodity: tobacco, wool, tea, rum, brandy, wine, rice, molasses, slaves, logwood, flour, pitch, beef, pork, mercury, brass, ironware, cotton, canvas and nails. The attraction of smuggled goods was their low, untaxed price. It was this aspect of the trade that would lead to conflict between Britain and Spain.

Spain claimed a monopoly of all trade with her American colonies, but the Spanish economy was unable to supply the rapidly growing number of South American colonists with the goods they required. Early in the eighteenth century, of the twenty-seven thousand tons of merchandise legally despatched to Spanish America only fifteen hundred originated in the Iberian Peninsula. The rest was supplied by France, England and Holland. By 1731 the Spanish situation had worsened and smugglers stepped into the breach. Their technique was relatively simple. Regular ships from South America, bound for Spain with cargoes of gold and silver, cochineal, cocoa, sarsaparilla, balsam, indigo, dyewoods, tallow, vicuna wool and drugs, would leave Havana, their final port before the Atlantic crossing. Over the horizon they would be met by smugglers, carrying with them all the goods the colonists wanted but could not obtain from Spain, to be bought at untaxed prices paid for by some of the bullion on board the Spanish ships. To try to stop this trade the Havana authorities set up the first *guardacostas* (coastguards). These tended to be hired privateers working on the basis of "no prize, no pay," so they were often unscrupulous and violent.

In 1731 an incident occurred that was to have far-reaching consequences. The British brig *Rebecca,* sailing from Jamaica to London, was intercepted by Havana coastguards and boarded by a particularly violent individual, Juan de Leon Fandino. In the melee that followed the captain of the *Rebecca,* Robert Jenkins, had an ear cut off. On return to England his case for compensation languished in the courts. In 1738 it was revived and Jenkins was brought to testify before a House of Commons committee. At the hearing Jenkins produced a box in which he said was his ear. Much political capital was made

out of the incident and public opinion was so outraged that in 1739 England declared war on Spain. It was a war that would become known as the "War of Jenkins' Ear."

When the war broke out a British naval captain, Lord George Anson, was recalled from Barbados where his mission had been to protect British shipping from attacks such as that on the *Rebecca*. Anson was to go on to become an admiral and to bring a number of reforms to the navy, including the classification of warships into six rates, the establishment of the marines, and the introduction of the blue-and-white officers' uniform. Meanwhile, in 1740 Anson was ordered to take six ships and fifteen hundred men to sail around Cape Horn into the Pacific and harry Spanish merchant shipping. Four years later he returned with so much plunder that thirty wagons were needed to haul it to the Tower of London for safekeeping. Anson's haul included 1,313,842 gold pieces-of-eight and 35,682 ounces of silver. Each crewman's share was well in excess of what he might have expected on departure from Britain, because Anson returned with only one ship and 145 men. The rest had perished not from their encounters with the Spanish but from scurvy. At the very beginning of the voyage, by the time they had reached landfall on the other side of the Atlantic, 200 were already dead. A year later only 323 men were left. The last would die in the third year of the voyage, leaving only enough to crew one ship.

The major problem with scurvy was that it weakened sufferers and left them vulnerable to other diseases. One of Anson's doctors wrote: "A most extraordinary circumstance—that the scars of old wounds, healed for many years, were forced open again; also many of our people, though confined to their hammocks, ate and drank heartily and were cheerful, yet having resolved to get out of their hammock, died before they could well reach the deck. It was also no uncommon thing for those who were able to walk the deck, to drop down in an instant on any endeavours to act with their utmost vigor."

The man who discovered the cure for scurvy did so as the result of work carried out only three years after Anson's return. His name was James Lind, and at the age of fifteen in Edinburgh he had been apprenticed to a surgeon. At the beginning of the War of Jenkins' Ear

the twenty-three-year-old Lind joined the navy as a surgeon's mate. In the English Channel, aboard HMS *Salisbury,* Lind carried out what was probably the first controlled clinical trial in nutrition. For two weeks he kept a group of twelve scurvy patients on the same diet: breakfast of gruel with sugar; dinner of fresh mutton broth and pudding; supper of barley and raisins, rice and currants. Six pairs of the men were each allocated a different daily supplemental diet: a quart of cider, twenty-five drops of elixir vitriol, six spoonfuls of vinegar, half a pint of sea water, two oranges and one lemon, and a medicinal paste made of garlic, mustard seed, balsam, dried radish root and myrrh. By the sixth day of the trial the men on the citrus diet had much improved. The others continued to decline.

In 1748 Lind left the navy, returned to Edinburgh to an honorary medical degree and set out to write a short paper on his experiment. His work ended five years later with the publication of a four-hundred-page *Treatise of the Scurvy,* dedicated to Anson. In the long run the navy would react to Lind's report by introducing a supply of lemon juice for every Royal Navy ship. In the nineteenth century the practice was extended to the merchant marine, where their use of limes earned the sailors the nickname "Limeys."

When Lind received his degree the leading medical figure at Edinburgh University was Alexander Monro, professor of anatomy at the new Faculty of Medicine founded there only a few decades earlier. Monro (whose son was to treat Flora Macdonald[98] on her return **98** 83 *157* from North Carolina) had impressive credentials, having studied in London, Paris, and in Holland at the University of Leiden, where he took lessons from the famous chemist Hermann Boerhaave. The large number of students attracted to Monro's dissection classes persuaded the university to come to an agreement with the city magistrates to supply the corpses of foundlings, stillborns, suicides, those who had suffered a violent death and those hanged for crimes. Unfortunately, supply failed to keep up with demand and led to the practice of grave-robbing. As long as the grave-robbing students left behind a corpse's shroud the removal of the body itself was not a criminal offense, although the activity caused such public outcry that Monro's windows were broken by a mob.

At the end of 1726 Monro published a major work, *The Anatomy of the Human Bones,* the first proper anatomy textbook, which contained minutely detailed descriptions. The book went into eleven editions and was translated into most European languages. In it Monro noted among other things that different nationalities could be identified by the shape of their cranium, that a man's stature decreases as evening approaches, and that the bone at a healed fracture is stronger than before the fracture. The extraordinary thing about the book was that it contained no illustrations. This was due to the fact that Monro's old teacher in London, William Cheselden (who got Monro elected to the Royal Society, was the queen's surgeon, friend of the great, famous for his fifty-four-second-long gallstone operations, and master of the Company of Surgeons) was himself planning to produce a book on bones, titled *Osteographica.* Cheselden's book was to have illustrations.

Osteographica was published in 1735 and ran to thirteen editions. The title page carried an illustration of the technique Cheselden had used to produce his drawings. It showed a camera obscura.[99] At the time, this consisted of a box, set into one side of which was a small lens. This produced an inverted image (of any object at which the lens was pointed) on the inside of the box opposite the lens. If the image were made to fall onto translucent paper or a thick ground glass surface it could then be traced. The technique made *Osteographica* one of the most accurately illustrated books ever published on the subject of bones. The camera obscura had been originally given its name by a short-sighted German astronomer named Johannes Kepler,[100] who had first used it in July 1600 to draw a partial solar eclipse in the market square of the Austrian city of Graz, where Kepler taught mathematics and astronomy.

In 1595, a year after his arrival in Graz, Kepler was struck by an idea so powerful he said he felt as if he had discovered the secret of the universe. The idea was not a new one, but it would lead to one of the most fundamental of all astronomical discoveries. Kepler was wondering why there were only six planets (known at the time) instead of twenty or a hundred, when he realized that this must have to

do with what was known as the "five perfect solids." This idea struck him in the classroom, where he had just drawn a circle in a triangle in a circle. Kepler realized that the ratio of the two circles was about the same as that of the orbits of Jupiter and Saturn. He looked for more geometrical figures that might generate other orbits and hit on the "five perfect solids." These were classical Greek solid geometric figures, each of whose faces were identical: the tetrahedron, the cube, the octahedron, the dodecahedron and the isocahedron.

Each one of these figures could be placed in a sphere and all of its corners would touch the inside of the sphere. Kepler applied the figures to the orbits of the planets. Inside a sphere representing the orbit of Saturn he inscribed a cube; inside that, another sphere (the orbit of Jupiter), inside which he put a tetrahedron; then the sphere/orbit of Mars; then a dodecahedron inside which he put the sphere/orbit of Earth; then an isocahedron, then the sphere/orbit of Venus; then finally an octahedron containing the sphere/orbit of Mercury. This explained why there were only six planets: their orbits fitted into the five perfect solids.

In 1597 Kepler published his amazing discovery in his first book, *Mysterium Cosmographicum*. Kepler was now obliged to check observational data to verify his grand theory, and this data immediately threw up an awkward discrepancy. The orbits of the planets were not circles but ellipses and these did not fit inside the perfect solids. The data also showed Kepler that the planets traveled their elliptical orbits slowly when distant from the sun and faster when closer to it. Also, each planet moved more slowly the farther it was from the sun. Why was this so? Kepler made the great leap of imagination and proposed that the sun released a force of some kind that drove the planets around in their orbits. Since the force might diminish as did light with distance it would drive the planets less powerfully (and therefore less quickly) the farther from the sun they were. In spite of this discovery Kepler remained rooted in medieval cosmology, calling the mysterious solar emanation a "Holy Spirit Force" that acted like a lash to spur the planets on. Kepler then went on to measure the "force" and produced his three great laws: that the planets travel

around the sun in ellipses; that a planet does not move at a uniform rate but in such a manner that if a line were drawn from the planet to the sun it would sweep over equal areas in equal times; and that the squares of the periods of orbit of any two planets are as the cubes of their mean distances from the sun.

At the end of September 1619 Kepler was working as provincial mathematician in the Austrian city of Linz when he was visited by a passing group of Englishmen headed by the earl of Doncaster, who was on his way to see the Holy Roman Emperor. The earl was accompanied by a chaplain who had read Kepler's work. The chaplain's name was John Donne, and one of his greatest poems had been written in reaction to the new cosmology. In the poem he wrote the now-famous lines:

> (the) new Philosophy calls all in doubt,
> The Element of fire is quite put out;
> The Sun is lost, and th'earth, and no man's wit
> Can well direct him, where to look for it.
> And freely men confess, that this world's spent,
> When in the Planets, and the Firmament
> They seek so many new; they see that this
> Is crumbled out again to his Atomies.
> 'Tis all in pieces, all coherence gone.

At the meeting in Linz Kepler is said to have given Donne a copy of his new book, *Harmonice Mundi,* to take back to King James I of England, to whom he had dedicated the work.

Donne's father was a well-to-do merchant and a member of the Ironmongers' Company. The Donne family was Catholic during a time of persecution, so Donne left Oxford without taking his degree, since this would have meant swearing the Oath of Supremacy and recognizing the queen rather than the pope as supreme authority over the church. Eventually Donne converted, took Holy Orders in the Protestant church, found powerful patrons and began a brilliant career as a preacher. By 1616 he was also a member of Parliament. In 1621 he was appointed dean of St. Paul's Cathedral in London, where

he began a series of sermons that made him nationally renowned. Huge crowds pressed into the cathedral every time he spoke.

In the 1620s Donne met one of his parishioners, Isaac Walton, who kept a linen-draper's shop and was a vestryman at one of the several churches for which Donne was responsible. Like Donne's father, Walton was also a freeman of the Ironmongers' Company. The two men became friends, and in 1626 Donne officiated at Walton's marriage to Rachel Floud. In 1631, when Donne died, Walton was present at the deathbed and nine years later wrote his *Life of Donne.*

When the English Civil War came in 1642 Walton was a fervent supporter of the losing Royalist faction. In 1649 Charles I was beheaded and the eleven-year period of the Cromwellian Commonwealth began. Those who had supported the king were imprisoned, hanged or had their property and (in the case of the clergy) livings confiscated. In 1653 Walton published the book that would make him famous, *The Compleat Angler,* aimed at the many defrocked clergy of Walton's acquaintance. The book was written partly to provide the out-of-work churchmen with recreation during their time of enforced idleness and partly because fishing would provide food for those of them now suffering from poverty. As Walton noted, angling was a fit activity for clergy since the Apostles themselves had been fishermen and the task of priests was to fish for souls.

The plot of *The Compleat Angler* takes the form of a journey by two companions from London along the River Ware and back again. The book gives instructions for catching trout, salmon, chub, grayling, pike, carp, bream, tench, barbel, gudgeon and many more. Walton added entertainment for anglers in the form of poems, songs with music, arithmetic puzzles, dramas, anecdotes and proverbs. In the fifth edition Walton added a chapter on fly-fishing, written by his friend and fellow-angler Charles Cotton. Cotton was the son of a rich landowner in Derbyshire, attended Cambridge University, and traveled in Italy and France. He greatly admired Walton, who had also been his father's friend, and the two of them often fished in Derbyshire on the River Dove, where Cotton built a small fishing house for them to use. It still stands today and above the entrance can be seen the entwined initials "CC" and "IW." Cotton's comfortable

lifestyle gave him time to write poetry and translate from the French. In 1671 he produced an English version of Corneille's *Horace* and in 1685 his last work was an English edition of the *Essays* of Montaigne, which still ranks as a masterpiece of translation.

Michel Eyquem de Montaigne, born in 1533, spent thirteen years as a magistrate in the court of Bordeaux. In 1570 at the age of thirty-seven he sold his magistrate's post and retired to his country estate where he lived in his library on the third floor of a round tower, leaving only for brief trips to Switzerland, Italy and Germany, and to serve two terms as mayor of Bordeaux. Montaigne's major contribution to European thought was to revive and make popular the ancient skeptic philosophy. On the beams of his study ceiling was carved the phrase, "All that is certain is that nothing is certain." The period in which Montaigne lived was fertile ground for the skeptic. His generation faced a problem that was new, urgent and fraught with danger: which form of Christianity was right, Protestant or Catholic? Each faith questioned the beliefs of the other. Protestants rejected the edicts of Rome and Catholics cast doubt on the literal interpretation of the Bible.

Montaigne's *Essays,* powerful exercises in skepticism, are unusually modern in their view. Montaigne was strikingly free from ethnocentrism and intensely interested in other cultures. He wrote about the newly discovered Indians of Brazil, giving a detailed description of their culture, and while remarking that they had "no trade, no knowledge of writing, no arithmetic, no magistrate, no political subordination . . . no riches or poverty, no contracts, no inheritance . . . no clothes, no agriculture, no metal," he refused to call them barbarians or savages, saying: "Everyone calls barbarous whatever is not customary with him." In an age rediscovering the Classics and discovering new parts of the globe Montaigne recommended the value of travel as a means of broadening the mind. Everywhere he went Montaigne sought to understand the local culture. In Switzerland he quizzed the Lutherans, in Verona the Jews, in Rome the flagellants, in France he questioned women accused of witchcraft. Prefiguring modern social anthropology, he said: "Every custom has its function."

Montaigne's work had a profound effect on a poor, provincial French writer named Pierre Bayle, who was eventually driven from France because he was Protestant. In Geneva he took courses in philosophy at the Academy and in 1681 moved to Rotterdam. There in 1696 he produced his great three-volume *Historical and Critical Dictionary.* The work was essentially a collection of biographies of historical writers and thinkers, and while Bayle included Classical figures in large part he dealt with those of his own time: humanists, Protestant theologians, and such recent philosophers as Spinoza and Hobbes. The *Dictionary* was based on Bayle's belief that all knowledge should be open to scrutiny and not simply passed on unquestioned from generation to generation. The work became a powerful weapon in the fight against intolerance.

Early in his Rotterdam period, in 1684, Bayle had begun to edit a monthly newspaper: *The News of the Republic of Letters.* This work put him in touch with a network of correspondents all over Europe. Two years later he published a letter supposedly written from the East Indies about the wars in Borneo between two queens, Mreo and Eneuge. The thinly veiled anagrammatic satire on "Rome" and "Genève" (that is, Catholics and Protestants) was written by another skeptic, Bernard de Fontenelle. Fontenelle settled in Paris in 1687 and began a literary career that shot him to fame with opera librettos, histories, comedies and poems. That same year he produced his best-known work, the first example of a scholarly work aimed at the general public, titled *Conversations on the Plurality of Worlds.* The book was a landmark in the popularization of science, but it raised dangerous questions about the relativity of knowledge because it postulated a nongeocentric universe. Fontenelle discussed the possible existence of other planets like the Earth, beginning the book: "It seems that nothing ought to interest us more than knowing how this world we inhabit is made, and whether there are other worlds like it which may be inhabited also."

In 1727 Fontenelle put a foot wrong with his *Elements of Infinite Geometry,* a work dealing with a level of mathematics about which he was not entirely qualified to write. There were, it seemed, mistakes in his math that attracted the attention of a major mathematical mind

in Switzerland who left Fontenelle in no doubt as to the error of his ways. Johann Bernoulli came from a Basle family that over three generations produced no fewer than eight mathematicians. Johann was apparently quarrelsome, quick-tempered and brilliant, and was said to be the man who made calculus understandable to the common man. His range was prodigious, including physics, chemistry, astronomy, optics and mechanics. Much of his time was spent working on differential calculus and corresponding with Gottfried Leibnitz, its coinventor (Newton did the same, independently). As part of Bernoulli's work in experimental physics he also investigated the recently discovered phenomenon of "mercurial electricity," first observed by the French astronomer Jean Picard[101] when in 1675 he noticed that movement of the mercury in his barometer produced a glow. Bernoulli was unable to explain the matter.

101 136 254

The man who did so was an Englishman, Francis Hauksbee. In 1709 he was demonstrator of experiments for the Royal Society under its president, Isaac Newton. In 1705 he showed the Society a nine-inch diameter evacuated glass globe that he had fixed to a device that would make it spin. As it rotated he pressed his hand against the glass and a purple light appeared inside the globe, so bright "that words in capital letters became legible by it." Hauksbee then experimented by rubbing evacuated glass tubes. These glowed, crackled and attracted small pieces of brass leaf, threads and wool. In 1709 Hauksbee published his findings, describing the glow and crackling noises as being akin to lightning and using the term "electricity."

After 1708 Hauksbee turned his attention to the phenomenon of capillarity: the way in which when a fine tube was dipped into a liquid the liquid crept up the tube. The narrower the tube the higher the liquid climbed. This also happened when the tubes were placed in a vacuum. Partly because of his link with Newton, and given the overpowering effect that the concept of gravity was having on all aspects of science, Hauksbee was convinced capillary action was related in some way to attraction. The particles at the surface of the liquid were clearly being attracted upward by the particles in the

glass. Newton supported this theory in one of his 1717 *Optics* essays. This was enough for a London vicar named Stephen Hales, who in 1727 was investigating the behavior of sap in plants. In his *Vegetable Staticks* published that year, Hales, who had been sticking glass tubes into plants and watching how sap rose into the tubes, claimed that capillary action was at work in plants and might even account for the behavior of blood in human veins.

In 1740 Hales was stimulated by news of a typhus epidemic among sailors on board ship off Spithead awaiting transportation to America to take up the study of ventilation. A year later he published *A Description of Ventilators,* which included the design of a ventilator he had invented for placing in the outside wall of a building. Two pairs of large bellows were worked by a centrally pivoted horizontal lever. The bellows were provided with inlet and outlet valves so that as the lever was raised at one end one bellows drew air in from the outside. When the lever was depressed the other bellows forced the air into the room.

Hales tested his machine in a granary close to his church in Teddington, though its real purpose was initially for use in ships. There was a high incidence of fever among sailors and this was thought to be due to "disease-causing" air. The ventilator would replace this "effluvium" with "good" air. Eventually, in 1756 ventilators were installed in navy ships and in prisons, but not before Hales had also installed them in two hospitals, one in central London and the other a Middlesex smallpox hospital of which Hales was a governor.

Ventilation proved not to be the cure for smallpox, a prevalent and generally fatal disease. Forty years later an English country doctor, Edward Jenner, found the cure. He had begun his medical career apprenticed to a country surgeon for six years, then enrolled at the anatomy school in London run by the two famous surgeon-anatomists, John and William Hunter. After two years Jenner, now aged twenty-three, returned to his home village of Berkeley in Gloucestershire and set up in practice. In 1796 he came across several cases of cowpox contracted by milkmaids during the milking process. The usual symptoms were the appearance of large pustules

accompanied by fever. Jenner knew about the Turkish habit of inoculation[102] against smallpox with the pus from smallpox pustules.
This tended to act prophylactically as a preventative against contracting the disease but it was an unpleasant and sometimes fatal
procedure. Jenner experimentally injected the eight-year-old son of
one of his workers with pus from cowpox pustules and then infected
the boy with smallpox. No smallpox symptoms appeared. Jenner
called his technique (after the Latin word for cow, *vacca*) "vaccination." It was an instant success, and by 1800 the practice had spread
throughout Europe and had reached America.

Most of the rest of Jenner's life was spent quietly in Gloucestershire, where he indulged himself in his passion for cuckoos. In 1788
he had been made a Fellow of the Royal Society following his publication *Observations on the Natural History of the Cuckoo*. In this he
explained how cuckoo chicks hijack the nests of other birds using a
hollow in their back to scoop up and tip out the eggs of the occu-
pant. The chick would also do this to eggs containing cuckoo sib-

102 121 224

Fig. 22: *Not everybody greeted vaccination with the same degree of enthusiasm.
A cartoon of 1802.*

lings. Just before his death in 1823 Jenner's last publication, on the migration of birds, was one of the first proper ornithological studies.

Jenner missed by three years the arrival of an American who would, so to speak, put ornithology on the coffee tables of the world. He was John James Audubon, the first great bird painter. Audubon had a varied career. Born in Haiti and brought up in France, he was sent in 1803 to Pennsylvania where his family owned a farm. In 1807, aged twenty-two, he set off to make his fortune in the West (at that time, Ohio and Kentucky). For thirteen years he moved from one financial disaster to another. The sawmill he opened failed, bankrupting him and an investor, the brother of the English poet John Keats. He tried running a store. It also failed. In Cincinnati he attempted taxidermy with some success. As he traveled he was also drawing and painting birds. In 1821 his fortunes changed when he landed the job of tutor to the daughter of a plantation family in Louisiana. In the five months that followed Audubon painted feverishly among the thousands of birds in the deep magnolia woods surrounding Bayou Sara, near St. Francisville.

When he had completed 435 paintings and failed to find a publisher, Audubon was persuaded to try England. Thanks to an influential contact, William Roscoe, within ten days of Audubon's arrival his drawings were on show at the Royal Institution. Audubon was an instant celebrity. Hundreds of people came to see the work, and he was lionized as the Romantic young woodsman from the New World. Audubon finally found a publisher in Edinburgh. By this time his plans for the work, to be titled *Birds of America,* had grown and he returned to America for more material. By now Audubon was an American national institution. Government schooners were placed at his disposal to take him to Labrador and other far-flung spots. In 1838 all five volumes of the great work were finally published.

In 1840 he received a letter from a seventeen-year-old boy named Spencer Fullerton Baird, describing a species Audubon had missed: the yellow-bellied flycatcher. Audubon invited the boy to visit and the two became friends. Ten years later the enthusiastic young naturalist had a specimen collection that filled two freight cars (2,500 American birds, 1,000 European birds, nests, eggs and reptiles, as

well as 600 skulls and skeletons of American vertebrates and fossils). The freight cars carried the collection to the Smithsonian where Baird was to take up his appointment as assistant secretary.

The 1850s saw the beginning of the great age of exploration of the West, and Baird was responsible for shipping back to the Smithsonian all specimens collected by the explorers and surveyors. The information Baird gleaned from the numerous expedition reports was encyclopedic, so it was to him that the government eventually turned for information regarding the possible purchase of Alaska in 1866. Baird advised Congress to ratify the purchase.

Of the hundred or more expeditions in which Baird was involved perhaps the most exciting was that led by Ferdinand Vandiveer Hayden. In 1867 Baird obtained Hayden a grant from Nebraska for a survey of the state's geological resources. The survey was extended and refinanced over the next four years, and in 1871 Hayden returned from the Rockies with stupendous photographs by William Henry Jackson that persuaded Congress to declare the area a special place: the first National Park in the United States.

It became known, after the river running through it, as Yellowstone National Park. And it contained the biggest geyser in the Western world: "Old Faithful."

CHAPTER 8

✖

Fire from the Sky

At the end of a bleak, wind-swept plain in the southern part of Iceland can be found one of the most extraordinary sights on the planet. Amid clouds of sulphurous steam and hot pools, every fifteen minutes *Strokkur* erupts, throwing a plume of scalding water seventy feet into the air. The word for this phenomenon, "geyser," comes from the old Icelandic word for "gush": *goysa*.

Geysers happen where the waters of an underground spring encounter hot rocks. This usually occurs in areas of volcanic activity and it happens in Iceland because of a gigantic, mile-long fissure known as "the thing that eats everybody": *allmannagja*. The fissure is part of a split in the Earth's surface that runs north-south the length of the Atlantic. As magma from the molten planetary core wells up through the split and hardens it forces the Atlantic tectonic plates apart at a rate of two centimeters a year. When the tectonic plates hit the continents around the edge of the oceans they are forced under the continental rim. The force of this impact causes buckling, throws up mountain ranges and on occasion causes cracks to appear. When this happens, magma is released to the surface by volcanic activity.

The first person to develop a theory to explain these planetwide disturbances was a German meteorologist named Alfred Wegener. Initially Wegener qualified as an astronomer but in 1905, deciding there were few astronomical discoveries left to be made (and anyway he lacked the advanced math), he took a job as technical assistant at

the Aeronautic Observatory in Berlin and began meteorological work with weather balloons and kites. He spent much of the rest of his life collecting meteorological data on four expeditions to Iceland and Greenland.

It was after the first (1906–8) that Wegener was struck by the way the coastlines of the continents on either side of the Atlantic fit together. In 1858 Antonio Snider-Pellegrini had published a map showing this fit, and an American, Frank Taylor, had theorized that the Atlantic had split open and forced the continents apart. In 1911 Wegener came across paleontological evidence that strengthened his views. Almost identical fossil snails had been found in Africa and Brazil. There was no evidence of a now-sunken land bridge that might once have joined the two places, so in 1912 Wegener made public his continental drift theory. At a geological meeting he proposed that the harder rock of the continents rode like ships on the softer rock of the mantle and that the continents had drifted apart, perhaps impelled by the centrifugal force of the Earth's spin pushing the land masses away from the poles, or perhaps moved by currents in the molten magma beneath the surface.

Wegener's hypothesis was met with derision, considered by geologists to be the work of a meteorologist unqualified to speak about geological matters. It would take fifty years of further discovery to confirm Wegener's basic thesis. Until then most geologists thought Wegener was seeing things.

Ironically, his other major field of study was mirages. As part of his meteorological work he studied these phenomena, one of which, the *Fata Morgana,* was already being observed in the Middle Ages. The best early description of the most famous example, seen across the Straits of Messina between Sicily and Italy, was written in 1643 by an Italian cleric, Father Angelucci, looking across the straits towards Messina on the Sicilian side: "The ocean which washes the coast of Sicily rose up and looked like a dark mountain range." In front of the mountain "there quickly appeared a series of more than 10,000 pilasters which were a whitish-grey colour . . . the pilasters shrank to half their height and built arches like those of Roman aqueducts." Before it all

vanished castles appeared above the aqueduct, each with towers and windows.

Mirages generally occur over flat surfaces like deserts and water and they are a complex product of air pressure and temperature, the temperature of the surface, the effect of gravity and the action of turbulence in the atmosphere. All these factors can combine to cause the light from a distant object to curve through the air and present a falsely positioned image to the observer's eye. In the *Fata Morgana* mirage the result is as Father Angelucci described, when the image can even originate in a flat object such as the sea and be transformed and distorted, defocused and moved in such a way as to create the famous shimmering "castles in the air" effect.

Fata Morgana is Latin for "Morgan the Witch." Morgan was one of the most powerful figures in medieval mythology and was thought to be the sister of King Arthur. Tales of the legendary sovereign of Camelot are generally reckoned to have originated in Wales with a sixth-century writer named Gildas. His work describes the fall of the late Romanized Celtic culture during the Anglo-Saxon invasions of England and records the Battle of Badon Hill, fought the year of Gildas's birth, at which Arthur is said to have fought. Scholars agree there was very probably a Welsh chieftain who fought the Anglo-Saxons invading Britain after the late fifth century and following the withdrawal of the Roman legions. In the early twelfth century the name of Arthur was appearing in the first *Histories of the Kings of Britain*. It is also at this time that the first mention of the Round Table appears. One interpretation of the legend is that it originates in Welsh mythology with Arthur as the sun god and the twelve knights representing the twelve months of the year. Be that as it may, by 1170, when a young French cleric named Chrétien de Troyes visited Glastonbury, in England (one of the places associated with the Arthurian legend), the stories of Camelot were well-known.

Chrétien appears to have been granted a benefice at the church of Saint Maclou in Bar-sur-Aube by Count Henry of Champagne, whose uncle Henry of Blois was abbot of Glastonbury. The abbot also had frequent contact with two of the authors of the *Histories,* William of

Malmesbury and Geoffrey of Monmouth, both of whom mention Arthur. So it may have been Chrétien's visit to England that provided him with material for his later poems about life at the Arthurian court and in particular the story of the "courtly love" affair between Lancelot and Arthur's wife, Guinevere.

In the courtly love relationship the man was the suitor, pleading his case in music and rhyme. The object of his affections would require him to undergo humiliations as proof of his love. The twelfth-century courtly love genre probably sprang from several sources. The first Crusades were bringing back from Constantinople stories of sensual delights, luxury and eroticism that had a powerful effect on people used to the deprivations of early medieval European life. At a time when marriage was primarily a matter of dynastic planning rather than passion, extramarital affairs were not unusual. Husbands often left wives for extended periods of time to go to war. Since adultery was a crime punishable by drowning, the platonic nature of the courtly love encounter may have been a means of sublimating sexual urges.

Perhaps the most intriguing origin of courtly love lies in the family relationships of Chrétien's employer Countess Marie, daughter of Eleanor of Aquitaine, who was herself the granddaughter of the first troubador, William IX of Aquitaine. The early twelfth-century troubador love-song tradition originated in an area of southwestern France which at the same time was in upheaval because of the activity of a heretical sect known as the Cathars.[103] One of the Cathar beliefs was that marriage was an undesirable relationship, since it tended to produce children. The Cathars condoned extramarital sexual relations intended only for pleasure and not for procreation. Cathars also accorded women equal status with men at a time when a woman could normally only exercise her legal rights through her husband or male guardian. Before marriage she was the property of her father and after marriage that of her husband. Cathar attitudes toward the sexual and social position of women may have acted to trigger the development of courtly love.

The mystic Cathars were reformers who criticized the church for retaining worldly possessions and attacked churchmen for lax and

immoral behavior. Cathars preached a return to the austere life of the early church Fathers. Cathar authorities, known as "the perfect ones," abstained from "impure" food (produce related in any way to procreation) such as meat, eggs and cheese. They also refused to kill any living thing. Sexual relations among *perfecti* were banned. They fasted on bread and water three times a week and observed special forty-day fasts three times a year. There were several reasons why the Cathar heresy attracted the particular attention of Rome. In the early twelfth century before the papacy had become centralized church authority was enforced through the local secular powers. In southwestern France many of these aristocrats were already Cathars.

Cathar beliefs struck at the heart of Catholic teaching because Cathars believed in two creators: God, good and perfect (the creator of the spirit), and Satan, evil and imperfect (the creator of the material world). Their argument was that a good Creator would not have made a material world so manifestly imperfect and full of evil. Cathars also believed that Jesus was merely an angel and that his human suffering and death were an illusion. Perhaps most important of all, the Cathars' appeal to the simple life and their attacks on the lifestyle of the Catholic clergy were winning converts among the poor.

For all these reasons Rome mounted a counterattack. In 1147 preaching missions by Alberic of Cluny, Geoffrey of Chartres and Saint Bernard failed. When Alberic preached in the cathedral at Albi (the center of Catharism) only thirty people turned up. Bernard was booed in the streets of Toulouse. So in 1198 Pope Innocent III declared the anti-Cathar Albigensian Crusade and then set up the Inquisition[104] to handle the long-term problem of heresy. The political [104] 50 *101* attractions of a Crusade in the southwest of France were powerful. The king of France wanted to extend his influence south of Paris, plenary indulgences would be offered to those on the Crusade, and there would be none of the risks usually attached to Crusades in the Middle East. The Albigensian Crusade was ruthless and highly effective. Thousands of Cathars were burned without trial, their castles and churches destroyed, and their property confiscated. In one of the many massacres, at Beziers, when the papal legate was asked how

Fig. 23: *An early fourteenth-century illustration of the fate of the Cathars, denied even the* coup de grace *before burning.*

Crusaders would know Cathars from innocents he is said to have replied: "Kill them all. God will know his own." Fifty years later the Cathar heresy had been totally expunged.

The Crusade had also struck indiscriminately at Jews, who were numerous in the area. The Jewish intellectual community had many links with Cathars and may have influenced the mystical side of the Albigensian heresy. The southwest of France and northern Spain were centers of a Jewish mystic sect known as Cabalists, most of them intellectuals of the rabbinate who practiced meditation and the recitation of mystical formulae that would put the practitioner into an ecstatic trance during which he would see visions of heaven. The formulae for the chant varied according to different Cabalistic practices, but one of the most powerful techniques employed was that produced in the last quarter of the thirteenth century by an erudite Spanish Cabalist, Abraham Abulafia. Abulafia's *Path of Names* attached numerical values to letters of the Hebrew alphabet in such a

way as to generate mystical relationships between words. The name-number equations showed, for example, that the number of the heavenly host was 301,655,172.

The technique of mystical word-number equations can most easily be described in English by giving the A–Z alphabet values from 1 to 26. The total letter-value number for the words "God is" $(7 + 15 + 4 + 9 + 19 = 54)$ adds up to the same as that for "love" $(12 + 15 + 22 + 5 = 54)$. Other mystical word relationships can be made in the same way. For instance, the number for "plague" is the same as "bad sky," suggesting a heavenly source of disease. "Holy Trinity" adds up to the same number as "Father, Son, Ghost." And "way of Cabal" is the same as "eternal peace." In 1274 Abulafia left Spain to travel and teach in Italy and Greece. Almost all his extant writings were completed in Italy, where he left his strongest and most lasting influence.

It was when a young aristocratic Italian scholar, Pico della Mirandola, became interested in Cabalism that Abulafia's ideas entered the mainstream of European thought and become a contributing factor in the development of modern science. Pico was Count of the small northern Italian town of Mirandola. Destined for an ecclesiastical career, in 1479 at the age of fourteen he was sent to study canon law at nearby Bologna University. Two years later he transferred to the University of Ferrara to study philosophy. Over the next four years he also visited Padua and Florence, meeting such major Renaissance intellectuals as Marsilio Ficino and Lorenzo de' Medici and being taught by the Jewish scholars Elia del Medigo and Flavio Mithridates, one of whom introduced him to the work of Abulafia and taught him Hebrew. Pico became obsessed with Cabalism and the Hebrew language. Between Abulafia's mystical numbers and the language of Israel Pico found a path to true faith. In his *Conclusions*, written in 1486, he risked death for heresy when he said: "There is no knowledge which makes us more certain of the divinity of Christ than magic and the Cabal."

Pico believed that the study of numbers would reveal truths about the universe and in introducing the idea into European thought Pico began the process that would end with the mathematical analysis at

the heart of science. Pico called this use of numbers "good magic," which would reveal relationships among all things in nature, stating: "By number, a way may be had for the investigation and understanding of everything possible to be known." *Conclusions* included a speech titled "Oration on the Dignity of Man," in which Pico took his belief in the ability to understand and control nature through numbers and turned it into the manifesto for the Renaissance. "Oration" foreshadowed what would become the scientific view of thinkers like Galileo.[105]

105 86 *160*

In 1490 in Florence Pico met a thirty-five-year-old, widely respected German scholar from the new University of Tubingen. Johannes Reuchlin was on the way to becoming one of the outstanding humanist scholars of the Renaissance. He was the first to teach Greek in Germany and had learned it from Greek refugees arriving in Europe after the fall of Constantinople in 1453. Reuchlin picked up a passion for Hebrew from Pico and took language lessons from Jacob Loans, a Jewish scholar who was private physician to the Holy Roman Emperor Ferdinand III. Over the next few years Reuchlin mastered the language and in 1506 produced the first manual of Hebrew grammar written by a Christian scholar. Reuchlin also took back to Germany Pico's fascination with the Cabal and the power of numbers. His *On the Cabalistic Art* was the first treatise on Cabalism by a non-Jew.

Like Pico, Reuchlin became convinced of the special value of Hebrew as a means of understanding Christian teaching. In 1508 he wrote: "I assure you, that no one of the Latins can expound the Old Testament unless he first becomes proficient in the language in which it was written. For the mediator between God and man was language, as we read in the Pentateuch; but not any language, only Hebrew, through which God wished his secrets to be made known to man." As Reuchlin's knowledge of Hebrew grew so did his belief in the need for the establishment of Hebrew faculties in European universities. This was a risky thing to suggest, given the anti-Semitic sentiment among many in the church. One of Reuchlin's opponents in this matter was a converted Jew, Johannes Pfefferkorn. In 1510 he asked Reuchlin to adjudicate in an appeal brought by the Jews of

Cologne against a court sentence ordering the burning of all Hebrew books. Reuchlin sprang to the Jews' defense and began a process that would finally bring him before a church court charged with heresy. The court proceedings dragged on for four years, and although Reuchlin was eventually acquitted, in 1520 he was ordered to pay the costs of litigation. Financially ruined and psychologically broken by the experience, two years later he died.

Reuchlin's defense in court had not been helped by a statement of support from his great-nephew Philipp Melanchthon, right-hand man to the church's greatest critic, Martin Luther. Melanchthon had first met Luther in 1518 when he arrived in Wittenberg, Germany (where Luther was a monk), to take up the post of professor of Greek at the newly established university. Luther, who only the year before had published the criticisms of Rome that would lead to the establishment of the Protestant church, attended Melanchthon's inaugural lecture, which was titled "The Improvement of Studies." It was a powerful, humanist appeal for a return to the original Aristotle and to the authority of the Bible. Melanchthon and Luther became instant friends. Both men shared the view that any reform of belief and practice had to start with education. A brief tour of Saxon schools convinced Melanchthon that root-and-branch change was urgently needed. He drew up a list of rules for the first-ever school inspectors. Schools were to be maintained by the civil authorities; teachers should be proficient in Latin and Greek; and schools were to be organized in three divisions: beginners, grammar-learners and advanced students. Melanchthon's rules also prescribed in detail the conduct of classes and the subjects to be taught. For the advanced class, these included Ovid, Virgil and Cicero, lessons in dialectic and rhetoric, prose composition, music and religious instruction. Melanchthon took the same modernizing approach to university instruction. He mounted an attack on the old Scholastic way of learning through disputation and worked out new statutes for faculties. This exercise was so successful that Melanchthon was called in to aid in the foundation of several new universities and to help reorganize older ones.

Not all Protestants (so called because they protested against Rome's negative reaction to Luther's theses) approved of Melanch-

thon's involvement with education. There was some criticism that his views were too liberal and that he had given way to Rome in many of his teachings. One of his particularly virulent critics was Andreas Osiander, who had been appointed professor of theology at the University of Konigsberg by the local duke, although not fully qualified for the job. Osiander issued pamphlet after pamphlet attacking Melanchthon for having forsaken true Lutheranism.

Osiander was interested in the mathematical sciences, and in 1540 when the first edition of Copernicus's first book (*Narratio Prima*) on the solar system was published, Osiander was sent a copy. The contents shocked him to the core. Osiander believed divine revelation was the sole source of truth, and the Bible did not describe the solar system as Copernicus did. The church taught the Aristotelian view of a cosmos with the Earth at the center and the sun and planets turning around it.

Copernicus's publisher was George Rheticus, a graduate of Wittenberg. When the full version of Copernicus's work was ready for publication in 1543, Rheticus was editing the manuscript in preparation for printing (at the Nuremberg press of Johann Petreius) when he was called away to the University of Leipzig to become professor of mathematics. He left the editing to Osiander, who first changed the title of the Copernican work from *On the Revolutions of Planets in the Sky* to the one by which is it still known, *On the Revolution of the Heavenly Bodies*. He also inserted a preface stating that while the author described a sun-centered system, the scheme was intended merely as a piece of mathematical convenience to make the work of astronomers easier and did not claim to reflect what was actually happening in the sky. This explained why Osiander had changed the title. The use of the word "planet" would have introduced the idea of orbiting bodies, which could include the Earth. Copernicus received a copy of the book with its new title and preface on his deathbed, when it was too late to do anything about it.

The next book Osiander received had been printed by the same Petreius Nuremberg press. This time the book was dedicated to Osiander himself. It was a text on algebra (*The Great Art*) written by an Italian physician friend of Osiander's, the inventor and gambler Giro-

lamo Cardano. The illegitimate son of a ne'er-do-well mathematician and lawyer, Cardano first studied at the University of Pavia, then taught philosophy while gambling away his leisure hours and writing a book, *Games of Chance*. In it he expounded the first law of probability: that throwing dice involved the impossible (throwing a seven with a single die), the certain (that one side of the die must fall uppermost) and the probable (that the first throw might be a six). If the impossible were set as zero and the certain as one then all degrees of probability in between could be calculated in fractions (that is, the chances of throwing a six is one in six). Later in life Cardano invented the universal joint still in use in the transmission shaft of every car today and known as the Cardan shaft. In 1525 Cardano qualified in medicine at the University of Padua and began a career as a doctor while working on what would be his magnum opus—*The Great Art* algebra book dedicated to Osiander.

In 1551 Cardano received a letter from the personal physician to Archbishop John Hamilton of St. Andrews, Scotland, asking if he would consider visiting the archbishop in order to treat his asthma, which had become so serious the prelate was unable to move from his house in Edinburgh and was suffering twenty-four-hour-long attacks once a week. Hamilton was no ordinary churchman, being the illegitimate brother of the earl of Arran, regent of Scotland during the infancy of Mary Queen of Scots. On June 29, 1552, after a journey from Italy lasting over six months, Cardano arrived with a new treatment for asthma that he had developed over the few previous years and was anxious to test.

Standard treatment for all conditions at the time assumed that the cure for any disease lay in one of two different conditions of the brain. Some physicians believed a healthy brain was "hot," some "cold." Hamilton's personal physician had been of the "hot" persuasion and this had led him to prescribe a cure that would make Hamilton's brain hot. Treatment confined the patient to rooms heated to stifling point and permitted only scalding food and mulled wine, in order to keep him in a constant sweat. Since the archbishop's lifestyle was already overindulgent the treatment made things worse. Cardano took the "cold"-brain approach, recommending cold showers,

walks before breakfast, plain and nourishing food, plenty of fresh air, lots of sleep, and periods of rest every morning ("but not with harlots"). Within two weeks Hamilton was so much better he persuaded Cardano to stay until September, whereupon Cardano departed for Italy much the richer, leaving a healthy churchman behind. Hamilton would not keep his health for long, thanks to the intrigue and turmoil that was to follow.

The contemporary political situation in Scotland was complicated by the fact that the country swung between Catholicism and Protestantism. In 1560 the Catholic Mary Queen of Scots,[106] for reasons of marriage absent from Scotland for twelve years (leaving the country in the hands of a regent), returned to the country on the death of her husband, the French king Francis. At this time Scotland was Protestant and Mary's Catholicism was accepted with the stipulation that she restrict her observance to her private quarters. Elizabeth, queen

106 62 128

Fig. 24: *A portrait of the young Mary Queen of Scots on her return to Scotland from France in 1560.*

of England, together with many of Mary's own advisers, now strongly advised a Protestant marriage, but contrary Mary (of whom the nursery rhyme speaks) decided instead on Henry, Lord Darnley, who was a Catholic. This raised Elizabeth's hackles, since through family ties both Mary and Darnley had claims to the English throne. Mary's grandmother had been Margaret Tudor, the elder sister of Elizabeth's father, Henry VIII. Darnley, Mary's cousin, was Margaret Tudor's grandson.

The marriage between Mary and Darnley was a disaster. Darnley proved to be a jealous, drunken lout who resented not being king of Scotland in his own right and who eventually connived at the murder of Mary's thirty-three-year-old Italian personal secretary, David Rizzio, claiming that the queen was having an affair with him. Mary retaliated by appointing the earl of Bothwell as her principal adviser. On the night of February 10, 1567, Darnley was killed in a huge explosion that wrecked the house in Edinburgh where he was recovering from syphilis. The conspirators were soon caught, having left behind them an easily traced empty powder barrel, bought candles at the last minute from a nearby shop and obtained fuses from soldiers of Darnley's own voluble guards. In 1571 Archbishop Hamilton would be hanged in his own vestments for complicity in the murder.

Meanwhile Bothwell divorced his wife and persuaded Mary to marry him. She was several months pregnant at the time, almost certainly by Bothwell. On May 15, 1567, Mary committed the ultimate folly, marrying Bothwell in a Protestant ceremony. This cost her the last vestiges of her political support in Europe. An army of Scottish nobles came against her and at the Battle of Carberry Hill, on June 15, she was captured. By the following year she had been taken across the border to an English prison and accused of treason for having claimed the English throne. Nineteen years of incarceration later, Elizabeth had Mary executed.

Meanwhile, Bothwell decided to flee the Scottish mainland. One of his titles (conferred on him only recently by Mary) was duke of the Orkney Islands, an archipelago well to the north of Scotland. Bothwell headed for Orkney with eight ships and a plan to set up "an empire of the sea." Unfortunately, the local Orkney sheriff decided

discretion was better than valor and refused him entry. The pursuing Scottish ships caught up with Bothwell and he was forced to make a run for it, eventually heading across the North Sea. As he came within sight of the Norwegian coast Bothwell had the misfortune to be intercepted and escorted into port at Bergen. Bothwell revealed his identity as Duke of Orkney. Things were going well when bad luck intervened. When the investigation into Bothwell's arrival began, one of his old flames, Anna Throndsen, turned up. Seven years earlier she and Bothwell had met when he was in Denmark and she had run away with him, first to France and then to Scotland. After years of living as his unacknowledged mistress, when Bothwell divorced his wife Anna expected marriage. So when Bothwell married Mary Anna went home in a rage. Now it was payback time. Her allegations of seduction and injury were enough to cook Bothwell's goose. He was moved to Malmö prison for greater security, while discussions were opened with Scotland about what to do with him.

Bothwell was visited in Malmö by the venerable French ambassador to Denmark (which ruled Norway and Sweden at the time). His name was Charles de Dancey, and he offered to take a letter from Bothwell to the French king and to intercede on Bothwell's behalf with the Danish authorities. Although Dancey was well-respected in Denmark there was little he could do for Bothwell. With Mary in prison nobody wanted the runaway Bothwell back in Britain to foment trouble. He was moved to a remote and rigorous prison regime in Dragsholm, Zeeland, where eventually he went mad and died in 1578.

Meanwhile Dancey continued a busy social life in Denmark, part of which involved his close friendship with the Danish astronomer **107** 135 254 Tycho Brahe,[107] a well-heeled young aristocrat whose family were friends of the king. Free to travel and indulge his passion for astronomical instruments, after initial studies at the Universities of Copenhagen, Leipzig and Wittenberg Tycho visited the great instrument-making center of Augsburg and began the serious study of the stars. In Augsburg he commissioned the construction of the latest model of quadrant, marked with single minutes of a degree, which he began to use to measure the apparent motion of the plan-

ets. Because of his father's illness in 1571 Tycho returned to the family home at Knutsdorp, Sweden, and went to live with his uncle at the nearby Cistercian monastery of Herrevad, where the two men set up a chemistry lab and worked on techniques for making gold.

On November 11, 1572, Tycho was returning from the lab when he looked up and saw something impossible: a bright new star in the sky. It was a supernova, and it was impossible because according to the pope and Aristotle the heavens were unchanging, so there could be no new stars. For thirty days Tycho measured the new star's position relative its nearest constellation, Cassiopeia. From any angle their angle of separation remained constant, indicating that the star was out in deep space together with the constellation. In 1573 in Copenhagen Brahe pointed out the star to Dancey and later that year he published the book he had now written about it, titled *On the New Star.* The book and its potentially heretical contents made Tycho famous all over Europe and established him as an astronomer of the first rank. Three years later the king of Denmark had given him the island of Hven (between Denmark and Sweden) and Charles de Dancey was there to lay the foundation stone for Tycho's great observatory, Uraniborg.

At Uraniborg Brahe produced a set of updated star tables dedicated to the Holy Roman Emperor, Rudolph, who was so impressed he asked Tycho to come to Prague as imperial astronomer. He also invited a young German astronomer, Johannes Kepler,[108] to be Brahe's assistant. A year later Tycho was dead, buried together with the metal replacement nose that he had worn ever since a duel in his university days. The existence of the nose is only known because it was mentioned by Tycho's assistant on Hven.

This was a mathematical young Dutchman named Willem Blaeu, who returned to Amsterdam in 1596 after his work with Tycho and turned his astronomical experience to good use by setting up a company dedicated to printing navigational data (for which a knowledge of stars and star tables was essential) and maps. With a shop on the Amsterdam waterfront, Blaeu was able to pick up the latest information from returning sea captains and keep his maps and tables up-to-date. By 1633 he had one of the most successful mapmaking houses

[108] 42 76
[108] 100 182

in Europe and had published charts of the four known continents, as well as books on cosmography, hydrography, topography and his own *Light of Navigation* manual for navigators. That year he was appointed official cartographer to the Dutch East India Company,[109] the greatest exploration and trading organization in Europe. He was to hold the job until his death in 1638.

Improved navigation and better maps were critically important to the East India Company, because cargoes from the East could be re-exported throughout Europe for profits of as high as 600 percent. Since the time of the company's establishment in 1602, more and more ships returned with luxuries for which Europeans would pay high prices: dyestuffs, pepper, silk, porcelain, tea, saltpeter, cinnamon, borax, musk and sugar. Voyages in search of these commodities were made easier by one of the cartographers whose maps Blaeu printed. He was a German named Gerard Kremer, also known as Mercator. Mercator solved a basic problem facing every navigator. Steering a straight-line course across latitude (north-south) lines that curved to converge at the pole meant that at the crossing of each line the compass bearing would change. In 1569 Mercator projected the globe onto a cylinder, which meant that the latitude and longitude (east-west) lines now crossed at right angles. This in turn meant that a straight-line course crossed all latitude lines at the same angle, making the navigator's life simpler. The fact that this map distorted the size of high-latitude locations such as Greenland was considered relatively unimportant. These were not the places to which commercial ventures went in search of profit.

In 1674 the first complete collection of charts to use Mercator's technique was produced by an Englishman, Robert Dudley, who titled the work *Dell'Arcano del Mare* (On the Secrets of the Sea). It was created for and dedicated to his employer, Ferdinando II,[110] duke of Tuscany. By the time of publication Dudley had lived in Italy for about forty years, ever since running away from England with his mistress, leaving wife and family behind. Dudley was the illegitimate son of the earl of Leicester, and since his mother's marriage to the earl had been secret and after her death the earl had married again,

208

family feuds put Dudley's inheritance in question. After his arrival in Italy, Dudley illegally assumed the title of Earl of Warwick, as a result of which all his English estates were confiscated. With his boats burned, he turned to boat-building, and impressed the Tuscan duke with his maritime knowledge (Dudley had spent several years with the English Navy). Dudley was given control of the shipyards at Pisa and Livorno, arranged for English ship-builders to work there and began to build warships for the duke. Dudley was also given the tasks of draining the marshes between Pisa and the sea, installing a fresh-water aqueduct to supply Pisa and building a canal linking Pisa and Livorno. He also persuaded the duke to declare the newly rebuilt city of Livorno (Dudley designed the harbor mole) a free port and "a place of universal toleration," thus attracting religious refugees of every stripe from all over Europe and vastly increasing the duke's fiscal revenue as Livorno rapidly became a highly profitable major international entrepôt.

Dudley's predecessor in water-management (and possibly, for a brief time after Dudley's arrival in Italy, his boss) was the celebrated engineer and architect Bernardo Buontalenti, who worked for the Medici family for over sixty years. Of his many architectural projects, perhaps the most famous are the Belvedere Fortress in Florence, the Villa Pratolino, and the fortifications of Livorno. But Buontalenti's special talent was with machinery. He began by designing water-lifting devices and complex water gardens with fountains and grottoes featuring water-powered automata. By 1589 he was in charge of the spectacular entertainments staged by the Medici on the occasion of a marriage or the arrival of a special visitor. In one case Buontalenti flooded the Pitti Palace courtyard to a depth of five feet for a mock sea battle. Buontalenti also designed fire-breathing dragons, exploding volcanoes, moving clouds on which gods were transported, collapsing castles, mountains, rocks and trees that rose and sank through the floor and thunder effects created offstage by rolling cannon balls down metal tubes. The plays that were presented included intervals, and in these short breaks a new musical form began to appear in which singers and dancers would be accompanied by

musical instruments as they enacted scenes to the accompaniment of Buontalenti's spectacular effects. Out of these early efforts came the first true opera, Peri's *Dafne*, staged in 1598.

Buontalenti's scenography was radically improved by another Italian who worked in Venice, named Giacomo Torelli. His contribution to stagecraft and design would remain standard procedure well into the nineteenth century. Torelli's use of machinery may have originated in 1640 during his brief period at the Venice shipyards, where the shipbuilders used a considerable amount of automation, with machinery operated by rope and pulley. Torelli's theatrical innovation involved cutting diagonal slits on either side of the stage floor. Through these slits Torelli erected small poles that supported scenery. Beneath the stage the poles were mounted on wheeled trolleys running on rails. The trolleys were operated by ropes wound onto a central drum. When the drum was turned with a counterweight all the trolleys would move at once, causing scenery to come on or off the stage with comparative rapidity. In 1645 the technique impressed an English visitor, John Evelyn,[111] who reported that in one of Torelli's plays the scenery changed no fewer than thirteen times. That same year Torelli was summoned to France by Giulio Mazarin, the Italian minister running the country for Louis XIII. At Mazarin's request Torelli introduced the French to what became known as the "theater of machines" and started a vogue for plays that included spectacular effects the machines made possible.

111 64 *135*

Giulio Mazarin was so popular he survived to serve under the next king, Louis XIV. A well-educated man, Mazarin had a passion for art and literature and provided pensions for Racine, Molière, Corneille and others. Mazarin's pride and joy was his collection of over forty thousand books, acknowledged as the best library in Europe. The books had been collected for Mazarin by his librarian, Gabriel Naudé, who in 1627 had published the first proper study of library science in a book titled *Advice on Establishing a Library*, which included instructions on how to choose, classify and arrange books, as well as hints on the decoration of a library, the treatment of staff and even on how to dust the books. In 1661 Naudé's book was translated into English by the same John Evelyn who had seen Torelli's play in

Venice. Evelyn then became an expert in library science and set up his own collection of books organized according to Naudé's principles.

One of Evelyn's friends was also interested in using Naudé's information to help him build a library of books that would help him with his grand scheme to reform the English navy. This maritime bibliophile was Samuel Pepys, and he had met Evelyn because of the latter's connection with navy hospitals. By 1685 Pepys was secretary to the navy and responsible only to the king. Pepys's reforms effectively founded the modern British navy and dealt with virtually every aspect of naval life on shore and at sea. He introduced formal training for officers, who would now be required to be able to navigate. Discipline, pay, pensions and medical treatment were regulated. Uniforms and saluting were formalized. Dockyards were modernized and the whole system of tendering for naval contracts was properly established. On board ship, guns and orndance were standardized and the number of a ship's complement now related to the size of the vessel.

Fig. 25: *Samuel Pepys, pictured with the manuscript of his song "Beauty Retire."*

Pepys persuaded the government to agree to supply the fleet with six months' stores in advance. Above all, he instigated the country's largest-ever ship-building program to ensure English supremacy at sea for generations.

The only aspect of naval life that Pepys did little to reform was the practice of signaling, which in the mid-seventeenth century was a primitive procedure. If a ship needed a delivery of wood it hung up an axe. A request to come to dinner was signaled by hoisting a table-cloth. In 1673 the first proper signal book appeared with colored drawings of fifteen flags and each of the positions to which they should be hoisted. By 1782 the number of flags had increased to fifty. By 1799 various patterns of three or four flags made it possible to send up to 340 signals and the signal book also included eighty last-minute manuscript additions. However, by this time the signaling problem was most acute on land. Communications between the Admiralty in London and the various naval ports had for centuries been done by courier at the speed of a horse. Delivery could take days, or in the case of foreign stations, months.

112 10 34
112 43 78
112 59 120

This problem was solved by Britain's French enemy, Napoleon,[112] in 1792. Surrounded on all sides by the Allies, Napoleon was desperate for a better way to communicate with his widely dispersed armies. On March 22 that year, the French Legislative Assembly was given a demonstration of a new communications system invented by a priest named Claude Chappe. Chappe's system involved sending signals by means of a twelve-foot horizontal wooden arm pivoted on a vertical beam on top of a tower. At each end of the horizontal beam was another three-foot beam, also pivoted. By means of pulleys and ropes all the movable beams could be made to take up a large-enough number of configurations to send a significant number of signals. These could be seen through a telescope by an observer on another distant, similarly equipped tower, who would then relay the message by the same means to the next tower, and so on. By 1794 the system was in operation over 210 kilometers, reporting in one instance on a military event only an hour after it had taken place instead of the ten hours it would have taken by conventional means.

That year a copy of Chappe's drawings happened to be in the possession of a French soldier captured by the British. The drawings then fell into the hands of the Reverend John Gamble,[113] a British 113 19 42 army chaplain, who promptly made a number of improvements and sent drawings to the Admiralty. To Gamble's chagrin, Chappe's idea had also reached the ears of Lord George Murray, who had also made improvements. Since Murray was a well-placed aristocrat it was his version the Admiralty proposed to adopt. In 1795, after successful trials on Wimbledon Common outside London, several chains of the new "semaphore" stations were set up.

By 1805 one of the chains extended as far as the major naval port of Plymouth, and a contemporary described the arrival of a message: "A single signal has been transmitted to Plymouth and back . . . [to London] in three minutes, which by the telegraph route is at least 500 miles. In this instance, however, notice had been given to make ready and every captain was at his post to receive and return the signals. The progress was at the rate of 170 miles in a minute, or three miles per second, or three seconds at each station; a rapidity truly wonderful."

Because of his work in prisoner-of-war exchange Gamble had also been able to facilitate the movement of people and documents through the English Channel ports, and it was thanks to this that in 1810 the patent for another French invention arrived in England. It was for a process devised by a champagne-bottler named Nicholas Appert for boiling food in a hermetically sealed bottle. This killed the bacteria in the food and kept it from putrefying for several months. The preserved food had tested by the French navy and was a great success.

When Appert's patent arrived in England it ended up in the possession of a businesssman named Bryan Donkin, who had an interest in an iron works and who realized that preserved food might last better and longer in metal containers. A canning factory was established by Donkin and his partner, John Hall, in 1812. By 1818 the partners were producing cans of cured beef, boiled beef, carrots, mutton and vegetable stew, veal and soup.

That year canned food formed part of the provisions taken by the Ross expedition to the Davis Straits in northern Canada. The expedition, headed by Captain John Ross and including his nephew James, aimed at finding the Northwest Passage. They failed, and in 1829 Captain Ross took a second expedition (financed by Felix Booth, manufacturer of Booth's Gin), which failed once again to find the Passage. However, on June 1, 1831, John Ross's nephew James crossed the ice on foot and reached the Magnetic North Pole. He identified the exact spot by suspending a magnetized needle on a thread and watching it assume a nearly vertical position. He promptly raised a flag and claimed the location (70.5 N, 96.46 W) in the name of King William, in spite of the fact that since the Magnetic Pole moves it was probably no longer exactly there even as he claimed it.

James was now bitten by the Magnetic Pole bug, and in September 1839 he headed his own expedition to Antarctica in search of the South Magnetic Pole. In January 1841 the explorers were stopped about three thousand yards short of their target by a mountain range rising in some places to twelve thousand feet. However, other expedition objectives were more than adequately met, as the expedition also discovered Victoria Land, the Ross Sea, McMurdo Sound and the Ross Ice Barrier.

The assistant surgeon aboard Ross's ship was a young man named Joseph Hooker, son of the director of the Royal Botanic Gardens in Kew. In 1872, after his return to England, Hooker, by now director at Kew, received a shipment from Brazil of seventy thousand rubber tree seeds. Vociferously encouraged by Charles Macintosh,[114] who had discovered how to liquefy rubber and use it for waterproof clothing, Hooker set about attempting to grow seedlings from the seeds. Only 4 percent of them germinated, and eventually 1,919 plants were dispatched to the Botanical Gardens at Peradeniya, in Sri Lanka. A few plants were also sent to Singapore, where they did not survive. A few seedlings also went to Malaysia.

Several years later the Malaysian plants had done well enough for rubber seedlings to be planted in Java. In 1884 the first commercial rubber-tapping occurred in the Sri Lanka plantations and from then

114 33 66

on the East became the prime source of British rubber. The industry rapidly expanded. By 1922, 85 percent of a total world rubber supply of nearly 380,000 tons came from the Eastern plantations.

During World War II the Japanese captured the plantations in the Malaysian archipelago and Sri Lanka remained the only source of Allied rubber supplies. This was a disastrous turn of events, since one of the principal uses for rubber in wartime was as a key ingredient in the manufacture of incendiary bombs. In July 1943 a rubber-benzol mixture (the rubber helped the benzol to burn more slowly and to stick to anything it touched) formed the main ingredient of three million incendiaries dropped on the German city of Hamburg, destroying the city and killing between forty thousand and fifty thousand people.

CHAPTER 9

⊠

Hit the Water

115 58 119 When Japanese forces took the Malaysian archipelago during World War II they left the Allies with an acute problem: how to run their war machine without plentiful supplies of rubber. For such things as tires and waterproof clothing essential to troops the problem was rapidly solved by the development of neoprene, an artificial rubber first discovered by an American chemist named Julius Nieuwland[115] and produced in an industrial process developed by DuPont.

This left one major problem unsolved: how to make incendiary bombs. These had previously used a mixture of rubber thickener, benzol and phosphorus, the rubber being used to retard the speed with which the benzol burned. A new thickener was needed. In 1940 when it began to look as if the war in Europe might turn into a prolonged conflict, the American government decided that science was likely to play a decisive role. The National Defense Research Committee was therefore established under Vannevar Bush, president of the Carnegie Institute. One NDRC division was to be dedicated to research into bombs, fuels, poison gases and chemical weapons. This division was placed under the command of James Conant, president of Harvard.

With the attack on Pearl Harbor in 1941 and the entry of America into the war, a Harvard professor, Louis Fieser, was asked to solve the rubber problem. The specifications were that the rubber substitute had to remain thick at temperatures as high as 150 degrees Fahren-

216

heit (for use in the tropics) and not become brittle at minus 40 degrees (in a bomb bay at altitude). It had to be tough enough to withstand an explosive blast without shattering and it had to survive lengthy storage without deterioration. Most important, it had to be adaptable to a simple field-loading operation.

In July 1942 Fieser had his product. It was called "napalm." By the end of the war output was more than 70 million pounds a year, and a total of 33 million bombs had been made. Each bomb consisted of a rod of high explosive that exploded, shattering the napalm container and at the same time releasing phosphorus, which then ignited the napalm. In the early stages making a bomb was simple. Napalm powder was stirred into gasoline or benzol in an aircraft fuel drop-tank and left overnight to thicken. Explosive and phosphorus were then added. On impact the bomb created a fireball, which burned intensely for ten seconds, giving way to a fire of reduced intensity that burned for up to ten minutes over an elliptical area thirty by ninety yards. Napalm was terribly effective, and in 1972 after adverse publicity surrounding its use during the Vietnam War, the United Nations passed a resolution deploring its use.

One of the key ingredients in napalm was palm oil, which had been available in large quantities since as early as the 1820s, when it was first imported (from Indonesia, the Philippines, Malaysia and Sri Lanka) as an ingredient for soap manufacture. The man who made soap-making into an industry was Michel Chevreul, director of the Gobelins tapestry factory outside Paris. Chevreul was an expert on fats of all kinds, thanks to his interest in the behavior of animal fats in yarn. It was Chevreul who persuaded a young French chemist named Hippolyte Mèges Mouriès to study fats. Mèges had already achieved some success with various inventions and discoveries: a remedy for syphilis, a technique for using egg yolk in leather-tanning, a new way of making bread, and effervescent tablet manufacture. In 1852 he turned to fats.

One of Europe's major problems at the time was population increase due to industrialization and the fertilizer-enhanced growth of cereal crops. Between 1750 and 1850 the European population had grown from 140 million to 266 million. The majority of these were

factory workers whose diet was nutritionally deficient, lacking in protein and fat to provide the energy they needed for work. By 1850 the fat supply was well below requirement. Beef suet would have filled the need, but it could not be spread. The demand for butter rose steeply and so did its price. Mèges was to resolve the impasse.

116 26 50
116 126 236
116 129 246
On Napoleon III's[116] imperial farms at Vincennes Mèges pressed beef suet at forty degrees Centigrade and obtained a fat that melted at five degrees. Churning this with milk produced a material that would spread on bread, which Mèges called "margarine." In 1871 he sold the patent to the Dutch firm of Jurgens, as well as to British, American and German manufacturers, and margarine went into production everywhere. Unfortunately supplies of beef suet soon ran out. A substitute had to be found that would be soft enough to spread but hard enough not to run. There was no such material available until 1897 when a pair of French chemists, Paul Sabatier and J. B. Senderens, discovered that vegetable oils were fluid because they had a lower hydrogen content than solid fats such as butter and lard. In 1902 a German, Wilhelm Normann, found a way to add extra hydrogen to oils. In its final industrial form the process involved pumping oil at around 180 degrees Fahrenheit into a closed vessel under pressurized hydrogen and then adding a catalyst consisting of fine particles of nickel deposited onto an inert powder called *kieselguhr*. The nickel catalyst caused hydrogen molecules to attach themselves to the oil molecules. As a result the eventual melting point of the oil could be determined (by how much hydrogenation took place), so that the hydrogenated oil would melt only at temperatures above that of normal use in margarine.

Kieselguhr is produced by grinding a friable sedimentary rock resembling chalk, and it has many uses besides hydrogenation, as an ingredient in toothpaste, ceramics, detergent, insulation and plastic. It is also employed as a filler in brick, paint and paper. One of its first uses was as the inert material holding nitroglycerine in sticks of dynamite. *Kieselguhr* is also known as "diatomaceous rock" because it is formed from the shells of diatoms, or plankton, which fall to the ocean floor when they die and over lengthy periods of time form sediments that then harden into rock.

This fact was discovered by a German researcher named Victor Hensen, from 1868 professor of physiology at the University of Kiel, who investigated the organ of hearing in grasshoppers' forelegs and went on to identify Hensen's duct in the human cochlea. Hensen's hobby was marine biology, and when he was a member of the Prussian Parliament he lobbied for funds for research programs that would benefit the German fishing industry. During this time it occurred to him that the most valuable contribution to fisheries would be one that assessed the productivity of the ocean itself. To this end Hensen decided to investigate the smallest organisms in the sea that might form the base of the food chain. In 1889, with the aid of specially modified silk millers' nets normally used to separate different grades of flour, Hensen set off on the great German Plankton Expedition to survey the whole of the North Atlantic.

Plankton (so-called from the Greek work for "drift") are tiny vegetable cells enclosed in a two-part shell, and they are the most prolific organisms in the sea. They are also ubiquitous, found in fresh and salt water, in mud or sand in shallow water or near the surface of the deep ocean. Plankton are so small that a jar of sea water contains millions of them. This meant that their numbers could only be assessed using statistical methods based on a representative microscopic count. The Plankton Expedition, on board the steamship *National,* lasted 115 days and criss-crossed the principal biogeographical zones of the North Atlantic as far apart as Greenland and Bermuda, the mouth of the Amazon and the Cape Verde Islands off the west coast of Africa.

Hensen made several significant discoveries during the expedition. Plankton exceed the mass of all other organisms in the sea. The high seas are generally poorer in plankton than are river mouths and coastlines. The deep-blue color of the ocean represents an almost complete lack of plankton. Most interesting and unexpected of all, Hensen discovered that tropical waters contained far fewer plankton than colder, high-latitude waters. This turned out to be due to the behavior of the ocean itself. Colder waters have an almost uniform temperature from top to bottom, whereas in the tropics (and elsewhere in summer) warm surface layers remain where they are and

when their nutrients are exhausted by the plankton the tiny organisms die of starvation. In the high latitudes spring and autumn gales disturb the water and bring up nutrients from below so at these times of year there is a constant resupply of food and the plankton thrive and multiply. Wherever upwelling occurs there is a large population of plankton for larger organisms to eat. This accounts for the extraordinarily rich fishing grounds off the coast of Peru, where anchovy feed on plankton and are then in turn eaten by tuna, whose numbers also increase.

The reason for this upwelling of cold, nutrient-rich Peruvian waters is a current about 550 miles wide running north along the Peruvian coast and named after the man who discovered it in 1802: the Humboldt[117] Current. The current is caused by a meteorological phenomenon identified in 1835 by the Frenchman Gustave-Gaspard Coriolis, who showed that the Earth's spin deflects objects moving on a north-south trajectory in the northern hemisphere to the right and in the southern hemisphere to the left. This causes the rotational direction of storms to be different in each hemisphere and accounts for the predominantly western direction of winds in the South Pacific. These winds cause the Pacific West Wind Drift in the ocean. When this oceanic movement hits the South American continent most of it passes south of the continental tip but some of it is deflected north by the coastline to generate the Humboldt Current.

It was in 1857 while investigating the pressure gradients in wind that the Dutch meteorologist Christoph Buys Ballot discovered the law named after him: that a person standing in the northern hemisphere with his back to the wind will have the low pressure on his left and high pressure on the right, and vice versa in the southern hemisphere.

Ballot had already made his name with an unusual experiment he had conducted twelve years earlier, on a railroad track near Utrecht. This experiment involved placing a number of horn players alongside the tracks. Ballot took up a position on the footplate of a train, which then moved along the track at forty miles per hour past the players, who all blew the same note. As the train moved Ballot was able to observe that the pitch of the note played on the instruments

117 73 144

appeared to rise as the train approached them and fall as the train passed and left them behind. This test proved what a professor of mathematics in Prague had said three years before. His name was Christian Doppler[118] and his theory was that if either the source of the sound or the observer were moving toward the other the ears of the observer would receive each sound wave faster. The pitch of the note would therefore rise because increased-frequency sound waves produce a higher note. Conversely, as one or other of the subjects retreated the sound waves would arrive less frequently and a lower-pitch note would be heard.

118 48 95

Doppler was primarily interested in this effect (now known as the Doppler Effect) as it appeared to manifest itself in the color of stars. In his paper *On the Colored Light of the Double Stars* he explained the presence of blue and red stars recently observed by astronomers. Because higher-frequency light was bluer, blue stars must be approaching the observer, and since lower-frequency light was redder, red stars must be receding. If the speed of light could be established, the velocity of these red- and blue-light-shifted stars could be worked out. This thought occurred to a French physicist named Armand-Hippolyte-Louis Fizeau (who also worked out the Doppler Effect some six years after Doppler, so the Doppler Effect is sometimes referred to as the Doppler-Fizeau Effect).

Fizeau was an accomplished astronomer, and in 1845 together with Leon Foucault[119] had taken the first ever daguerreotype photographs of the solar surface. In 1849 Fizeau developed an ingenious way of calculating the speed of light. He spun a large 720-tooth cogwheel on its axis and shone a beam of light between the teeth. The light beam was reflected by a mirror set some five miles distant. At a certain speed (12.6 revolutions per second) the speed of the passing teeth was such that they coincided with the crests in the reflected light waves and the light disappeared. Working out the math relating to the frequency of the light, the speed of the wheel, and the distance to the mirror, Fizeau was able to say that the speed of light was about 196,000 miles per second (only 0.05 percent from its actual speed).

119 40 75

Fizeau married the daughter of Adrien de Jussieu, the last in a line of French botanists. Jussieu succeeded his father as professor of

botany at the Natural History Museum in Paris and made a minor contribution to the development of vegetable taxonomy. As a young boy at school in the Lycée Napoleon he struck up a lifelong friendship with Prosper Mérimée, the son of the secretary to the Ecole des Beaux-Arts. Prosper was a sexually precocious young man and was involved in at least one scandal while still at school. His first mistress appears to have been one of his mother's painting pupils, an Englishwoman seven years his senior named Fanny Lagden, who dedicated her life to him and was buried in his grave in Cannes.

In the 1820s, after receiving a law degree, Prosper spent time among the Parisian bohemians, including Stendhal and Alexander von Humboldt, and met the Viollet-le-Duc family, with whose son he would work in later life. Mérimée began his literary work in 1822 with a historical drama about Cromwell. In 1828, while recovering from a gunshot wound received during a pistol duel with an aggrieved husband, he wrote the work that would make his name: *The Chronicle of the Reign of Charles IX,* one of the great French Romantic novels. In 1830 Mérimée visited Spain on a tour of museums and at one point while traveling on a stagecoach fell into conversation with a fellow passenger, the Count de Teba. The count invited Mérimée home to Madrid, and it was there that he met the countess and her little five-year-old daughter Eugenia, with whom he became fast friends. It was reportedly while he was staying with the family that the countess told Mérimée a story about a gypsy girl who stabs her lover in a jealous rage. Later Mérimée turned the tale into a novel that would become famous when its plot was used by Bizet for his opera *Carmen.*

Returning from Spain, Mérimée became a government bureaucrat and in 1834 was appointed inspector general of historic monuments. It was a job that delighted him. Over the next eighteen years he toured France, restoring some of the country's greatest architectural treasures with the aid of his young friend and architect Eugène-Emmanuel Viollet-le-Duc. In all they restored more than four thousand monuments and buildings, including the great Gothic cathedrals, the Roman theaters of Arles and Orange, the Palace of the Popes at Avignon, the Abbeys of St. Denis and Cheroux and the me-

dieval castles of Blois and Chinon. In 1853 Mérimée's little Spanish friend Eugenia, now grown up (and known in French as Eugénie[120]), married Napoleon III and became empress of France. She immediately persuaded the emperor to grant Mérimée a life senatorship and an annual pension of thirty thousand francs.   120 46 88

That year, Mérimée mounted a vitriolic attack on the judges who had issued an arrest warrant for Guillaume Libri-Carucci, a friend of Mérimée's and inspector general of French libraries, for stealing rare books. Libri had fled to England taking with him a large number of rare books. Libri was an Italian, and in 1850 Mérimée had gone to London to visit another Italian friend to discuss the possibility of Libri gaining a position on his staff. Mérimée's London friend was named Antonio Panizzi. In 1823 he had arrived in England after fleeing Italy to escape a death sentence for his membership in a revolutionary nationalist group known as *carbonari*. This secret organization, many of whom were imprisoned or executed, was fighting to rid Italy of Austrian occupation, and Panizzi was one of its most senior members. In England he managed to get a job as professor of Italian language and literature at the newly founded University College, London. In addition to this badly paid post he also became assistant keeper of books at the British Museum. His appointment would one day change the life of scholars all over the world.

In the ninety years since its opening in 1753 little had changed at the museum and its services to the public had become woefully inadequate. Most people now regarded the library as a haven for the idle rich. In 1831, when Panizzi was appointed to the Department of Printed Books, it was the least important section of the museum, containing only 240,000 books housed in rooms closed to the public. In 1837 Panizzi was appointed as keeper and immediately began to lobby for more funds. He played on the British sense of national pride, making unfavorable comparisons between the British Museum and other national libraries. The technique worked, but it took until 1846 for action to be taken by Parliament on Panizzi's request for extra money. In the expansion that followed Panizzi found himself with a space problem. He sketched out an idea for the solution: a great circular reading room to be built in the courtyard of the British

Museum, whose walls would contain bookshelves. After the opening in 1857 the reading room became a Mecca for scholars worldwide.

The British Museum had been founded in the first place to house the collections of Sir Hans Sloane, a doctor and antiquarian. After studying in France, where he met the great naturalists, including Pierre Magnol (after whom the magnolia was named), in 1687 Sloane sailed to Jamaica as personal physician to the newly appointed governor Monck. In the two years Sloane spent on the island he avidly studied its flora and fauna, geography, meteorology and local folklore. In the search for new plants for use as drugs or food (he collected over eight hundred), his attention was particularly taken by chocolate. Later he produced the recipe for chocolate mixed with milk, the precursor of the modern chocolate drink. In 1712, after his return to London, Sloane became physician to the king, then president of the Royal College of Physicians, and finally president of the Royal Society following the death of Isaac Newton.

By 1753 when he died his collection of "curiosities" was well-known as "Sir Hans Sloane's Museum." By the standards of the time the collection was very large (twenty-five hundred items, twenty-five thousand coins and medals, and seven rooms full of books) and was regularly visited by leading scholars. In Sloane's will he stipulated that if the nation did not buy the collection from his heirs for twenty thousand pounds within one year of his death it would be offered in turn to the Royal Academies of Science at St. Petersburg, Paris, Berlin and Madrid (each would have a year to decide). After this the collection would be sold to the highest bidder. The British government responded by establishing a lottery to raise the money, and the British Museum opened its doors only six years later. Until 1805 admission was by ticket only and groups were escorted.

Hans Sloane was also an innovative physician and took a leading part in experiments with inoculation for smallpox, a killer disease at the time. In 1716 the Venetian consul at Izmir communicated to Sloane details of a procedure used in Turkey. Sloane did little about it until Lady Mary Wortley Montagu returned to England from a two-year stay in Turkey as wife of the British ambassador. While there she **121** 102 *190* had witnessed the inoculation[121] procedure and had became so en-

Fig. 26: *The British Museum, designed in Neoclassical style by Sir Robert Smirke. This present building dates from 1852.*

thusiastic she had her own son inoculated. Part of the reason for her interest was that the disease had already killed her brother and she herself had contracted smallpox in 1715. Thanks to Hans Sloane she had survived, though losing her famous looks in the process.

Lady Mary was the daughter of the Earl of Kingston and had for some years been well-known both for her beauty and her wit. Later in life the poet and satirist Alexander Pope would become infatuated with her, but when the relationship turned sour the two became mortal enemies.

During her stay in Turkey Lady Mary first studied the language and then begun to travel about, disguised in voluminous Turkish costume. Thanks to her sex and rank she was accorded the rare privilege of visiting aristocratic Turkish ladies in their harems, where she learned much about Turkish life and customs. It was during these visits that she came across the practice of inoculation. The Turks would deliberately infect small children with pus from smallpox pustules. Over a few days the children would develop swellings and a

number of pustules but then these would heal and the inoculated subjects would never again contract the disease. Lady Mary wrote: "I am patriotic enough to take pains to bring this useful invention into fashion in England; and I should not fail to write to some of our doctors very particularly about it, if I knew any one of them that I thought had virtue enough to destroy such a considerable branch of their revenue for the good of mankind." On her eventual return to England Lady Mary set about persuading all and sundry to take up the matter. Princess Caroline had her two children treated and then everybody else followed suit.

While in Turkey Lady Mary also wrote a collection of essays now known as the *Embassy Letters*. She had apparently never intended them for publication, but after her death a copy of the essays was passed to a printer and the work became public. The letters are delightfully written, full of fresh and vivid descriptions of what Lady Mary saw and thought as she wandered the gardens and palaces of Turkey: "I allow you to laugh at me, for the sensual declaration in saying that I had rather be a rich effendi, with all his ignorance, than Sir Isaac Newton with all his knowledge."

One of her observations related to the profusion of tulips to be found in Turkey. Her visit coincided with an upsurge of tulip mania among the Turks. There were more than thirteen hundred varieties of the flower, with such exotic names as "Beauty's Reward," "Dawn Pink," and "Lover's Dream." The French ambassador wrote back to Louis XV describing the way the palaces were bedecked with the flowers: "The trellises are all decorated with an enormous quantity of flowers of every sort, placed in bottles and lit by an infinite number of glass lamps of different colours. These lamps are also hung on the green branches of shrubs which are specially transplanted for the fête from neighbouring woods and placed behind the trellises. The effect of all these varied colours, and of the lights which are reflected by countless mirrors, is said to be magnificent. The illuminations, and the noisy consort of Turkish musical instruments which accompanies them continue nightly so long as the tulips remain in flower." The tulip had first been introduced to Europe in 1645 when a Flemish scholar, Ogier de Busbecq, brought seeds from Istanbul to Vi-

enna. He also brought the wrong name for the flower. In Turkey the tulip is called *lalé*, but when Busbecq asked what the flower was called he was told it was a "tulipand-flower." *Tulipand* is the Turkish word for "turban," and his informant was describing the shape of the flower. So in the West the name became "tulip."

The Swiss horticulturist Konrad Gesner became the first naturalist to describe and illustrate a tulip in his 1651 *Book of German Gardens*. After spending time teaching Greek at Lausanne Academy, in 1541 Gesner settled in Zurich as professor of natural history and set up a medical practice. Most of his time was spent writing. In 1555 he began work on the two-volume *Opera Botanica,* for which he drew nearly fifteen hundred illustrations. Gesner was the first botanist to recognize the importance of floral structures as an aid to systematic classification. He was also the first to stress the importance of seeds, showing that they often revealed connections between apparently unrelated plants.

Gesner was also interested in bibliography, and in 1555 published the three volumes of his *Universal Library,* a monumental work that contained a list of all books published since the invention of the printing press a hundred years earlier, as well as a catalogue of authors arranged alphabetically together with brief descriptions of their works, and a giant dictionary divided into twenty-one subjects (including grammar and philology, dialectics, medicine, astrology, geography and theology). The third volume included an account of the 130 known languages and translations of the Lord's Prayer in twenty-two of them. Gesner also wrote on the importance of the use of textual analysis to understand ancient texts such as the Bible. This endeared him to his godfather, Ulrich Zwingli, the man who led Switzerland to Protestantism.

Zwingli had an uneventful early life, matriculating at the University of Vienna and becoming ordained as a priest in Constance, Switzerland, in 1506. He then spent ten years as a serving cleric in the small Swiss town of Glarus. There in 1515 he met the man who was to change his life: the great Dutch humanist Desiderius Erasmus. Erasmus introduced Zwingli to the historical, analytical approach to the study of biblical texts. Zwingli began to take an increasingly crit-

ical attitude to the way the Catholic Church conducted itself and preached the faith, and his fame as a scholar began to spread. On January 1, 1519 (his birthday), partly in recognition of his publications, Zwingli was given the post of "people's priest" at the Great Minster in Zurich and found himself in a position of power. In a city of only six thousand adults the pulpit was stage, loudspeaker, radio, newspaper, television and Internet combined. One eminent church administrator was said to have advised his supporters that if they wanted to influence policy they had to be sure to get their proposals accepted "before the preacher stands up in the pulpit."

Zwingli's break with the Catholic authorities came over the next four years with his attacks on belief in purgatory, the invocation of saints, monasticism, indulgences, tithes, ecclesiastical vestments, the Mass, Latin services, music, baptism, transubstantiation and celibacy. His most public act of defiance, other than getting married in 1522, took place on the evening of the first fasting Sunday in Lent, March 9 the same year. That evening a group of Zurich citizens disregarded Catholic teaching that forbade the eating of meat during the festival and ate smoked sausages. This event took place at dinner in a private house at which Zwingli was present, although he himself did not eat the offending sausages. Two weeks later his sermon was titled: "Regarding the Choice and Freedom of Foods." In it Zwingli cited the Bible as supporting the view that Christians were free to eat all foods since these were in themselves neither good nor bad. In this way Zwingli reduced the act of fasting to a matter of private conscience, expressing the humanist belief that matters of faith should be left to the individual, who would be guided by revealed truth. In 1525 the Zurich Town Council introduced new, stringent "Zwinglian" laws against prostitution and new regulations for social behavior and dress. It became a civil offense to blaspheme, play card games or dice or to wear silk, gold, silver, velvet and low-cut shoes. In 1530 a general curfew closed all inns at 9:00 P.M.

Zwingli brought about one other major change to life in Zurich. For centuries it had been a Swiss custom to send young men off to fight as mercenary soldiers. Fighting was popular and admired in Switzerland, where life at home was hard and monotonous and

where the lack of cultivable land offered little opportunity for younger sons. Swiss mercenaries had long been held in high esteem throughout Europe. They had developed a particular fighting style, thanks to their use of pikes. A Swiss pike "square" of several thousand men massed together and moving as one, ready by sheer weight of numbers to roll over an enemy formation, or to stop suddenly and angle their pikes outward in defense, was well-nigh invincible. Enemy cavalry could do little, since before they were able to cut down a pikeman they could be impaled on his pike. Zurich had a long-term agreement to supply mercenaries to France, and Zwingli persuaded the Canton Council to revoke it.

The pike square was already on the way to obsolescence. A few years before, at the Battle of Marignano (in which Swiss mercenaries had fought for the French against the Spanish) a new firearm, the arquebus, had radically changed the nature of war and rendered the pike square ineffectual. Toward the end of the seventeenth century other new developments in weaponry accelerated this process.

The first was the flintlock musket. It was designed so that pressure on the trigger released a sprung arm carrying a flint, which then struck a small, serrated metal plate. This caused the flint to shoot

Fig. 27: *Swiss mercenary pikemen (wearing their white cross) fighting for the French at the 1525 Battle of Pavia, Italy.*

sparks into a pan filled with powder at the same time as the action also opened the pan cover. When the powder in the pan ignited it lit the full charge of powder inside the barrel and fired the ball.

The slightly later development of a prefilled paper cartridge (the musketeer opened it with his teeth, poured the powder into the barrel and then inserted the ball on top of it) sped up the rate of fire to two or three rounds per minute. This was twice as fast as the earlier matchlock musket, in which the powder was ignited with a smoldering fuse. With no further danger of accidental discharge from sparks (which could happen when matchlock musketeers stood close to each other), the new flintlock permitted soldiers to stand less far apart. This in turn led them to discard the old broad-brimmed hats and full-skirted coats in favor of slim-fitting clothing. The flintlock enabled close ranks, firing by rows, to maintain a hail of fire.

The second innovation was the new bayonet, which consisted of a blade attached to a metal sleeve that fitted around the muzzle leaving the musket free to fire with the bayonet still attached. The infantryman was now pikeman and musketeer in one. He could shoot at the pike square from a distance and then move in with the bayonet to finish the job.

These innovations combined to reduce the need for Swiss mercenaries. The French minister for war, the Marquis de Louvois, realized that the new weapons and the tactics involved in their battlefield use were going to require soldiers to be better-trained than ever before. Such training was going to take several years, so the new army was going to have to be professional and permanent.

The idea of a standing army had already been developed to some
122 63 129 extent in England, Holland[122] and Sweden, but Louvois made his force fully national and introduced organizational measures that made the French army perhaps the most advanced on the Continent. Louvois created a quartermaster's department with a commissariat staff to supervise the price, quality and transport of supplies. This in turn led to improvement in the roads over which the army traveled and to the establishment of strategically placed magazines for arms, ammunition and food. Louvois also found a man who was so good at drilling the troops his name became a household word: Jean Mar-

tinet. Other changes included the issue of uniforms, the rationalization of medals and awards, an organized promotion system, regular pay, codes of discipline and the construction of the Hôtel des Invalides in Paris for those crippled in action.

Toward the end of the century an Italian immigrant to France added one final element to the military mix by introducing the first marching music. In 1661 Jean-Baptiste Lully was appointed superintendent of court music to Louis XIV and began to write music for dances in which the king would perform starring roles. In 1672 Louis added a school of dance to his Royal Academy of Music. One year before, Pierre Beauchamp had been made royal dance master, and it was he who facilitated the development of ballet with his new system for learning steps called "choreography."

By the time Beauchamp retired in 1687 he had laid the foundations of *danse noble* and made the French style of dance and the terminology it employed standard until modern times. In 1701 a book by Raoul Feuillet replicated much of Beauchamp's work. Titled *The Art of Describing Dance,* it described the "track notation" of Beauchamp's choreographic technique, which used a line to indicate the path to be followed by the dancer. Black dots to right and left of the line indicated the positions of the feet. Additional strokes and symbols indicated arm movements and any extra ornamentation to be added. The new choreography would be in use for nearly a hundred years. By 1706 Feuillet had been translated into English by a dance master named John Weaver.

Weaver had already established himself in London as a theatrical dancer in pieces performed supplementary to the action of a play. In 1702 he had produced his *The Tavern Bilkers* at Drury Lane Theater. This work was described by a contemporary as "the first entertainment that appeared on the English stage where the representation and story was carried on by dancing, action and motion only." In 1717, Drury Lane also saw the production of more of Weaver's danced mimes: *The Loves of Mars and Venus* and *Harlequin Turned Judge,* among others. Drury Lane Theater was at the time in fierce competition with the newly redecorated Lincoln's Inn Fields Theater managed by John Rich, who experimented with pantomime and

dance. In 1728 Rich staged a new production by the relatively un-known author John Gay, titled *The Beggar's Opera*. It combined dance, popular song, comedy and political satire, and the story line contained a thinly veiled attack on Prime Minister Robert Walpole. On January 28, 1720, *The Beggar's Opera* attracted an opening night crowd of twelve hundred. Before the season was over the ballad-opera had been performed an unheard-of sixty-two times and was a smash success. It was said at the time that the satirical *Beggar's Opera* "made Rich gay and Gay rich."

Satire was a popular genre in a time of transition from rule by monarch to rule by Parliament, when corruption was rife. This was the heyday of Alexander Pope[123] and Jonathan Swift,[124] two of the greatest masters of satire in English literature. Gay knew both of them and for a brief time in 1714 they were all fellow members of a private writers' association named the Scriblerus Club. Scriblerus members met informally at each other's lodgings to eat, drink and re-gale the assembled company with pieces satirizing the great and the powerful. The official purpose of the club was to write the memoirs of a fictitious individual named Martin Scriblerus, but the real intent was to publish pieces under his name attacking the follies of the self-styled intellectuals of the day. Targets abounded in a period when people still believed in witchcraft, the philosopher's stone and astrology.

The club member who did most of the wining, dining and enter-taining (because as the royal physician he could afford to do so in his grace-and-favor apartments at St. James's Palace) was Dr. John Ar-buthnot, whose other obsession, besides satire, was statistics. In 1692 Arbuthnot published *On the Laws of Chance*, in which he made his famous remark: "There are very few things which we know, which are not capable of being reduc'd to a Mathematical Reasoning; and when they cannot, it is a sign that Knowledge of them is very small and confus'd." In 1710 he wrote *An Argument for Divine Provi-dence*, in which he attempted to demonstrate that providence and not chance governed the sex of a child at birth. From a study of the mor-tality tables (births and deaths) for London over a period of eighty-two years he calculated that there were many more births of boys

than girls. Since this was against the laws of chance Arbuthnot suggested that because men lived riskier lives than women the higher male numbers showed God was making sure enough men would survive to renew the population.

This first known example of statistical inference attracted the attention of continental scientists and in particular that of a young Dutch mathematician, Willem 'sGravesande. 'sGravesande met Arbuthnot during a one-year visit to England in 1715, when he also met (and impressed) Isaac Newton, whose work he was already teaching in Holland. Newton was evidently not the only one to be impressed by 'sGravesande's work. At one point the great French thinker Voltaire made a special trip to visit him in Holland to get his opinion on the book Voltaire was writing about Newton.

At the time, Voltaire was in residence with the love of his life, the beautiful and brilliant Marquise Emilie de Châtelet, at the Château de Cirey in Eastern France. The house was a long way from Paris, where over the previous fifteen years Voltaire had established his reputation as France's greatest writer and found himself in serious trouble with the authorities for his outspoken views. There had been particularly negative reaction to his *Letters Concerning the English Nation*, written in 1729 after a three-year visit to London (where he had attended the funeral of Isaac Newton). The book praised the liberty accorded writers in England and made unfavorable comparisons with the absolutist regime in France.

In 1733, after numerous love affairs, Voltaire met Emilie. His memoirs begin with the sentence: "I was weary of the idle and turbulent life of Paris, of the crowd of fops, of the bad books printed with official approval and royal privilege, of literary cabals, of the meanness and rascality of the wretches who dishonoured literature. I found in 1733 a young lady who felt more or less as I did, and who resolved to spend several years in the country to cultivate her mind, far from the tumult of the world." Voltaire went with Emilie to Cirey and they set up house together. Emilie's husband was an army officer who was almost permanently absent and who seems to have approved of his wife's liaison. Each of these two workaholics had a separate study, and Voltaire also kept a small lab. Both were writing

about Newton's work. Voltaire was producing a popular version and Emilie was tackling the mathematics. In spite of the fact that Voltaire and Emilie lived informally and did not believe in servants, the cream of the European intelligentsia was soon beating a path to their door. Staying at Cirey was not a relaxing experience. At all hours of the night and day guests were expected to take part in magic lantern shows, philosophical discussions, plays and poetry readings. In 1738 Voltaire's *Elements of the Philosophy of Newton* went into print and was an immediate and sensational success. In London it gained Voltaire election to the Royal Society. In 1758, a few years after Emilie had died, Voltaire bought a villa at Ferney in Switzerland and retired "to cultivate his garden." It was there in 1765 that he received an intriguing letter from an Italian scholar about the souls of snails and worms.

The writer, Lazzaro Spallanzani, was professor of natural history at the northern Italian University of Pavia where he had for some years been investigating the regenerative properties of certain animals: snails, worms and salamanders. He had discovered he could cut pieces off these creatures and the missing parts would grow back. In the case of some worms this might sometimes result in the regeneration of two separate creatures. This created a theological problem, because if souls were indivisible then when two worms were created out of one and each of them had a soul, where did the extra soul come from? Spallanzani said it must always have been present in an egg of some kind. The remark started the whole of modern reproductive physiology.

The other work in which Spallanzani made startling advances related to the contemporary view, held primarily by the English microscopist John Needham, that there was a "vegetative force" present in the minute organisms that could be seen down a microscope. This, Needham claimed, would account for the presence of maggots in cheese, moths in carpets and so forth. According to Needham such organisms were created spontaneously by the vegetative force in the cheese and the carpets. Spallanzani disagreed and set about proving Needham wrong. In 1761 he took a flask of dirty water in which he had previously seen microscopically small organisms, boiled the

water in the flask and then melted the neck of the flask to seal it. Some time later he broke the neck and quickly examined the water under his microscope. The organisms in it were dead. But even as he watched live ones appeared. Since these organisms only appeared after the flask was opened, Spallanzani concluded they had to have entered the flask from the air. This was almost exactly the same experiment for which Pasteur[125] would get all the credit a hundred years later.

125 54 114
125 3 27

Spallanzani's reputation was so great that he inspired the character of the "wizard-scientist" in a German story written by E. T. A. Hoffmann and immortalized in Delibes's ballet *Coppélia*. Hoffmann began as a lawyer and became in turn a theater manager, then a writer of ballets, operas and novels. Hoffmann's novels were among the first "psychological" stories, grotesque tales full of doppelgangers and psychopaths. Some of the plots went into musical form in Wagner's *Die Meistersinger*, Offenbach's *Tales of Hoffmann* and Tchaikovsky's *The Nutcracker Suite*.

In 1816 Hoffmann was appointed counselor to the Berlin Court of Appeal. Two years later he was in charge of an investigation regarding the activity of Friedrich Jahn, who was accused of secret and treasonable association with intent to overthrow the government and subsequently jailed for six years. Jahn was a nationalist who had reacted to Germany's defeat at the hands of the French in 1806 by starting a movement to persuade Germans from every principality and state to unite and establish a single, liberal nation. Jahn's technique for rallying supporters was to set up gymnastic clubs with the aim of inculcating youths with the sense of discipline, comradeship and obedience that would be required for the wars that undoubtedly lay ahead as Germany asserted herself. Jahn's clubs sprang up all over Germany and soon became hotbeds of subversion and free speech.

In 1819 the political murder of a prominent German conservative, August von Kotzebue, brought a crackdown by the Prussian authorities that closed the gym clubs and suppressed free speech. One of Jahn's followers, Adolf Follen, was arrested and tried for distributing subversive literature. Although Adolf would eventually be acquitted, his brother and fellow liberal Karl decided in 1820 to flee the coun-

Fig. 28: *An early nineteenth-century German gymnastic club. The athletes usually dressed in loose cotton jackets and trousers.*

try, first to Switzerland and then in 1824 to America. In 1825 he settled in Cambridge, Massachusetts. As soon as he arrived he began gymnastic exercises with the students at Harvard, and in one of the university dining halls opened the first college gym in America. At the same time two more gyms opened nearby, one in Boston and the other in Northampton, both run by fellow Germans. By 1850 there were a hundred gym clubs in America run by German refugee immigrants, most of them liberals or socialists.

One of the first American organizations to adopt gymnastics as part of its program was the YMCA, the first of whose branches opened in Boston in 1851. That year the YMCA received a letter from a man in Geneva who was the corresponding secretary for a group of young Swiss Christians, suggesting that such groups form an international association. In 1855, partly at his instigation, the first World Conference of YMCAs occurred in Paris, attended by representatives of Belgium, France, Britain, Canada, Germany, Holland, Switzerland and the United States. The conference established the World Alliance of YMCAs. Henri Dunant, the Genevan who had suggested the conference, was the main author of its charter.

126 26 *50*
126 116 *218*
126 129 *246*
Four years later Dunant found himself in the small northern Italian village of Solferino for a meeting with the French emperor Napoleon III,[126] who was about to watch a battle between his army

and that of the Austrians. Dunant stayed to watch, too. On June 14, 1859, 350,000 soldiers from both sides met and proceeded to slaughter each other. Over forty thousand men were either killed or wounded. Dunant, watching from the hill, was appalled by the savagery. When the battle was over, in the nearby town of Castiglione delle Stiviere, Dunant organized the townsfolk to help the wounded of both sides. For three days and nights Dunant and his helpers tried desperately to save hundreds of young men from death.

Three years later Dunant published *A Note on Solferino,* in which he wrote: "It ought to be possible in peacetime to get together trained helpers who would care for the wounded after a battle. People who would be ready to go and help wherever and whenever they were needed. . . . Countries at war should recognise these helpers and give them all possible assistance. . . . A meeting must be held where these ideas could be discussed." After intense lobbying of the kings, queens, generals and prime ministers of various European countries, in 1864 Dunant succeeded in arranging a meeting in Geneva, where the Red Cross was formed and the Geneva Convention on the treatment of wounded soldiers was signed.

For the Red Cross one of the earliest and most urgent operations required on the battlefield was the blood transfusion. This generally involved the difficult process of joining donor and recipient blood vessels and usually ended in the inexplicable death of the recipient. The mystery was solved in 1900 by an Austrian physician named Karl Landsteiner, when he discovered that blood from one person could cause another's red blood cells to "clump." Clumping could cause blockages in the capillary system, bringing damage and even death. Landsteiner found that blood contained two "factors" that could cause clumping. He named the blood groups containing the factors "A" and " B." People possessed either one, or both, or neither. So a person's blood group was either A, AB, B, or O. In 1900 Landsteiner mentioned this idea in a footnote and won the Nobel Prize.

The Nobel Prize would also go to the man who solved the other half of the transfusion problem: the difficulty in uniting blood vessels. He did so with a technique that was astonishing in its simplicity. He used three sutures to join the blood vessels at three equilateral

points around the vessel's circumference. Then he pulled on two of the sutures, causing the edge of the vessel between them to straighten, and sewed the straight edges together. He then repeated the action twice more and released the vessel to spring back circular, and joined. The name of the medical stitcher was Alexis Carrel, and like Landsteiner he spent time at the Rockefeller Institute for Medical Research in New York. Carrel's ultimate aim, in finding a way of suturing blood vessels, was to be able to carry out organ transplants. For this he also needed to be able to keep a separated organ temporarily supplied with oxygen and nutrients.

The man who made this possible in 1930 worked for several years with Carrel before perfecting a sterilizable glass perfusion pump with which Carrel was able to keep a kidney alive for several weeks. The pump-maker was Charles Lindbergh, who three years earlier had completed the first ever transatlantic crossing in his monoplane

Fig. 29: *Charles Lindbergh, standing before his monoplane* Spirit of St. Louis, *in May 1927, just after his epic flight.*

Spirit of St. Louis. Lindbergh married the daughter of U.S. Ambassador Dwight Morrow. After the wedding Morrow went to London to attend a disarmament conference. One of the things the conference did was to reaffirm the constraints imposed on the German navy by the 1919 Versailles treaty. Germany was limited to building three new ships, all of them under ten thousand tons' displacement.

The first, *Admiral Graf Spee,* was launched in 1936. *Graf Spee* circumvented the intentions of the disarmament agreement because she and her two sister ships packed the punch of a full-size battleship and went faster and farther than a cruiser. Scarcely had World War II begun before *Graf Spee* sank nine British ships and took their crews on board her supply vessel *Altmark. Graf Spee* was finally run down by the British in December 1939. After a brief firefight the German battleship took refuge in neutral waters off Montevideo harbor, Uruguay. The Uruguayans had given the ship four days to leave, and the German High Command ordered the captain to scuttle her. The British turned their attention to *Altmark.* Two months later she was found in a Norwegian fjord and the British prisoners were rescued.

Hitler took this invasion of neutral territory as an indication that the British were about to invade Norway, so he advanced his own invasion plans. On April 8, 1940, the Germans invaded Norway. Three weeks later they had placed an exceptionally tight security ring around the hydroelectric power station at Vermork in the Rjukan valley to the east of Oslo. They had done so because hydroelectric power was essential to a top-secret Nazi research project that involved a special kind of water.

One essential factor in causing a nuclear chain reaction is to be able to slow down the passage of a neutron so that it does not pass through the nucleus of an atom of uranium in a trillionth of a second. At a slower rate there is more chance that it will collide with the nucleus of a uranium atom and split it, releasing particles that will in turn split other nuclei and so on. When uncontrolled, this "chain reaction" process is what causes a nuclear explosion.

The material which can slow the initial neutron bombardment was produced at Vermork. It was called "heavy water," because with the use of a gigantic amount of electricity water could be "reduced." This

would leave it with a heavier-than-usual amount of deuterium, an element occurring naturally in water. If the heavy water were placed between the source of the neutrons and the uranium nuclei, the deuterium atoms would act to slow the neutrons enough to trigger a chain reaction.

This was why on the night of February 27, 1943, a group of Allied commandos (all of them Free Norwegians) entered the Vermork plant and blew it up. When they hit the water, Hitler was denied the material that might have given him an atomic bomb.

CHAPTER 10

×

In Touch

On March 25, 1951, *The New York Times* ran a front-page report carrying the astonishing news that Argentina had successfully operated a nuclear fusion reactor. It appeared that in the late 1940s the Argentine dictator Juan Peron, increasingly estranged from his own scientific community, had set up an isolated island laboratory for Ronald Richter, a German scientist. In this laboratory on February 16, 1951, according to an Argentine press release, "There was held with complete success the first tests which, with the use of this new method, produced controlled liberation of atomic energy." No further details were available.

The reaction of European and American researchers was predictably skeptical. The harnessing of fusion power presented extraordinarily technical problems, only one of which was to reproduce the conditions on the surface of the sun where at temperatures in excess of two hundred million degrees Fahrenheit the process of fusion converts mass into energy at the rate of five million tons a second. In the solar environment lightweight hydrogen nuclei are so hot and moving at such high rates that when two of them collide they fuse. The union forms a nucleus of heavier helium, and as it does so releases large amounts of energy in the form of light, heat and neutrons. The sun's gravitational field is so massive (three hundred thousand times greater than Earth's) that it holds together with a density ten times that of lead the incandescent gas in which the reac-

tions occur. So the hydrogen nuclei are packed together long enough to ensure that collisions happen with great frequency. Fusion therefore requires three conditions: long confinement time, high density and heat.

These were some of the considerations in the mind of an American scientist named Lyman Spitzer, Jr., when he heard of the Argentine announcement during a skiing holiday in Colorado. During the lengthy intervals spent on the ski-lift Spitzer was stimulated enough by the news to give further thought to fusion, because as an astrophysicist he was acquainted with the stellar fusion process and had earlier become involved in theoretical work on the project to develop a hydrogen bomb.

Spitzer knew how it might be possible to heat a gas to the necessary temperature because he had recently read work by the Swedish physicist Hannes Alfven regarding the influence of magnetic fields on hot gases in the cosmos. A superheated gas would become electrically charged ("ionized"), and its ionized particles would then be attracted to magnetic fields. Spitzer also knew that no material on earth could withstand two hundred million degrees Fahrenheit. The theoretical solution to the problem was to contain the hot, charged gas (known as a "plasma") in a magnetic container. A month later Spitzer presented his ideas for an experimental fusion generator to the U.S. Atomic Energy Commission in Washington, D.C. The device, called a "stellarator," was designed to heat the plasma by inducing a current into it and containing the superhot plasma in a closed, figure-eight-shaped tube inside which a complex grid of magnetic fields would be generated. Spitzer's stellarator was the first of several experimental fusion reactors that would be developed from then till the end of the twentieth century.

The value of developing a successful fusion reactor some time in the twenty-first century is hard to exaggerate. The high-energy neutrons released by the fusion process could be used to generate heat to boil water whose steam would drive electric power turbines. Today the most recently developed fuels for the fusion process, deuterium and tritium, are found in abundance. A fusion reactor is safe because in the case of catastrophic failure the magnetic confinement environ-

ment collapses and the fusion process stops immediately. Fusion power plants would also produce no pollutants and could substantially reduce the amount of fossil fuels at present being burned in conventional power plants. There would also be little or no problem with nuclear waste, since fusion produces very much less radioactive by-product than the atomic fission process.

Superconductivity could make fusion even more attractive. Superconducting materials might permit the transmission of electricity at virtually no cost, since cables made of superconducting materials would offer millions of times less resistance to the passage of electric current than conventional cables. In terms of power transmission this would mean that over long distances no intermediate booster power stations would be needed.

Superconductivity was first discovered in 1911 by a Nobel Laureate, the Dutch professor of experimental physics Heike Kammerlingh Onnes, while working at Leiden University in Holland. Onnes was obsessed with extreme cold, and the cryogenics work of his lab was soon to lead the world. Once helium gas had been liquefied by James Dewar in 1898 Onnes decided to use it in the investigation of what he thought might happen when the temperature of certain materials reached close to absolute zero, or minus 459 degrees Fahrenheit. It had been theorized by Walter Nernst in Berlin that as a pure metal became colder its resistance to electricity should become smaller and smaller until at absolute zero it disappeared completely. After early experiments with platinum and gold Onnes became aware that the slightest trace of impurities in the material would reduce the extent to which resistance fell. Onnes realized that the best metal to use would be mercury, since it is liquid at room temperature and is easy to distill and redistill until an extreme degree of purity is reached.

In 1911 Onnes discovered that the resistance of mercury dropped sharply just above the boiling point of helium (and well above absolute zero). Just below this temperature the mercury resistance disappeared totally. Experiments with a superconductive coil of lead immersed in liquid helium produced an extraordinary result. Once a current had been set up in the lead ring, even after the power had

been switched off, so long as the lead ring was kept at superconducting temperature the current remained in the lead. Onnes called this a "persistent current" and went on to maintain such a current for a period of two years until he discontinued the experiment.

The liquefaction of gas, so helpful to Onnes, had first been done thirty-four years earlier by a Swiss researcher named Raoul-Pierre Pictet and simultaneously by a Frenchman named Louis Paul Cailletet, whose contribution to cryogenics was triggered by an accident. Cailletet became involved with gases while running his father's blast furnaces, when he became interested in ways of retrieving the materials in the fumes given off by the smelting process. In 1877 he began work on liquefaction. At the time there were six gases considered to be permanent (gaseous in their natural state): oxygen, nitrogen, hydrogen, acetylene,[127] nitrogen dioxide and carbon monoxide.

Cailletet began with acetylene, and it was at this point that the accident happened. He had theorized that a pressure of sixty atmospheres would liquefy the gas but before this pressure was reached his apparatus sprang a leak and the pressure on the compressed gas suddenly fell. Cailletet had been watching the glass cylinder in which he was compressing the gas and noticed that at the moment the pressure had suddenly fallen a faint mist had appeared. He immediately realized that the fall in pressure was causing the condensation of the gas and producing small liquid droplets. Armed with this knowledge he now succeeded in recreating the same pressure-drop conditions with the atmospheric gases, beginning with oxygen. On December 2, 1877, he compressed oxygen to about three hundred atmospheres, first reducing its temperature to minus 27 degrees Centigrade by surrounding it with evaporated sulphur dioxide. When Cailletet released the pressure in the same sudden manner as had happened in the acetylene experiment, the oxygen condensed and formed liquid droplets.

In 1889 Cailletet's interest in other aspects of pressure was unexpectedly served by the construction of the Eiffel Tower[128] on which he subsequently installed a nine-hundred-foot manometer, running up the tower. The manometer consisted of a transparent tube filled with various liquids. The lower end of the tube was connected to a

127 39 74
127 57 119
128 79 150

pressure source and the upper end left open to the atmosphere. Cailletet was able to calculate the total pressure exerted by each of the liquids tested.

The tower made possible other air-pressure-related experiments when its designer, Gustav Eiffel, dropped small, variously shaped plane surfaces with fine wires attached to them to measure the speed of their fall and experimentally confirmed that air resistance increased as the square of the surface of the object moving through it. In 1906 Eiffel built a wind tunnel at the foot of the tower and for the first time proved that more lift was generated by air flowing over the camber of a wing than striking its underside.

Eiffel knew a great deal about the movement of air because by the time he built the tower he was France's greatest engineer, specializing in high-level railway bridges over gorges and rivers in France, Portugal and Indochina. Eiffel's bridges were miracles of delicate iron tracery, capable of withstanding high wind-loads. By 1886, when the French government decided to build the tallest tower in the world as a centerpiece for the 1889 Paris Exposition, Eiffel was the only engineer with sufficient expertise in wrought-iron to do the job. Given the likely wind-load stresses on the tower cast-iron would have been too brittle and steel so flexible it would have produced an intolerable amount of sway.

Eiffel's specialty was latticework, and the Eiffel Tower is a beautiful example. Eiffel reduced the metal structure to the absolute minimum consistent with safety. He also achieved absolute precision (rivet holes, for instance, had to be placed within one-tenth of a millimeter) by placing the tower foundations on hydraulic jacks that would raise or lower each of the tower's sixteen columns accurately enough to be sure that the piers were absolutely horizontal. This ensured that by the time the structure had reached its full height of nearly one thousand feet it was still exactly vertical.

It was Eiffel's wind-load expertise that had won him a rather special commission just before he got the contract for the tower. The project was nothing less than an attempt by the French government to bring political stability to the country through the ceremonial donation of an extraordinary gift to the United States.

The plan originated with Frédéric Bartholdi, who in 1871 was sent to the United States as the agent of a small but influential group of moderate Republican intellectuals who were concerned that France was in danger of social upheaval following the recent defeat at the hands of the Germans. This had led to the flight of the emperor Napoleon III[129] and the inauguration of the Third Republic. French democracy was on shaky ground, with monarchists calling for a return to the days of the empire, revolutionaries who wanted an extreme left-wing state and the moderates caught between the two. Bartholdi's plan was to rally French public opinion to the moderates with a very public act linking the fledgling French republic with the great transatlantic democracy whose independence the French had virtually assured a hundred years before with troops and money.

129 26 *50*
129 116 *218*
129 126 *236*

The political link with America would be forged by ensuring that contributions from both countries would pay for the construction of France's gift: the Statue of Liberty. And as the statue was to stand exposed to fierce gusts in New York Harbor the ideal person to build the statue's support structure would be Gustav Eiffel. When the Statue of Liberty was finally dedicated on October 28, 1886, the American cofunding was almost entirely due to last-minute efforts by Joseph Pulitzer, owner of the *New York World*. Pulitzer lobbied strenuously to gain public support for the project, which many saw as an irrelevance, by printing in his newspaper the names of every donor, no matter how small the amount given. This would later generate the myth that the statue had been paid for by schoolchildren.

The French intended the statue to be described as "Liberty Enlightening the World," the idea being that it would act as a powerful and very visible reminder to all Americans of the quality of French culture and of America's political debt to France. At one stroke the entire political meaning of the statue was changed by a young Jewish poet named Emma Lazarus. In 1883 well-known authors were invited to write verses about the statue and to permit their poems to be auctioned. Lazarus wrote the poem, which was then chosen for recitation at the dedication ceremony and later inscribed on a plaque placed on the statue's pedestal, the section of the monument built and paid for in America. The last lines of Lazarus's poem turned the

Fig. 30: *Emma Lazarus.
Her poem about the Statue
of Liberty was titled "The
New Colossus."*

Statue of Liberty from a French icon into the symbol of America as
the home of freedom:

> "Keep, ancient lands, your storied pomp!" cries she
> With silent lips. "Give me your tired, your poor,
> Your huddl'd masses yearning to breathe free,
> The wretched refuse of your teeming shore,
> Send these, the homeless, tempest-tost to me.
> I lift my lamp beside the golden door!"

Lazarus did one other thing that placed her in the history books.
Almost singlehandedly she started the Zionist movement to establish
a Jewish homeland in Palestine. Her efforts were triggered by the
horrifying news of the 1881 anti-Semitic pogroms in Russia and Ger-

many, when thousands of Jews died in violence during which their homes were destroyed and their possessions confiscated. Forty thousand of the survivors emigrated to the United States, where Lazarus spoke out strongly in newspaper articles and poems against the persecution the new Jewish immigrants had already suffered and against the conditions in which they were being held on Ward's Island before entry to America.

In 1882 she wrote: The Jews . . . "must establish an independent nationality." That year she heard from an Englishman who had for three years been taking practical steps in the same direction. Laurence Oliphant, an English non-Jew, wrote to Lazarus from Palestine, where he had been trying to obtain suitable land and the permission of the Turkish occupying authority to build settlements for European Jewish refugees. His letter to Lazarus was an appeal for her help in getting the U.S. government to ask the Russians to persuade the Turks to allow Romanian Jews to settle in Palestine.

130 34 67 In 1888 Oliphant married Rosamund Dale Owen,[130] niece of the man who had brought the Smithsonian Bill to the floor of the U.S. Senate. Before the couple could retire to their new home in Palestine Oliphant died. He had had an extraordinary life. Beginning as a lawyer in Sri Lanka, where his father was the British chief justice, in 1853 Oliphant had taken up travel writing and was hired by the *London Daily News* to cover the runup to the Crimean War. In 1854 Oliphant traveled in Canada and the United States. The following year he reported on the siege of Sebastopol for *The Times* of London. Another trip to the States followed. In the decades that followed Oliphant visited China, Japan, Korea, Italy, Poland, Moldavia, Albania, France, Germany and finally Palestine.

In 1857 while in China he served as private secretary to the eighth Earl of Elgin at the time when Elgin was using gunboat diplomacy to force the Chinese to accede to British demands that they open up China to foreign trade and accept the legalization of opium (which the British would then import to China from India, as payment for goods). The Chinese agreed, then reneged on the deal, so Elgin was obliged to return to China and force the imperial government into submission by bombarding the Summer Palace in Peking. Elgin

found the violence, especially the damage to the ancient palace, extremely regrettable.

Elgin's father had held similar views about historical monuments. In 1799 the seventh earl was appointed ambassador to Turkey. In keeping with the new craze for things ancient and Greek (and with the help of Sir William Hamilton,[131] antiquarian and husband of Emma, who ran away with Lord Nelson), Elgin obtained the permission of the occupying Turkish authorities to erect scaffolding around the Athenian Parthenon. The purpose of the scaffolding was to make plaster casts of various carvings. Elgin was also given permission "to take away any pieces of stone with old inscriptions or figures thereon." The Parthenon, on the Athenian Acropolis, was a Doric temple built between 447 and 432 B.C.E. and was the crowning glory of Pericles' program of public works designed to establish Athens as an imperial city at the head of a confederacy of city states. 131 13 37

By the beginning of the nineteenth century the glory that was Greece had all but vanished from Athens, by now a dirty, provincial slum city of perhaps twelve hundred houses. The Parthenon itself was in ruins. It had been turned into a mosque in the fifteenth century, then became a gunpowder magazine subsequently wrecked by a lightning strike that exploded its contents. In 1687 Venetian artillery had blown off the temple roof and destroyed parts of the colonnade. By 1800 the Turks were carrying off large pieces of the temple and statuary to grind up for lime to make mortar. When Elgin saw the magnificent (and still relatively undamaged) frieze running around the entire temple inside the colonnade and the untouched metopes (four-foot panels, carved in high relief) on the exterior he decided not to make plaster casts of them but to take away both metopes and frieze for safekeeping.

The removal of what would become known as the "Elgin Marbles" took more than nine years at a cost that almost bankrupted Elgin. His actions did not meet with universal approval in England. In *Childe Harolde* Byron[132] described Elgin as "the last, the worst, dull spoiler" taking "the last poor plunder from a bleeding land," and in 1815 he wrote an entire poem about Elgin's stripping of the Parthenon, describing Elgin as "cold as the crags upon his native 132 30 61
132 60 122

coast. His mind as barren and his heart as hard." However, there was little argument that the marbles were, in the words of the evidence presented before the House of Commons Select Committee set up in 1816, "the finest things ever to come to this country." In the end it was decided that the government would buy the marbles from Elgin for the sum of thirty thousand pounds and place them in the British Museum. Elgin was in no position to refuse, but he had spent an estimated seventy-four thousand pounds on removing, transporting and storing the marbles, and the cost of the entire venture would financially ruin his family for the next two generations.

One of the experts called before the 1816 Select Committee had been Sir Thomas Lawrence, who argued in support of the decision to purchase. By this time Lawrence was the country's most famous portrait painter, his recent sitters including the Prince Regent and the Duke of Wellington. Lawrence had begun as a child prodigy, earning large fees for portraiture by the age of eleven. In 1787 he was enrolled at the Royal Academy and began to paint the rich and famous.

Fig. 31: *Lawrence painted Queen Caroline, who was an accomplished sculptor, with her chisel in hand.*

Lawrence rapidly became known for his inability to treat his subjects with the fawning respect to which they were accustomed. On one occasion when his subject, the tsar of Russia, complained how unreasonably long the work was taking Lawrence replied: "Sir, I can't be reasonable!" In 1789 Lawrence was invited to paint Queen Caroline and Princess Amelia, whose portraits were then exhibited to great acclaim in the Royal Academy exhibition of 1790. Two years later Lawrence was appointed painter to King George III.

This was at a time when the King's health was failing. His surgeon was a Scotsman, John Hunter, who had reached the age of seventeen before he could read and then went to Glasgow to study carpentry with his brother-in-law. When the latter's business failed, in 1748 John was sent to London to stay with his older brother William, who ran an anatomy school. John was an immediate success, revealing an astonishing dexterity and skill in dissection. Before the end of his first year he was given the job of preparing the "subjects" (usually the bodies of executed criminals) for each dissection lesson. After eleven years with William, John spent three years as an army surgeon and wrote *A Treatise on Blood, Inflammation and Gunshot Wounds*. He then married Anne Home (who wrote librettos for the composer Haydn) and published the first scientific work on the treatment of teeth. In 1774 Hunter became a director of the Humane Society,[133] set   **133** 5 *28* up a highly successful practice and began to indulge in his various hobbies. These included hedgehogs, the structure of whales and codfish hearing. In 1759 the Hunter anatomy school had taken on a new pupil, named William Hewson, and in 1762 when John retired because of ill-health, Hewson, who had attended William's lectures and lodged with John, took over as assistant and then as William's partner.

In 1774 Hewson was to die from an infection, four years after marrying a woman named Mary Stephenson. In the 1750s and 1760s Mary had taken in lodgers, one of whom, on two separate occasions, was Benjamin Franklin.[134] He had been in England on the first occa-   **134** 15 *38* sion, from 1757, to argue the right of Pennsylvania to raise certain taxes and on the second (and more historic) visit to argue against the British right to tax the American colonies without granting them representation in Parliament. After failing in this second endeavor

Franklin returned to America and became a leading figure in the events leading up to the Declaration of Independence in 1776. In the years that followed William Hewson's death Franklin tried again and again to persuade Mary Hewson to come to America to be with him, on one occasion writing: "Your joining me . . . will surely make me happier, provided your change of country may be for the advantage of your dear little family. When you have made up your mind on the subject, let me know by a line, that I may prepare a house for you as near me, and otherwise as convenient for you as possible." In 1786 Mary finally went to Philadelphia and spent three and a half years looking after Franklin until he died.

Franklin gained a deservedly international reputation for his research into the nature of electricity. Work for which he is less well-known was related to the numerous occasions on which he crossed the Atlantic either to England before Independence or later as U.S. minister to France. In 1769 Franklin had heard rumors that the fast ships on which transatlantic mail was dispatched did well en route from America to Europe but were unaccountably slow on the return, taking up to two weeks longer to complete the journey. When relations between America and England became more strained in the period immediately before independence this postal delay became a critical matter. Franklin sought the advice of Captain Timothy Folger, a relative of his mother who had for years commanded whaling ships out of Nantucket. Folger told him of a mysterious "river of the sea" that whalers knew about, which ran up the East Coast of America and then off toward Europe. The whalers used this current to enhance their speed going east and on their return zig-zagged back and forth across it to avoid delay.

On several of his transatlantic trips after 1775 Franklin investigated the mysterious current. From early morning to late evening every day as he crossed the ocean he measured the temperature of the water in and around the current by lowering a corked bottle to below 210 feet, where the pressure forced in the cork and the bottle filled. The bottle was then quickly drawn up and the water temperature measured. In this way, Franklin was able to trace the

boundaries of the current whose water turned out to be up to six degrees Fahrenheit warmer than the surrounding sea. Thanks to this temperature profile Franklin was able to map the current. His chart was the first detailed map of the Gulf Stream.

Franklin took his temperature profile of the Gulf Stream in Fahrenheit degrees because by then the Fahrenheit scale was in fairly general use. This had not long been the case. As late as mid-eighteenth century it was not uncommon for there to be as many as a dozen different temperature scales. But at a time when science and technology required ever more precision this disorganized state of affairs was not helpful. The problem was solved by Daniel Gabriel Fahrenheit, an instrument-maker born in Danzig and sent to learn business in Amsterdam. In 1707 at the age of twenty-one Fahrenheit left the city for ten years of travel around Europe, visiting other instrument-makers and scientists, first in Germany and then (in 1708) in Denmark. In Copenhagen he met the ex-mayor, a talented scientific amateur named Ole Roemer, and was able to watch him at work. In 1717 when Fahrenheit returned to Amsterdam to set up as an instrument-maker he took with him the notes he had made of Roemer's work.

Using a mercury thermometer, Roemer had taken the temperature of the armpit of a healthy male and marked the level of the mercury. He then marked the spot to which the mercury fell when the thermometer was immersed in a freezing water. Since the temperature of a mixture of salt and ice was considered to be the coldest possible, he called this zero. Fixing an upper limit (boiling water) at 60, freezing water came at 7.5 (one-eighth up the scale), and a healthy armpit came at 22.5 (three-eighths up the scale).

Fahrenheit decided in the interest of greater precision to expand Roemer's scale, multiplying each number by four. This set freezing at 30 and armpit temperature at 90. To eliminate the awkward fractions this would cause and to maintain divisibility by eight, he moved the freezing point to 32 and armpit temperature to 96. The later, minor change of armpit (blood) temperature to 98.6 set the modern thermometer scale, which we attribute to Fahrenheit because Ole Roe-

mer's own notes were destroyed in a fire and little was known of his thermometer work for two hundred years.

However, Roemer was known at the time for other, more cosmic matters. Earlier, in 1671, while he was still involved in astronomical studies, a passing French astronomer had persuaded him to work as his assistant during a visit to the Danish astronomer Tycho Brahe's[135] observatory at Uraniborg on the island of Hven (between Denmark and Sweden). The purpose of the visit was to check the observatory's exact coordinates as part of a major French program to update astronomical tables such as those Brahe himself had produced. Roemer then went to Paris and spent several years developing an extraordinary idea that had occurred to him while carrying out observations on Hven.

One of the exact coordinates in the sky Roemer had measured for the French was the position and time of eclipse of Io, one of Jupiter's moons. Precise moments of celestial time such as these were of great value to mariners, as they allowed exactness in calculating longitude position at sea, which is determined by the time a celestial event happens compared with when it would occur at home port. The difference between the two times at which the phenomenon was observed told a navigator how far east or west he was. It was during the observations of Io that Roemer began to wonder why the time at which the eclipses occurred varied with the distance between Jupiter and the Earth. He came to the momentous conclusion that these differences must be due to the fact that the speed of light was finite (and not instantaneous, as had been believed ever since the time of Aristotle). The image of the eclipse must therefore be taking longer to arrive at Earth the greater the distance from Jupiter. Calculations based on this assumption led Roemer to announce on November 21, 1676, that the speed of light was 140,000 miles per second.

During the previous two years the man who had persuaded Roemer to come to Paris, fellow-astronomer Jean Picard,[136] was concerned with more down-to-earth matters. Between 1674 and 1675 he played an active role in assuring a constant water supply for the king's new château at Versailles.[137] In 1671 Louis XIV had started to build a great royal palace with magnificent gardens on the site of his

135 107 *206*

136 101 *188*

137 89 *161*

father's relatively modest hunting lodge. The construction of Versailles and its gardens took thirty-six thousand workers twenty-six years.

Picard's water problem related to the fact that Louis wanted the latest fountains and water-powered amusements in grottoes all over the palace grounds. Water was also needed for the hundreds of thousands of plants, trees and shrubs in the gardens The hydrological difficulty was that Versailles turned out to be higher than the surrounding ground. This awkward fact was revealed by Picard, who used an adaptation of his astronomical telescope to survey the different levels with extreme accuracy. Thanks to this a complex network of canals and aqueducts was subsequently designed and brought water from reservoirs and springs in the surrounding countryside. From 1683 on, the Versailles gardens were being adequately supplied.

This was good news to André Le Nôtre, the gardens' designer, who must have been an exceptional person, since he was described by contemporaries as "honest, honorable and plain-spoken." It was even said that Le Nôtre achieved an almost personal relationship with his sovereign, the Sun King. Le Nôtre's Versailles gardens, built for an absolute monarch and unequalled in their size and complexity, were intended to reflect the concept of the king's supreme control. At a time when exploration was opening up the world and science was revealing the secrets of the cosmos, Versailles represented another aspect of man's newfound power. Untamed countryside no longer surrounded society with mysterious and uncontrollable chaos as it had done since medieval times. Elegant lines of trees and carefully delineated flowerbeds now shaped and constrained the elements. The king also controlled nature.

His chief minister wanted that control to extend further. In the late seventeenth century Jean-Baptiste Colbert[138] was busy trying to retrieve the French economy from the near-bankrupt state in which Louis XIII had left it. As part of his plan (which included revamping the whole of French industry so that France would no longer need to import goods), Colbert made a complete reorganization and reform of the French navy. Colbert's dream was that France would become a

138 84 *159*

world power ranking with England. His ambitious ship-building program included the introduction of draconian afforestation laws. For centuries the woods had been decimated by charcoal-burners and fuel-collectors. The new regulations now preserved the trees for ship-builders alone (one side-effect would be to drive the iron industry to seek other sources of fuel and ultimately to develop ways of using coal that would power the Industrial Revolution).

It was thanks to the continuing scarcity of wood that the inspector general of the French Navy in 1732 was an already-recognized botanist. Henri-Louis Duhamel du Monceau had begun life as a chemist, but after a visit to England in 1729 to study ship-building concentrated much of his attention on wood and forest management. His first book, published in 1747, was about ships' rigging. At the family château of Denainvilliers, between Orleans and Chartres, Duhamel experimented with the latest English agricultural techniques and started one of Europe's first arboreta, gathering specimens from all over the European continent and from America. Duhamel's treatise on trees and shrubs was widely influential in the early importation of new plant species. In 1750 he translated the

Fig. 32: *Duhamel's legacy. An eighteenth-century French print from a book on forest management.*

English agricultural expert Jethro Tull's seminal work on *Horse-Hoeing Husbandry,* adding to it from his own experience. Earlier in the century Tull had seen French peasants hoeing their vineyards, and when he used the technique in England found he could produce a wheat crop from the same ground for thirteen consecutive years without the need for expensive manure. Ironically, this French innovation publicized by an Englishman now formed the basis of Duhamel's *Traité de la Culture des Terres* ("Treatise on Cultivation"), which was in turn translated into English in 1759 as *A Practical Treatise of Husbandry* by John Hill, assistant gardener at the new Royal Botanical Gardens in Kew, London. Hill was also the author of a catalogue of some thirty-four hundred species of plants being cultivated in Kew at the time.

In 1761 an English architect and author named William Chambers asked his publisher to send him a list of the latest books on gardening (likely including Hill's work and his translation of Duhamel), because Chambers had just been commissioned by the dowager princess Augusta, King George III's mother, to carry out architectural work at Kew. Chambers was already famous for his books, *Treatise on Civil Architecture* and *Designs for Chinese Buildings,* which had led to his earlier appointment as architecture tutor to the Prince of Wales, who was now the king. Chambers had learned about Chinese style between 1742 and 1749 when he was in China working for the Swedish East India Company. These voyages convinced him to quit commerce, and in 1749 he moved to France and Italy for six years to study architecture.

In response to Princess Augusta's commission Chambers designed more than twenty buildings for Kew Gardens, chief among which (and still standing) was the Pagoda, an octagonal ten-story structure 163 feet high, more of a rococo statement than a true Chinese reproduction. The building caused a sensation and set the fashion for architectural *chinoiserie.* Pagodas popped up in parks all over Europe in Potsdam, Munich, Tsarskoie Selo, Chanteloup and Oranienbaum. Thanks to his links with royalty, Chambers was appointed architect of the works together with Robert Adam, and in 1784 he became surveyor-general, titular head of the architectural profession in En-

gland. In 1774 he and Adam were commissioned to work on Somerset House, a grandiose new public building in central London. In 1782 the two men hired a Scottish stoneworker, Thomas Telford, who would later describe Chambers as "haughty and reserved."

Telford was a self-taught journeyman stonemason with ambitions to be an architect and planner, and he spent two years working at Somerset House, learning all he could. After leaving Chambers and Adam, Telford built a dockyard house, remodeled a castle, designed a prison, a church and a hospital and became Shropshire's county surveyor. His civil engineering career began when he was appointed to work on a network of new canals linking the rivers Dee, Mersey and Severn. The aqueduct he built for this project at Pontcysyllte in Wales is one of the engineering triumphs of history. The canal is carried one thousand feet across a wide, deep valley in a cast-iron trough eleven feet ten inches wide, containing the aqueduct and the tow-path and supported on nineteen slender stone pillars, each 127 feet high. Sir Walter Scott called it the greatest work of art he had ever seen. Even today it is impressive and beautiful.

In 1801 Telford was commissioned to build the great Caledonian Canal through the Highlands of Scotland. During the eighteen years this took to complete Telford also built 920 miles of new roads and over one thousand new bridges, transforming the Scottish economy by making possible stagecoach services, regular mail and newspaper delivery. This in turn boosted commercial activity, which increased land and property values. By 1820 Telford was the first president of the new Institute of Civil Engineers. When he died in 1834, popular and admired, he was buried in Westminster Abbey.

His only failure had been the design he entered for the competition to build a new London bridge. Telford's idea was for a single, six-hundred-foot, cast-iron span rising to sixty-five feet above the river, with a roadway forty-five feet wide, and weighing six thousand tons. In 1816 when the government consulted a group of eminent scientists and engineers on the subject their opinion was that the bridge was brilliantly conceived. Unfortunately, in order to avoid too great a rise at the crown of the arch (necessary to facilitate the passage of shipping), Telford planned high-level approach ramps supported by

brick colonnades running along either bank of the river. The cost of the land on which these ramps would be built was too great and Telford's design was rejected.

A member of the ad hoc bridge review group (which also included James Watt[139] and ironmaster James Wilkinson) was Thomas Young,[140] one of the most innovative and versatile scientists of the day. Young was a prodigy. By the age of two he was literate and at four he had read the Bible twice. By the age of nineteen he was proficient in twelve languages, ancient and modern. He had also mastered calculus and read Newton's *Principia Mathematica* and *Optics,* and Lavoisier's *Elements of Chemistry.* At this point he began studies to qualify as a physician and then attended Cambridge, where he was known as "Phenomenon" Young. In 1801 he was appointed professor at the Royal Institution in London, where his work was to prepare popular lectures on science and the mechanical arts. He also made major advances in the study of color vision and perception, and in deciphering Egyptian hieroglyphics.

In 1799 he had also begun the study of light, and in 1807 he published a paper describing a series of experiments in which he had shone candlelight through a lens, then a pinhole, and finally two narrow slits. Beyond the slits, where the light fell on a sheet of paper, Young saw a series of light-and-dark patterns that he concluded must have been produced when the light coming though the slits recombined. Since the effect of this recombination was to produce what appeared to be interference patterns similar to those produced by interacting ripples of water, Young announced that contrary to all contemporary opinion he believed light traveled in waves through some kind of "luminiferous ether."

This ether was of course invisible and intangible (and ubiquitous, since light also traveled in a vacuum). The search for this mysterious "ether" would bedevil the work of scientists for most of the nineteenth century. In 1888 a German physicist named Heinrich Hertz conducted a series of experiments to see if electromagnetic radiation traveled through the ether as did light waves. Confirmation came with his discovery of radio waves. Hertz had been directed to this research by his professor at the University of Berlin, Hermann von

139 16 39

139 37 68

140 91 163

Helmholtz, a leading figure in European science. Helmholtz had studied physiology under Johannes Müller, who wrote the *Handbook of Physiology*, a milestone in the history of European medicine. Müller (and then Helmholtz) rejected earlier, quasiphilosophical approaches to physiology based on speculative Romantic thought, relying instead on the empirical evidence of observation and experimentation. One of Müller's greatest contributions to neurophysiology was to encourage the view of the nervous system as a unit.

Strangely enough, it was in matters such as nerve function that Müller clung to a view that seemed to contradict his belief in empirical evidence. Müller was a Vitalist, holding that it would be impossible to reduce the life processes to the mechanical laws of chemistry and physics. Vitalists believed that the organism as a whole was greater than the sum of its parts and that some kind of "force" coordinated the physiological action of organs, nerves and tissues to produce the harmonious behavior that characterized an organism. Vitalists held that this force was not susceptible to experimental quantification. Müller used the nerve impulse as an example.

His pupil Helmholtz disagreed violently with the whole Vitalist approach and set out to disprove it. In 1852 he published evidence from experiments he had conducted on a frog's sciatic nerve. Using a myograph, Helmholtz recorded the effect of sending an electric current into the nerve. The muscle contraction that followed nerve excitation was recorded with a lever that moved with the muscle spasm and traced a curve on a smoked-glass surface moving at a uniform speed. The vertical component of the curve was proportional to the contraction of the muscle and the horizontal component was proportional to time. Helmholtz found not only that the nerve impulse occurred in a finite period but also that it moved at the relatively slow speed of about ninety feet per second.

Vitalists ignored the findings. By 1900 the leader of the German Vitalist movement was a physicist, chemist and philosopher named Ludwig Klages, who was a disciple of Nietzsche and a devotee of antirationalism. For Klages the intellect was a superimposed power, constraining the naturally intuitive and "prophetic" mind. In his work over and over he exhorted psychologists to turn away from ra-

tionalism toward "divination." In Monaco in 1905 Klages founded a center for the study of "Characterology," an alternative form of psychology that assessed personality through what today would be referred to as "body language." Klages and his followers claimed that intuitive analysis of the conflicting elements of a person's character as shown by movement and expression would reveal what lay behind what he called "the mask of courtesy."

In an extension of this approach to the study of character (which together with characterology he offered as a tool for personnel selection), Klages also published a book on graphology, the study of handwriting. The book was a runaway success and went into fifteen editions. Klages maintained that handwriting offered added insights into character, since it was affected by the different driving forces in the personality. Thus, for instance, large handwriting indicated either enthusiasm or a lack of realism, whereas small handwriting indicated either lack of enthusiasm or realism. Sloping writing reflected either congeniality or rashness. Vertical writing indicated either rationality or aloofness. The choice of either the positive or negative characteristic in each case depended on the rhythm, depth and richness of the script. This final feature could, however, not be measured but only intuitively perceived. Given the irrational element in Klages's thought, it is not surprising that his characterology and graphology were most extensively used by the Nazis to select their SS officers.

Klages's graphology drew attention to the extreme individuality of each person's handwriting. Thirty years after the Nazis had adopted his theories the extreme individuality of handwriting was presenting problems to the United States Post Office Department, at the time facing an unmanageably massive growth in business mail. By the early 1960s it accounted for 80 percent of all correspondence, and the amount of mail was growing rapidly. The single greatest contribution to this growth had come from the introduction of the computer. In permitting the centralization of accounts it generated a vastly increased amount of billing, bank deposits and receipts, credit card transactions, Social Security payments and other business items traveling through the postal system. There was an urgent need to streamline the process of sorting and delivery. On July 1, 1963, the

Post Office Department introduced the five-digit ZIP ("Zone Improvement Plan") Code. The first number in the code indicated a broad geographical area (for instance, zero referred to the Northeast and nine to the West); the following two digits referred to areas of population concentration or areas using a common transportation system; the final two digits referred to small post offices or postal zones in larger, zoned cities. In the 1980s the U.S. Postal Service added four more digits, permitting sorting and delivery to be automated to the level of an individual building.

Automatic processing of mail began in 1965 with the installation at the Detroit Post Office of a high-speed Optical Character Reader. This first-generation machine read the line of typed or block-capital letters carrying the name of the city and the state ZIP Code, then sorted mail into one of 277 pockets. However, each address had to be checked by an agent before delivery. In the 1980s more sophisticated machines were developed capable of reading an individual ZIP Code and spraying the relevant machine-readable barcode on the mail, which could then be sorted by computer. At the end of the century, still constrained by what Klages had called the "extreme individuality" of handwriting, even the most advanced, "multiline" OCRs were still only capable of reading block-letter handwriting or typed letters.

Some of the earliest research in optical character recognition started in 1952 with research into systems to assist reading by the blind carried out by the Cognitive Information Processing Group at MIT. This early research shared a common origin in cybernetic[141] feedback theory with the guidance technology described at the beginning of this book's journey on the web of knowledge: the electronic personal agents[142] that will keep us in touch with the world in the twenty-first century.

141 2 23

142 1 22

Bibliography

CHAPTER 1

Bradley, Ian. *William Morris and His World*. London: Thames & Hudson, 1978.

Carson, Gerald. *Cornflake Crusade*. London: Victor Gollanz Ltd., 1959.

Corbin, Diana Fontaine Maury. *A Life of Matthew Fontaine Maury*. London, 1888.

Guilfoyle, Christine, and Warner, Ellie. *Intelligent Agents*. London, 1994.

Hibbert, Christopher. *Nelson*. London: Viking, 1994.

Holmes, Frederic Lawrence. *Claude Bernard and Animal Chemistry*. Cambridge, Mass: Harvard University Press, 1974.

Jameson, Eric. *The Natural History of Quackery*. London: Michael Joseph, 1961.

Masani, P. R. *Norbert Wiener*. Basel, Boston, Berlin: Birkhäuser Verlag, 1990.

Spencer, Colin. *The Heretic's Feast*. London: Fourth Estate, 1993.

Sultana, Donald. *Samuel Taylor Coleridge in Malta and Italy*. Oxford: Basil Blackwell, 1969.

Taylor, Anne. *Annie Besant*. Oxford: Oxford University Press, 1992.

CHAPTER 2

Batty, Peter. *The House of Krupp*. London: Secker and Warburg, 1966.

Dibner, Bern. *The Atlantic Cable*. New York: Blaisdell, 1964.

Hyman, Anthony. *Charles Babbage*. Princeton: Princeton University Press, 1992.

Leupp, F. E. *George Westinghouse*. Norwood, Mass.: Norwood Press, 1919.

Mackenzie, Thomas B. *Life of James Beaumont Neilson, F.R.S.* Glasgow: West of Scotland Iron and Steel Institute, 1928.

McLaren, David J. *David Dale of New Lanark*. Milngavie: Heatherbank Press, 1983.

Mitchell, F. *Tank Warfare.* Stevenage, Herts.: Spa Books, 1987.

Moon, John F. *Rudolf Diesel and the Diesel Engine.* London: Priory Press Ltd., 1974.

Rosenberg, Nathan. *The Britannia Bridge.* Cambridge, Mass.: MIT Press, 1978.

Seeligman, T., Torrilhon, G., and Falconnet, H. *Indiarubber and Gutta Percha.* London: Scott, Greenwood & Sons, 1910.

Stigler, Stephen M. *The History of Statistics.* Cambridge, Mass.: Harvard University Press, 1986.

Vaughan, Adrian. *Isambard Kingdom Brunel.* London: John Murray, 1991.

CHAPTER 3

Baines, Edward. *History of the Cotton Manufacture.* New York: Augustus M. Kelley, 1966.

Blackmore, John. *Ernst Mach.* London: University of California, 1973.

Carmichael, Leonard, and Long, J. C. *James Smithson and the Smithsonian Story.* New York: G. P. Putnam's Sons, 1965.

Crocker, Glenys. *The Gunpowder Industry.* Haverfordwest: Shire Publications Ltd., 1986.

Gernsheim, Helmut, and Gernsheim, Alison. *L. J. M. Daguerre.* London: Secker & Warburg, 1956.

Hackmann, Willem. *Seek and Strike.* London: H.M.S.O., 1984.

Harris, Neil. *Humbug, the Art of P.T. Barnum.* Chicago: University of Chicago Press, 1981.

Lewes, Vivian B. *Acetylene.* London: Macmillan, 1900.

Pannekoek, A. *A History of Astronomy.* London: George Allen & Unwin Ltd., 1961.

Phillips-Matz, Mary Jane. *Verdi.* Oxford: Oxford University Press, 1993.

Quinn, Susan. *Marie Curie.* London: Heinemann, 1995.

Sawyer, L. A. *Liberty Ships.* New York: Lloyd's of London, 1985.

Style, Jane M. *Auguste Comte.* London: Kegan Paul, Trench Truebner & Co., Ltd., 1928.

White, Michael, and Gribbin, John. *Einstein.* London: Simon & Schuster, 1994.

CHAPTER 4

Blackstone, Sarah J. *Buckskins, Bullets, and Business.* Westport, Conn.: Greenwood Press, 1986.

Bortoloan, Liana. *The Life and Times of Titian.* London: Hamlyn Publishing Group, 1968.

Bradford, Ernle. *The Great Siege.* London: Hodder & Stoughton, 1961.

Cluny, Hilaire. *Louis Pasteur.* London: Souvenir Press, 1965.

Hatch, Alden. *American Express.* Garden City, N.Y.: Doubleday & Co., Inc., 1950.

Main, Gloria L. *Tobacco Colony.* Princeton: Princeton University Press, 1982.

Neillands, Robin. *The Hundred Years War.* London & New York: Routledge, 1990.

O'Malley, Charles D. *Andreas Vesalius of Brussels.* Berkeley and Los Angeles: California Press, 1964.

Ordish, George. *The Great Wine Blight.* London: J. M. Dent & Sons Ltd., 1972.

Sharov, Alexander S., and Novikov, Igor D. *Edwin Hubble.* Cambridge: Cambridge University Press, 1993.

Shaw, Stanford J. *The Jews of the Ottoman Empire and the Turkish Republic.* London: Macmillan, 1991.

Shennan, Francis. *Flesh and Bones, The Passions and Legacies of John Napier.* Edinburgh: Napier Polytechnic, 1989.

Smith, Melvyn. *Space Shuttle.* Sparkford, Somerset: Haynes, 1989.

Warner, Marina. *Joan of Arc.* London: Weidenfeld & Nicholson, 1981.

CHAPTER 5

Bull, Angela. *The Machine Breakers.* London: Collins, 1980.

Clayton, Michael. *The Jeep.* London: David & Charles, 1982.

Clifford, M. N., and Wilson, K. C. (eds.). *Coffee.* London: Croom Helm, 1985.

Goldsmith, Margaret. *Christina of Sweden.* London: Arthur Baker Ltd., 1933.

Gordon, Alistair. *John Galt.* Edinburgh: Oliver & Boyd, 1972.

Grendel, Frédéric. *Beaumarchais.* Trans. Roger Greaves. London: Macdonald and Jane's, 1977.

Hughes, J. Trevor. *Thomas Willis.* London: Royal Society of Medicine Services Ltd., 1991.

Hutchison, Harold F. *Sir Christopher Wren.* London: Victor Gollancz Ltd., 1976.

Lande, Dr. Lawrence. *Introduction to John Law.* Edinburgh: University of Edinburgh Centre for Canadian Studies, 1989.

Longford, Elizabeth. *Byron.* London: Hutchinson, 1976.

Oppenheimer, Jane M. *Essays in the History of Embryology and Biology.* Cambridge, Mass.: M.I.T. Press, 1967.

Parker, Geoffrey. *The Military Revolution.* Cambridge: Cambridge University Press, 1988.

Pattison, Mark. *Isaac Casaubon.* Oxford: Clarendon Press, 1982.

Robinson, George W. *Autobiography of Joseph Scaliger.* Cambridge, Mass.: Harvard University Press, 1927.

Winegarten, Renée. *Mme de Staël.* Leamington Spa: Berg Publishers Ltd., 1985.

CHAPTER 6

Aitken, Hugh G. *Syntony and Spark—The Origins of Radio.* New York and London: John Wiley & Sons, Inc., 1976.

Barchilon, Jacques, and Flinders, Peter. *Charles Perrault.* Boston: Twayne Publishers, 1981.

Campbell, Malcolm. *Pietro da Cortona at the Pitti Palace.* Princeton: Princeton University Press, 1977.

Houghton, Raymond. *The World of George Berkeley.* Dublin: Eason & Son Ltd., 1985.

John, William D. *Pontypool and U.K. Japanned Wares.* Newport, Monmouthshire: The Ceramic Book Co., 1953.

Koepke, Wulf. *Johann Gottfried Herder.* Boston: Twayne Publishers, 1987.

Lavine, Sigmund A. *Allan Pinkerton.* London: Mayflower Paperback, 1970.

May, Stacy. *United States Business Performance Abroad: The Case Study of the United Fruit Company in Latin America.* New York: National Planning Association, 1958.

Nordon, Pierre. *Conan Doyle.* London: John Murray, 1966.

Rolt, L. T. C. *The Aeronauts, A History of Ballooning.* Gloucestershire: Alan Sutton, 1985.

Rowse, A. L. *Jonathan Swift, Major Prophet.* London: Thames & Hudson, 1975.

Smith, Charles H. *A. F. Wallace on Spiritualism, Man and Evolution.* 1992.

Stafford, Fiona. *The Sublime Savage. A Study of James Macpherson and the Poems of Ossian.* Edinburgh: Edinburgh University Press, 1988.

Stanton, Phoebe. *Pugin.* London: Thames & Hudson, 1971.

Vining, Elizabeth Gray. *Flora MacDonald.* London: Geoffrey Bles, 1967.

CHAPTER 7

Allan, D. G. C., and Schofield, R. E. *Stephen Hales*. London: Scholar Press, 1980.

Burke, Peter. *Montaigne*. Oxford: Oxford University Press, 1994.

Chancellor, John. *Audubon: A Biography*. London: Weidenfeld and Nicolson, 1978.

Dickinson, Robert E. *Makers of Modern Geography*. London: Routledge and Kegan Paul, 1969.

Fisher, Richard B. *Edward Jenner*. London: André Deutsch, 1991.

Hartcup, Adeline. *Angelica*. Harmondsworth, Middlesex: William Heinemann Ltd., 1954.

Kidler, Peter. *Richthofen*. London: Arms + Armour Press, 1994.

Koestler, Arthur. *The Watershed: A Biography of Johannes Kepler*. Lanham, Md: University Press of America, 1960.

Mackworth-Praed, Ben. *Aviation: The Pioneer Years*. London: Studio Editions Ltd., 1990.

Marriott, Ernest G. *Izaak Walton*. Nottingham: Nottingham Flyfishers' Club, 1986.

Morley, Geoffrey. *The Smuggling War*. Stroud: Alan Sutton Publishing Ltd., 1994.

Roddis, Louis H. *James Lind*. London: William Heinemann Ltd., 1951.

Stone, George W., and Kahrl, George M. *David Garrick*. Southern Illinois University Press, 1979.

CHAPTER 8

Blumenberg, Hans. *The Genesis of the Copernican World*. Trans. Robert M. Wallace. Cambridge, Mass.: M.I.T. Press, 1987.

Boase, Roger. *The Origin and Meaning of Courtly Love*. Manchester: Manchester University Press, 1977.

Craven, William G. *Giovanni Pico della Mirandola*. 1981.

Crone, Gerald. *Maps and Their Makers*. London: Hutchinsons University Library, 1953.

Dan, Joseph. *The Early Kabbalah*. Mahwah, N.J.: Paulist Press, 1986.

Dodge, Ernest Stanley. *The Polar Rosses*. London: Faber & Faber, 1973.

Gade, John Allyne. *The Life and Times of Tycho Brahe*. New York: Princeton University Press, 1947.

Holmes, T. W. *The Semaphore*. Ilfracombe, Devon: Arthur H. Stockwell Ltd., 1983.

Kardross, John. *The Origins and Early History of Opera.* Sydney: University of Sydney Press, 1957.

Manschreck, Clyde Leonard. *Melanchthon.* New York: Oxford University Press, 1970.

Ore, Oystein. *Cardano.* Princeton: Princeton University Press, 1953.

Schwarzbach, Martin. *Alfred Wegener.* Madison, Wisc.: Science Technology Inc., 1986.

Spitz, Lewis W. *The Religious Renaissance of the German Humanists.* 1963.

Turrill, William B. *Joseph Dalton Hooker.* London: Thomas Nelson & Sons Ltd., 1963.

Wormald, Jenny. *Mary Queen of Scots.* London: George Philip, 1988.

CHAPTER 9

Beattie, Lester M. *John Arbuthnot.* Cambridge, Mass.: Harvard University Press, 1935.

Besterman, Theodore. *Voltaire.* Oxford: Basil Blackwell, 1976.

Brown, Pamela. *Henri Dunant.* Dublin: Wolfhound Press, 1991.

Everdingen, Ewoud van. *C.H.D. Buys Ballot.* Antwerp, 1953.

Halsband, Robert. *The Life of Lady Mary Wortley Montagu.* New York: Oxford University Press, 1960.

Killingray, David. *The Atom Bomb.* London: Harrap, 1983.

Lawson, Joan. *A History of Ballet and Its Makers.* London: Sir Isaac Pitman & Sons Ltd., 1964.

Lumsden, Malvern. *Incendiary Weapons.* Cambridge, Mass.: M.I.T. Press, 1975.

MacGregor, Arthur. *Sir Hans Sloane.* London: British Museum Press, 1994.

Miller, Edward. *Prince of Librarians.* London: The British Library.

Millington-Drake, Egen. *The Drama of Graf Spee and the Battle of the Plate.* London: Peter Davies, 1965.

Smith, Maxwell A. *Prosper Mérimée.* New York: Twayne Publishers, Inc., 1972.

Stephens, W. P. *Zwingli.* Oxford: Clarendon Press, 1994.

Stuyvenberg, J. H. van. (ed.). *Margarine: An Economic, Social and Scientific History.* Liverpool: Liverpool University Press, 1969.

Uerberhorst, Horst. *Friedrich Ludwig Jahn and His Time.* Munich: Heinz Moos Verlag, 1982.

Bibliography

CHAPTER 10

Bourde, André J. *The Influence of England on the French Agronomes, 1750–1789.* Cambridge: Cambridge University Press, 1953.

Cahan, David (ed.). *Hermann von Helmholtz and the Foundations of Nineteenth-Century Science.* Berkeley, Calif.: University of California Press, 1993.

Checkland, Sydney. *The Elgins.* Aberdeen: Aberdeen University Press, 1988.

Clark, Ronald W. *Benjamin Franklin.* London: Weidenfeld and Nicolson, 1983.

Cohen, Ernst Julius. Kammerlingh Onnes Memorial Lecture, in *Journal of the Chemical Society*, 1920. Vol. 1, pp. 1193–1209.

Cohen, I. B. "Roemer and the first determination of the velocity of light," in *Isis*, 31 (1940), pp. 327–79.

Dorsey, N. Ernest. "Fahrenheit and Roemer," in *Journal of the Washington Academy of Sciences*, 36, No. 11 (1946), 361–72.

Harris, John. *Sir William Chambers.* London: A. Zwemmer Ltd., 1970.

Harriss, Joseph. *The Eiffel Tower.* London: Paul Elek, 1976.

Hazlehurst, F. Hamilton. *Gardens of Illusion: The Genius of André Le Nostre.* Nashville, Tenn.: Vanderbilt University Press, 1980.

Levey, Michael. *Sir Thomas Lawrence.* London: National Portrait Gallery, 1979.

Qvist, George. *John Hunter.* London: William Heinemann Medical Books Ltd., 1981.

Rolt, L. T. C. *Thomas Telford.* Harmondsworth, Middlesex: Penguin Books Ltd., 1979.

Taylor, Anne. *Laurence Oliphant.* Oxford: Oxford University Press, 1982.

Vogel, Dan. *Emma Lazarus.* Boston: Twayne Publishers, 1980.

Index

⬨

Index

Dutch East India Company, 80, 137
dyes, 66–67, 80

eclipses, 76, 93, 94, 182, 254
Eddington, Arthur, 93
Edict of Expulsion (1492), 103–4
Edison, Thomas, 48, 49, 147
education, 15, 16, 162, 201–2
Ehrlich, Paul, 11
Eiffel, Gustave, 245–46
Eiffel Tower, 150, 244–45
Einstein, Albert, 92–93, 94
electricity, 11, 38–39, 48–49, 70–71,
  74–75, 142, 146–47, 188, 242–43,
  252, 260
electrophoresis, 169–70
Elements of Chemistry (Lavoisier), 259
Elements of Infinite Geometry (Fontenelle),
  187–88
Elements of the Philosophy of Newton
  (Voltaire), 233–34
Elgin, James Bruce, Earl of, 248–49
Elgin, Thomas Bruce, Earl of, 249–50
Elgin Marbles, 249–50
Elizabeth I, Queen of England, 111,
  204–5
Embassy Letters (Montagu), 226
embryos, 142–43
emotion, 25
Enfantin, Prosper, 89
Engel, Ernst, 57
Enterprise, 164–65
Erasmus, Desiderius, 227
Essays (Montaigne), 186
Estienne, Henri, 126–27
Estienne, Robert, 126
ether, 92, 259
Eugénie, Empress of France, 222, 223
Evelyn, John, 135, 210–11
evolution, 142–46
excise taxes, 112–13
*Explanations and Sailing Directions to
  Accompany the Wind and Current Charts*
  (Maury), 29–30

factories, 54–55, 59, 67, 178, 217–18
Fahrenheit, Daniel Gabriel, 253
Fahrenheit scale, 253
Fairbairn, William, 62
Fandino, Juan de Leon, 179

fashion, 121
fast food, 116, 117
fasting, 228
Fata Morgana, 194–95
fats, 217–18
Featherstonehaugh, Harry, 37
feedback, 23–24, 262
Ferdinand, King of Castile and Aragon,
  103–4
Ferdinando II, Duke of Tuscany, 160,
  208, 209
Fessenden, Reginald, 147–48, 149
feudalism, 157
Feuillet, Raoul, 231
Field, Cyrus W., 30–31, 63
Fieser, Louis, 216–17
fighter planes, 171–73
fishing, 185, 219
"five perfect solids," 182–83
Fizeau, Armand-Hippolyte-Louis, 221
flak jacket, 50
flintlock musket, 229–30
flying shuttle, 41, 80–81
Fokker, Anthony, 171
Folger, Timothy, 252
Follen, Adolf, 235
Follen, Karl, 235–36
Fontenelle, Bernard de, 187–88
Forfarshire, 28
Formigny, Battle of, 100
Fort McHenry, 124–25
Foucault, Leon, 75–76, 221
fountains, 134–35, 254–55
fractionating tower, 118–19
France, 110–11, 138–41, 159–60, 229,
  230–31, 233, 235, 245–46, 255–56
Francini, Tommaso, 134–35
Franklin, Benjamin, 38, 164, 251–53
French Revolution, 121
frit, 80
Fromanteel family, 114
"Fruits of Philosophy" (Knowlton),
  44–45, 67
fungicide, 96–97
furfurol, 48, 49
fusion, nuclear, 241–43
fustian, 80

Gaelic, 154
Galileo, 160, 200

Index

Index

Macie (Smithson), James, 68–69, 70
Macintosh, Charles, 66, 67, 214
Macintosh, George, 66–67
McParlan, James, 166, 167
Macpherson, James, 153–54
Magendie, François, 25, 26
Magna Carta, 152
magnetic fields, 242
Magnetico-Electrico Celestial Bed, 38
Magnetic Pole, 214
magnetism, 11, 142, 242
magnitude of brightness, 94–95
Magnol, Pierre, 224
mail delivery, 97–99, 149–50, 261–62
Malta, 33–34, 35–36, 105–6
Malthus, Thomas, 144
manometer, 244–45
manteau d'armes, 109
manuscripts, 126–29
maps, 207–8
marching music, 231
margarine, 218
Marignano, Battle of, 229
Mariotte's Law, 161
Mark V tank, 52
marriage, 196
Martin, Dick, 27
Martinet, Jean, 230–31
Marx, Eleanor, 43
Marx, Karl, 43
Mary, Queen of Scots, 128, 204–5, 206
Maryland, 112
Masked Ball, A (Verdi), 87
Masnadieri, I (Verdi), 86
matchlock musket, 230
Maurice, Prince of Nassau, 129–30, 133
Maury, Matthew, 29–31
May, Phil, 150–51
Mazarin, Giulio, 210
Medical and Surgical Sanitarium, 46
medicine, 106–7
Mèges Mouriès, Hippolyte, 217–18
Melanchthon, Philipp, 201–2
memory, 15, 16, 23
Mendelssohn, Felix, 85
Mendes, Dona Gracia, 104, 105
Mengs, Raphael, 175
ME 163 fighter, 96
Mercator, Gerardus, 208
mercenaries, 228–29, 230

mercury, 76–77, 188, 253
Mérimée, Prosper, 222–23
methane, 119
Mill, John Stuart, 91
Millardet, Pierre, 96–97
milling machines, 83
mirages, 194–95
modus operandi (MO), 166
Mohammed Ali Pasha, 87–88
Moissan, Henri, 74
Molly Maguires, 166
money, 110, 138–39
money orders, 97
Monk, Maria, 31–32
monomethyl hydrazine, 96
Monro, Alexander, 181–82
Montagu, Mary Wortley, 224–26
Montaigne, Michel Eyquem de, 186–87
Montgomerie, William, 64
"Moral Physiology" (Owen), 67
Morgenthaler, Hans, 117
Morris, William, 42–43
Morrow, Dwight, 239
Morse, Jedidiah, 31
Morse, Samuel, 21, 31–33
Morse Code, 31, 64, 147
mortality tables, 232–33
Movement of Waters, The (Mariotte), 161
Muhlberg, Battle of, 108–9
mule, 41, 81
Müller, Johannes, 260
Munroe, Charles E., 50
Munroe effect, 50
Murad IV, Sultan, 111
muriate of potash, 80
Murray, George, 213
Mushet, David, 65–66
musket, 83, 130–32, 229–30
Muslims, 102–6
muslin, 81
myograph, 260
Mysterium Cosmographicum (Kepler), 183

Nabucco (Verdi), 86
napalm, 216–17
naphtha, 67
Napier, John, 113
Napoleon I, Emperor of France, 34, 35–36, 87–88, 141, 164, 212

Index